Murder at the Table of Fools

The Lonely Detective Solves the Roach Murder

CHARLES E. SCHWARZ

iUniverse

MURDER AT THE TABLE OF FOOLS
THE LONELY DETECTIVE SOLVES THE ROACH MURDER

iUniverse books may be ordered through booksellers or by contacting:

iUniverse LLC
1663 Liberty Drive
Bloomington, IN 47403
www.iuniverse.com
1-800-Authors (1-800-288-4677)

ISBN: 978-1-4917-4783-4 (sc)
ISBN: 978-1-4917-4784-1 (hc)
ISBN: 978-1-4917-4782-7 (e)

Library of Congress Control Number: 2014917451

Printed in the United States of America.

iUniverse rev. date: 10/14/2014

DEDICATION

To the women most helpful for this work

mother, Agnes

wife, Emily

Our Mother, Mary

CONTENTS

CHAPTER 1

Five are Poisoned

At twilight, five of us were poisoned at the sports banquet, four of us survived, and one didn't. At a banquet for participating sons and their fathers celebrating Deptfield Midget Football season's end, five fathers sat down at banquet table number 12, a large circular table with eight place settings. Technically we hadn't sat down, but were standing with drinks in hand. We'd tipped our chairs against the table, claiming our places. At the center of the table were cheese bits, crackers and salsa. All five hands quickly hit the center and we were soon stuffing our mouths with salsa on crackers. All five of us were poisoned. Of course at the time we thought we were suffering from a case of food poisoning, which was literally right, although in fact it was wrong.

As the emergency ambulances dumped us off at the hospital, it was first feared there had been a mass food poisoning at the midget football banquet. After midnight, medical and police officials realized we were the only ones poisoned and declared it a deliberate poisoning, probably by a deranged person.

Unfortunately, a banquet hall crowded with hysterical mothers screaming for their children's safety caused the children to imitate the hysteria and join in with fulsome screams and flowing tears, especially from the cheerless cheerleaders. Initially, with all the chaos in the venue—firemen, EMTs, police, and children running to and fro, and mothers rushing to grab elusive excited children more interested in the uniforms than in a mother's protective grasp—naturally it was assumed the children were the target of either a terrorist attack or a lone deranged mass murderer. This led to TV media's first news alert, during which the anchor breathlessly announced possibly a hundred children had been poisoned with probably ten or more dead. Updates would follow, even if there was nothing to update, and an in-depth analysis would follow each update.

Arriving at the hospital emergency room we underwent forced stomach pumping, a horrendous exercise that only pedophiles deserve, and were forced to swallow foul, exotic purple, green, and chalk solutions no one bothered to identify. Finally, flat on our backs, more dead than alive and wanting more to die than to live, we were rolled into a wardroom.

During the night one of the five of us received disproportionate attention with frequent visits from nurses, interns and even doctors. He was in the bed next to me by the window. I felt sorry for the poor bastard. That he was being paid so much medical attention said he was very rich, very famous, or very sick. As the rich and famous would never find themselves lying next to me, I figured he was deathly ill and sympathized for him while simultaneously being glad it was him and not me.

The morning found the four of us survivors bedded in the same large hospital room, three beds against one wall (one poignantly empty) and against the opposite wall two beds and a lavatory. In the bed opposite me was a complainer, a continuous complainer: his stomach hurt, his throat hurt, his IV needles hurt, his head hurt, his ass hurt, but most annoying was his consistent complaint of having to pee. To any passing upright figure, to his intercom, to each of us, to the ceiling, and to all other parts of the room he whined about having to pee. Flat on my back, nauseated, and feeling like hell, all I heard was, "Damn it, I've got to take a leak." Three minutes of silence, then, "It's backed up so far I can spit and cry piss." Brief silence, then, "Oh Lord, the pressure! The pain! I can't stand it a minute longer!" A short interval, then, "If someone doesn't come soon, I'll explode." To my curt suggestion he use the bizarre, long-necked plastic bottle that had been conspicuously placed next to our beds, he replied that he couldn't find it and that even if he could, just reaching for it would break the dam.

In the bed next to me by the door was another complainer. Not only didn't he have a urine bottle, he was missing a bedpan, his water carafe was empty, he hadn't received any pain pills, and he definitely knew why he had been so singularly neglected.

The bed with the flooded bladder told him to shut up or he'd go over there and personally fill up his water jug.

An argument flared up between the two as to who was more neglected but quickly dissipated, as the opponents were too weak to sustain their bile.

During the night visions of urine stained beds and the ever-present, ugly, pungent hospital smells weaved in and out of my consciousness as I slowly dipped into a light sleep. Suddenly the lights came on and a herd of white stampeded past my bed and huddled around the poor soul by the window. Whispers—urgent whispers, then scary whispers, then sad whispers, then whispers of finality—came from the silhouettes outlined on the privacy curtain.

Suddenly the curtain was thrown back and the parade of white rushed out. The somber doctors were followed by worried white-garbed females, and bringing up the rear of the sepulcher train was a human form encased in a white sheet on a gurney being pushed by black orderlies dressed in white.

As the white parade passed him, Full Bladder yelled for relief. "I'm so backed up I can cry, and if I do it'll be tears of piss."

Before the door closed I saw flashing lights from the corridor and heard the members of the media shouting, demanding a few words about the guy under the sheet. They asked hopefully whether he was the football star player on the Jets who had been reported to be a guest speaker at the banquet.

When the door closed and the room lights were turned off my adjacent complaining neighbor mumbled to the dark room, "Who does that bastard know to get all that attention? I know why I'm not getting any attention. It's because—"

The urine bed said, "I'm warning you, keep it up and I'm going to pee. And it won't be in my bed."

The other complainer complained, "Damn it. Why don't you use the bathroom? You're right next to it. Me, they put facing it. All I have to look at is a shit house. I know why they put me opposite the—"

"Shit. I'm begging. Someone get me a urine bottle. If I get up I'll lose control."

Suddenly the outline of a nurse appeared in the doorway before disappearing into the dark shadows in the direction of the urine whiner. Whispers, the rustling of sheets, then silence. After awhile she said, "I can't stand here all night."

"I can't do it in front of a woman," he whined.

"Fine. When you're finished, put it on your night stand, and don't, I repeat, *don't*, spill it."

She left.

Silence—more silence—then the bladder yelled, "You guys are listening! I can't go with everyone listening!"

"Crap," my complaining neighbor cried. "Did you expect her to hold it for you? No one would give me a urine bottle and I know why."

Sarcastically I asked the bladder if he wanted us to leave the room until he finished peeing.

To placate us, he said, "Okay, okay, I'll try."

Silence—more silence.

"Damn it!" I yelled. "Will you piss so I can get to sleep? I can't sleep waiting to hear you pee. Just piss!"

More silence.

"Well?" I asked.

"*You* try to piss lying down. It's unnatural."

The patient next to the bladder put forth a cheerful idea for our future. "Wait 'til you have to take a shit in the bed pan."

We all mumbled, "Shit." I prayed for constipation.

More silence.

"Damn it!" I said. "After all that complaining and bullshit about peeing, you're empty."

"No man. It's just I've been holding it so long my muscles are locked tight. I can't relax them."

"It's me!" my complaining neighbor shouted. "You don't feel safe pissing in front of me. My presence threatens you. I'm being insulted. The man will not pee in front of me."

The puzzled bladder asked, "What the hell are you talking about?"

"You know! You know! You damn well—"

He was silenced by the sound of rushing water, a veritable endless downpour. After what seemed like ten minutes of listening to the waterfall in the dark, silent room I started to giggle. My neighbor giggled. We all laughed until the bladder stopped peeing, pleading he couldn't laugh and pee at the same time. His observation broke us up.

When he finally finished peeing, a benign silence reigned in the darkness. Suddenly we heard a dreadful sound, a plastic bottle falling to the floor followed by the noisy gurgling of escaping fluid. Again we lost control, laughing loudly, and our laughter increased with each cry of despair from the bladder, who kept moaning, "Oh shit, I can't reach it! Oh shit, it's all over the floor! Oh shit!"

Suddenly the lights went on and two young nubile nurses came running in. Their youth and beauty, wrapped in white, flowing uniforms, announced the lithesome spirits of a forest glen. Their upturned cute kissable noses had been designed to smell only the perfume of wild flowers, their green eyes to gaze solely upon singing bluebirds, their slender smooth porcelain hands to be caressed only by cool, clear waters of woodland streams, their flawless soft white cheeks to be lightly wrinkled only in gentle, innocent mirth. Now, in that drab room, those innocent, delicate angels looked down at that ugly long-nosed phallic bottle dispelling its gross cargo and then at the bladder, who was frozen in shame, half-in, half-out of bed, his hairy bare ass peeking out from his hospital gown, one wet hand in— Well, it was a disgusting scene made ten times worse by the two angels who had been forced to see it.

Glaring at the struggling miscreant, who was trying simultaneously and unsuccessfully to upright the urine bottle, get back to bed, cover his ass, wipe his hand and become invisible, one angel said, "Mr. Brothers, ring your bell if you need assistance in relieving yourself."

"I *did* ring," apologetic Brothers whined, "but no one came."

She corrected him. "But we are here."

The other angel pointed a graceful forefinger at the ever-widening puddle and said, "Look at what you've done."

Cringing under his sheet, looking as if death would be a welcome release, he murmured, "I'm sorry."

Turning to the room, the white nymphs condemned us for laughing at Mr. Brothers because he had spilled his urine.

Slipping farther under my covers, I desperately wanted to explain that we were not gross, callous, insensitive men, but were eminently worthy of their good opinion.

They left us to our shame and discomfort. We'd have felt tenfold more dirty and guilty if those heavenly spirits had stooped so low as to clean that vile mess. They didn't. Thank goodness, a middle aged, fat, ugly woman in a blue uniform came in with a mop and pail and disinfectant spray. The remainder of the night passed in sleep.

The morning after our poisoning was given over in trying to quiet our stomachs and minimize our discomfort in absorbing the medical fluids. Intravenous needles were pumping into us from a control panel as complicated and ominous as any Frankenstein movie prop. All the while I continuously prayed to enter a forgiving, dreamless, painless sleep, an easy injection away and cruelly forbidden me.

The four of us were in a large, melancholy hospital room. At one end of the room, over radiators were three closed, sealed dirty windows that framed a depressing vista of three similar dirty windows imbedded in brick five feet away. Opposite the windows, the room's closed oversized door buried us alive from the ongoing flow of life outside the room.

Enduring the first day's miseries none of us was in any condition to socialize; however, our helpless, hapless, hopeless condition didn't deter others from taking advantage of our condition to pounce upon us. Nurses—cruel, brutal, callus women ruthlessly and without seeking consent or permission—sadistically inserted needles everywhere and anywhere while complaining of vein sizes and uncooperative attitudes. They sucked from impoverished veins test tubes of blood and peered at our empty, long-nosed urine vats while shaking their heads at the lack of results, then demanded more blood and that the urine vats be filled instantly. They administered enemas and forced vomiting, then saved the sickening results in carefully labeled assorted vials and bottles. The administered enough medically induced pain to satisfy the Marquis de Sade on a day he felt perky and playfully adventurous.

After those white birds of prey flew from our room of pain, the gods visited. Fat, clean, sleek, pompous, disdainful doctors walked about our beds, nodding sagely at our charts, nodding comprehensively at our complaints, nodding sympathetically at our pain, nodding wisely at our describing symptoms, nodding encouragement to that bed and murmuring hope to this bed, and extending empathy to all with air pats of healing hands. Singularly or in groups they glided in and out, doing nothing.

All this was costing my health plan ten dollars a smile and fifty a nod, with pats going at a hundred.

After the expensive starched-white coats departed, before we could draw a relaxed breath an excited crowd of expensively suited men and women charged in as if it was a Black Friday sale at Marcus Neman. Separating into couples, each of which approached their predetermined patient, they were unsuccessful in attempting to don somber, caring, concerned expressions. Instead, their inner excitement showed in glistened eyes and wet, salivating lips reminiscent of a drunkard approaching an open bar.

My couple identified themselves as Flower Wiser and Damien Donaldson, Senior Chief Supervising Agent from the Homeland Security Agency. In case I could possibly doubt their status, they quickly flashed gold- and silver-encrusted badges as if fearing the shine would blind me.

Flower sat, and Damien remained standing.

Having grown heavy, possibly flabby, and definitely obese while fighting the terrorists flowing in and out of New York City airports, Damien eyed Flower's chair wistfully.

Flower, no delicate bud herself, resembled a lobby large urn topped with a head of disorderly weeds and she wasn't moving an ass's inch.

With absolutely no concern for my condition, Flower asked whether I could answer a few questions.

Before I could consult my sour stomach and my tender butt to answer, Damien quickly asked whether I'd seen any sinister activity at the children's banquet table.

Flower amplified. "Or any suspicious characters engaged in suspicious activities."

Damien quickly said, "We definitely aren't targeting any foreign Muslim-looking persons, and in canvassing your mind you should take the broadest view in trying to isolate and identify possible terrorist poisoners."

Flower added, "Or possibly a deranged person engaged in erratic behavior."

I asked, "Was it a terrorist attack?"

"We haven't definitely determined that," Flower reluctantly confessed.

"Any children poisoned?"

Begrudgingly Damien admitted, "To date, after a thorough examination, no child has exhibited any effects of poisoning."

After eventually determining that our well of knowledge of suspicious characters was as void as our scrubbed and empty stomachs, they left amass. Before the door shut I heard someone Flower called Geraldo tearfully gasp when she answered his question: "Yes Geraldo, it could be a terrorist attack on little children. The investigation is still ongoing." To some of Geraldo's mumbling, Flower said she'd be glad to be on his special.

The door closed as Donaldson emphatically stated, "You can't interview the surviving men on how they feel about being poisoned, especially on camera."

Having been emptied from the mouth, butt, and every vein by lunchtime, we were suffering not from hunger, but from empty stomachs and tender, enema-bruised rumps. Suddenly, huge food trolleys were rattling down the corridors with the promise of colorless, tasteless, formless, non-nourishing hospital food. Our stomachs growled in response.

The patient closest to the door complained he knew why our room was being served last. The urine guy was busy playing with his urine bottle under the covers. The guy in the bed next to him, diagonally across from me next to the window, was combing his hair and telling us he knew why we were going to be the last served and gave an inexplicable leer and a thumbs-up gesture. The sterile made-up bed where the guy was wheeled out last night, still empty, remained ominously silent.

"Damn!" the urine patient complained. "I just can't do it in the prone." He sat up on the edge of his bed and closed his curtain. He began a discharge just as a young, attractive food server entered, trays in each hand. After serving me and the guy with the comb to the accompaniment of a rushing mountain stream, she pushed aside the urine guy's curtain to get at his bed table. He screamed but the stream kept flowing. The other complaining guy complained about being served last, and of course he knew why he was last.

Hungrily and hastily uncovering our food dishes we were shocked to find the entrée was a half-bowl of bland, tasteless, thin, almost clear beef broth. The appetizer was a half-cup of cherry flavored Jell-O. It was so watery they must have dragged a single bleeding cherry screaming across a kitchen vat of boiling gelatin. The only bright spot was a Dixie cup of vanilla ice cream frozen solid.

The guy in the urine bed, half-in, half-out his hospital gown, got up and gently carried his filled bottle shakily toward the bathroom. Sheepishly he apologized. "I jerked when she suddenly opened my curtain. Got to wash my hands, so I might as well empty— Oh shit."

Our attractive female food server, accompanied by a freckle-faced sweet sixteen year old candy striper walked into the room, almost bumping into him. He rushed into the lavatory, splashing as he went.

The sweet candy striper said, "Ugh."

The attractive food server said, "Disgusting," then announced that a mistake had been made in our lunch.

For a brief, delirious moment, mushroom-covered T-bone steaks anointed with A-1 sauce and accompanied by French fries playing peek-a-boo in ketchup puddles jumped to mind, only to be ruthlessly squashed as she quickly and unceremoniously took away our ice cream.

The complainer next to me told her he knew why he was not only losing his Dixie cup but why they took his first after he was served last.

The hair combing, thumbs-up gentleman was tenacious in holding on to his ice cream. It took arguments, scolding, pleading and finally a tug of war before the food server was able to pry the Dixie cup out of his hands. The lucky dog, I noticed he managed to swallow two spoonfuls before the ignoble surrender. In defeat, he winked slyly to the food server and said he knew why she had made the mistake. She took a quick glance at the pisser's table, then quickly returned to the thumbs-up's bed, reached under his covers and, after a brief and lively struggle, extracted a second Dixie cup. She scolded him. "Stealing another's food! *Really*, Mr. Palante!"

With the subtlety of a burlesque comedian he said, "It's your love I'm out to steal. I'll be here all day, so you'll know where to find me, in bed, in pjs."

She left quickly. The candy striper was giggling.

The lavatory door opened and a head peered out. "They're gone?"

"Yeah," I answered, "and so is the ice cream."

Assured, he ran to his bed and closed his curtain.

"Do you have a bladder complaint?" Palante, the patient with the Casanova complex sarcastically asked, then said, "It's going to be hard making out with the nurses with you peeing, spilling, and stinking up the place all the time. Man, pee is a love turnoff."

"It's all this IV. The fluids just go right through me."

"Well put a cork in it. Every time a good-looking nurse comes in you're spraying all over the place. Get any pee on my side of the curtain and I'll rub your face in it."

Bladder's said, "Screw you!"

Casanova Palante replied, "Don't you wish you could." Then he asked us if we noticed the food server reaching under his covers. "Before she grabbed the ice cream, she grabbed me you know where." He grinned.

No one answered.

Undeterred, he continued. When he started to get graphic about the imaginary grabbing, everyone told him to shut up.

Everyone had their privacy curtains drawn, trying to digest a dab of Jell-O and a smidgen of watery beef broth in quiet repose. Late autumn's warm yellow sunlight filtering through the window's drab yellow curtains gave the room a quiet library ambiance. I gave grateful thanks for my stomach's calm, it being content to go about its business without complaint. I started thinking about a TV, where one was and how could I view it, and debating whether to risk disturbing my complacent stomach with the horrendous struggle it would require to reach the bedside phone to order a TV. My stomach decided it and I were unequal to the effort.

CHAPTER 2

A Visitor

During a quiet moment of repose my curtain parted and Woodruff whispered in his whiny voice, "Ed? Ed McCoppin, you in here? It's me, Woodruff."

Damn, it was the worse time for a visitor and he was the last person I wanted to see. My partner, Detective Woodruff Biden of homicide—the most pompous, disliked, self-righteous hypocritical liberal on the force, if not on this earth—was the last person anyone would want to see. Like a mosquito, he was sure to disrupt sleep and bite at the most tender place. Handsome, thirtyish, born to wealth, which he exuded in dress, voice, attitude and carriage, he peered between the curtains while his annoying broad smile indicated his happiness at my misfortune. With all miserable hypocrites, if you know their true nature they become transparent. I saw Woody's soul as plainly as if it lay at the bottom of a cup of the hospital's clear beef broth.

Once inside my hospital space, after carefully folding his heavy cashmere overcoat, he placed it over my feet. The coat's costly quality pressed heavily on my feet. His tie, suit, and shirt said money, and it said it so quickly you knew Woodruff was rich before he opened his mouth and said hello in that irritating Harvard accent. Sitting between my elbow and my shoulder he forced me to twist my head to look up at him as he looked down at me.

The reason I had been assigned as this character's detective partner can only be ascribed to either malevolent superiors or malicious fate. My consuming ambition from the day we met to this day was to get another partner. But since he was my partner, common courtesy, common decency, and common sense said I must play the hypocrite's game: hide my feelings and be friendly. The difference between us was that my hypocrisy was a foreign import I was forced to wear; his, of domestic manufacture, was readily and easily worn. I could and did shed my imported facade as uncomfortable cloth. He did not or would not or could not shed his hypocrisy because there was nothing beneath it. Underneath his current socially accepted attitudes, beliefs and platitudes he had no core, no being. The best way to describe our differences was that I knew when I was being hypocritical, and he didn't. I was uncomfortable when I was being hypocritical, but he wasn't. In truth, if accused of hypocrisy he'd be honestly shocked and insulted at such an unwarranted charge; I'd be embarrassed.

He brought a small bouquet of flowers, a nice gesture, but it was no more than his sense of himself as being a thoughtful, sensitive person, demanded. It was not for me, but for himself, his self-esteem demanding no less. He would not visit a hospital without bringing a suitable gift.

Of course, the flowers were an unsuitable gift. A male police partner doesn't give his male detective partner flowers no matter what the occasion, at least not while he's breathing. I gave the appropriate thanks I didn't feel, which he waved aside with manicured nails, (*Damn! What homicide detective gets manicures?*) and mentally gave himself sufficient thanks for his thoughtfulness for both of us.

Making polite inquires about my health, he was almost successful in hiding his disappointment on hearing my fulsome lies about feeling great and my false promises of a quick recovery. To annoy him further and to exacerbate his disappointment, I exaggerated and underlined my lies with a happy face. Twenty feet of intestines could be hanging out of my ass, and to him I'd gaily laugh and be cheerfully optimistic rather than venting my pain and causing his bubble of joy to grow, barely obscured behind his empathetic attitude. Of course, he had to be cheerful and happy over my reported good health, so we threw false smiles at each other and exchanged exaggerated false cheer.

We remained uncomfortable in our good cheer until Woodruff, recovering from his disappointment over my fast recovery and trying to spread a cloud over my bed announced, "One guy at your table, Jim Scott, didn't make it. Died last night."

I didn't respond. I really didn't care and I wasn't up to bringing up any hypocritical caring.

Trying to cause a relapse to my good cheer, he continued. "Did you know it wasn't food poisoning? I mean the food itself wasn't spoiled."

"No?" That surprised me. All during the excruciating pain of enemas and stomach pumps, and despite Homeland Security visits, I still thought it was just bad food. The salsa generated in some illegal's Mexican's kitchen was my chief suspect.

"Yeah, your table was the only one to go down." He liked that thought and to hide it, frowned a little. "It was the salsa; cockroach powder was sprinkled on it."

"Roach powder?!"

"Yeah, cockroach powder."

For him the enjoyment was tripled. He enjoyed the idea of my poison being cockroach powder. He took enjoyment at my evident discomfort and in being the messenger who had caused my pain. Pressing his advantage in chipping away at my cheer, he said, "I wonder why you didn't taste something wrong with the salsa?" What he meant was how could I be so stupid to eat the poison. I was responsible for all my pain because I was careless and stupid. His self-serving inference was that he never would or could be so unobservant or stupid as to eat cockroach poison.

I explained, "The salsa was hot, real jalapeno-pepper hot, mouth-ripping, eye-tearing, drink-guzzling, and ice-cube-chewing hot. None of us could resist the challenge."

"Well, since you're my partner and also one of the victims, they put me in charge of the investigation."

"They" were the politicians and politically connected police hierarchy who socialize with Woodruff's wealthy parents. Five men poisoned at the father-son midget football banquet with one dead was a headline case guaranteed to receive a lot of newsprint and TV interview time. It promised a sure promotion and was a plum assignment, so of course Woody got it.

He made it sound like "they" were forcing a reluctant virgin to sacrifice her honor to save mankind. In reality he was a cheap whore forever running after a five-dollar trick. He hadn't come to see me but because of the case; shouldn't have surprised me, but it did; shouldn't have disappointed me either, but it did.

Unnecessarily he said, "It's a big case, has to be solved. The city can't have a mass poisoner loose. Imagine the panic; imagine if he strikes again, maybe putting roach poison in a school cafeteria lunch: children writhing in horrific pain and dropping dead from roach poison." He said "roach poison" as often as he could, knowing it revolted me. Leaning over me like a priest hearing a dying man's confession, he whispered, "Terrorists."

Smelling his mouth mint, I grunted, "Heh?"

"Keep it quiet. The media is on the terrorist's trail."

"So?" I said, my breath, I hoped, telling the tale of a night of vomiting.

Backing away Woody whispered, "Besides Homeland Security, the FBI and the CIA are getting involved."

Incredulously I asked, "Could it be a terrorist attack? A midget football banquet in Queens, New York?"

"On TV, the president will personally address all the country's midget football parents... in fact, all parents"

"Why?"

"Why! Shit, every son's mother is scared; every son's grandmother is frightened."

"Why?"

"We've got to reassure the country their children are safe."

"I got poisoned. Only adults got poisoned. It's got nothing to do with children."

"Mac, you can't be that naive. What is more newsworthy? What's really scary? A hundred children almost poisoned with cockroach poison by a terrorist organization, or five guys who were drinking stupidly eating some roach-poison-laced salsa? Shit, one's exiting and gets great news ratings; the other is, 'What a shame! So what? Probably they were drunk.'"

Once in a while Woody made sense. He could see the hypocrisy of lies in others and still remain blind to what was within himself.

With me flat on my back I knew he'd have been assigned a new partner. I thought, *With any luck, his current temporary partner will be made permanent and I'll be free of the backstabbing SOB.* "Who's your partner on this?"

"A rookie... young, innocent to the techniques of homicide investigation. With NYPD needing to educate rookies in the sensitive correct police procedures, I volunteered to mentor my new partner. I think we'll work well together and mesh well as a team. They (*There's that word again*) want me to teach the rookie all the correct legal police investigative procedures but without the discriminatory prejudices and illegal shortcut techniques prevalent in the past." His liberal façade was so thick and comfortably worn, he was the only white cop in America who still believed OJ and Casey Anthony were innocent.

He was looking so happy about his new rookie, I nobly volunteered, "If you'd like to make the new team permanent, it's all right with me."

"Never, Mac, never. Your assistance has been great. Hey, I couldn't have solved the, er... past cases without your help."

He really thought he didn't need me. Woody could lie with the best of them. He believed half of his lies, and he totally believed that everyone else, especially me, believed all of them.

Deciding to bring a little truth to the surface of this stagnant, stinking pool of polite BS, I said, "Woody, I don't assist you. We're partners. You're detective first grade and I'm second grade, but as far as I'm concerned the distinction starts and stops at the pay differential. Second, I solved the recent Hoboken Indian Ax Murders (Lonely Detective Volume II) case, despite the interference of all your politically correct crap. And don't forget, it was thanks to your testimony that I was suspended for six months without pay and the ax murderer got off."

"Mac, Mac, don't upset yourself. You're sick. You know I had to testify truthfully. It was you who used the, er..." He looked about our curtained tent searching for possible eavesdroppers. Then he took a deep breath, leaned close to me, and risked whispering, "You *did* use the N word. If you have racist prejudice, it's your problem, your sickness, and your sin. If you deal with it and come to terms with it, you can cure yourself of your hateful prejudices. I certainly am unable to condone such ignorant attitudes, and I'm prepared to fight such crude prejudices with education and unbiased truth. As your partner I was hoping to re-educate and sensitize you to the plight, the suffering, poverty, and prejudices that people of color experience every day in our racist society."

"Damn it, Woody, you should have lied for your partner and nailed that murderer."

"Me? Lie? And under oath? Mac, that's something I could never do. My lord, what would happen to our judicial system if people didn't take their legal oaths seriously?"

"Look, Woody, you SOB, no one wants to work with a guy who stabs his partner in the back. I'll be glad to get a new partner, one who backs me up and doesn't take credit for my work. I solved the Indian Ax Murders and you took the credit and the promotion."

Woody was unable to believe anyone would think ill of him, and if by perversion that rare person did believe ill of him, the reason had to lie within the person, never in Woody himself. Self-deception was his ego-enhancing magnanimity of forgiveness and understanding. "Mac, you're ill. You're lashing out from a sick bed. After all, let's face it: someone may have tried to kill you. You, not the children, could have been the target."

That thought had not disturbed my peace 'til this moment when a considerate, sensitive Woody tossed his rock into my quiescent mind.

"And the idea that you're so personally disliked that someone would risk killing four others just to bring you down is a terrible burden for you to bear. I understand your pain and anger. If it helps you to deal with it, go ahead and strike out at me. I know it's not at me; it's at the hurt inside you. If attacking me gives you relief, go ahead. My affection for you is strong enough to forgive and forget your pain-inspired attacks."

I half-expected him to rip open his expensive shirt, bare his pigeon chest and with suffering eyes raised to heaven, start praying to the secular non-god he worshipped. Instead, true to form, he continued his self-serving rant.

"Mac, you must cleanse your mind of thoughts of enmity towards me and look into your heart. That's where your corrosive hate and envy lie; that's where, scouring with the Brillo of self-honesty, you must remove and cleanse yourself of your racist hate, of envy of me and my success, and your terrible preoccupation with money. All must be excised. Take responsibility for your life; don't blame others for your misfortune."

"Damn it, Woody, get your ass out of my room! I'm sick of the sight of you and I'm tired of listening to your BS."

"I'm here for you, Mac. Use me; abuse me if it helps you achieve mental health."

I tried reaching for the water cravat to throw at the asshole but the damn thing was a thumbnail's length out of reach.

In his persona of sensitive caregiver, he took the carafe, poured a glass and started to hand it to me. Then, seeing my eyes were red lights stopped the glass mid-air before I could grab it and throw it at him. "Better not give you this, Mac; don't know if the doctors would want you to drink water." And he drank it.

As he sat in silence, I closed my eyes, mentally willing him out of my space, out of my job, out of my life. I really, really didn't like the bastard.

Finally, he sighed. I heard it through closed eyes and obstinately refused to open them.

He coughed. I snored. He cleared his throat. I snored louder. He sneezed. I snored even louder. He touched my hand. I moved it away while giving out the loudest, most obvious artificial snore I could project from the prone position.

"Mac, I know you're not asleep. Heavens, if you were asleep I'd be the last person to wake a sick man, but we both know you're not."

Can't fool him, being a detective first grade. Like all educated fools, he could never get the message within the message.

"Mac, this is a murder investigation. We have to catch the man or men who did this. He or they are insane, of course; he or they need extensive psychological help. Without professional help, he may do it again; he may even hurt himself."

Like all liberals, he slipped into his favorite mode of thought—empathizing and excusing the criminal—which never failed to drive me up the wall. I opened my eyes. "What's the story on the poisoning?"

He dodged the question. "Well, the main purpose for my visit is to see a sick friend in the hospital. However, I do have another purpose: to interview you, to find out what happened at the banquet and the events leading up to your eating cockroach poison, and er... spilling your guts all over the place settings."

Whether it was the sound of the bladder patient filling his bottle for the tenth time or not, Woody announced, "Say, do you have a bathroom here? I've got to wash my hands."

Screw his euphemism. "You can wash your hands in the bathroom, and if you've got to pee, you can also do it in there." His dislike of my pee remark gave me some satisfaction.

CHAPTER 3

Woody's New Partner

As I lay there, seething with dislike for the hand-washing pompous ass, my curtain opened and an extremely cute nurse peeked in. She was mid-twentyish with straight, shoulder-length, sinfully shining black hair, green eyes highlighted with eyebrow liner, eyelashes thickened licorice black, full lips painted deep red, perhaps too red for the afternoon. In fact, her good looks were startling. Her extensive expensive facial make-up suggested midnight, low-cut clinging silk gowns, dances, champagne for two, carriage rides ending in romantic early morning trysts in a Park Avenue penthouse duplex, not a hospital room a little past two in the afternoon. Out of place, her make-up had an effect: if she was plain looking, she'd appear stupid, but being attractive, she appeared fantastic.

I invited her into my cubicle hoping to talk to her. Well, actually to flirt a little. As she entered, I realized she was definitely no nurse. She was wearing a fashionable, tailored, brown and red tweed jacket and a skirt that de-emphasized her waist and brought out her ample hips, fronting for a firm, round behind. The ruffled, white silk blouse bubbling out past the unbuttoned jacket and flowing over the jacket's lapels suggested large, soft, white breasts undulating just beneath the surface, while a thin black ribbon tight about her throat said, *I'm sensual, forbidden, dangerous, and wouldn't you want to see me standing over you wearing just the ribbon?*

Hopefully not ogling while she stood over me, briefly I enjoyed mentally picturing her in just the ribbon. I looked at her up and down, over, around and especially at the fluffy white silk suggestively hiding and outlining fulsome breasts. As she stood so close and high over me, with her breasts so purposefully there, wordlessly proposing damnation in playing at domination, I decided I wouldn't mind experiencing some of that domination. In fact, I hoped she'd pull a whip from behind her ass and pounce.

"You're Ed McCoppin, Woody's old partner. I'm Detective Ronni Deutsch, helping Woody. Do you mind if I call you Eddy? I'm Ronni, with an 'I'."

Shit, why do women have to go so quickly to first names? Annoyed at her ignoring my title while stating and underling hers, I emphatically said, "Detective Ed McCoppin."

Ignoring my correction, she asked, "Where's Woody? I've got the reports we need."

I nodded in the general direction of the bathroom. "He's washing his hands."

Speaking of the pompous ass, the lucky bastard ducked into our little tent and smiled at Ronni. As he turned to me, his smile became a self-satisfied one implying, *Don't you wish you were me and I were you?* After introducing Ronni Deutch he needlessly mentioned my marital status before waxing in a self-congratulatory manner over how politically correct he was in demanding a young rookie woman as a partner and how happy he was they had assigned Ronni. Lest, Heaven forbid, we suspect his joy was sexually motivated, he ticked off Ronni's qualifications on his fingers: she had graduated from college as a sociology major, concentrating in dysfunctional families (*In contemporary America are there any other type of families?*); she'd worked almost a year in the city's Social Services department, but feeling unfulfilled, unchallenged, underutilized and (unsaid) an underpaid paper pusher, she quit; she'd graduated from the police academy in the top twenty, and after working a year at a nothing desk job, was promoted to detective third grade and at the ripe age of twenty-five was second banana in a headline case. As obnoxious Woody ranted over her zero qualifications I thought of the men with seniority working, suffering, and studying for years still walking or riding the streets. *Damn affirmative action and liberals like Woodruff who in doing something completely wrong can turn it into a courageous moral right thing.* Of course he wasn't shafted; doing the courageous right thing cost him nothing; it was easy sainthood gained the politically correct way.

Woody continued, "No offense, Mac, but you know I've been desperately pleading they assign a minority to me. For too long our society has excluded women, blacks and other ethnic...."

He wandered off into his 'I'm a rich liberal who loves the poor minorities,' speech, a noble St. Francis of Assisi who doesn't feel the need to give his money to the poor. I'd heard it a thousand times and now he was launching into it for busty Ronni's benefit.

To deflect the conversation away from him, I turned to Ronni. She had moved her chair to my elbow, allowing me an opportunity to inspect her close up. Her ocean green eyes were outlined and encircled by a shoreline of black. I said, "So you graduated in the top twenty of your class."

She smiled with teeth so bright, white, expensively capped and orthodontically even that they resembled my grandmother's dentures. She touched my arm, a touch more firm than gentle. It might appear to a casual observer to be a caring, sympathetic, gesture motivated by a nurturing attitude, but it wasn't. It was a conscious, deliberate sexual feint on her part, a physical increment on the sexual continuum sexually attractive women employ to secure interest in themselves. In earnest tones and with an earnest facial expression, she said, "I worked hard, very hard, at the academy. I'm determined to be a success in police investigative work and be a career model for other women. Woody and I agree the department needs an infusion of women and minorities to give a greater sensitivity to and understanding of the underprivileged, while presenting a representative diverse police image to a diverse American public."

Crap. She has the same bullshit line as Woody. But as sociology major could she possibly say anything else? The difference was, he believed it and she didn't. More accurately he believes it as long as it doesn't work against his interest, and she doesn't believe it unless it works for her interest.

"Top twenty," I said, both to say something and to keep from saying what my intellect wanted to say. After all, it's hard to say "bullshit" to a twenty-five year old with peach smooth cheeks and sparkling green eyes peeking out of dark, man-made caves, and whose soft white hands were tipped in purple and alternating gently patting and holding your hand.

Woody, standing behind her and patting her shoulder, tried to present the strong masculine figure encouraging a woman who is encouraging a sick, weak, impotent man-child lying in bed. I felt I was at the bottom of a food chain. In the ensuing silence, Ronni handed some reports to Woody, who scanned them and handed them back.

Men love silence, women are made uneasy by it, and liberals, being good talkers, passionately hate it, so Woodruff broke it first. "Look Mac, we don't want to stay too long and exhaust you. Just give us a run down on last night's banquet and I'll let you rest while Ronni and I question the other victims."

I deeply resented his treating me as an outsider, a civilian, especially in front of Ronni. If I gave him what I knew, he'd brush me off and keep all his information from me. Given his incompetence, he'd also screw up the case, and given his influential friends, at the end somehow he'd make me responsible. I wanted to be an insider, part of the investigation. I gestured towards the reports Ronni was protectively clutching to her breasts like so many nursing babies. "Woody, old partner, first fill me in on what's in the initial reports."

We started to dance around who would show his hand first, with Woody expressing concern for my recovery and wanting to relieve me of any worry. Ronni seconded his touching concern for me by casually patting my shoulder, rubbing my forearm, holding my hand, and keeping the reports tightly nipple nursed.

I promised working would hasten my recuperation.

Woody worried whether the doctors would allow it. He said maybe he should confer with them and get back to me.

I prescribed mental stimulation to divert my attention from my current physical condition, telling them a mind can only have one occupant at a time.

Inappropriately, Ronni giggled. "With men the occupant is usually a woman."

Revealing something of herself? I suspect she'd uncovered her soul and I saw it.

Looking down at her wistfully, Woody hoped he was hearing a suggestive future for him.

Abruptly I said, "Woody, tell me what you found out. Neither of us will get anywhere playing cute with each other."

One thing about Woody—he never gives in, only grants favors. "Okay Mac, don't get so worked up, you'll have a relapse. If you want to know so badly I guess it won't hurt to give you some information."

A concerned, nurturing Ronni seconded Woody. "If you feel you're getting tense or upset, just say so. We'll stop and come back later." She made me feel like I was minutes from receiving the last rites.

Woody said, "There were eight of you at the table."

I interrupted, "I only saw five including myself."

An annoyed Woody frowned while Ronni said, "Eddy, don't interrupt Woody. It distracts him."

Shit. She's acting like he's Moses on high and I, an irreligious ignorant idolater refusing to recognize his divine anointment. And where did this Eddy stuff come from?

Woodruff smiled, "Thank you, Detective Ronni." He turned to me, "There were three missing from table 12: Antonio Geroni, Murry Zapp and Thomas Applegate. Applegate, the team's coach, decided to move from table 12 to sit at the main table with the children."

"Why? What reason did he give?"

"He felt a coach should be with his players."

"And when did he decide on this sports etiquette thing?"

Ronni answered just to show she was part of the conversation. "During the afternoon. He forgot to remove his name tag from table 12, so for all intents and purposes everyone thought he was going to be at your table."

"Who was the second missing one?"

Ronni continued. "Tony Geroni was out working on an emergency plumbing job."

"Suspicious! What about the last no show, Murry Zapp?"

"Zapp had a silly argument with Jim Scott, the one who died, over whose son was the better football player. Out of pique, he moved to table 11."

"Very suspicious," I said. "So the five who—"

Woody said, "Mac we mustn't jump to hasty conclusions. The three not at table 12 are under suspicion as well as being possible victims. We've—"

"So five of us got it and it was Jim Scott who died last night?"

Lightly hitting my biceps, Ronni said, "Please Eddy dear, don't interrupt. It isn't courteous."

I felt like a Grateful Dead groupie screaming obscenities during a Bach concert in Prince Albert Hall. *And what's with this "dear" and "Eddy" and "Woody" and "Ronni?" It's all just too damn girly cute.*

Magnanimously, Woody said, "It's all right, Ronni. Yes, the dead man was James Scott, a tire changer for a Pep Boys auto supply store. Died during the night. Wife hasn't been informed yet. Can't locate her."

Turning, Ronni looked up. "You tried, Woody. We'll find her and tell her together. Even the Homeland Security boys have failed."

Possessively patting her back between her shoulders, he located her bra fastener for future reference. The stroking appeared unconsciously given and unnoticed by Ronni, but everyone reading it correctly was able to deny the messages and maintain their innocence and purity.

I told him, "Look, Woodruff, five people were poisoned. One died, and the rest of us have recovered. What made him so special?"

Ronni shushed me and playfully slapped my shoulder, for again I had interrupted.

Pontifically, Woodruff pronounced, "Ulcers" as if he personally had done the autopsy. "Bad case of ulcers. The hot salsa ripped them open and the cockroach poison went right into the bloodstream." He smiled over "cockroach poison" as his gaze caressed Ronni's shiny black hair. "The rest of you upchucked most of the salsa before you could digest a fatal dose of the cockroach poison. Using hot salsa to mask the taste of the cockroach poison was very effective. However, unfortunately from the murderer's point of view, the toxic chemicals in the cockroach powder combined with the salsa's hot peppers became a purgative mixture, causing everyone to throw up. If the cockroach poison had been in the mashed potatoes, you'd be dead now."

"So what's the lowdown on my fellow patients?"

Once again telling me not to interrupt Woody, Ronni was making me feel as if I was telling dirty jokes during the Sermon on the Mount. Playfully and lightly slapping the side of my neck, more a caress than a slap, she blew my composure.

"Ronni, if you slap my hand, biceps, shoulder or neck again I'll spank you." Both they and I were taken back by my threat. It was a Freudian slip. I meant to say I'd slap her back.

She was angry. The first words out of her mouth were about sexual harassment, the second string was about sexual intimidation, and the third was about sexist pigs. She concluded with a personal, exaggerated evaluation of herself. "Mac, you just *wish* you could spank me."

Woodruff was aghast, both for me saying what the dirty hypocrite was thinking and hoping to do ever since he'd met her, and for the career and legal implications of what she was saying. In saying them, she was threatening not only me, but possibly in the future, him. Scared, he said anxiously, "Mac, you don't need sexual harassment charges after facing race charges in the Hoboken Indian Murder Case." To her, he said, "Ronni dear, it would help neither our investigation nor your career profile if we all became enmeshed in a sexual harassment scandal."

We all backtracked, with Woody as usual preening himself as the voice of reason in a world tormented with irrational emotions.

However, clearly she had frightened him. Plus, now she knew threats of sexual harassment over spanking talk scared him. If playful Woody actually did the deed with her, she could simultaneously enjoy it and gain the whip hand over him.

Waving a hand at my closed curtain, I again asked, "What information do you have about them?"

Woody told me the dead Pep Boys tire man, who had been in the bed on my right, was married with one child. The guy in the bed on my left, the one always complaining, was an Arab named Abdullah Hassan Malcolm V. He drives a gypsy cab and lives with a common law wife and her three children, all of whom are in the hospital waiting for visiting hours. The Casanova diagonally in the bed across from me was Paul Palante, a married school maintenance man with two kids. The guy opposite me, the pisser, is Ray Brothers, owner of three McDonald's franchises. He's separated from his wife, and he has a daughter and son.

In return, I told them all I remembered of the salsa eating disaster. "I was the last of the five to get to the table. Palante, Abdullah, Ray Brothers and Scott were already there, standing around sucking on their drinks. No one really talked, just exchanged nods or a few words of polite camaraderie."

Feeling I had given the two sufficient nothings to merit tossing a question back to them, I asked for more information about the three who weren't at table 12.

With Ronni busy checking the files nursing at her breast, Woody abruptly summarized. "Coach Tom Applegate, a security analyst for a brokerage house, as you know, ate at the main table with his team. The only one really absent was the plumber, Antonio Geroni, who at the last moment skipped the banquet, claiming he had an emergency leak. He's being investigated, of course."

It was obvious Geroni was high on Woody's list. He gave additional details on table 12's other missing diner, Murry Zapp. "Ed, get this— Murry Zapp is a friend of Jim Scott's. In fact, they work together at Pep Boys. Zapp was originally slated to sit next to Scott at table 12, but he suddenly changed to table 13."

Ronni stopped fidgeting with her folders to add with a sociologist's profundity, "The question is why he made the change. He'd better have a good reason. If he doesn't have one it could put him high on our suspect list." Deciding to put her oar deeper into our conversational waters Ronni asked, "Who ate the salsa first?"

Woody added, "And who ate the most?"

Ronni continued Woody's thought. "And who ate the least?"

I mentally weighed the amount of salsa on each cracker and counted the number of crackers thrown down each throat, then told them what I knew.

"Palante was first. Then Ray Brothers, the McDonalds guy, dived in. He said the Golden Arches should add burritos and bankrupt Taco Bell. Abdullah, the black guy was next. They were all pursing their lips and screaming at each other how hot it was. They were trying to cool their mouths off with their drinks, when the murdered Pep Boy, Jim Scott, announced he loved spicy food but shouldn't eat it because he had a bad ulcer. But he said the hell with it and dove into it with vengeance. It was searing their lips, and they were howling and drinking cold beer. It was like they had to try some, just to see how hot is hot. It was hotter than hot.

"The guy with the ulcer was the first to complain and started to get sick. The rest of us quickly followed. Everything after that was a blur of pain and vomit." I looked at Ronni. "What happened to the three no shows at our table? Their absence looks suspicious."

Brushing aside my question, Woody asked if I knew anything about the men who got sick.

"I never talked to them 'til that night, though I had seen them at my son's football games. Who had access to the table while it was being set up? Who put the salsa on our table?"

Woodruff ignored my question. "Did anyone act suspiciously at table 12 or during your treatment in the emergency room?"

"I don't know. I was too sick to notice. Which wives or daughters were at the dinner?"

"Everyone's," he airily responded, then repeated, "Who ate the least salsa?"

"I did; however, it was so hot that no one had more than a couple of crackers before the pain hit. Whose wife set up table number twelve?"

"Mac, there's no help there. Ray's daughter put out the butter and his wife did the rolls, Palante's wife put out the place settings of plastic plates and utensils, and Geroni's wife, the no show guy, put out the glasses, followed by Abdullah's wife who put out the water pitchers. Applegate's wife put out the table numbers, and Scott's wife put out the paper tablecloths."

"And the salsa? Who put it out?"

"Mac, I'm sorry to say, but one of the wives thinks it was Pam, your wife, who put out the salsa. But she's unsure. In fact, given it was her husband who died, she was confused and hysterical at the initial interview at the banquet."

Ronni added, "Actually she was totally incoherent. Her impression has to be discounted."

"Don't tell me you suspect Pam."

Leaning forward so his body English would show how earnest he was, Woody said, "Hell no. Never. There is no way Pam is a suspect."

"But the FBI?" Ronni added. "Homeland Defense, State Police, they don't know your wife, so...."

I pressed for further salsa details. "Who brought the salsa to the banquet? Did all the tables get bowls of salsa?"

Evasive Woody expressed concern over my getting too excited.

Ronni, to show independence or to exhibit inside investigative knowledge, revealed that our table was the only one favored with salsa.

To maintain their status mentor to rookie, Woody confirmed Ronni's revelation and added, to make certain of their hierarchy, "I determined only one bowl of salsa was brought into the banquet hall."

"We don't know who brought it into the hall," Ronni amplified to erase any suspicion that she occupied a subservient role.

Her addendum forced Woody to reveal that the salsa bowl was on a side table covered with Saran Wrap with Ritz crackers next to it.

Ronni shot back, "With a typed note saying it was for table 12 from a well wisher."

I was happy to be an audience of one. As they played their one-upmanship game, I was able to gain information I ordinarily would have to sweat bullets to mine.

Finally out of information, each paused. In the ensuing awkward silence Woody held out for a good three seconds before asking a typically stupid question. "Did you notice anyone not swallowing?"

Sarcastically I responded, "If someone did, he wouldn't get sick and be lying here, and we'd have a pretty good idea who the murderer was"

Demanding inclusion, I asked if he was holding out on me.

Apologetically Ronni pointed out I must be considered both a suspect and a victim and good police procedure forbade sharing information with suspects or victims. Woody could get into trouble if it became known.

A smiling Woody ruminated out loud over how as a police detective I had to have many enemies, especially after the Hoboken Indian Case.

Angrily I retorted, "Yeah, including every member of every narrow-minded liberal overlapping special interest group: civil-rights groups, pseudo politically correct groups, and every group that protects the so-called rights of animals, feminists, abortionists, Indians, minorities, criminals, handicapped people, children, or students. Their ever louder, never-satisfied, ever-expanding so-called rights defy rational thought."

During my tirade both Woody and Ronni remained quiet, nervously looking around. When I stopped, with an inhale Woody whispered, "Keep quiet. People could hear."

Standing up, a horrified Ronni said, "You shouldn't say such things against people's rights! Are you a hater?"

"Screw hate. You can't hate stupidity; you can only be disgusted by it. The only group without rights is the white man."

"Don't say white!" Woody pointed towards Abdullah's bed.

Ronni, shaking from anger or horror, shouted, "Males!"

Misunderstanding, Abdullah shouted, "Mails!" followed by his complaining everyone was getting mail except him and he knew why.

Nervously both Woody and Ronni started making tentative movements to leave. Ronni said, "Mac, don't say anything now. Just rest and get well. Let me and Woody work the case."

Woody said, "Mac, you've got a lot of anger in you. Don't let your anger destroy you. I'll keep you informed of my progress."

Ronni wanted to correct him, but he turned to leave.

I called him back and used his desire for Ronni and his desire to gain the prestige of solving this high-profile case and his need for inside information about the victims. "Listen," I said. "Let the wives visit their husbands one at a time. I can listen to their conversation, and I might pick up a clue." I was thinking, given that poison is a woman's first choice as a death instrument, and as all the wives were at the banquet preparing and serving food, they had to be the main suspects. Besides, a strange guy putting a dish of salsa out would have stood out so much he'd now be sitting in the joint, arranging book and movie deals.

Ronni's enthusiastic support for the idea quickly erased Woody's concern over violating privacy rights.

Believing the tired, tried and true axiom, 'the love of money is the root of all evil,' I asked Woody who was the richest among the victims. No one was even close to the pisser, who owned three McDonalds franchises.

Ronni added that he was separated and his wife is the custodial parent of their son and daughter.

Woody said the son was the sole beneficiary of all three McDonalds grease pits and his three point four million life insurance policy with the mother as executrix.

I knew the kid from the football games. He was a chubby nine year old who played the line on the 85-pound team. The opposition usually walked over him and I suspect Mom did the same and would until he was in his thirties when she'd turn the job over to his wife.

After my two aggravating pills left, orderlies moved Brother's bed over to where the deceased Pep Boy Scott had been so I could eavesdrop on his and his wife's conversation. Of course, Abdullah, the complainer on my other side near the door, who had been consistently demanding to be moved next to the window, went ballistic seeing the pisser moved there. He complained it didn't make sense seeing that the pisser, Ray Brothers, who passed more water than a yacht in the America's cup race, now had a longer trip to the bathroom. Besides, since he'd asked for the window spot before anyone else he should get it. By all rights, the window bed should be his and he knew why he didn't get it. When no one paid attention to him he complained about being ignored and swore he knew why he was being ignored, hinting none too subtly about a dark, evil, giant racist conspiracy underway against him. Keeping his privacy curtain tightly drawn, he continually shouted his complaints through the curtains.

CHAPTER 4

Eavesdropping on Big Mac

It was half-past two when Eleanor, Ray's soon to be ex-wife, twenty years beyond her twentieth birthday and fifty pounds heavier than on her wedding night, came in followed by their daughter, twenty years younger and fifty pounds lighter, which still didn't make her a lightweight, but being young made her a voluptuous replication of her mother.

Ray's bed had been pushed up against the window, so Eleanor and daughter had to sit between Ray and me. To give them confidence in their privacy I imitated sleep.

After the perfunctory greetings, kisses, and floral presentation Eleanor explained that little Willie, their nine year old son, couldn't come because of schoolwork.

Ray said, "Bullshit."

Both mother and daughter had worked the banquet, so naturally Ray asked them if they had seen anything or anyone seasoning the salsa.

Neither admitted to having seen anything, and they asked Ray if he knew anything, saw anything, had any ideas.

He had none except he had to go to the bathroom. All conversation stopped. I almost fell asleep while he was going but was brought up short by the sound of flushing and then of Abdullah complaining about being opposite the shithouse and having to hear disgusting bowel and bladder sounds, the flushing of water, and smelling sick room smells a sick man should never have to smell.

Back in bed, an angry Ray gave a sanitized account of his previous night's difficulties and embarrassments to his wife and daughter. Naturally, this led to his inquiry about a private room. He wanted his wife to move him to a private room and damn the expense. He couldn't take another night with us complaining about and laughing over his difficulties, especially when he had fallen out of bed and hurt himself. He told them we were crude, low-caste, no-class men and it's no wonder someone had tried to kill one of us.

It appeared one of us was responsible for his being poisoned. Again, his wife asked if he had seen anything and he swore there had been nothing to see. After all, everyone had eaten the poison. He questioned his daughter Courtney as to what her duties had been.

She said, "I was carrying the ice and butter pats to the tables."

"Did you put butter on my table?"

Virtuously she answered, "All tables had butter bowls, eight pats in a full bowl of ice."

"Honey, I want you to think hard. When you put the butter on my table was the salsa there?"

"I really don't know. It took so much time, counting out the exact number of butter pats and spooning the ice. I didn't have time to notice anything."

Impatiently the mother said, "Ray, for heaven's sake, she didn't see anything, period. The police told us the poison was roach powder mixed in the salsa and your table was the only one to get it, so if she saw anything suspicious about salsa she'd have mentioned it."

"Eleanor, damn it, the effing poison was there and someone put it there."

"Ray, not around Courtney. Watch your language. You can be so crude."

"Look, Eleanor, she does it and we both know she does it, so the name of what she does shouldn't shock her."

That upset both of them, the mother denying the fact, the daughter denying the name; apparently doing it in love sanitized it.

Ignoring the daughter, Ray buttressed his accusation of Courtney's conduct with several male names, describing several explicit situations he had encountered that admitted to no other explanation. From the hurt and anger in his voice, it was obvious his sixteen year old daughter's fornications were sore wounds, which with the slightest irritation bled profusely.

He concluded his tirade by saying that's why he'd left all his money and restaurants to his son.

The mention of fiduciary matters brought a new attack from the wife about separation expenses and him neglecting his daughter with both his love and his money. Of course the emphasis was on money. The wife concluded her attack with hard, quiet words pushed through clenched teeth, that even she could have been provoked into wishing the poison was more effective. "Every selfish man who deserts his wife and children deserves any and all misfortune fate serves him."

"Maybe you're the poisoner," Ray said, not seriously but out of anger. It was obvious he couldn't believe he was the target.

Well, I must confess deep down that I didn't feel I was the intended victim either. Normal people, feeling they are good, feel they don't deserve enemies and are shocked to discover hatred directed at them. On the other hand, paranoids readily see enemies and happily greet them, glad to be justified.

"Listen," the wife said, defending herself, "I was tossing the salad and putting it into individual salad bowls, and if you think tossing salad for almost fifty men is easy, *you* try it."

"Did you put them out? The salad bowls?"

"No. I just told you I was tossing salad. I had my hands full of lettuce, tomatoes, radishes and red peppers, and plastic packets of dressing. The salad was to be served after everyone was seated. Someone else was to put out the salad bowls. I just mixed it."

"So you didn't see anyone at my table who—"

A svelte woman arrived, eight years older than the daughter and eight times more attractive. "Ray, my darling, I couldn't wait any longer. How are you, sweetheart? I brought you, oh—"

For a long moment, silence reigned.

I peeked through my eyelashes and then opened my eyes wide. I recognized the woman; she was in the cash bar drinking. She was Ray's girlfriend, the other woman, and the one in second place, trying very hard for a first place finish. Shit, I thought. "Shit," Ray said.

Daughter Courtney gasped, "It's her! It's Amber!" like she was saying "It's shit!" and the wife looked at Amber as if the mistress was a dog shitting on her expensive Persian rug.

Ray said, "Shit .What are you doing here?"

"I was concerned and afraid for you, Ray. I love you. I had to come."

I don't know about Ray, but I suspect the rest of us thought *Bullshit*. She was protecting her expected territorial possession of Ray and his McDonalds franchises.

Eleanor asked Ray, "How did she turn up so fast?"

"I called her to bring me some clothes," he said.

He was lying. No one was able to make any calls from the room because Woody had seized all the cell phones and disconnected the land phones, which annoyed Homeland Security, as they had established quasi-legal wiretaps. Only after two days of listening and getting silence, and after one day checking their tapes, did they realize Woody had cut them.

When I saw her drinking at the cash bar, wearing a red cocktail dress—a provocative red flag of sexual danger moving through throngs of fathers sucking up drinks and waiting to enter the dining room—I wondered who she was and who she was with. From her dress, her makeup, her hairdo, her body movements and her expression, I knew she certainly was not a wife or a mother. Now in the hospital, in sexual attack mode, she was wearing a violet skirt that fell short of her knees by two inches and a white blouse, both wound tight.

With such a tramp not only possessing immediacy of ownership but physically eclipsing and sexually dominating her, Ray's wife couldn't and wouldn't stay; the contrast was too painfully clear. With daughter in tow they left, both snarling their hopes for Ray's speedy recovery.

After they left, Ray scolded his mistress, saying she should be more discreet.

She said, "Look Ray, you're through with that old cow." He winced at old cow but let it pass. "And we're trying to build a future together. All Eleanor is interested in is your money. I think she was hoping to find you lying here dead."

"Amber, let's get off these subjects and give me a kiss. I've been through hell."

Dutifully she gave him a kiss and from all the noise and its duration it included lips, tongue, teeth and tonsils. I think he wanted comforting affection and she was diving into his mouth, desperately trying to generate excitement, or maybe extracting gold, possibly both.

With annoyance and discomfort, coming up out of her mouth, breathing hard he pushed her away.

To even-out his insulting push, she complained he needed mouth wash. That hurt but he let it pass. "Look Amber, if anyone asks if you were at the banquet, just say no. It'll be simpler."

She asked why she should, though I suspect she knew why.

"Because of the insurance, the three point five I took out, and you're the beneficiary. Remember a couple of months ago I told you about it?"

I remembered the three point five to his son and wondered if there ever existed a three point five to either one. Hearing you're the beneficiary of three point five mil, you can't be so crude as to ask to see the policy.

She made a face like she was searching her memory for some trivial forgotten fact before she purred quietly, "Oh yes, I think I remember you mentioning something about insurance."

He flared at her, "You should! You're the one who pushed me to get the policy. And remember, it's important not to let Eleanor know you're the beneficiary. If she found out, all hell would break out."

"Ray, if you love me you'll want to protect me. It's not the money, it's to give you peace of mind knowing if anything happened to you, you'll be able to rest easy knowing I'd be taken care of. I don't understand why it has to be kept so hidden. It's always best to be open about everything."

Not wishing for more emotional upheaval to be tossed on him he murmured apologetically, "Well, my strawberry swirl, it's a motive."

"Ray, baby puss, you don't think I'd—"

Of course not, my tender quarter pounder, but the police...." He let the sentence hang for a moment then asked, "You didn't leave the bar and go into the banquet room did you?"

She hesitated a moment—a moment that said yes—but she said no.

Ray said, "I was a fool to let you talk me into allowing you to come. Shit, if my wife saw you... well, you know how precarious my visitation rights are, and my future alimony payments are still in negotiation."

"I wouldn't do anything to jeopardize your relationship with Willie, your son. Ray, you've got to believe that."

"My little McNugget, you know I trust and love you."

He may have, but I didn't trust her nor the wife. Both had motive and means. The weapon—well, anyone who had cockroaches had it, and roaches were the city's universal long-term squatters.

Hoping to reassure him of her love and innocence she reached under the covers to shake hands with her biggest ally, but he shook her off. "Not now, my little French fry. The big Mac isn't up to action today. Why don't you go see about getting me a private room and a TV?"

On her way out, Palante, in the opposite bed, cried out, "Hey sweetheart, reach over here and grab a big whopper. The burger king is open for business."

She froze him with a look and skewed him with a comment. "You look like a Ronni to me."

I may have envied Ray his three McDonalds, but I wouldn't take the three women in his life nor his bladder for ten franchises.

CHAPTER 5

Knocking on Woody

The door to the ward had barely closed on Amber before Woody slid in to see whether the wife, mistress, or daughter had made any verbal slip-ups, like admitting they had poisoned the salsa, or that their homes were infested with cockroaches.

Woody barely got his thousand dollar slacks onto the seat when the complainer suddenly pulled open his curtain, which he had previously kept closed tight as a fortress wall. Abdullah Hassan Malcolm the 5th, complaining he was the only one not allowed visitors, then stated he knew why. Glaring at me and at Paul Palante, who was studiously combing his hair, and glaring at the bathroom door as it closed on Ray's back he said, "I know why I wasn't given the window bed. I know why I'm the one looking at the bathroom. I know why I was placed in the room's worst bed, have no water, no bedpan, no urine bottle, and no pain pills last night. It's because I'm an Afro American and this is a racist hospital."

Unfortunately, for his love of complaining, he was scheduled to receive the next visitor and be subjected to my eavesdropping.

Staring open-mouthed at him, Woody mumbled, "He's not Arab; he's black." Then glancing at me, a very frightened Woody whispered, "Mac, for heaven's sake, say and do nothing racist to anger him. With your background of previously politically incorrect talk it'll be our careers if you get us into trouble upsetting a sick black man. Look, just lay there. No, better, I'll get you transferred out of this ward." Then he cast a furtive glance at Abdullah even as he feared his glance might be interpreted as a racial insult. "Maybe I should move *him*, maybe to a private room ... No. That could be read as segregation... to a semi-private room with another black." He liked that idea for a second, then rejected it. "No. It would be seen as a loathsome example of a ghetto." Finally he said, "What should one do in a racially sensitive situation?" Then he remembered he was talking to me. "Look whom I'm asking advice on a delicate racial situation."

That annoyed me. He was the most prejudiced, closed-minded idiot I'd had the misfortune to meet. "Look Woody, he's not going and I'm not going. We're following the original plan. You allow the relatives to visit each of the victims, one at a time, and I listen in. Hopefully we'll gain some useful info. After all we still don't know who the targeted victim or victims were, nor whether there was any specific reason for the attack. Remember, this still could be a terrorist act or the action of a demented mind." I tossed in terrorism and insanity to get Woody's mind off race.

Still scared but not knowing what else he could do that wouldn't somehow be construed as racist, Woody relented. "Okay Mac, but remember race has entered into the mix. There well could be an armed Montana militia right wing fascist racist hate group who targeted a very specific person...." He gave the slightest nod toward the next bed "Because of his ethnicity. We could be dealing with a hate crime."

Like all liberals, Woody lived in constant fear that the couple of dozen bizarre militant bearded kooks living in the woods of Montana were fully capable of and just months away from overthrowing the government in a bloody insurrection. If Woody and his liberal friends weren't constantly vigilant, the government would fall within a year. "Look," I said, "any modifying action you take can will be interpreted as racially motivated, and truthfully it would be."

"But you'll be right next to him." Again he quickly nodded towards the next bed. "If you do something insensitive or use words that could be construed as hateful, no matter how innocently intended, it will destroy your career."

"And since you're connected to me," I reminded him "you'll be guilty of racial insensitivity by association."

Woody winced. The sin of all sins in his mind was to be insensitive. Brutal murder could be explained away and excused, but never can one be excused of being insensitive.

I continued, "All you can do is act like 'you know who' isn't very special color wise, solve the case as quickly as possible, and hope the race card doesn't show face up."

Begrudgingly, he accented. "Okay, okay, but Mac, if you use the N word I'll personally bring charges against you and devote all my influence in getting you discharged from the force and convicted of hate speech. Do I make myself clear?"

Oh, the land of free speech. You can say anything as long as it doesn't offend anyone.

Since previously in the Hoboken Indian Ax Murder he had done just that, after I said "the N word," obviously he'd do it again, so I nodded and told him to move my bed closer to the "special" person and send up his family.

He got up and hissed, "Say nothing and do nothing. Not a gesture, not a look, not a sound that could be interpreted as, well... do nothing, say nothing, look at nothing."

CHAPTER 6

Abdullah

After a troubled Woody left, an attractive nurse with two orderlies switched Ray Brother's window position and gave it to Abdullah and under the pretext of straightening my covers, moved my bed even closer to Abdullah's. Receiving this attention Abdullah complained how, next to the window he was furthest from the bathroom and with the sunlight falling on his bed he wouldn't be able to nap, and Brother could hop out of bed and with two steps land in the toilet as well as enjoy the restful shade. Loudly and continuously he shared his insights. "I know why: he's white and rich, and I'm black and poor." Turning towards me rhetorically asked, "Why is she fussing over you? Look, your pillow is being fluffed, your covers are being straightened and I'm ignored. I still haven't got a bedpan. I know why. I'll tell you why. I'm not afraid to say why. It's because I'm a proud Afro-American, that's why."

The nurse asked him if he needed a bedpan. Abdullah haughtily answered, "It's too late. You've shown your racism and now you're trying to insult me by implying that I need a bedpan, that as a black man I'm not civilized enough to use the bathroom. I'm a proud black man and all your racist attempts to demean and rob me of my pride in my black race will fail. I tell you—"

She slammed a bedpan on his bedside table and walked out leaving him with no one to tell about his extreme racial suffering.

He was about to vent all his grievances about the window to the window once again when his common law wife came stomping in, a black woman with enormous, flabby weight hanging heavily on an average-height frame. Huge slabs of fat hung under her arms, and bales of blubber clung to each hip. Fortunately, her blubber-filled ass extended sufficiently to the rear to counterbalance the massive, rotund breasts away from her four chins by a good foot, allowing for an even keel. As black as Abdullah, as large as a truck, as loud as a laugh track trying to make a TV comedy show sound funny, Dagmar Miller easily pushed our beds apart with her hips to stand next to Abdullah's head.

Abdullah tried to get in the first words, knowing from experience with her he would have to talk first or not at all. He whined, "This is a racist hospital, sweet butter, I'm not getting the treatment or the attention the white patients are getting."

Standing over him, peering down, a huge cliff of soft mud threatening to avalanche at the slightest provocation, she shouted, "You damn fool! Going to a simple banquet you get yourself poisoned? Who's gonna drive the cab? You can't expect me!"

He whined, "Honey butter, I almost died. I think it's a racist plot to get rid of the only black father at the banquet."

Grabbing a chair and sitting down, she shouted, "Get off that racist shit and tell me what I'm gonna do for money. The welfare is a good week away. You better get well damn quick and get your sorry ass out of that bed and into your cab. There are children to feed. Do you expect them to eat that Muslim scrambled bullshit talk?"

"Creamy butter, Louis Farrakhan knows—"

"When that light skinned nigger puts money in my hand instead of trying to take it out, I'll listen, but 'til then, who's gonna drive the cab? When are they gonna discharge you?"

Abdullah weakly complained, "My melting butter, I almost died last night. Shit, you shouldn't yell at me. It's not my fault I got poisoned, and look how far I am from the white man's shit house! It's way over there. It's a plantation in here. Oprah should make a movie of my pain."

"*You* went to that honkey dinner, didn't you? Didn't I tell you don't go to whitey's stuff? If you listened to me and drove your cab last night you'd be all right and there'd be money in the house."

"Butter finger, I had to go to show the white racist bastards I wasn't afraid and someone had to be there for Winslow. He was a cinch for the MVP trophy. Without my boy that milquetoast team—"

"Pride, that's your trouble. Instead of supporting your family you're out eating with white trash and getting yourself poisoned."

Beaten down, Abdullah was quiet.

She didn't like his silence and snapped, "Heard it was roach poison. Shit, you're one dumb nigger to eat roach poison. I've been putting that stuff around my apartment since I was six and I never ate any. I've got sense."

"Damn it, Dagmar, I'm a sick man. I almost died and here you are badmouthing me, and me in a sick bed! You shouldn't do that!"

His accusation struck Dagmar as justified so she took a different tack. She moderated her conversational voice though she was still loud enough for the entire room and the bladder in the bathroom (Ray was still there, if not doing business, hiding out) to hear without effort. "I'm angry 'cause I'm so scared and frightened over what happened to you. Don't you know I'm worried to death about you? Rufus, you know you're my man."

"Butter syrup, how many times did I tell you my name is Abdullah now? Don't use my slave name."

"Rufus, just you stop that Muslim nonsense and tell me how I'm gonna pay Jimmy. He's talking threats and we both know his talk ain't just talk." Inching as close to Abdullah, a.k.a. Rufus, as her massive breasts and two-yard wide waist would allow, Dagmar whispered, "Jimmy is just crazy enough to put roach poison in your food."

He seconded her thought. After a period of silence he said, "Damn it, Dagmar, why do you bring Jimmy into my sickness? How can I get well with you worrying me about Jimmy?"

"Well fool. If you're stupid enough to lose his money at a crooked dice game you got only yourself to blame."

"Sweet butter, I know the game is honest and after I get out of here and sell the rest of the bags—"

"Quiet fool! Cops are all over the place."

"Listen my farm-churned butter, talk to Jimmy. Explain my situation. Tomorrow I'll be out of this racist hospital. After I pray in the Mosque for my deliverance from the white devils I'll be driving the cab and selling you know what. A week from now Jimmy will be paid, and with your welfare check and my disability coming in, things—"

"Fool's fool. Your mind is so filled with that Mosque crap. Now listen carefully: You've been poisoned. You almost died."

"Sometimes it felt like it."

"You may never fully recover."

"Don't say that,"

"You may never be able to make love."

"Shit, don't even think it."

"You may never be able to work."

"Saaay, cocoa butter, do I see where you're going?"

"You suffered great pain."

"Amen to that. Now I'm walking next to you."

"No one knows the future consequences of roach poison."

"Allah, protect me. We're marching in step."

"The mental damage— Maybe you'll be a worse fool than you are now."

"Love butter, don't call your muffin a fool."

"Maybe you'll act the fool in public, staggering around, falling down, like all those homeless drunks and druggies."

He joyfully shouted, "My heavenly tub of buttery love, you got a lawyer!"

"Of course I did. I haven't got my mind on racist this or racist that. My mind is on the children and the money I need to take care of them."

Suddenly a frightened Abdullah cried, "Dagmar, you didn't turn on me? You didn't make any salsa and figure on suing everybody and maybe selling the bags yourself?"

"Fool, drop the bags, and remember, we're not married."

"There's always common-law."

"Well the lawyer says we should get married and you should adopt all my kids."

"Pancake butter, you know I don't believe in that white racist marriage shit. We've got love. It's better than a piece of paper from the white man."

"Love counts for shit if it's not legal. The lawyer says it's best if you got a legal wife and lots of legitimate children. It means ten times the money and doubles our chance of winning if we get married right away. With an O.J. jury, with no chance of losing, we could even borrow from Jimmy."

"Butter of my toast, what about your welfare? What about mine? We could lose a lot of white bread if we get married."

"Listen fool, you better not have trouble with marrying me. I've given you the best eight years of my life and two of my six are yours. It's time you stop borrowing your butter and finally man up and buy it."

Hopefully he countered, "It won't look good if I go back to work. Maybe I'm so disabled I'll never be able to work again."

"Fool's fool. All that gypsy stuff is under the table as well as the cash sales from you know what. As far as whitey is concerned, you haven't worked a day in your life."

Abdullah sighed. "Man, if they only knew how hard I do work." After a long moment of silence he asked, "You got a black lawyer? I won't have a white lawyer. We got to go with the brothers."

"The brothers' contingency fee was forty percent of any settlement. The white honkey's was thirty-five percent. You choose which one."

"Butter cup, you're right, we can't let a brother rip us off. If a brother tries that, he ain't no brother. Go with the honkey. It's a shame we blacks don't treat each other as well as whites treat each other."

"Well I've signed with the honkey. His name is Donny O'Malley, and he's preparing the papers where we're suing everybody, and I mean everybody. We'll be rich after this."

He winced. "Did you have to pick an Irishman? Couldn't you get a Jew?"

"Fool. He's associated with a Goldstein and I suspect they are both Italians."

After a thoughtful pause, Abdullah commented, "Butter cake, you have to give thanks to Allah for lawyers." He held out his hands to her.

She purred, "And thanks for contingencies, my sweet lovable fool." Leaning over she poured about a hundred pounds of soft black butter into his arms, leaving a good two hundred pounds in the tub and whispered, "Praise and love for contingency fees."

They continued exchanging dreams of large sums of free money and wet sounding kisses. I turned away, thinking the common-law wife, a very practical mother, definitely was not smitten by her Muslim sheik. *Would she poison the fool in order to generate a large lawsuit? Could she be so devious as to poison the salsa just enough to induce a marriage proposal and it was only unfortunate bad luck that someone with a bad ulcer had died?* She had the motive and certainly the opportunity. Everyone had noted her huge, dark presence dominating bowls of white potato salad and macaroni salad. At the banquet she had stood behind the food table, ladle in hand, arms akimbo, scowling at the bowls and anyone walking by. An expert on roach poison, would she know how much to give to sicken a normal person without proving fatal?

Leaving, she admonished Abdullah not to say anything to anyone and not to sign anything, "Play dumb, you fool," were her last words.

Hearing all this selfish, greedy, self-serving crap made me tired and not a little depressed. So I patted my growling, queasy, empty stomach and hoped to see my own wife soon. *Maybe Pam can smuggle in a hamburger.* The thought made my stomach leap with joyous anticipation, but in mid-air, thoughts of greasy meat crashed it into my colon.

CHAPTER 7

Joy Scott

As planned, Palante and his Casanova bed were exchanged with Abdullah's position and brought angry comments from the rich McDonalds guy, complaining there was too much moving about, talking and visiting in a ward and demanded to be moved to a private room. The Black Muslim gypsy cab driver complained about being shoved around like an 8 ball bouncing off the cushion and he knew the reason why. The lady's man suggested all this bed moving was just an excuse for the nurses to come into the room in order to flirt with him. To join in the general complaints I observed that all the moving about was the hospital's attempt to jack up an already outrageous bill. Everyone said "Amen" to that.

I was barely settled in my bed when a screaming, yelling, crying, hysterical woman came running into the room. If she was the Casanova's wife she definitely was overreacting. Turns out she was Scott's wife, the guy who punched a one-way ticket on Michael Jackson's Never Never Land train, and she was still overreacting. After running about in circles, peering at each of us, she threw up her hands and yelled, "It's true! It's true! Poor Jimmy! My poor Jimmy is dead!" Then she lowered her voice and growled, "And all of you are alive. Is it fair? Is it right? All of you are alive and my dear, poor Jimmy is dead!"

I hoped what she thought was unfair was that Jimmy was dead, not that we were still alive, but I was fairly sure she'd feel better if the corpses were stacked five high. Bringing my bed to a sitting position, I saw a frumpy mid- to late-thirties woman in a worn, ill-fitting dress, no makeup, hair awry, arms flapping at the ceiling as if trying to fly, and staring at me. I debated whether a decent dress, make up, a hairdo, and a more feminine posture would make her attractive, but I decided although the changes would help she still wouldn't rate a full head turn. Quietly, to justify my existence to her accusatory stare, I said, "He had an ulcer; that's why he succumbed and we didn't."

She yelled, "What ulcer? The stupid doctors talked to me about ulcers. My husband was perfectly healthy and now he's dead. He left home a happy, healthy father to attend his son's football banquet and six hours later I'm told that he had ulcers and he's dead, the only one out of five. And now I'm a widow and his son is fatherless. How could his happen?" Suddenly she let out a horrific scream. "I'm alone! I'm destitute! My son has no father!" I guess poor dead Jimmy didn't rate a scream. All her screaming about pain and anguish was for herself, her son and her financial situation. *Was her affection for Jimmy or for his utility in her life?* Suspecting the latter I didn't feel I was being overly perceptive.

Two nurses hurried into the room, ostensibly to attend to her hysterics, but actuality to remove her from the room. They couldn't budge her. Determined to hold the stage, in turn she yelled rhetorical questions at each patient. To the supposedly disabled black gypsy cab driver and dealer in mysterious baggies, she cried, "Who cares for widows and orphans? Who cares? Does anyone care? Answer me!"

Holding the corners of his bedspread chin-high trying desperately to hide behind it, Abdullah helplessly answered, "I don't know... welfare people?"

The nurses told her they knew who cared. And with each one gripping an arm hard, one pulling and the other pushing, they confidentially whispered to her, "The psychiatrists... the doctors... they care. They're anxious to see you. Let's just go outside."

Turning a tear-stained face to me she dramatically yelled, "Who will support a widow and her child? Who will feed us, shelter us? Are we to be thrown into the street, homeless, starving, eating from dumpsters, sleeping in cardboard cartons, and living in gutters? Who, I ask you? For heaven's sake, tell me, who."

She made a move towards me and I fearfully slid under the covers. "I don't know." For my physical safety I refrained from adding that I really didn't give a damn.

The nurses, putting more energy and less finesse into their pushes and pulls, told her the hospital's social service office on the third floor was anxious to help her with her financial and personal problems and desperately wanted to see her.

She turned to Palante, the lothario, demanding he tell her who would help her recover from this tremendous emotional trauma. She was devastated, her entire life destroyed by hot salsa. Adrift, alone with only her son for comfort and companionship, which was too much of a burden for a child to carry, she tearfully screamed, "Who can help me, a friendless widow, alone, all alone in a cruel world? Do you care?"

Scared, Palante was holding his pillow in front of him. He told her she wasn't his type and he was happily married.

Putting their shoulders into their pushes and pulls, the nurses still could only deflect her as, fighting against the white drag, she made her way towards Brothers, the McDonalds franchise. The nurses were shouting to her that there was a support group for women whose husbands had come to a violent end meeting at that very moment in the basement. Since they'd experienced the same kind of loss they cared very much. They would be her friend, and they were serving coffee and donuts.

Ignoring this source of companionship, the widow, standing at the foot of Brothers' bed, shouted, "Why me? Why my husband? Why *my* family?" And each "why" brought an accusatory pointed forefinger aimed between his eyes. After turning around with a stretched out hand passing a pointed accusatory finger over our beds she again asked Brothers, "Why me? Why *my* husband? Why are you all alive and healthy?"

The rich are never inhibited in speaking their minds to their financial inferiors so he said what everyone in that room was thinking. "Madam. I don't know why and I don't give a damn why. I just know I am alive. Please leave. I have to go to the lavatory."

"You're alive!" she spit out with hate. "I'm a dead woman. I've no life now with poor Jimmy dead."

Brothers responded, "Don't look at me to give you life. I have to go."

Shaking off the nurses' grip, she approached the side of his bed. "Why are you so lucky and I so unlucky? Answer that! Why you? Why not me?"

An intimidated Brothers defended his luck. "Your husband's eating excesses and his inherited constitution created his ulcer, and his lack of character kept him from refusing to eat food that was poison to his stomach."

"Pompous ass! People who profit the most from luck believe in it the least. I, who have been unlucky all my life, continually believe in it."

The two nurses energetically told her she was lucky to be in this friendly hospital, where caring physicians, empathetic psychiatrists, compassionate social workers and loving, sensitive support groups resided in abundance.

Ignoring them and calming down, turned she turned and apologized to the room. "I didn't come here to rant and rave like a mad woman but to ask you, did he suffer? Did he speak of me, his family? What were his last hours like? I can't leave until I know. Was there any pain?"

Crap, I thought. *What do you think with cockroach poison burning his gut out?* "No," I said, loudly and emphatically.

The nurses, noticing my line of attack, swore we were all treated for pain relief, given injections, and administered pills. There was no pain in this room. There was no pain in this hospital. Her husband had no pain.

From beneath his covers the black guy yelled, "What's all this shit about pain killers? I didn't get any and all the white people here are getting high on painkillers. They let the poor black man suffer in pain, facing the white man's bathroom with no bedpan, no water, and no urine bottles. Well, I know why."

Everyone ignored his complaints as Jimmy's wife continued. "Did he say anything? You know, about me? About his son? What were his last words?"

He had no last words but the situation cried out for last words. So after pausing to see if anyone else was going to speak I filled the awkward silence with her husband's last words. "He talked of you and his son. How lucky he was to be married to you. How happy he was living his life with you. What a joy it was to have you as his wife."

"And his son, Jeffrey—what did he say about Jeffrey?"

"Ah, his son... he was so proud of Jeff. He never stopped talking about his son, praising him, and enumerating his athletic abilities. At the banquet he was fulsome with love for his son, but at his last moments, here in the hospital, dying, he spoke exclusively of his undying love for you, his beloved wife."

The lothario, trying to give credence to my painfully obvious bullshit, interjected, "Yeah. Between munching hot cockroach-salsa-loaded sandwiches he'd say his son did this, then he'd eat a cracker, then his son did that, and then load up another cracker with cockroach salsa. Then it was his wife was the greatest."

The widow, filtering out the salsa and ignoring the cockroach stuff, swallowed whole the rest.

The McDonalds franchise told the widow her husband talked about how he loved to take his kid out for McDonalds nourishing, healthy hamburgers after the games.

The black complained that Jimmy never talked to him at the banquet nor at the hospital and he knew why: for the same reasons he got no pain pills and spent the night looking at the white man's bathroom without a bedpan, no water, and no attention while whitey was getting high.

Satisfied, she cried real tears. Whether it was for her husband or out of emotional appreciation for the scene she had created was in Limbo.

I felt it was sad. No, not sad... pathetic.

Suddenly she left, spraying tears in her wake. Everyone felt the tension ease and in silence thought we were indeed twofold lucky, to be alive and to be free of her. I was exhausted from all the wives and still had no clue who, if any of them, had put cockroach poison in the salsa. I still had the lothario's wife and my own to endure. Exhausted, I looked to renewing my injured body and calm my unsettled mind with sleep. I felt I could speak for the room when I concluded wives can drain and numb the mind. Women live for and thrive from emotional turmoil; men hide from it and can die from it.

CHAPTER 8

Pam McCoppin

My wife Pam came next, somberly dressed in a brown skirt, a white blouse and a tan overcoat. Above average in bust and curves, at thirty-four she still has a great face marred with only a few minor wrinkles, which she easily fills in with makeup. She arrived with no scenes—no shouting or sobbing or screaming—just a simple kiss and a quiet hug. She shifted a chair closer to the bed, tugged at the privacy curtains, smoothed the covers, and gently patted the pillow. With some fear in her eyes, and a hint of concern in her voice she inquired how I was.

Lying, I said, "Okay."

"Do you need anything?"

I enumerated some personal hygiene things: underwear, pjs, a robe, paper and pen, and some comfort food, possibly a Twinkie.

She nodded, mentally noting each item, and asked what the doctors had said.

"Nothing," I told her. After all, I was only the patient. "As they passed my bed, they did smile at me."

When she asked if I was involved in the investigation, evasively I pointed out as a victim I certainly was involved.

She went on to tell me how Michael, our ten year old son, was taking my near murder by poison wonderfully well. He was excited, telling all of his friends about the banquet: the ambulances, stretchers, and police, grown men crying and writhing on the floor and vomiting, everything in mass confusion. He said it was the most fabulous sports banquet, the greatest. Ah, the reason young boys grow up to be heroic soldiers.

When I questioned her about what she had seen at the banquet she related the mass confusion, how several hysterical cheerleaders were rolling about on the floor, screaming in pain, giving every indication of suffering food poisoning till someone pointed out they hadn't eaten anything. It was a hard sell as neither the girls nor their mothers wanted to admit they were suffering more from mental problems than physical problems.

After we were removed from the hall and the hysterical girls were slowly and reluctantly cured of histrionics, the organizers made a courageous decision that the banquet, having been paid for, would continue less five fathers. Naturally there was a pall over the whole affair, especially since no one cared to eat any of the food despite the caterer's tearful entreaties that the food was good and the organizers repeatedly saying the food was paid for. Unfortunately, the caterers and organizers practicing abstinence didn't encourage food consumption. However, despite the unfortunate preface, all present put up a brave front and applauded each child as they bravely walked up to receive individual trophies.

Pam had followed the ambulance to the hospital, leaving my son with a teammate's parents so he could pick up his award.

I complained, thinking he should have come to the hospital with his mother and screw the award. I felt hurt, both at him for valuing the trophy more than he valued his father and at his mother for letting him. I could have been dying, and she was making arrangements so the kid could get his award.

In justifying her actions, Pam explained how much the award meant our son, how his presence at the hospital would be more a distraction than a help, and that he had to get to bed because tomorrow was a school day; however, she had stayed at the hospital till three a.m. when the wives were told everything was going to be all right and they could go home. That is, every wife except poor Mrs. Scott, wife of the dead Pep Boys worker who, when told of her husband's death, became hysterical and had to be given sedatives to calm her down. Once the other wives were reassured, they all left the hospital.

In an investigative mode, I asked how many wives were at the hospital.

"Well, there was some woman in red called Amber; the dead man's wife, Joy; Palante's wife, Dorothy; and the McDonalds guy's soon to be ex, Eleanor; and me. The black man's wife, Dagmar, volunteered to stay behind to comfort the children and take pictures of the children picking up their awards."

Still stung over my son's lack of concern and my wife's toleration of it, I kept repeating between pouts he should have been at the hospital last night and he certainly should have been here today, even if he had to miss school.

Patiently she explained that boys often can't be expected to have an adult's sense of reality and are unable to grasp the concept of death, never mind the death of a strong, dominant figure in their lives such as a father.

My annoyance increased with the psychological bull she was spinning and was inflamed by the slightly condescending way she was saying it; it's most irritating to be dipped down deep in bullshit as if it was an elevating revelation to you. Angrily I told her, "It's not what the kid thinks, knows, wants, or is interested in that's important; it's what we know he must learn; it's what we want he must want; it's what we say he must say, that's important. Damn, Pam, you keep looking at things through the kid's eyes. It's the kid who's got to see through *our* eyes, so he can see that reality is not centered around his ass."

She defended him with, "Ed, the boy's ten. You're expecting too much."

"You're expecting too little. He should have come to the hospital last night and especially today. He's learned the wrong lesson, that his award is more important than his father."

Pam ended the conversation as she usually did when we disagreed, by speaking in silence of her sadness, her annoyance and her righteousness, and of my ignorance and stubbornness. As usual, I couldn't and wouldn't respond to her silence.

Too tired to continue, conscious I was spoiling a visit I'd been looking forward to and aware we were starting to sound like the other couples (who I believed we were above), I let the silence flow too long. I didn't know how to switch to another topic, and I didn't feel like switching anyway.

Finally rising, she asked if there was anything else I needed. To my "no" she said she and Michael would visit tonight and bring the items I needed.

The way she said it, flat, matter of factly, had me wanting to scream, "Shit, don't bother," but I didn't for fear she wouldn't bother. Her visit, too short to be affectionate, ended too politely for closeness, with the parting kiss too light; it was an appearance kiss, a kiss meant to make me feel lonely, a kiss to hurt me, and it was successful.

CHAPTER 9

Dorothy Palante

The last wife to visit, the Lothario's, was a surprise. I was half expecting a thin, mousy, unattractive, unassuming woman, or maybe a stout, muscular, overbearing, no-nonsense butch female, but she was of modest build, modestly attractive, and modestly dressed—a modestly normal wife in her late twenties.

After they exchanged kisses, her cheerfulness increased with each of her husband's accounts of women chasing after him. She smiled when he talked about nurses coming on to him, saying he was being too sensitive. When he mentioned Ray's mistress in red eyeing him at the bar, she giggled, saying he was mistaken. To his account of the food server grabbing for his privates, she laughed and said he was being silly.

After acknowledging his attractiveness and magnetic charm, she said he shouldn't misinterpret caring women's attempt to help him. She explained that most women respond to attractive, appealing men such as him with helpful attention and caring concern, and that he should accept the attention as the natural outpouring of feminine mothering.

Agreeing with all the attractive, appealing stuff, Palante argued strongly against her conclusion, using the food server's grabbing under the covers as his salient argument.

Laughing an infectious laugh that made anyone who heard it unconsciously smile, she argued that maybe eating the ice cream could bring on a serious relapse, and out of concern for his health the food server had gone after the ice cream Dixie cup. "Only a person who was really concerned for you would have reacted with such determined haste. She was frightened you'd foolishly hurt yourself."

Palante grumbled about the food server spending an awful lot of time finger crawling and hand grabbing under his covers just to get a Dixie cup and maybe he could sue for sexual assault.

Dorothy waved that aside. "Dearest, you worry too much about women's attention to you causing me distress. You were afraid I'd hear about her ice cream search and accuse you of something terrible, but I trust you. You don't have to explain. It doesn't matter what other women do. I know my husband loves only me and I have nothing to worry about." She smiled and, holding his hand, moved the conversation to their children, an infant girl and their nine year old football player.

Though not complaining about the kids' absence, Paul did complain about a woman dressed in red hitting on him the evening before in the bar. "I tell you Dottie, she was constantly staring at me, her eyes begging me to go over and buy her a drink."

With good-natured laughter, Dottie told him the woman was merely trying to be friendly with the fathers.

Brushing that aside, Palante complained when he walked past an attractive mother who was in charge of serving meatballs she had whispered she'd take care of him and winked. Clapping her hands, Dottie said it proved her point. He was so good-looking, women just wanted to take care of him. "She was planning to give you extra meatballs."

Of course, the more she tried to allay his fears of sexually predatory women going after his body, the unhappier he became. The more she reaffirmed her trust in him, the more irritable he became, and the more she reiterated her trust in women's benevolent, nurturing nature, the more annoyed he became. Her oath of unswerving faith in his love and faithfulness positively angered him.

After a while, their conversation left Fantasy Island and settled on reality's rocky mainland in the form of hospital bills and who is going to pay them and how large they would grow and whether being in a room containing four patients would curtail that growth. While she talked money they didn't have to pay for hospital bills, Palante talked about money they would get via lawsuits. While she voiced hope that their Pep Boys health insurance would pay it all, he was busily walking down Abdullah's path, counting free millions enticingly hanging from the low-hanging branches of nearby imaginary trees.

Though worried over the bills she remained cheerful and optimistic as he, although planning to spend unearned millions, seemed inexplicably angry and depressed. Finally, as she took her leave, she stopped at the door and turned, flashing a broad smile at each man and saying she sincerely hoped for our speedy recovery. As a final gesture she blew a kiss to Palante.

She made me feel good with her unforced laughter, her guileless smiles, and her honest good spirits. Whether or not she actually believed her own asexual explanations of Palante's bizarre accounts of sexual solicitation, erotic invitations, blatant molestations and downright deviant attacks by every female within ten yards of him—especially given the absurdity of his complaints—I couldn't say, but listening to her I'd guess she didn't. She was a woman who believed people were basically good, and she humored the eccentricities of her husband.

For the next two days we stayed in the same room despite McDonalds pleas for a private room and Abdullah's demands to be moved into an all-black, all-Muslim room, but definitely not one segregated by race or religion.

We stayed two days because that was our medical insurance plans would allow. The hospital's arguments and doctor's learned opinions of dire medical consequences accruing to us if we left in less than ten days disappeared when the money people said two days and no more. With us remaining obdurate about not personally paying for more treatment, hospital administrators and our sage doctors suddenly agreed we could be safely wheeled through the front door and deposited at the curb. During the two days, wives, children, friends, relatives and co-workers visited. Nurses, hospital functionaries heavy with paperwork to be signed and concerned lawyers with more paperwork came around as they deemed necessary, and on that odd rare occasion, even a doctor dropped by to extend an uplifting comment and an encouraging smile at reports on our urine flow and the fact that we possessed a pulse.

By far the most frequent personages flowing in and out of our ward room at any time of day or night at their convenience were anxious authoritarian types: Homeland Security, anxious and suspicious over Abdullah's antecedents, tactfully worked around each of those antecedents as if each was a covered land mind; the CIA, secure in the knowledge no one knew specifically what the hell they actually did, turned up in overly expensive Italian threads. Their questions carried the intensity of exotic intrigue: Where were our passports? Any quick vacation trips to the Bahamas? in recent trips out of the country did we touch Morocco, converse in Tunis, or say hello to Libya on the way to Baghdad? Ray Brothers and Abdullah were the stars in their eyes. Ray for all the trips and cruises to exotic locations and Abdullah with his Farrakhan Muslim connection.

The FBI, in dark suits, with ear plugs, black briefcases, and microscopic voice recorders, strolled in briskly, secure in the knowledge they were the FBI and everyone was or should be impressed. Ray Brothers and I received most of their attention: I, for possibly being the target of retaliation for past arrests, and Ray for possibly being the target of some obnoxious obesity haters trying to save children from the evil seductive snares of Big Mac.

The State Police came in too, nervously dressed in civilian clothes, though a colonel or general did come now and then, resplendent in uniform, and asked mundane, inconsequential questions: Whom did I suspect? Had I seen anyone sprinkling powder on the salsa?

And Treasury Agents, so satirically expensively dressed in comparison the FBI, circled around Ray's bed vowing to uncover his hidden ill-gotten loot and seize it even if it was stuffed up his ass.

The ATF people in stenciled bulletproof vests were the most obnoxious, worrying over who had machine guns squirreled away, who owned assault rifles, who had intimate connections with Idaho militant terrorists, who had explosives stashed somewhere, and who smoked cigarettes where they shouldn't, putting children in danger of TB. They tossed aside our strident denials that we were any of those things as crafty subterfuge. One agent with a paunch, a superior attitude and reading glasses perched atop a bald head, standing arms akimbo in the center of the room, announced he was the agent in charge. If anyone smoked, marijuana excepted, or used drugs, raise their hand. Abdullah confessed to using a little medicinal Acapulco Gold because of his bad back.

Foolishly Palante confessed to taking an occasional chew of tobacco, which horrified the ATF crew. The leader cried out "Mouth cancer!" A female agent who was four years from retirement and looked at least ten years past, shouted, "He's disgusting!" She pounced on Palante's bed, ripping and tossing aside covers and sheets, mattresses and pillows, then shouted to a shaking Palante to give up his plug and expose his spit cup. When she started to scrutinize his hospital gown with menacing intentions, he screamed and ran into the bathroom. Unfortunately Brothers was there making his hourly pilgrimage. The two men, screaming like girls engaged in a sleepover pillow fight, were an embarrassment to the room.

Abdullah shouted for a private room, a non-segregated one containing only brothers. I went submarine, only my nose showing above the covers. With a forefinger gun pointing at me, the ATF head warned dire things would happen to anyone caught with tobacco products, especially without tax stamps. After they left, a trembling Palante and Ray Brothers slowly exited the bathroom whispering "Are they gone?" and "I wanna go home."

Woody and Ronni questioned me, asking for hints as to whose visitors could, would, might and may have done it. I had nothing to add. All subsequent visits by relatives were repeats of the first, except that Abdullah was seating personal injury lawyers whose corrupt seductive talk of easy money started to get me thinking.

CHAPTER 10

Woody Visits Again

On my first day home, third day since the poisoning, as I lay on my couch, Woody visited me ostentatiously out of concern for his partner because Woody is a caring, sensitive guy; actually he was stymied on the case and he was hoping I had gleaned some informational tidbits from my fellow patients. Again he brought flowers, this time audaciously colored flowers longer in stem, wider in circumference and more densely packed, much to Pam's delight and my annoyance. Trying to stroke me for favors with a bouquet was absurd; however, he possessed no imagination so it was typical of him.

Gushing over the flowers with the usual predictable comments, Pam ran into the kitchen to find an appropriate vase.

Smiling and in a sympathetic voice, Woody inquired about my health and commented on my healthy looks, then transmitted wishes for my speedy recovery from Ronni and others at the precinct, and he did so with all the emptiness those wishes signified. If that wasn't annoying enough, Pam bustled back into the room, still gushing over the beauty of the flowers, and placed the vase on the coffee table so the carnation and rosebuds blocked my view of the TV.

Grandly waving aside her thanks, Woody kept up a repetitive chatter, telling how much I was missed at work, asking how my health was, and averring that I shouldn't rush back to work but should take advantage of a long paid convalescent leave. Knowing how he enjoyed the vivacious Ronni as his new temporary partner, that last bit rang true. With the false complaining voice hypocrites employ, he complained about the responsibilities the important roach business had placed on his shoulders. Additionally, despite his reluctance and without him having sought the honor, he'd been placed in charge of managing the police contribution to the upcoming National Memorial Service, a task that created heavy demands on his time. "It's a very important position," he said, a half-statement, half-question that demanded the listener return the expected validation—"Oh yes, it's very important"— implying that he was both very capable handling important affairs and highly regarded by superiors.

I refused to stroke his ego, so Pam took it upon herself to be polite and gave him what he expected. He turned to her and asked her opinion about a ten foot high memorial floral arrangement depicting the NYPD shield. Was it a good idea? Was it in good taste? People like Woody who ask your opinion aren't actually asking for it. The idea is their own, so ipso facto it's positioned beyond your ability to critically evaluate it, leaving you with the single option of rendering your affirmation.

Pam, attuned to his verbal dance, gave Woody's idea a resounding "Amen!" though whether out of politeness or belief neither I nor she knew.

Barely acknowledging Pam's memorial floral confirmation, Woody turned to me and said (not asked), "Mac, you'll be there on stage along with Pam and your son Mike. It's still to be decided whether the boys should stand together in their football uniforms or with the parents."

"A memorial!" Pam enthused, then said, "What shall I wear?" as if it really mattered.

To the sudden idea of a memorial and my assumed attendance, I said, "What memorial? What the hell are you talking about?"

"The memorial! Everyone is going to be there. It's shaping up to be the event of the year."

"Woody, I didn't hear about any public memorial service."

Pam explained, "Mac, it's been constantly on all the TV news programs."

"Pam, you know I don't waste time watching news programs designed for idiots."

"Oprah and Dr. Phil will be there," she said, as if Sts. Peter and Paul were making a stage appearance.

Lest I become ecstatic over the idea of such grand personages being physically present, Woody clarified. "They'll probably be present through electronic hookups via television; Oprah will extend comfort and sage black advice to the suffering families, and Dr. Phil will give healing counseling to mothers and children traumatized by the mass terrorist attack."

An increasingly excited Pam added, "And Mac, Dr. Phil has offered free therapeutic counseling to a select group of children on his TV show."

Whispering, Woody confided he'd heard from an unofficial but impeccable source that actually Phil's therapeutic counseling was going to be extended over an entire week of TV shows." He grinned, then continued. "In addition to that, Oprah, besides just extending sympathy, comfort and advice will give a complete makeover for the cheerleaders and their mothers on a three-hour prime time TV special. The first hour will detail the difficulties encountered by today's young women and mothers: obesity, low self-esteem, manipulation by men who are terrified by successful women, glass ceilings, being valued only as a sex object, raising children as a single mother, and the special difficulties black women encounter in a racist, sexist society. The second hour will cover the cheerleaders getting a complete makeover while being lectured by learned experts about the evils of early marriage and the impact of dietary disorders. And get this: they'll also be counseled to be open to diverse dating and told to engage in only protected sex."

I stopped listening and made up my own version. I could only assume that after the makeovers the cheerleaders would be paraded on stage to the applause of a rapturous audience. No doubt the mothers would receive the same makeovers in the third hour along with dietary recipes from volume six of Oprah's Certified Cookbook series that bitch-slap the taste buds into flights of ecstasy and not only don't carry calories, but cause you to lose calories as you chew. Of course, Oprah, with her alligator-tear-pond eyes, would warn everyone of anorexia and bulimia lurking to snare and infect the unwary girl. Then all the cheerleaders and mothers would receive free Oprah cosmetic kits valued at $29.00, available at only the best stores, free shoe and dress ensembles from the Oprah clothing line exclusively sold at Target and, to move the audience to ecstatic rapture, absolutely *everyone* would receive a gift of Oprah's new book on how she succeeded in a racist society.

The audience would go wild, hand waving as if they'd found redemption and discovered the good. Several ladies would faint and have to be carried from the studio. The cheerleaders would do cartwheels and the mothers would hug each other and anyone else within reach. Needless to say, a smiling Oprah would be teary eyed with happiness at all the help and joy she was bestowing.

Woody's voice forced its way back into my consciousness. "If Phil and Oprah's TV extravaganzas aren't sufficient to march America down the road to recovery, Ellen DeGeneres will host an afternoon special from her modest, cozy (forty million dollar) home. She'll devote the first hour to helping girls and mothers find strength to fight obesity and come to terms with their true sexuality, so they discover that women don't need men to be happy."

And I suppose at the end of the special Ellen and her partner would give the cheerleader girls hugs and kisses with the profound advice they should be open to exploring their true self, I thought. But that isn't what I said. "What the hell is all this crap?"

Both looked shocked that anyone would cast a negative light on all that is known to be TV good: TV good to the eye, TV good to the ear, TV good to the emotions, TV good to the universal expected goodness. What next? The emperor is naked?.

Pam reminded me it was Oprah, Dr. Phil, and DeGeneres as if I hadn't grasped the significance of the names.

Adding to the crap pile, Woody told us Scott's widow and son may be on *The View* to be interviewed extensively on the widow's feelings on losing her husband, the son's adjustment difficulties, and their thoughts about lax laws regulating cockroach poison.

Pam hopefully gasped, *"The View?* Are they going to be at the memorial?"

Regretfully Woody said, "No," explaining, "They're currently committed to a month-long series of shows interviewing battered women living in physical fear of their husbands. They're cruelly manipulated, subjected daily to physical abuse of the worse kind, and continually raped and subjected to other gross, unspeakable sexual deviations, all of which will be fully discussed and explored in detail. They will explore how abused women are robbed women of their self-confidence, leading some of them to desperate acts, like of stabbing their husband twenty times after pumping ten bullets into him. *The View* will be explore women's feelings on being subjected to such horrors, then applaud them for their courageous plans to rebuild their lives after the life-affirming experience of terminating the abusive relationships."

"Crap," I said to put a period to this nonsense.

Pam scolded me for my use of such crude language.

Woody noted, "Mac, you've got to watch your language."

I told them I wasn't going to any crappy public memorial despite the electronic presence of Dr. Phil.

Woody was surprised. "You've got to attend. The department expects you to represent the police as a victim. Your presence will show crazy conspirators the roach poison wasn't a government-inspired plot."

Justifying my intention of not going I mentioned a dislike for bland, nondenominational, sectarian services in which God is mentioned but never drops down from the clouds.

With pride Woody quickly corrected my concern. "It's going to be a total secular memorial. Mac, rest assured neither God nor religion will be brought into the service."

"If God and the possibility of an afterlife is excluded, what's the purpose? It becomes just a bullshit farce."

Upset, Pam again chastised me for using such language, especially in describing a memorial service.

Interjecting himself in Pam's and my dynamic as our arbitrator, Woody magnanimously gave me forgiveness. "It's all right Pam. Remember, Mac has been through a lot and isn't completely himself."

Being criticized by my wife stung, but Woody's forgiveness was beyond toleration. "Without life after death, a memorial is merely people who knew the deceased engaging in gratifying self-flagellation by sharing memories based on conjecture or hopeful wishes all woven around pious platitudes. Also, why do people who have absolutely no connection with the deceased want to celebrate the life of someone they don't know? I mean, the guy could be the incarnation of Satan?"

Pam asked where this attitude of mine was coming from and said if I was adamant about not attending, certainly she and Mike would still go to the memorial service.

Where is she coming from giving me this hurt? Unconsciously I assumed she would stand by me and not with Woody, Oprah, Phil, DeGeneres and The View.

Woody informed me that my attendance wasn't a voluntary option but a departmental order; not to comply could cost me rank, even my job.

"Rank? Job? Shit Woody, why didn't you say so? Pam and I will be glad to attend. Should I come in uniform or what?"

"It's undecided. I'm having an urgent meeting with the top brass and the PR people about that. Some view you in uniform as threatening to women and racist to blacks; others maintain that it emphasizes the department's innocence by showing your victimization."

Remaining dumb to his uniform quandary and the awkwardness created by my disinterest with it had Pam speaking for me. She told him she knew I appreciated him stopping by, knew his visit had raised my spirits, and knew I wanted him to stay for lunch. When he demurred, stating the press of important business (Woody never had unimportant business) she knew how disappointed I was. Finally Pam, knowing Woody and I wanted to be alone, discretely closed the door to the family room and left us.

When I asked Woody how his investigation was going, I wasn't surprised to hear his predictable meaningless patter relating how he and Ronni were working well together as a team and how she was a great help in making the memorial arrangements. To get the gas bag to the point I pressed him about any investigative progress he'd made during the three days I was laid up.

As if stating positive progress he answered with his negative progress, explaining that they were close to eliminating al Qaeda, the IRA, and Shining Path terrorists, though it still could be right wing Aryan zealots or religious anti-abortion hate groups. After trying for a hand pat, which I successfully avoided, he asked if I had any thoughts about the case. "In particular, did you learn anything, no matter how insignificant, from the victims or their visitors in the hospital? Did you gain any insight into the various government investigating agency's thoughts from the tenor or direction of their questions to the patients?"

Summarizing, I said, "Idiots, excitable idiots." I left the appellation unspecified: government agencies, visitors, patients, whoever.

Woody said, "I understand your feelings but they're the government; you've got to respect them. Now, regarding allegiances to subversive groups in particular, did anyone indicate membership in or sympathy for any terrorist groups? Or most important, explicitly or implicitly, did anyone express racial hatred?"

I answered, "No. Wait, on second thought the black guy, Abdullah, was into Black Muslim Farrakhan shit, though I doubt his common law would let him give them any money, never mind do anything for them."

Nervous, Woody leaned forward and ordered me in his most offensive officious manner to leave the Afro American to Ronni and himself. "And all Muslim terrorists must be referred to as al Qaeda radicals, not Muslims."

"Well," I asked, "what did you find out about the three missing guys? That Tom Applegate, the coach who was busy with the trophies at the head table, looks promising. You said you were zeroing in on him."

"Mac, Ronni and I certainly concentrated on those three, both as possible targeted victims and as perpetrators who conveniently absented themselves after putting cockroach poison in the salsa. Unfortunately none are members of any right-wing extremist groups. However two of the three, Applegate and Murry Zapp, both in attendance, didn't dine on the cockroach powder, do listen to the dangerous lunacies of Rush Limbaugh, and very significantly, Applegate, a member of the Libertarian Party, is against paying taxes."

I told him to drop the cockroach word.

Acting surprised, Woody condescended. "Mac, since you're a professional I didn't think my specifying the poison as cockroach would bother you, but seeing your sensitivity I won't mention it again."

Mentally I bet myself a good steak dinner against a bowl of oatmeal mush he'd say it again. He ignored my advice to forget the nonsense about the right-wing connections. He mentioned that Applegate's wife's car had a Right to Life bumper sticker.

I asked why Tony Geroni wasn't at the dinner.

As if sharing a bit of deep knowledge accessible only to higher intellects, Woody informed me, "Yeah Mac, I'm suspicious about this Tony Geroni guy. A self-employed plumber, he said he was unexpectedly called out on an emergency job on the night of the banquet. Unfortunately, we can't verify it. The phone records show he did receive a call early that evening. He promised he'd join his wife and son at the banquet, but before dinner, he went to answer an emergency call only to find no one was at the address. Returning home, he said he was too angry over the wasted time to go to the banquet. Geroni swears a competitor made the call because he's the only one in the area who answers late-night emergencies." With a sigh, Woody said, "So where he was is unverifiable, and remember, his wife expected him to be at the dinner at table 12, so she can't be eliminated. It's safe to eliminate him as a poisoner since he wasn't at the banquet, but he still could be the target."

Sarcastically I said, "More negative progress." Then I asked about the libertarian Applegate. "Did anyone see him around table twelve?"

"No. We've definitely made more negative progress in the cockroach crime. (Won a steak dinner.) He didn't approach any of the tables. Right up to the time you all upchucked the cockroach poison (won myself a desert) he was constantly observed arranging trophies at the main table. He's not the poisoner but could still have been the intended victim."

Since I had him talking, I asked about Murry Zapp. "What reason did he give for moving from table 12 to table 13?"

"Being Scott's supervisor, Zapp felt it would be inappropriate for Pep Boys management to sit and eat with a Pep Boys employee."

"Pep Boys supervisor!" I exclaimed.

Not recognizing my sarcasm Woody explained, "Yes, in charge of the entire tire department. Scott only changed tires."

"I find that explanation ridiculous."

Woody shrugged, "It's corporate protocol. Certainly we may see it as undemocratic, but you have to understand some insecure people need to exercise the meaningless perks of office over others to enhance their self-esteem."

I thought, *Yeah, like politicians... and some defective detectives I could name.* I said, "Woody, put a sock in that crap." Once he gets soapy going on daytime pseudo psychological talk show crap he can go on for hours. "Does Zapp's wife have a motive?"

"Divorced. Carol, his ex, says their break-up was friendly, despite his infidelities. She initiated the divorce in order to be able to move on with her life and resume her career at the Dollar Store." He tried to stop, but the momentum from his prejudices was too strong to brake. "Now that's her story, but Mac, during the initial interview she manifested all the psychological clues of being a battered woman living in fear of an abusive philandering husband."

In Woody's TV mind, half of America's women were battered, the second half obese, the third half sexually manipulated puppets controlled by the men in their lives, and all women—although unencumbered by testes—were as strong as men, even better than those ruled by testes.

I asked if he had any concrete evidence of abuse suffered by any of the husband's wives.

"They all deny being abused women which, as you know, is the classic symptom of the battered women's syndrome; they're too ashamed to confront and admit being subjected to abuse by their husbands."

Unable to rationally counter such nonsense, I listened to a as Woody contemplated that Zapp's ex-wife was his best suspect, a politically correct suspect, a beaten and battered wife striking back against her violent tormentor, a scenario some sensitive, politically correct governors would respond to with a quick pardon.

Woody sighed. "Well, I've got to get back to work." And slapping his knees, he rose.

I could have gotten up to see him out, but I didn't. I've seen him hug people too often to risk it.

Since it was a cold cloudy November day, Woody buttoned his English imported trench coat and plaintively asked, "Are you sure you've got no information for me?"

"No."

Hearing Woody getting ready to leave, Pam came in to again ask him to stay for lunch. She got a no and a hug and we both received that empty offer people love to extend of help if we ever need it. In return, he received Pam's sincere gratitude for his thoughtfulness in visiting us, and gushing over the top, her thanks for the flowers and her assuredness that she would look forward to the memorial service.

The door slammed and I felt as I always do when Woody leaves: irritable, annoyed and vaguely dissatisfied. My only hope was that Ronni, if she bedded him, would become his permanent partner in both senses of the word.

Taking the doctor's orders of bland food too literally, for lunch Pam prepared a cup of tomato soup out of Campbell's kitchen. Having won a steak and desert dinner with Woody's cockroach mention, I decided to trade the rare porterhouse for a cheesesteak hoagie. Sitting around in my pajamas at lunchtime on a battleship gray day sucked out all my energy and I felt I was being buried. If I didn't get dressed, get out, and fill my stomach with a nasty greasy fat-filled cheesesteak I'd be dying on the couch watching *Oprah, Oz, Phil* and a studio full of middle-class, middle-aged mindless white broads reacting with horror, excitement, tears and joy to all the nonsensical manipulating show biz bullshit.

Pam didn't fight my decision to go out, which disappointed me. I wanted and expected my wife to baby me, but she simply asked when I'd be back. I said about six and dressed warmly, for November in New York could be nasty.

CHAPTER 11

First Visit, Jim Scott's Widow, Joy

The greasy cholesterol loaded cheesesteak hoagie with a couple of cold beers went down with more pleasure than having sex with an entire NFL cheerleaders squad. Unfortunately once it was down, my stomach, being inhospitable turned ugly as if waking up, and instead of cheerleaders found a squad of angry gay-pride marchers tramping up and down on their way to the colon. Deciding to work through the queasiness, I launched my personal investigation to discover who had poisoned me. It was very personal and I knew Woody, with his liberal mind set couldn't get past his prejudices to find his shoes in the morning if Ronni moved them to the other side of the bed. As for the FBI, CIA, ATF, Homeland Security and Anti-Terrorist Task Force industriously working to uncover phantom terrorists, I had no hope for their success and disregarded the entire alphabet.

While wolfing down the cheesesteak, I made a list of possible victims, knowing if I could locate the intended victim, the poisoner would be obvious. To discover the victim I had to discover the motive connecting the murderer to the victim. Given that opportunity was apparently available to everyone, the connection had to be through motive. The victim had someone, probably a wife with both strong financial and/or personal reasons to kill. Also, the murderer had to have a strong, desperate personality to poison not only her husband but also a whole group of innocent men. I wondered whether the Pep Boys salesman, Jim Scott, the only one who died, was actually the intended victim? Or possibly did the wife of the school maintenance Casanova, Paul Palante actually believe all his bullshit and decided to get revenge? Or maybe like any rational person, did she just get so sick and tired of listening to it, decide to scrub all the bullshit from her life?

Ray Brothers, the pisser, was a prime candidate to be murdered: rich with an angry separated wife, a slutty daughter, a grasping mistress, three McDonald's restaurants and a seven-figured life insurance policy.

There was the Black Muslim gypsy cab driver, Abdullah Malcolm, a.k.a. Rufus, whose common law wife Dagmar had lawyers suing even before she saw him in the hospital. There was also the mysterious gambler, Jimmy, to whom Rufus owed money as well as the shady drug business he was running out of his cab.

And of course Tom Applegate, Zapp or Geroni could have been the intended victims and saved only by chance. Of the eight planning to be at table 12, only one victim was out of consideration, me.

Walking out of the greasy spoon I felt I had to do something, no matter how frivolous, rather than return home and listen to my stomach's complaints and my wife's never ending verbal concern over my health and our appreciation for Woody's consideration. Gathering my overcoat tight about me against the November cold I knew the address of the only person who actually died was a ten-block walk from the greasy spoon. The walk did my stomach no harm. In fact, the cool invigorating air in the lungs and the walking hip exercise soothe the lower regions, calming whatever was going on down there.

At about three in the afternoon I arrived at Jim Scott's house, which was surrounded by police barricades to keep out the desultory crowd of curious onlookers. On either side of a cracked cement path leading to the Scott's front door were two rounded mounds announcing this was the entrance to a special place .A mound of stuffed Teddy bears and polar bears holding hands with numerous little dolls stood bedraggled on one side. On the other side, a large congregation of wilted flower bouquets sounded a forlorn note. Scattered about both mounds were candles of various heights, numerous childish crayon drawings, butterflies being the more decipherable, and printed notes expressing condolences and hope.

Several local and national TV personalities addressing cameras with turned down lips and misty eyes were sadly reporting on the tragic death, on how the neighborhood is grieving. Accompanying cameras panned the crowd providing a chance for TV immortality with inappropriate waves and smiles. A fortunate few were gifted with a ten-second interview during which they expressed with tearful sorrow, in the expected approved manner, their inexpressible pain and the fear of how such evil could happen in America. An enterprising mother struggled to hold up her five year old daughter who stimulated by her mother's off camera pinch in the butt gave an appropriate loud howling responses was rewarded with two interviews, one national. Hugging the squirming daughter the mother struggling to keep her tears dammed related, as a single mother she lived in fear for her precious girl's life and she gave thanks for the near escape of all the children at the banquet. The interview ended with the camera lingering as the dam broke and both mother and daughter near collapse had to be supported by onlookers.

Flashing my badge to the cop, I passed through the barricade.

Although residing in my general neighborhood, the late Jim Scott's address was several steep steps down in house values. Best described as a bungalow, a tired weary bungalow, possessing a small fenced-in front yard containing more bare dirt then brown dead grass. A rusting bicycle was leaning up against a wooden porch housing more litter and junk then empty space.

The house itself boasted of nine hundred tired square feet squatting on an eighth of an acre in a neighborhood where its lack of size and upkeep were not remarkable. Knocking on a glass storm door I was surprised with Murry Zapp coming to the door asking, "Yes, what can I do for you?" Looking over my shoulder he smiled, waved at the camera and crowds before realizing the event's somber import, corrected himself and frowning gave a pathetic characterization of a shrug conveying 'what can one good person do in a chaotic world of evil?'

Turning to me, sorrow for the state of the world vanished as irritably he stated, "I'm Murry Zapp, a friend of the family, and I'm not giving any interviews. If you want an interview arrange it with my lawyer, Mr. O'Malley."

Introducing myself as a fellow banquet sufferer he paused, gave the crowd another sad smile, another poignant expressive shrug and invited me in.

He was fortyish, in a short sleeve blue Pep Boy uniform shirt, short sleeved to show the biceps inflated to a noticeable extent. Obviously working out and though two inches shorter than I, he probably carried fifteen pounds more weight, muscle weight. I figured the guy having just gotten a divorce and looking at the candles prodigious flame atop his last birthday's cake got scared and now was desperately running from the fire to recapture his twenties. All I could say is lots of luck. Given his receding hairline, I was willing to bet he was popping hair growth pills and Viagra, along with his steroid intake hoping to attract a thirtyish, hell a twentyish "Bay Watch" babe. Given a chin that's receded just a little less than his hairline, and a large nose as wide as it was as long, suggested if serious about doing the make-over, a visit to a plastic nose man wouldn't be a waste of money.

Deciding my best approach would be as a fellow victim expressing condolences to the widow, rather than push the detective gambit asking official questions, I told him I was Ed McCoppin and sitting at table twelve next to Jim, wished to express my condolences to the widow.

Zapp grunted an acknowledgement, "Yeah, I recognize you now," before yelling to the back of the house, "Joy, someone who was at poor Jim's table is here to see you."

Coming from the back bedroom she looked a hell of a lot better than she did in the hospital. The black dress was tight enough to reveal a pretty trim figure with neckline just low enough to tell the world she wasn't shortchanged in that department and yet remaining sufficiently modest to allow her to call you a sick pervert for looking at and noting her bounty . With her light brown hair with tinges of blonde advertising a very competent neighborhood hairdresser, the only mar to the whole looks package was an average face now with a lot of time invested in make-up, was rising beyond not bad to damn good.

We all sat down on furniture that had seen better days, and those better days were cheap days. As a cultural telltale sign, we sat in a semi-circle seven feet away from a thirty-eight inch TV. Joy introduced the rejuvenated forty year old as Murry Zapp as Jim's supervisor at the Pep Boy's Store. He quickly explained he came to see if he or the Pep Boy's organization could help Joy in her time of need.

Turning to me, in somber tones he related how all the guys in the tire installation division were devastated by poor Jim's sudden demise, with everyone at Pep Boys agreeing Jim was one hell of a great guy; a wonderful co-worker who never shirked a tire installation nor faked a tire balance. In case I had any doubts, as Jim's overall supervisor, he personally knew this was true, intoning, "No tire goes on a car unless I personally okay it. For me, driving on safe tires always comes first." Piously he added, "It's sort of a religion for me."

Believing he was modestly impressing me, I gave him a couple of nods to indicate a vague understanding of his commitment to auto tire safety. *I wondered if he really believes this shit or was he just shoveling it for public consumption, more likely needing to believe he believed.*

Asking my name, the widow apologized saying with all that has happened she forgot it, but she never had it. To get the conversation away from Murry and his highly prestigious awesome responsible job she asked if the TV news people were still outside. Murry and I reassured her they were there in full force as well as a sympathetic crowd of well wishers.

Getting up she peeked out the front window's blinds to assure herself the customary crowd accruing to tragic public figures was present. Turning back she complained, "They're like vultures feasting on my misery. If only they would leave me alone." After peeking out again she asked Zapp, "Do you think I should step outside for a few moments, say a few brief words expressing my gratitude for how all their outpouring of love has been a great comfort to me in my devastating loss, and tell them I'm praying to God for the strength to be strong for my son. Maybe at the end, clutching a floral bouquet to my breast or carrying one of those stuffed Teddy Bears say a few words to those TV people before going inside the house."

"Shit, no, Joy, er, excuse me Detective McCoppin," came from Zapp. "Although it shows, in the midst of your tragic loss how deeply you care for others and appreciate their love, remember, O'Malley commanded all interviews are to go through him."

"But the people are so sad, and the TV people look so needy for a few words."

"O'Malley empathically said no public statements."

"I don't know, couldn't I just go out on the porch and thank everybody. We could watch it on the 6 o'clock news."

"O'Malley would have a heart attack. He's in deep serious negotiations with several network talk shows. You've got to keep your words sacred and secret 'til O'Malley says you can speak, who you can speak to, and what to speak."

Walking back from window peeking, a vexed widow inquired if I knew when the police were going to release her husband's body.

I told her I had no idea.

Without any sign of queasiness, the widow told me, "You know, they've been doing autopsies on him since the morning he died, and watching enough TV police dramas I know poor Jim's insides are being kept in disgusting jars." She paused.

A solicitous Murry gave her, "Ugh, it's terrible to think of that Joy."

With honesty equal to his I contributed, "Especially happening to a loved one."

"Cremation, that's the only answer." She said it firmly as if we were going to strenuously argue against it. "I know his parents will raise holy hell about it. But what's the use of spending all that money on caskets and burial plots, when poor Jim's insides have been excavated out and only the husk ... er, skeleton is left."

Zapp seconded her observation, adding, "Poor Jim has probably been scooped out so much there's nothing left but an empty shell. Joy, er Mrs. Scott, cremation definitely is the only sensible course. Besides, you'll need all the money you can save for yourself and Jeffrey to live on. Everyone knows Jim's Pep Boys life insurance policy of a hundred thousand won't go too far with today's prices. Today you have to pay over two hundred for a safe tire, including balancing."

After a moment's thought he added to the hundred thousand, "I want you to know the boys at the tire department; in fact all the guys at the Pep Store, including the battery guys are taking up a collection for you and Jeffrey."

First she enthused, "Really? That's wonderful," before realizing the pitiful sum she'd realize.

Zapp continued with some pride, "To date we've collected over two hundred and forty dollars and money from other Pep Boy stores is still coming in."

The widow gave a second "Really that's wonderful," in a tone saying the collection as well as the amount wasn't really wonderful. After hearing of the two forty we sat in awkward silence

Joy broke the silence by offering us coffee and cake. With a quick consultation with my stomach I told her no, nothing for me but Murry Zapp either because he wanted to escape the awkward silence or really wanted coffee and cake saying yes, told the widow not to get up, he could help himself, and walking to a door adjacent to the TV asked, "This is the kitchen, isn't it?"

The widow, who had not given the slightest indication of getting the coffee and cake gave a yes, and told me apropos of nothing that her son, Jeffrey, was at her grandmother's. She asked, "How is your son bearing up under the horror of witnessing my husband's death?"

I gave her a lukewarm 'okay,' hoping to communicate a devastating son teetering on the delicate edge between lifelong trauma and sanity. Sadly I reflected to myself, my touching death's hand hadn't caused my son Mickey to interrupt his life in any appreciable degree.

Somberly she nodded back at me saying as if it was of any possible interest to anyone, "I'm okay." Then taking back the 'okay' she continued, "Devastated as you can understand, although it's worse for Jeffrey. He saw his father die. Can you imagine how my boy must feel; at an event he's been looking forward to since September, an event that was going to be so happy for him, to suddenly, inexplicably, turn into an unimaginable horror; his father dying at almost his very feet."

She paused to enjoy both the drama she was picturing and the feelings she was successfully evoking within herself. To spur her on I gave out several sympathetic "I know"'s. On the fourth 'I know' she continued, "Jeffrey will need extensive psychological counseling, possibly for years, if he's ever to recover from the trauma he's undergone to enable him to live the life a normal boy has the right to expect."

As I gave her a few more 'I know' she paused, this time to think.

She brushed aside my polite false concern. "You're a detective; do you think poor Jim's death could have been an accident? If it was an accident, the Pep Boy insurance policy would double to two hundred thousand, which would be a big help to pay for Jeffrey's analysis."

"Well Mrs. Scott, given it was poison, and cockroach poison at that, and not spoiled food, it's hard to see how it would be an accident."

"Murry thinks whether it's an accident or murder, the double indemnity clause will be enforced. Apparently being a murder, insurance companies consider it an accident. He also suggested a lawyer for a wrongful death lawsuit. Grieving, I'm just too confused to think clearly. I've got to concentrate on Jeffrey's future which is why kind Mr. O'Malley, in getting in touch with us was a blessing. He offered to represent me at this difficult time."

I identified, "He's a lawyer."

Not liking 'lawyer', Joy continued, "He's been so helpful. With the accidental death and all the questions I'm so confused. Murry and Justin have been so supportive."

"Justin O'Malley?"

"Er, yes, Detective McCoppin, er …… can I call you Mac?"

"Sure."

"Please call me Joy. With my husband definitely not the intended victim, his death must be considered accidental. What do you think?"

"I don't know, Mrs. er .. Joy."

"Do you think my husband was the intended victim? I can't think of anyone who disliked Jim, never mind want to kill him. Is there any information as to who was the intended victim? Or was it like the TV says, a random Muslim terrorist attack?"

"Can't say right –"

"You know, the FBI was here. Well dressed, polite, as was the CIA. The CIA corrected me when I referred to Muslim terrorists. You must say al Qaeda. Even Homeland Security people turned pale when I said Muslim and the AFT Agents quickly left the house saying they didn't hear me say it. Anyway, the CIA lost interest when I told them we hadn't left the City in ten years, never mind the country, and have no middle or Far East relatives. Isn't it a shame, ten years with no vacation trip.

"The most obnoxious were the Homeland Security people, two fat slobs who wanted permission to search the crawl space for explosives, and the attic for assault rifles. They acted as if we had a swat team's arsenal lying about despite the AFT having spent half a day going through the house finding nothing. Given the Homeland couple's obesity I couldn't see how they could crawl under anything or climb up anywhere."

I agreed, the Home Land people were offensive.

Leaning towards me she asked, "Confidentially, are you joining the rest of table 12 in Justin O'Malley's class action suit? Or maybe you don't want to say."

After explaining I hadn't signed any papers, I gave her some silence. Nodding to the front window she continued, "You know that sometimes when you have a big public catastrophe like mine, a lot of people and organizations get together to help the victim's families. Do you know of any citywide charitable collection going on to help raise money for poor Jim's devastated fatherless son and his wife racked with grief now all alone?

"What do you think of my launching a website, a Facebook page about my and Jeff's suffering to keep people up to date on our suffering and to inform them where they can donate money to help me? A scholarship fund for Jeff could be a possibility."

I had to tell her I had been ill and housebound and this being my first day outside I had no information what-so-ever as to what anyone is doing to help her and her son.

After a pause, annoyed she said, not asked, "You'll be at Jim's memorial service celebrating his life," then asked what had I heard about the arrangements.

To show I was in the loop I mentioned Oprah, Dr. Phil, *The View*, and De Generes being electronically present, maybe even in person and there was to be a large floral arrangement from the police department. I stopped to let her appreciate the names.

Her response was, "They all want to have an exclusive interview with me and Jim's son. The nice Justin O'Malley is handling the negotiations."

Didn't like the house, didn't like the room and furniture, didn't like Zapp and definitely didn't like Joy, so I didn't feel the need to go polite. "Negotiating financial arrangements."

Ignoring financial, Joy amplified, "There is the question concerning the position I and Jeffrey will occupy on the stage. O'Malley believes stage center, with the rest of the children in uniform ten feet behind, and a floral arrangement should be presented to me, and the electronic personages should talk directly to me, the widow, and fatherless Jeffrey."

I asked where the other parents would stand.

"Well O'Malley thinks they should be in the audience. Of course, in the first row. Pointing out the visual poignancy would be diluted if not lost with a crowd of parents milling about the stage."

After honestly agreeing my preference to sit in the audience, preferably near an exit, to get her to my only purpose of visiting this very sad house was to find something out about Jim. Thinking, well hoping drugs, gambling, pole dancers, I asked the grieving widow if Jim had any disturbing habits.

"Hell, bad habits? Jim? You've got to be kidding." She said it with such emphatic force it sounded like it was a fault of Jim to be free of addictions to drugs, gambling, alcohol, and women. "If you knew Jim you would know he was what I'd would call a 'should man.'"

Confused, I interrupted, "Er… a man all women 'should' marry?"

From the strange look she gave me it was obvious that wasn't what she had in mind when she described her husband as a 'should' man. "Oh, yes, he certainly was an ideal husband, and I thank heaven that we got married, but when I say 'should' in describing Jim, I mean he was a man who lived his life like he should. 'Should's dominated and directed his life. He went to work everyday because he should go to work every day. He put Jeffrey into the football program because he should, and went to Jeffrey's football games because he should go. He went to church every Sunday because he should, he rooted for the Mets and the Jets, because he should. He bought a house for Jeffrey and me because he should. He saved a little money each week, as he should. We went to all the places we should go to, zoos, ballgames, and saw movies we were told we should see. He gave money to United Way because he was told he should. He even went bowling on Thursdays because he felt he should get out once a week with the guys and should let me have a night to myself.

Never arguing with me, always agreeing because he shouldn't argue with his wife. He moderately exercised because he should. He didn't eat foods bad for him, eating only foods he should eat. He voted because you should. In fact, Jim had no vices because he …"

I concluded for her, "shouldn't have any"

With a wry smile she continued, "You know, it's just occurred to me, the first and only time Jim did something he shouldn't have done, eating spicy food with an ulcer, and he got punished. It killed him."

Murry Zapp came into the room complaining that he couldn't find the coffee, there was only one piece of pound cake left and as it was getting late he best get back to the store adding with a laugh, "When I'm not there, tire balancing goes to hell."

Standing, with teary choked up thanks for our visit from the widow, Murry and I made our way out. Outside the gate near the curb, Murry apologized to the pushy made up media girls holding tight to mikes, telling them his lips were sealed. Walking through the crowd, some old grandmothers, laying gentle hands on us, murmured comforting 'I'm so sorry' or 'Be strong' or "I'm praying for you" with one asking for my autograph. We finally freed ourselves from people who enjoying sharing other's pain.

Before cutting Zapp loose I asked, if he was a good friend of Jim's, why did he move to a different table.

"Well, Detective, you understand, at work I'm management, and poor Jim being an hourly employee precluded any type of real intimacy. I did organize the Pep Boys bowling team for the guys as morale building, being Captain of the team for almost three years, but problems developed. The guys were getting too familiar with me on the job. Can't maintain management discipline at the workplace if there are unwarranted jokes about your average. However, I met with Jim at the games where our sons were playing and by working in the same store and being in the same profession, we'd stand together watching the boys. I want to tell you I was really proud of my son Harold and I did question the positions the coaches played him. Unfortunately, being, divorced, and not being able to see the kid a lot, I never made it an issue, still Jim and I were very upset at how the coach was utilizing our sons' talents."

"What about moving to table thirteen?"

"Oh yeah, table thirteen. In fact, with all the throwing up I was one of the first guys at your table helping everyone out. Let me tell you, it was pretty disgusting and dam messy.

"Hell, talk about luck. Can you imagine if I was sitting at table twelve? Well anyway, it was the management-employee relationship thing where feeling if I got too close to Jim socially, it might jeopardize our relationship at work. Besides," and he took a step closer to me, "in confidence, just between you and me, Jim had his dark side. I know for a fact he frequently beat his wife, and often forcibly raped poor Joy when she wasn't in the mood. Let me tell you, Joy will be better off without him. I just hope financially she'll be able to make it. Tell me, do you think the owners of the hall, the Midget Football League or the caterers could be held responsible for Jim's death? O'Malley's talking millions but can you really believe anything a lawyer says?"

I told him there didn't seem to be much money there and the caterer and hall can always declare bankruptcy.

"Well Detective, it's just that I would like to see Jeffrey and Joy taken care of. O'Malley is very optimistic for Joy. What do you think her chances are, and are you going to join in the lawsuit?"

I gave him an "I don't know," followed by a "have a nice day," and putting a "good-bye" to our conversation, turned and started to walk the ten blocks to my house with a stomach making its presence known and it wasn't saying bon appétit.

CHAPTER 12

Ronni

I barely got to the end of Ray Scott's block when a red BMW sports car pulled up.

Leaning over the passenger seat, Ronni yelled for me to join her. Looking at my watch, noting 4:20, and with the November sun pale and cold still hanging tough at the earth's edge, I figured what the hell. Besides, curious as to what she and Woody were up to, I hoped to gain some information.

Greeting her through the passenger window I casually glanced over the toy car's roof to be surprised in making eye contact with an attractive thirtyish woman across the street. She immediately dropped her eyes and hurriedly walked in the direction of Jim Scott's house.

Even at the best of times, in the best of weather, when looking my best and feeling my best, female eyes locking into mine is in the realm of fantasy, but on a cold windy day, with my color paler than the setting November sun, I put fantasy to bed and wondered about the unromantic interest I held for the woman. Something to ponder. However at the moment it was Ronni and my difficult struggle in getting into her BMW, an ordeal similar to trying to get a stack of ten sheets of paper in an envelope designed to hold nine. Finally with bent knees peeking well above the dashboard, my nose an inch from the windshield and head dangerously close to the roof's interior, I succeeded in closing the door without losing any flesh or clothing. Breathing heavily from the exertion I asked what she wanted.

With a smile best described as perky, she asked if I had been visiting the Scott's house. Seeing I was fifty yards from the Scott's depressing dirt and weed filled front yard, I took it as a rhetorical question which could honestly be answered and not give too much away.

Turning full face to me she confessed that Woody asked her to visit Mrs. Scott, and in the process of extending police department's sympathy, woman to woman, find out if Jim Scott had any enemies. Lest I think Woody was shifting unpleasant work to her, she justified her solo visit on chauvinist grounds, how a woman could better relate to another woman in her time of intense suffering.

Continuing excusing Woody's absence, she said he had to attend a very important meeting at police headquarters, important because they were organizing a task force in which Woody and she would be in charge of the initial investigative data gathering unit, the IDG.

Resisting the temptation of giving her a few "oh gee"s, "how wonderful"s, I pumped her for any miscellaneous minor information, knowing if she and Woody had any important information she would keep it hidden better than her nipples, which thanks to a tight green silk shirt were in sharp outline, and with the shirt's plunging V, they were only an inch or so from seeing daylight. Sensitive, never looking down, keeping my eyes locked on her face, yet I was able to note one nipple's outline was facing straight out, the other turned slightly inward. Did I say she looked hot on this cold dreary afternoon?

Turning face, shoulders, hips and the other things towards me, she told me the salsa brand was the hottest manufactured by Ortega. In addition to the roach poison, it had additional jalapeno peppers added by person or persons unknown. She and Woody made the brilliant deduction; the same hand adding the hot jalapeno peppers was the same hand that added the poison. The salsa was placed on a side table near, but separate from the long serving tables.

I asked her a ridiculous question, "Did anyone see who put the salsa down on the side table?"

She took the question seriously mentioning everyone was moving around so much preparing the meal, fathers carrying drinks and greeting each other, energetic children running between tables, they couldn't get any definite information as to who was around the side table. Not only that but the poison salsa could have been brought there in a plastic covered bowl hidden under a jacket, beneath an apron, and easily surreptitiously put out without anyone really seeing him or her.

Leaning towards me, moving nipples one inch closer to daylight and freedom, with hand on my knee, a solicitous Ronni asked how Pam and I were getting along. She gave the words to me in an apologetic voice and sympathetic facial expression implying Pam was a possible, even chief suspect, I should have been provoked to defend Pam, but my expected outrage was muted by the inch close nipple and the gentle seductive hand/knee grip invitations. The two opposite inputs my interest in new acquisitions cancelled protecting prior accusations.

Bringing us back to table 12 I told her, "If I remember correctly, the salsa and crackers were in the center of the round table, and all the chairs were undisturbed. No, some of the guys had leaned their chairs up against the table, reserving their table position."

She dismissed my later observation saying they had a 15 foot square mark-up of the entire banquet hall including chairs and plates, and were now busy trying to position all the catering workers, volunteer mothers, fathers and children using scale figurines.

I gave her a "really?" thinking of the model train set I was planning for a surprise Christmas gift for my son, and out of curiosity asked, "Who built it?"

"The task force commissioned a company that does miniatures for movie and TV to construct it on a rush order basis." In confidence she added, "Let me tell you, it cost over five hundred thousand."

Sarcastically I commented, the money was well spent.

Smiling, ignoring the sarcasm, Ronni exploded a bombshell, "Mac, do you know you weren't supposed to be seated at table 12. You were assigned table 13."

My unfeigned surprise led her to add, "You didn't know! Woody and I thought you might have switched place names."

I told her clearly I hadn't, and wondered why in heaven they thought I did.

"13, Woody figured a person with your prejudicial attitudes, you know, er --- stereotypical belief system, you're probably superstitious and wouldn't want to sit at table 13."

"That's totally ridiculous. Look, just reflect on what Woody said about me and tell me who thinks in stereotypes."

She didn't think, just plowed ahead, "I argued with Woody over you being responsible for switching the name places. We both agreed if you hadn't done it out of superstition, then someone else did it deliberately for the sole purpose of moving you to the poison table."

More interested in getting the person's name I stood in for, I omitted pointing out, if I was the intended victim it might have been easier to just plant the poison on table 13. I mumbled a few 'yeas' then asked her whose name was switched with mine.

"A Mr.Zapp was originally assigned to table 12, next to the unfortunate Mr. Scott. Apparently they were good friends and coworkers so Jim Scott originally requested they sit together.

"Mac, do you realize what that means. Someone placed poison at table 12, then seeing your name wasn't there switches your place with

Zapp's. Woody and the task force feel this name switching could be a strong indication you were the targeted victim."

I felt I had to throw some sense at her. "Maybe this nut guy Zapp didn't want to sit next to Scott and switched our names, or Zapp, putting the poison out on 12 moved to table 13."

Graciously giving me the point she leaned back against the driver's door trying to look seductively relaxed and without a bed or pillow in sight still was successful. "We thought Zapp could be our man but in interviews he maintained he didn't make the switch saying Scott and he were friends, but Pep Boy Corporate ethics demanded the switch. Being Jim's supervisor he shouldn't socialize with an employee whose work he oversaw."

My pressing down the passenger window as the BMW was steaming up with stale exhaled breath and some great smelling perfume, Ronni, taking the hint pressed hers down. Watching her two inch blood red nails carefully pressing the control down, through her opening window I saw the same thirtyish woman staring at us. Again, we made eye contact. Again, she hastily looked away and hurriedly walked away, but now in the opposite direction.

What we did to the windows encouraged Ronni to comment in a very sensual voice accompanied by flirtatious facial expressions how very hot and how close we were in the car. She almost fell over herself making sure I got the double entente.

Knowingly giving her my best make-out smile I said, "It certainly is." When women flirt it's a fundamental sex commandment, men must respond in kind. Not responding appropriately you are cast immediately out of pink land into the neither world of inconsequential despised neutered persons.

"Look Ronni, I know you and Woody are working on this case non stop (and picking up some heavy overtime money) so could you give me any information about those who didn't make it to the banquet and were to sit at table 12."

All kittylike she coyly whispered, "Well I don't know if I should, after all you're not assigned to the case and maybe Woody would disapprove."

I remained silent waiting for her to open the department's mail.

A little annoyed that I didn't waste time begging she told me Tom Applegate, though assigned to table 12 decided at the last minute to sit with the little football players at the head table, and the other person missing from table 12, Tony Geroni had weak justifications for not being at our table.

"Well Mac," leaning deep into our conversational space, into my personal space, she explained, "Geroni hasn't a verifiable alibi, saying he received a phone call about a nonexistent emergency plumbing job. When he got to the address he found it was an empty lot. What's significant Mac is the wives didn't realize their husbands wouldn't be at table 12. Geroni's wife Blossom believed, after finishing the job he would attend the banquet. Carol, Zapp's ex wife was unaware of his decision to switch tables, so their wives could have poisoned the salsa."

Using our problem as an opening, she leaned further into creating a very intimate space mentioning Applegate's wife Robin also was ignorant of her husband's move to eat with the players.

Shit, I thought as I leaned back hard against the passenger door, *she'll be in my lap next, though I knew it was all 'come on' meaningless bullshit. Hopefully she took my leaning back as male bashfulness and not rejection.* Rejected women, even if meaninglessly engaging in flirtation, will turn nasty on a dime.

She didn't get nasty, gave a pout that could easily pass for a kiss pucker. "Our problem is our inability to eliminate any men of table 12 as possible victims, even those who weren't there. In fact, with everyone's wife running around the hall, hours before and during the banquet's start, it's impossible to eliminate anyone. If we could say so-and-so was not the intended victim, we could cross off the wife."

Her lips were so close I could see the down hairs on her upper lip and the drying cracks in her lipstick. I agreed the approach to the problem is to find the intended victim and then you know the murderer. It was obvious, but all conversations are exchanges of the obvious to facilitate mutual understand and agreement; to step out of the expected is to create chaos, confusion and conflict and destroy friendship.

To my relief she retreated several conversational space zones remarking it was Woody's view and he suspects I was the intended victim.

"Don't tell me he thinks my wife tried to kill me?"

"No, of course not," she replied, but so quickly I knew Woody was not only entertaining the idea, he was dancing with it. "We're trying to find any connection between your past cases and those people who were there. Woody says if we can find a mother, wife, girlfriend whose son, husband, boyfriend, you arrested, we'd be more than halfway to solving the case."

Women who continually quote a man to a man are sure to tick off the recipient, and I was getting heavy bites with Woody ticks.

She gave me a pause to think about what she and Woody had thought. During this time deciding to extricate myself from her, her Woody, her car, her meaningless flirtatious overtures and her stifling silly presence and perfume, I wondered how best to do it when suddenly her eyes lit up. Giving a little girlish screech, and patting my bony knee she said, "Mac, I've just had a fantastic idea. Why don't you and I drive over to Ray Brother's house and interview him and Courtney, his current girlfriend."

A furtive glance at my wrist revealed it was 4:45, the tired sun had left the scene but the sky had not pulled down the curtain so the stage was still lit. What the hell, I agreed, "Fine."

CHAPTER 13

Brothers and Courtney

On our drive to Ray Brothers' house, in statement form, Ronni went over her plan of attack for us, adding a question mark at each statement's end to make her plans more palatable to me. "We'll initially interview them together?"

"Okay."

"Then asking the girlfriend to show me the house, we'll separate and I'll interview her while you interview Ray?"

"Okay."

"After we interview them, woman to woman, man to man, we'll make some excuse to separate them again. This time I'll interview Ray Brothers and you talk to his mistress Courtney?"

"Okay Ronni, sounds good to me." My third okay wasn't affirmative enough and she gave me some silent room 'til I gave her a more emphatic, "Yeah, it all sounds good to me."

Satisfied she gave me back a "Good" either as a reward or a period.

We were silent for the remaining drive out of Scott's neighborhood, passing through mine and into the plush upscale neighborhood only dentists and fast food franchise owners like Ray Brothers can afford. Pulling into his driveway Ronni and I silently gave the house and the grounds an admiring appreciation. It may not impress twenty-year-old millionaire rock idols, or politicians who, though scrupulously honest and with wholehearted devotion help the poor and suffering little people, somehow inexplicably always manage to retire filthy rich. but it certainly impressed me.

A large square red brick edifice with green ivy audaciously crawling hand over hand up the sides of the house to slyly peek into the windows, I easily visualized my house fitting inside this brick structure's foyer, and not blocking the entry. Unlike Scott's front yard, there were no dirty brown bare spots, only large swatches of crew cut green grass curving around trimmed islands of dark brown mulch lying at the feet of stately evergreen trees. The driveway led to a three-car garage dwarfing Ronni's BMW. Crawling hand over hand, foot over foot out of the sporty BMW I had the feeling we were miniatures entering a life-size world.

Ray escorted us to a living room, explaining we were lucky to catch them home, given this was his first day he was able to go to work. Apparently Courtney talked him into making it a short day and to celebrate his return to health by eating out. Suddenly large double doors opened allowing the lady in question to make her entrance, wearing a tight light blue sheath dress with a single strand of pearls, which I'm guessing were genuine. The dress's split almost to her hip bone enabled her to walk and shake more easily.

We arranged ourselves on the furniture with upholstery costing more than poor Scott's house. Even sitting at a distance of ten feet I'm sure Ronni could have given an accurate appraisal of the pearls, dress and shoes.

Getting up from the brocade ten foot couch, Ronni gave Courtney a girlie hug and justified the intimacy by murmuring how terrible it must have been for Courtney to almost lose the man she loves. With such an opening, Courtney could do no less than carry on with the theme, heroically enumerating all her fears, her suffering, her mental anguish over the last four days. Laughingly she explained her appetite disappeared in sympathy with poor Ray's eating difficulty, and only now with his reemerging could she look at food, hence the reason for dining out. Her litany of pain didn't evoke sympathetic appreciative comments or looks from Ray.

To move the conversation to the purpose of our visit, I mentioned that I had just come from seeing Joy, Jim Scott's widow.

Ray hurriedly interrupted to show that although he did not intend to visit the widow, he was still a very caring individual. "Must be terrible for her to lose her husband like that, right before her eyes. One can only imagine what she's going through."

With no one interested in expanding energy to do any imagining, Courtney, leaning back in a loveseat, turning soulful eyes to Ray murmuring the trite, "If it happened to me, if it was Ray rather than that poor ridiculous Pep Boy salesman, I don't know how I could continue living. Ray's my whole life."

There was a pause as we all recognized the insincerity of her statement, all but possibly not Ray, who beaming at her went to her and standing behind her rested his hand on her shoulder.

Ray asked Ronni if the police had any suspects in regards to who tried to poison him, er, us.

I let Ronni tell him the nothing in so many words; they couldn't publicly announce the progress they are making; they had some serious suspects; all the resources of the department are being focused on this particular investigation; arrests were imminent; the survivors could rest assured no other attempts on their lives will be permitted, (As if someone gave permission to kill Scott.); the NYPD was working closely with the FBI, CIA, AFT and Homeland Security

Ronni continued saying any help Ray could give would be of great assistance which allowed her to move easily into asking Ray if he saw anything suspicious at the banquet, anything no matter how insignificant that he may have forgotten and now, after the event, in retrospect, remembers.

If Ray had any ideas or remembrances, I would have been one surprised detective. Staring at the living room's drape drawn eight foot windows he gave his brief mental search the pantomime of great thought. Turning to us, patting Courtney's shoulder, he confessed he had no ideas, except to suggest a crazed lunatic or Jim Scott had a serious enemy, possibly a disgruntled Pep Boy customer. He then ended gifting to us his weighty judicious opinion, "If I were you, I would check out that Scott fellow."

Turning to Courtney I asked, if she had attended the banquet, and if she did, did she notice anyone acting suspicious.

It was a race between Ray and Courtney as to who was to deny her attendance at the banquet. I gave it to Ray by a nose.

Acting surprised, Ronni asked why Courtney hadn't attended the banquet with Ray and his son.

With hard lips, sharp mouth corners, Courtney dropped her tearful caring scared girlfriend looks and became the other woman. "Because Eleanor, Ray's soon to be ex wife was going to be there, and Ray didn't want us to meet fearing we'd make a scene at his son's banquet. Something I would never do, embarrass dear Ray in front of his son." Leaving unsaid the thought that that was most certainly what Eleanor would do.

Twisting her head back, reaching up, holding Ray's hand she told him, as far as she was concerned, there was no need for him to worry. She'd never never start an argument with Eleanor. Then turning back to us she confided, "Eleanor is a very bitter woman and I can understand that. I know how devastated I'd be if Ray ever left me." Turning her head back to him, confessing her undying love she announced her early demise if he ever left her.

Ray, as embarrassed as I was with her public verbal display of affection, murmured, "I would never leave you, my little chicken Mac Nugget. Never."

All conversation had to stop, for at that moment Ronni and I were two theater goers watching a great tender love scene and it would seem to be the height of callous insensitivity to speak while the two experienced actors, well rehearsed in their script, demanded a pregnant pause.

Eventually someone had to break the scene and Ronni did, changing the subject. "Courtney, I can't get over how beautifully you've decorated your house."

Well, that intro led to discussions of what Courtney purchased, where Courtney bought them, what difficulties Courtney encountered in buying the whatever, and Courtney's invitation to take Ronni on a tour of the house. A fast "yes" and the two of them vanished out the double doors leaving Ray and me staring at each other, not knowing what to say.

Well, that's not quite true. I knew what I wanted to say and said it. "Ray, I'm here not as a detective but as a fellow victim who's trying to find out what happened. I'm sure both of us would like to know. You don't think you were the intended victim and I certainly don't believe I was. Just coming from talking to Scott's widow and Zapp, his tire supervisor, I can tell you they're convinced Scott wasn't the intended victim either, but someone was. If you had a crazy person running around that banquet hall with poison salsa, why was our table the only one picked out? You would think a mass murderer would try to kill as many people as possible and drop poisoned salsa on every table."

He politely nodded at every punctuation mark but his eyes kept sliding from me to the double doors.

"Ray, I really believe one of us at that table was the target and the rest of us merely accidental victims. The murderer, in killing five, possibly eight men, hoped to hide his intended victim thereby obscuring his connection."

Walking from behind Courtney's love seat to a straight back chair near a bookcase filled with hard covered books (no soft covered books in this house) he said, "You know Mac, what you say makes sense, but I tell you, I wasn't the intended victim. If you really want my opinion, that black guy, that gypsy taxi driver was probably the most likely one. I don't want to sound like a racist, but the guy's a racist, and I wouldn't be surprised if he was mixed up with some nasty illegal business, probably drugs. Do you remember what happened at the end of the last game, when that white Lexus drove into the parking lot as everyone was leaving, and two big black guys came out and started yelling and hitting that Abdullah person. If it wasn't for that big fat wife of his yelling, screaming, and throwing punches, I think those two guys would have killed him right there."

Shit, how did I forget that? "Yeah, I remember that incident, and believe me, the police are looking into Abdullah's background very carefully. But Ray, one thing is troubling me, causing me to look at you and Courtney with suspicion. I know Courtney was at the banquet."

"No way. Do you think I'm crazy? With my wife there? If Courtney walked in, there would have been an immediate fight. I mean yelling and screaming, you wouldn't believe. I gave emphatic orders to Courtney she was not to come in. She drove me to the banquet, dropped me off and went back home. I don't know who told you she was there, but she wasn't. Besides, I know she wanted to go back to her dress shop to do an inventory check."

"Ray, we can't get anywhere if you keep throwing crap at me. Not only did others see Courtney, but I did. For damn's sake, she was wearing a firehouse red dress and looking like a million bucks, was circulating so much at the bar she looked like a Communist flag waver at a May Day Rally, so don't tell me she wasn't there."

"You saw her?"

"Ray, she was impossible to miss in that red dress. For heaven's sake, she was a walking fire. I saw her talking to your daughter's boyfriend, so he and your daughter knew Courtney was there."

Surprised he asked, "Was it the black one?"

"Yeah, with tattoos, gold earrings, pierced nose, lips and eyebrows."

"Yeah, a gold mine's supply of dangling body piercing jewelry. Damn it Mac, I could kill that creep Derek. It tears me up to think he's…well, with my daughter."

Letting the black boyfriend slide I said, "Yeah, but let's get back to Courtney."

For a long moment Ray struggled to drag his mind from the strange things black Derek was doing to his daughter. Finally getting him back to Courtney, the woman he was doing strange things with, he gave up his denials. "Yeah, she was there. Told her not to come in, but the woman is so in love with me and jealous of Eleanor, sometimes emotionally she doesn't think. Her jealousy and insecurity are understandable. I had been going with her before I left Eleanor so of course my wife thinks I left her because of Courtney. I don't know. It may be true. Well anyway, it was one hell of a separation, something I would never want to go through again: the emotion, the lawyers, the money, the disruption of your life, and it never ends. When I go to watch my son play football, I have to go to the far end near the goal post with Courtney because Eleanor is planted at the fifty yard line. If you don't think it's a struggle to keep Courtney from marching down the football field and sitting on the fifty yard line in front of Eleanor you know nothing of women. I spend more time and energy watching Courtney then watching my boy play the game.

"You know Mac, looking at this house, the furniture, the three cars in the garage, you'd think I had life by the balls, but I tell ya, my life stinks. My wife hates my guts, my daughter is going downhill, hell forget downhill, she's down in a swamps, sleeps with everybody, even blacks, thinking she's fantastic because she does, hates me, calls me a racist and blames me for anything in her life she doesn't like, and my son Willie who I dearly love, is turning into a soft spoiled mama's boy. I push sports and believe me, it took a lot of argument to get him into a football program. His mother wanted soccer. I don't need to tell you, boys need to give hits and to feel hits, and football is great for that."

We saw eye to eye on that, and trying to keep our man to man rapport I told him so, then proceeded to ask if anything recently happened which could have a bearing on the poison.

He hesitated, "Well, I wasn't going to mention it, but right before the banquet I discovered one of my counter workers, a seventeen year old black kid was passing out free hamburgers to his friends late at night, and in another store I found some fifty year old broad, who I made night manager and was planning to move her up to day manager, was ripping me off at the register. I tell you, an employer has to trust his employees. Do you know what would happen to business if every employee was like those two? Chaos, that's what would happen. It's not laws that keep chaos chained but culture. We have a cultural expectation of honesty. South of the border, well you know what goes on down there."

"I suppose you fired them."

"Yeah, the afternoon of the banquet. I told them they were through, but since I had assigned them to help serve my donated McDonald's burgers and French fries to the kids at the banquet, they worked that last night."

"Well there are two possible people with motives against you."

"People don't kill because they're fired. Well I suppose it could be seen as motivation but realistically, fast food job, I don't see ...."

He was sinking into a pensive melancholy mood, so it was time to remind him of his insurance. "Ray, you know the three and a half million dollar insurance policy you've got on your life with your children as beneficiaries could be seen as supplying your wife with a motive."

Ray whispered, "Quiet with that. Courtney thinks she's the beneficiary. If she finds out otherwise I'll have to buy another policy just for her."

"So Eleanor and Courtney also have motives."

He got angry. "What the hell are you talking about? Eleanor would never kill me, her children's father, and Courtney loves me."

"They were all at the banquet. Either of them could easily have dropped the poison salsa bowl on the side table."

He waved the idea aside with a sweep of his hand telling me what I was saying was ridiculous.

I continued to press him, specifically about Courtney, asking him, if she felt he wasn't going to marry her, then there's a probability she'd believe she'd be supplanted in his affection by another woman who would become the new beneficiary of that three point five million policy. "Ray, if she doesn't believe you're going to marry her, she's got a three point five million reason to permanently terminate your relationship."

He seriously thought about it, not about Courtney poisoning him, but what I said about his precarious relationship with Courtney. He got up and going to a well stocked bar asked if I'd like a drink.

"Yeah," then my gut kicked my brain in the ass, "Er, on second thought, no Ray, my stomach is still too delicate to handle booze."

Giving me a "Right, I'll pass too," and sitting down he continued, "You know Courtney really loves me. I know the truth of that as well as I know the truth that we're sitting here in this room. And I love her." Pausing, leaning forward in his chair he lowered his voice as if I was his confessor, "First it was, you know, we had to move in together, then never ending importuning to get a divorce so we could get married. She's been hinting, hell, nagging about us getting married, but I tell you, after going through one hell of a separation I'm leery of getting legally involved with another woman. I've even kept Courtney's dress shop in my name so any profits or tax losses will not be encumbered"

"Courtney has a dress shop," I said.

"The dear needs an outlet for her creative energy, and she wants to start a new career."

"Well anyway Ray, If you're absolutely positive of her love for you, and your love for her, why the hesitation of getting a divorce and marry Courtney?" What I didn't say was possibly his hesitating was the knowledge of being a fifty year old physically unattractive guy, with three McDonald's franchises, and she, a mid twenty year old hot looker who likes money and hasn't any, and is very worried about her future after thirty."

Laughing like an indulgent parent confessing to spoiling a child Ray admitted Courtney seeing herself as a dress designer wanted to start her own dress boutique. Shrugging his shoulders, he added, "So I figured, what the hell, having some spare change I figured why not invest it in a mall dress shop. I'm sure Courtney will make a success of it. Seeing how well she dresses, you have to know the woman has great fashion sense. True, it's losing money now but you can't expect to make money in your first year of business despite being opened for the Christmas season. Hopefully the second Christmas season will turn a profit. Of course, if not, we might have to take a tax write-off on the whole thing."

His 'second Christmas' was said with a sad sense of reality, a grasp of the inevitable failure. Courtney should remember when love costs too much it's recycled. Sex, like food, is necessary, and like food, is always cost evaluated.

The women returned chatting and laughing as if they were long lost high school best friends reunited after a long separation. Ronni came over to me gushing, "Ed, you should see their beautiful home. Courtney has done wonders in decorating."

From the glint in Ronni's eyes and from her animated expression I knew she really was excited about the house, and in her mind was planning how she'd decorate her house once she gets someone to buy her a million plus home. Maybe Woody, but from my deep affection for dear Woody I wished her good hunting but thought, *yeah lady, lots of luck there.*

Obviously Ronni's mind had been sidetracked from business, as she was starting to describe how the master bedroom closets, larger than her bedroom, were organized.

To get her back on track I told her, "Ronni, I believe you told me you wanted to get Mr. Brother's official statement."

"Huh? We could do that later. You should see the master bathroom. Besides being a walk through shower it's got six shower heads and …"

Pointedly looking at my watch, which was nearing six, I told her it was getting late, and I knew she wanted to take Mr. Brothers somewhere private and get his statement.

Finally getting the message, looking a little deflated, Ronni turned to Ray, "Oh, yes, Mr. Brothers, is there somewhere we can go to get your official statement as to what you saw and did on the night of the banquet."

Ray complained, "I've already given five official statements at the hospital to all the different investigators, and more since I've come home. There is nothing I can add."

Undeterred Ronni smoothly told him people often remember small details days after an event which they might have overlooked when giving initial statements close to the tragic event. "You know, Mr. Brothers, the trauma you were subjected to could have loomed so large in your mind as to overshadow or obscure small, less significant details. It's those details I'm hoping to evoke."

Her argument seemed reasonable, so grunting his assent they went to Ray's study, leaving Courtney alone with me. She immediately played the hostess offering me a drink. Once again, the mind said yes, and again the stomach emphatically vetoed it with another kick. The greasy cheese steak marching down my colon was making a noisy stink about the trip.

"No, thank you Courtney. Ray was telling me you opened a dress shop in the mall."

She lit up and enthusiastically started to describe the dress shop's mall location, its interior design and lighting, the special sales she's running or will run, various designers' creations she was carrying, all for a good five minutes 'til she mentioned the upcoming Christmas rush, which gave me an opportunity to mention Ray's comment that he hoped the second Christmas would be more profitable.

Her excitement waned, and her lowered penciled eyebrows, like thunderclouds, halved her blue shadowed eyes. "Of course this Christmas will be better. We opened only two months before Christmas and barely were able to get stocked when Christmas was over. This Christmas will be better and the following Christmas will be fantastic. What everyone must remember is it takes several years for a dress shop to establish a name and a loyal following, especially when you are aiming for upscale sophisticated women shoppers. Everyone in the dress retail business knows that."

Thinking the dress shop would see a third Christmas was as probable as me seeing my million this Christmas, I changed the subject, "Courtney, I have to tell you in all fairness I saw you at the banquet. You were circulating at the bar, and someone else also saw you."

"Dam it, it was Palante. That creep hit on me at the bar. Can you imagine, at his kid's banquet, with his wife in the next room, the guy comes up to me, accusing me of 'staring' at him, then telling me he can't let me buy him a drink, as if I wanted to buy the weirdo a drink. Men buy me drinks, I don't buy men drinks."

I wondered if the passage of twenty years would change that. With our culture's feminist evolutionary path it was almost certain.

"Well since we agree you were at the banquet, and Ray didn't want you there, why did you go, and what did you do there?"

Knowing why she was there, a lioness protecting the kill she stole from another, I still wanted to see how she would explain it.

Her story was simple. After dropping off Ray, instead of returning home she sneaked into the bar section of the hall. She never left the bar but kept an eye on Ray. If his wife started to fight with him she would be there to protect him adding, "You know men are at such a disadvantage in fighting with women."

"You never went into the banquet room?"

"No, in fact I was waiting outside the building when they carried you men out on stretchers. Of course I was devastated but I can tell you right now, I saw his ugly wife smiling, and that slut of a daughter laughing and hugging some gold festooned black creep as they put poor Ray into the ambulance. If someone is responsible for the tragedy … well never mind, I don't want to accuse Ray's wife and daughter. Ray still has benevolent feelings towards them and I respect those feelings no matter how misplaced and totally unreciprocated they are."

As she finished, Ray and Ronni returned. Getting up politely for Ronni's entrance, and walking over to her to advance our leave-taking process, Ronni, ignored my gambit and sat down asking Courtney and Ray their thoughts about the memorial service and were they planning to attend.

Quickly reacting, Ray said he didn't like the idea, but he wasn't able to get out his reasons for not attending before Courtney announced they would be going. She thought It was a great idea and asked if it was true the memorial would be televised. Receiving a 'yes' from Ronni, Courtney went into wardrobe considerations. She had the perfect dress in her boutique: dark blue silk with just the right vertical silver threads, not showing too much, just a respectful bodice, respectful yet attractive..

Still standing, hoping I could start the leaving process as my heart was down visiting a quarrelsome stomach, Ronni mentioned *Oprah, Dr. Phil, The View* words. Ray took my hint and stood up as the seated girls reciting celebrity names, each accompanied by a programmed commentary, opening with the ever traditional weight gambit over Oprah's losses, followed by Whoopi's gain, before commenting Dr. Oz's new exciting book on relationship wisdom. With them starting to open Katie Couric's insights into troubled and abused women, in desperation Ray was forced to announce Courtney and he had to dress for dinner.

As Ronni walked to her car Ray held me back just outside the front door, "Mac, I just want you to know, neither my wife nor Courtney want to kill me. True the wife is bitter but it's directed against Courtney, feeling she's breaking up our marriage."

"Is she?"

"Of course not. Women love to think they control men. It's a fundamental dogma with them. No, Courtney didn't capture me, didn't drag me away from Eleanor. I was ready for a change and fortuitously hot Courtney came into my life at the right moment."

Ronni gave the BMW's horn a short tap.

Smiling at me Ray said, "Look it's cold out here and I'd better get inside. But one thing I want you to realize, Courtney really loves me."

I couldn't resist, "Would she, if you didn't own the McDonald's stores, but only worked there?"

"Yeah, know what you're saying and we both know the answer. To be fair, if she didn't look great and wasn't great in bed, would I want her? And we both know the answer to that. Mac, face it, romantic love is a teenage thing. At our age it's sex for money. Probably later it will be convenience and companionship."

Before he ducked back into the house I asked him, "So Ray, does she really love you?"

Shrugging he gave a silly smile.

What I should have asked, did he really love her, but we both knew the answer without asking. Just before closing the door, leaning to me he whispered, "Has the name Desiree surfaced in the investigation?"

"Desiree!"

Reading my answer in the exclamation he told me to forget Desiree. "The name means nothing," and he closed the door.

Means nothing? Meant something, to be mentioned.

CHAPTER 14

Ronni's Three Little Surprises

Seated in her car prior to driving me home Ronni asked what I learned from Ray and Courtney. After telling her about the dress shop and Ray's plans to close it after Christmas as a losing proposition, I asked what she learned, mentioning we're partners and it was time to share information.

In a tone saying, as a male I could never access feminine nuances, she observed, "Courtney is pushing Ray hard to get a divorce and marry her. She half suspects Ray may go back to his wife while also fearing the possibility he may be seeing another woman. (*Ah ha, Desiree.*) She's one frightened woman desperate for security of a wedding ring. Also found out she has a white bib apron in the kitchen which, wearing over her dress, she could have easily mingled in with the rest of the women serving food."

"What about Woody? Has he found out anything?"

"Well we've been very busy. Given this may be a terrorist attack there are many investigating committees to be set up within the organizational structure. The City and State police, as well as the FBI, CIA, AFT, Home Defense people and the Pure Food and Drug Department, the Agricultural Department, the--"

Interrupting her litany of all the agencies pertinent or not to the case, all sitting at the hungry media's feet feeding them sound bites desperately begging for the media's love and attention I told her, "It's a plain homicide by poison."

Teacher to a failing obdurate student she angrily responded, "The media has declared it a possible terrorist attack against America's children and against football, our most popular sport."

I commented, "If the media cries 'terrorist attack' the government must answer; if the media shouts 'save the children' the government must respond. There is a difference between PR and what really happens. You're making it sound like the PR dance is real, and everyone must follow the media's analysis as if any of their ideas had a connection to reality. Of course the pompous rich bastards can and do create reality for the unreflective unwashed masses."

She countered, "Just how would you answer last night's *60 Minute* special containing interviews with the angry little ten year old black football player boy, and the sweet white teary eyed nine year old cheer leader telling Diane Sawyer how traumatized they were."

I shrugged and she slapped my indifference with a triumphant, "You can't possibly know what is really happening." She went on, "How about TV's *Night Line*, *News Line* and *Date Line* interviewing the mothers and wives who, with fulsome tears desperately employing hankies and tissues in an unsuccessful attempt to staunch the water shown in close-ups revealing in detail their pain as they plead for the government to do something."

Sarcastically I mentioned, "It's all a lie," then asked, "What about O'Malley's law firm giving interviews in, near, and about hospitals and football fields. What about soccer moms and doctors crying on the TV news programs about how football is dangerous, never mind the deepest of deep thinkers; sociologists, educators and psychologists talking about male aggression and how it would be a better world if men took up cooking and nursing children."

Patiently, mother to child, insider to outsider she said, "Woody and I have a better perspective on this case. Sarcasm and negativity doesn't help solve this horrendous murder. Mac, cynicism is not an attractive attitude."

"Okay, okay," I cried, "I surrender. It's getting hot in the car. Let's get going."

She had to give the last shot. "In fact, Woody and I have a critical meeting tonight to set up an organizational flow chart delineating the areas of authority various investigational agencies are allowed to follow.

"And later I'm attending an important meeting which will establish the committee that will collate the data from each of the investigative agencies and teams into a coherent whole so as to get the big picture."

I didn't answer, thinking, *oh yes, the big picture, the long term view, the overall -, just more BS.* Looking at the dark streets as we drove out of the land of the rich into my neighborhood, the land between the rich and the poor, thinking committees; the breaks to progress, the escape parachutes for responsibility, I looked forward to warm food and the gentle comforting of my home. Turning into my street, a street lined with large bare trees whose obvious longevity gave mute testimony to my house's age, Ronni slowed and gave me her three little surprises.

The first was her stating she thought we'd make a great team, buttressing this opinion saying she felt working together we handled the Brothers' interview smoothly.

I gave her a noncommittal 'yeah' not knowing where she was going only to have her follow it up with surprise two, a complimentary opinion of my detection abilities and how I was highly thought of in the department.

Before I could crawl out of the BMW, surprise three, her resting a gentle hand on my kneecap, and with the warm caring sensitivity a woman extends to her child or lover cautioned me to be careful, warning me I could have been the intended victim. In fact, she told me several task forces viewed me as the possible prime target with the black gypsy cab driver Abdullah Malcolm and the rich Ray Brothers a distant second and third respectively in the minds of the newly formed City's Response against Poisoners Task Force, the C.R.A.P. Task Force.

Managing to extricate myself from her car, leaning down to say goodnight, her last words dripping with womanly concern sounding like an extended come-on, "Mac, again for my sake take care of yourself." Then she issued a modification to the come on, "Everyone is worried about you."

I gave her 'thanks,' but it was thanks for nothing, knowing certainly I'm able to take care of myself and if in trouble feeling I'd not only be the chief worrier, I'd be the only one.

Walking to my house I mulled over her three surprises thinking, what the hell is the scheming bitch up to now? She'd no more work with a second grade detective then a democrat would cut my taxes, and I knew the upper reaches of the department, if they did have any knowledge of me, didn't like me. My fellow workers were a different matter. With them I felt if not in high esteem there was some esteem, esteem that stopped short of any appreciable act of worrying about me. As for the sexual invitation and its implied RSVP I'd give it a pessimistic non response. She wanted my vote, but would she pay for it.

Turning to watch the BMW turn left at the corner I noticed the misted up windows of a late model car parked two houses down. Crap, I thought, lovers making out parked right on the street. Shit, was I so old and miserable in begrudging the guy's lucky to be making out that I couldn't give him a mental right on. Then it suddenly dawned on me, the stupid city's task force idiots, they've named themselves CRAP.

CHAPTER 15

A House is Not a Sanctuary

White observing Ray Brothers' house was not a home, and noting Courtney was not a wife, and Ronni was not a companion but an annoying flirt, I walked into my home. Approaching the front door of my house with each yellow lit window promising warmth, I felt I was a refugee escaping a sad alien land returning to my sanctuary, to my home to my wife and son, and my home's familiar furnishings, each an important particular in forming my essential personal reality. What was needed was a satisfying meal, my easy chair, the paper, then to bed for healing repose.

Walking into the living room, thinking I left my stress- causing reality outside to fester in the November night's dampness, only to find the outside cold infected my home with trouble rising from my easy chair. Liquor filled glass in hand, a false smile in place, Woody welcomed me as if I was the visitor. My felt surprise instantly turning into irritation causing my outburst. "What the hell are you doing here?"

His bonhomie aggravated my attitude. My 'hell,' brought an explanation: he came with Psychologists Dr. Paris Start and Dr. Lovey Leeper, experts in treating people in crisis.

Finding my sanctuary defiled I demanded, "What the hell are they doing here? Where the hell are they?"

To hurl anger at Woody is merely blowing wind at the back of his ego's sail. "Easy Mac, keep calm, they're in the kitchen counseling Pam."

Confused, my repeating, "Why the hell are those characters here,", had me accepting Woody's presence as a given.

Affluent Woody, free from financial concerns, irrationally worried about the cost to the poor, believing those in the financial subbasement are constantly worried about costs, he reassured me the consulting would cost me nothing. He said, "It's free," like one would say 'Open Sesame' to a world of riches.

His inference I lived in the subbasement when knowing I lived my life on the second floor pushed me to counter, "Nothing's free. The interconnected chain of giving away free stuff ends with me paying for the free stuff with my taxes."

Playing the host in my home, Woody advised me to calm down, sit down, have a drink. "Drs. Start and Leeper are helping Pam get in touch with her repressed feelings in order to successfully deal with the traumatic episode she just experienced."

I couldn't get past him inviting me to sit down, have a drink, and his paternalistic attitude towards my wife issued to me while I stood in the interior of my home, my back to the front door, looking inside the living room. Only after maneuvering around a standing Woody and taking possession of my living room was the trauma crap able to come to the fore. "What the hell is this trauma bullshit? Woody, I was the one poisoned. I'm good, never felt better." The later was a downright lie.

Fighting to keep the high ground he told me to sit down, have a drink, I was overreacting.

Sitting in my easy chair saying I didn't want a drink, though really needing a stiff one, Woody, standing, maintaining his prominence said, "Understand Mac, the gut is still delicate. Roach poison can really tear up the insides. You really shouldn't take the risk. You don't want to throw up on your living room rug."

Damn it, a double bind. If I continue refusing a drink I'd be acknowledging his prognosis and advice. If I took the damn drink I was obeying his original suggestion. In either case I was subservient to his words. I stewed in silence, inexplicably angry with Woody. The present situation only warranted annoyance; the fury I felt resided outside the current situation, possibly some irrational thing about my life.

As previously stated, girly Woody hating silence broke it. "We've got the FBI doing background checks on everyone at the banquet. It's still too early to rule anyone out." With a smile easily interpreted as a jocular foray at my expense he inquired, "How's your past? Hope you've got nothing that's naughty and not nice."

Like every man, having past sins, seeing no humor but a threat he enjoyed delivering, how could I respond to his attack delivered under the guise of companionship humor. Laugh with the interrogator's jest and endure self depreciation? Or denying the humorist's thrust and maintaining innocence suggest I took the humorist jab seriously and therefore suffered additional guilt of hypocrisy.

Playing dumb I commented, "Have they uncovered any relative information on the banquet attendees?"

"Too early. They've done a forensic profile of the killer."

Realizing he wasn't going to share, I prodded saying dismissively, "It's all a waste of time." At the time I was deep into the land of negativity and perversely enjoying my visit.

My negativity forced Woody to defend profiling. Sitting down facing me, teacher to mistaken student, he confided. "Just between us, although the FBI profiler suggests the poisoner is between 15 and 50, they narrowed it to 20 to 40 as the most probable age range. Probably a woman, who as a young girl had experienced physical, mental, and/or sexual abuse by a dominant male in her life. She's white, could be black, and most likely has a grievance against someone at table 12."

My sarcastic 'really' Woody taking it to be an honest 'really' continued, "Of course the forensic profile people haven't eliminated a deranged psychotic mass murderer who could be male or female but most probably male."

Continuing my sarcastic vein I added, "Who has had a past traumatic experience with the Pop Warner Football League."

Not surprising he missed the vein, "Both terrorists and psychotics always attack innocent people out of misplaced anger festering from past traumatic childhood experiences."

With just a few degrees of sincerity I asked if the FBI was able to eliminate al Qaeda.

Leaning back in his chair, excuse me, my chair, touching finger tips to form an arch, Woody, as if possessing important secret confidential information told me, "Mac, you've got to understand, there's a limit to the confidential information I can confide to you. As far as the investigation is concerned, you could be the primary target of the killer."

To prod him summarizing I said, "So the FBI has dropped the terrorist idea."

Not wishing to give me an inch Woody added, "Homeland Security and CIA are still actively pursuing the terrorist angle as the FBI and State Police are concentrating on a deranged psychotic killer who, by unfortunate happenstance, picked your son's banquet. They and the National Security Agency, at the moment, are running extensive data searches for any similar mass poisoning worldwide. I can tell you this, Facebook, cell phones, credit cards, MySpace have no secrets from us."

With his giving the data search a high level of optimism, mendaciously I had to ask about the search's success.

He gave me an optimistic, "Not yet," as if the yet was moments away from becoming a Cinderella successful moment.

Continuing to combat my negativity Woody confided the Department of Agriculture was checking on the salsa ingredients in cooperation with the Pure Food and Drug people who had experts looking into the factory preparation of the salsa. The Poison Control people have already traced the roach poison to a Mexican manufacturing company.

Leaning even closer to me whispering as if telling a dirty joke in mixed company, he told me, "You know, South of the Border may not have our strict health regulations. The poison may have been bad. Toxic impurities could have found their way into the roach poison."

Incredulous I stated, "You're saying the poison, being tainted was made poisonous."

"Exactly. We're pulling all roach poisons off the shelves to see if contamination has been injected into the roach product in any consumer venue."

"Ridiculous," I said wondering where the hell was this consumer venue coming from?

Woody agreed to the word but not to the meaning. "Yeah, it's ridiculous the amount of time and resources all these investigations are absorbing, but justified in giving the critical situation we're dealing with."

Woody's 'we' was always just a nudge from becoming an 'I'.

"Mac, hear this, Congress is starting to hold hearings as to the advisability of holding hearings and which House should take the lead and what specific committees will hold the investigative hearings. Mac, I can tell you, the full force of the government is being energized by these attacks on America's boys and girls."

Hearing murmuring voices from the kitchen I yelled to Pam, "What is going on out there?"

Woody answered for her, "It's the crisis psychologists helping her."

"So, she's not a suspect."

Woody's, "Certainly not in my view" suggested in other's views she was a murderer and I was her victim.

Hoping there was some iron ore residing in Woody's bullshit, I asked what else he has uncovered. Again my hope was stillborn as Woody told me initially everyone thinking 'spoiled food' the first responders concentrated on eliminating the possibility of improperly prepared salsa. " Anyway, Mac, Pam can't be eliminated, but knowing Pam and having the greatest admiration for her I know to even consider her as a poisoner is ridiculous.

"Although you still could be the targeted victim poisoned by a victim of your past arrests."

"What the hell is this about victims of past arrests? The creeps were all guilty as sin."

"Calm down Mac, don't upset that stomach of yours. When we finish doing the background checks on the men at table 12 and any and all women connected with them, we'll see some real progress.."

Woody paused, and in the pause I got up, poured two fingers and sat down. I didn't offer Woody a refill.

Replying to my discourteous non offer he grandly announced he didn't want another drink as if an offer was imminent. He had a lot of critical work still pending where a clear head was needed implying my head could be befuddled with booze. With refusing what was not offered he added a barb, "Mac, with your pumped out stomach better go easy on the liquor."

I had no comeback save taking a good inch off my drink.

"Mac, I heard you visited Scott's widow. We frown on you visiting the victim's family. Sill with the damage done, did you learn anything germane to our investigation?"

Germane! Venue! Why the hell use those words if not to impress an illiterate inferior, and he still employs his regal 'we'.

Woody sounded as if he headed the FBI, the CIA, AFT and CRAP, along with the entire police department.

I withheld my impression of the widow being a selfish money hungry bitch, and the Zapp character a pompous idiot probably sniffing after the widow; if unlucky he might get lucky and be damned. I gave Woody my fulsome praise for the widow's courage in holding up under her tragic loss which he, expecting to hear, swallowed whole. I gave him Zapp as one hell of a sensitive caring fellow who, out of benign motives was trying to help the widow. In Woody's mind everyone was sensitive and caring except those who not blessed with optimism, were condemned to live in dark negativity never to see people's goodness and a future filled with Kumbia.

I asked what Ronni said about our visit with Ray Brothers and his mistress Courtney; did she gain any information.

"Ronni was there! She was at Brothers! You were there with her!" escaped before his face saving, "She was there on my orders. I'm just surprised she took you along. I'll have to talk to her about that. You understand any information she gained must remain confidential. Since you were there I'd be interested in your impression of Ray and Courtney's relationship and their relationship with his separated wife. After all, being the only rich person at 12 he has to be one of the main suspected victims after you."

I gave him the 'love' he expected. Ray loves Courtney, has a deep appreciation for his wife Eleanor. Courtney is devoted to Ray, devastated by his near death experience and as for Eleanor, their separation was amicable and Eleanor, glad Ray has found happiness with Courtney wishes him and Courtney all of the best.

A little reality edged out from Woody's primrose mind. "Some separations can get pretty ugly." He paused, and in the intermission I got a three inch refill promising my stomach some chicken rice soup later. On my way to my chair, Woody confided the Security Exchange Commission is working closely with McDonald's Corporation Headquarters.

"You're not serious. The SEC and Big Mac."

"Certainly, any connection between bad food and McDonald's, no matter how tenuous could affect the market. Big Mac's security people are fully committed to finding out if Ray was the target and if so was it because of bad food or bad service at one of his franchises."

To match Woody's unintentional stupidity I sarcastically asked if anyone was investigating an obesity connection. Have they found any connection of fanatical obesity fighters and the roach poison.

"Shit, do you think so! An attack on McDonald's high calorie low priced meals?" was Woody's startled response. In the pause, while he nursed this new idea I added another finger to replace the finger I demolished while promising my stomach herbal tea and a couple of wafer cookies, with early bed and four aspirins, and the hell with the label warning. With drink in hand, making my way to my easy chair, concentrating on the glass and my steps, my free psychiatrist Dr. Start and Leeper marched out of the kitchen.

CHAPTER 16

Something Free

Rising to greet my two uninvited free psychologists, any previous aplomb gained in dealing with Woody's intrusiveness dropped past zero into the negative integers when I saw the duo.

Dr. Paris Start's rotund physiology impressed me as a white bowling ball, finger holes forming a happy face beneath short tight lesbian butch gray hair. Her girth supported by two short stumps precluded walking. Waddling as if the living room floor floated on roiling seas, smiling at me, her eyes traversed the room for the nearest vacant easy chair.

Her companion Dr. Lovey Leeper could, if one wanted to be unkind, be referred to as a walking tall fifty year old ghostly pale cadaver. Youthful facial flesh of a bygone epoch collapsing formed caverns, crags and canyons of the present vista. I'm sure in the past, how far back I cannot guess, he must have smiled, but never having the unique pleasure of witnessing that memorial event you could only wonder what grotesque jest gave it birth.

I remained standing hoping to physically bar their invasion of my living room. For Dr. Paris Start my attempt at barring her was a nonstarter. Her five feet, possibly an inch or two higher if one was inclined to be generous, deftly danced around me and occupied Woody's vacant chair. Sitting, she appeared taller without shedding a pound of width.

Lanky cadaverous Dr. Leeper was content to stand, just inside the living room, preparatory to lecturing all those before him.

Woody, on rising to greet Dr. Start lost his chair, and not wishing to admit the loss by seeking an alternative chair announced his departure, but not to the cold outside. He mentioned as if interest to the room, "I better see how Pam is doing," and left to go to my warm kitchen and my wife. Hell, felt lucky he left me with my pants.

Ensconced in an easy chair, Dr. Start invited me to sit down in my living room, not asking, more the casual 'take off your shirt' demand doctors issue preparatory to an exam.

Sitting down, in their face, I finished the remaining finger of my three fingers. Both noted my finger licking with concerned frowns.

Dr. Start began by asking I call her Dr. Paris, and could she use Mac.

Didn't have a chance to deny the intimacy as standing, Dr. Lovey Leeper, still critically eyeing my empty tumbler, quickly asked, after the recent banquet events did I feel the need for the support of liquor.

My animosity to these intrusive characters smothered all politeness, "No. Don't feel the need for a drink, which is why I can and am having another one." To give emphatic punctuation to my comeback I got up and defiantly poured four fingers, and was startled by how little remained in the bottle.

Sitting down with Dr. Paris on my left and cadaverous Dr, Lovey still standing on my right, they had me at criss cross disadvantage. Smiling, overly plump Dr, Paris gave out unwarranted affection; Dr, Lovey gave the appearance a stern lecture was about to commence.

Paris happily told me my wife was bearing up very well with all she's undergone. Lovey informed me, as if Pam was a stranger to me, how strong and courageous she was.

Biting off a finger just to spite them, they noted the bite and exchanged sinister glances suggesting a problem drinker was in the room.

Still standing, Lovey Leeper, without lecture notes, told me I shouldn't feel guilty. My first suspicion they felt my guilt was over a drinking problem was put aside with Paris Start telling me guilt feelings due to surviving a terrorist attack was natural and I shouldn't be ashamed of the feeling. Her silly smile, his cold stare implied my guilt was over my living and another dying was such a weight on my spirits I needed spirits to raise my spirit.

Confessing my heart held no sense of guilt, only held the wonderful sense of being lucky, had them exchanging looks.

Paris gave Lovey a nod.

Lovey returned a shrug.

Accompanying the nod and shrug each magically produced leather notebooks.

Still standing at his unseen podium, Lovey Leeper somberly instructed me on how denying feeling of guilt could be a sign of deeper psychological problems.

Nodding, Paris exuding affectionate care as if we were related by blood, mentioning repressed guilt was extremely unhealthy, adding people experiencing her psychological therapeutic treatment in dealing with repressed guilt are eventually freed from their guilt feelings.

Lovey noted how many respected articles in psychological journals not to mention the authorities, Dr. Phil and Dr. Oz unequivocally support how people feeling guilty in not dying when others die can under extensive intensive psychological treatment regained their joie d'vivre.

With my unsaid feelings 'better Scott than me,' eyeing the remaining three fingers yet being unsuccessful in wiggling my toes indicating feeling below the knee left the room, I gave the finger a pass. With not a little pomposity I told them I felt no guilt, felt only God's gentle caring hand in my life making me feel special.

God's gentle hand had both scribbling in their leather notebooks.

"Repression," the bowling ball rolled over to the cadaver who amplified, "Serious unconscious repression." With that one word diagnosis written and shared between them they immediately issued a coauthored prognosis; my unacknowledged repression would manifest itself in debilitating mental illness accompanied by continued nightmares, insomnia and certainly sever health problems due to excessive drinking.

Paris Start enumerated a likely future of perverse sexual addictions, possibly involving flagellation and certainly impotence.

Sternly lecturing, Lovey indicated an almost certain future of drug and alcohol addiction accompanied by dreams where under intense analysis will eventually be interpreted by himself as fears of castration, as well as the inability to relate to others.

Paris amplified on the theme; my repression will certainly cause depression and incontinence and was just days away, if not moments away; individuals smothering and repressing unknown guilt was the sexual tap root nourishing all personality disorders. Both eyed my three fingers as if they were unclean.

Celebrating my ability to give them the finger I bit off another finger.

Smiling, Paris inquired how was my marriage; were Pam and I experiencing any difficulties.

My answer, 'we have a great marriage,' wasn't the answer they wanted and needed.

Lovey Leeper corrected, "No marriage is without problems. Difficulties are normal in a healthy marriage." Unsaid, the contra positive, unhealthy marriages are the ones that have no difficulties.

Paris' take on my marriage and marriage in general was the universal repression of marital problems; and my fear and antagonism to face mine was psychological proof of deep seated serious difficulties in my marriage.

Not replying to their word game, eyeing the front door, I willed them to miraculously pass through it. Void of divine power I sought refuge in taking another finger bite. Damn it, the hand's previous fingers kept me anchored to the easy chair. Instead of energizing me the liquor enervated my spirit. With caring concern, Paris vicariously queried about my sexual health: was I experiencing flatulency, difficulties in the bedroom.

Seeing my shock, Lovey Leeper quickly added in tones indicating though he was the virile exception, it was certainly nothing to be ashamed of; all men experience some sexual impotence.

They heard my 'what the hell are you two idiots talking about' exclamation as an affirmation of their astute insights of repression. By studying deep profound tomes of psychology treating how repression causes your problems and by expounding on the causes previously unknown to you, motivating your actions in life, they can change your life from shitty poor to wonderfully good. Their aim is to make you normal. But who wants to be known as unexceptionally normal. What counts against their claims is the universal mental and social dysfunction of psychologists. From intense interaction employing incomprehensible indefinable jargon with similar minded experts they knew my psyche, your psyche, all psyches. There wasn't a psyche they weren't capable of conversing with on an intimate level save their own. Ignorant, Start and Leeper plunged into their prejudices to uncover my true meaning. Their protective shell of belief allowed them to interpret my exclamation not as I meant but what they wanted it to mean. I was astonished at their absurd irrational belief in their ability to consciously divine what was 'til now hidden from my conscious.

There was only a faint fingerprint of liquor in my glass. Erasing it, I debated whether to deal myself another hand. It was obvious Paris was now more interested in my sexual performance than Lovey. Hell, she was more interested than I was. Eagerly she pressed for details: how often, what duration, and was intensely interested in hearing about any erectile dysfunction.

Unsteadily I rose, planning to show them the door. However, inexplicably found myself pouring out two fingers, conscious I was working on my second hand and holding an empty stomach. Lovey Leeper astutely observing my finger obsession, my slightly unsteady attempts to walk mentioned to the room he had extensive experience in treating problem drinkers, had successfully made them healthy, happy, abstainers leading productive lives once he exposed their repressed feelings from childhood he gave out this modest accomplishment as if he was addressing a room of alcoholics collecting their disability checks and not me personally. Still, he who hears Leeper's words take heed and act accordingly..

Realizing my drinking was a little past the line separating social drinking and sloppy drinking, reflexively, defensively, I covered my guilt with an attack. For someone to say you have a problem, to a person who knows there is no problem, but suspects in this instance the problem looks real, was sure to bring an angry denial. I growled, "I'll drink when, where and how much I want and will you two get the hell out of my house, er my home."

With my polite upbringing and of civil disposition I thought telling them to leave would offend and affect them. Unfortunately my words went unheard. Lovey Leeper, moving a few steps into the room, with a slight bend of his head confided, all that I say to them was sacrosanct. By law, by professional ethics, by oaths taken with hand upon their doctoral theses, their lips were closed as if they were dead and embalmed to all things confessed. Neither threats, law, torture could pry the slightest innocuous confidence from them, never mind extreme degenerate confessions.

Paris told me to trust them as I would a priest in the confessional except they will never condemn any repressed sin no matter how depraved. I acknowledged. Being nonjudgmental, they never inflict annoying penalties to obtain forgiveness save to rip the childhood repressed event causing adult dysfunctions from your unconscious and into the light of consciousness. When it is revealed, your life is cleansed and made normal.

They ignored my commenting. No one wants to be normal, if normal means unexceptional. In fact, people go to extreme bazaar lengths to gain some resemblance of uniqueness, even suicide.

Continuing, Paris proudly answered they do not recognize sin, only repressed feelings especially traumatic feelings of a childhood sexual nature.

Lovey interrupted, "I should explain my colleague is the disciple of Freud. On the other hand I believe Jung had a better grasp of the human psyche." After imparting that clarification he retreated behind his symbolic podium. "Current modern advance intellectual thought that separates the individual from his evil deed knowing the deed was done due to maladjustment, ignorance and repression; one cannot view the individual through his deeds. There are no evil people only evil actions. Denounce the deed, save the individual by giving good mental health."

"Look, what the hell bullshit are you giving me. Look, there's the door. Use it."

Both wrote in their notebooks, sagely nodding to each other, wrote down more, looked sadly at me, then jotted a few more lines of observation before Leeper demanded, "Now, "Tell me about your anxieties. Is our presence a cause of your anxiety? Do we threaten you? Do you fear exploring your feelings about us and thereby need a drink to stifle those anxieties?"

Quickly Paris Start asked if I, seeing them as two blades of a scissor, feared castration from their presence.

Obviously annoyed at Paris' interruption, Lovey continued his train of thought as if Paris' train, a local, needing to be quickly shunted to a siding to allow his express to pass unhindered. "Anxiety takes many forms, the fear of going outdoors."

Paris, clarifying, "Agoraphobic," then added, "Erotophobic," which Lovey quickly interpreted as sexual anxiety.

Remaining standing I yelled with a minor slur how I wanted them to leave, with the insertion of a hell of a lot of explicatives.

Picking up his psychic lectern, Lovey took two defensive steps back. Trying to cross her legs which kept slipping apart, Paris had to settle for crossing her arms beneath billowing breasts. Professorially she told me, "Your manifest antagonism towards any attempt of therapeutic treatment indicates numerous serious anxieties caused by multiple repressions hidden in your mind's subbasement, all needing to be dragged out into the light of consciousness and be seriously addressed."

Pulling out a leather diary Lovey Leeper suggested further treatment at his office could be offered Tuesday and Thursday at one. "Of course the additional consulting wouldn't be free, but your City's health plan covering all expenses, it actually would be free." The last word was said as if it warranted a drum roll followed by a 'praise be'.

His solicitation was sufficient to move Paris to plant her feet securely on the floor preparatory to levitation and say, "Your anxiety originating from deep repressed sexual childhood trauma needs to be treated by a skilled Freudian practitioner." A large spiral diary previously hidden in the chair's cushions magically appeared. "Being unmarried (no surprise)

I'm able to receive clients in the evening. I see from my day planner I'm free on Thursday, six to seven or perhaps Friday, seven to eight. You must never let concerns over therapeutic appointment times interfere with your commitment to regain good mental health. As a dedicated health professional I'm willing to sacrifice my personal life to insure my patients can recover a sexually fulfilling life. What about any weekend, day or night? And remember, it's free."

A frowning Lovey stated, "In any treatment Mr. McCoppin receives, Dr. Start will not divulge what happened in the therapeutic session to his wife. However I feel he should be alerted to Mrs. McCoppin's unhappiness in her marriage, her suffering deep feelings of being unappreciated. In my professional opinion I'm sure I can resolve these marital difficulties. Given their seriousness I'm willing to make time to treat you as a couple along with individual sessions for each of you. I'm confident I can resolve these repressed difficulties with only six months of treatment, intense treatment, and of course it's free with your medical coverage."

After a momentous struggle, rocking back and forth with the support of the chairs' arms, Paris Start rose. Passing me she shared her professional opinion my marriage was sexually dysfunctional adding, "More marriages break up due to difficulties in the marriage bed. If you can find the courage to attend my sexual awareness seminar alone or with your wife, I can assure you of bedroom bliss unencumbered with any sexual repression."

Astounded at the confidences Pam shared with these two loony birds I couldn't summon the appropriate anger.

Facing each other they were ready to do word battle over my mental health and who would cure it free of cost. Garnishing with explicatives never heard nor allowed in my home 'til then I shouted they are to leave,

leave immediately. My "Get the hell out," was interspersed with justified descriptive nouns, 'idiots, morons, imbeciles'.

Can ignorant fools, believing with fanatical faith in their profound wisdom, concomitant with their belief that all others holding different opinions are necessarily ignorant fools, can ever take offense at the ravings of the unenlightened; being misunderstood, being called stupid are profound confirmations of their intellectual majesty.

Easily removing a finger from my glass I walked through Lovey's magic lectern to chest bump him towards the front door. With his residing on a higher if not highest intellectual plane, the physical contact came as a shock. Without verbal resources necessary to counter the physical, he graciously announced he had to leave for there were other patients, suffering survivors from a poisonous death in dire need of his counseling. At the door sill he asked if Dr. Paris Start was leaving. Sharing a defeat is half way to success. With the two of us at the door we waited as Paris wiggled her way to us.

Watching her torturous process Leeper shared a confidence; apparently my wife was concerned over our marriage dynamics. Where that came from, why it came, I couldn't grasp, though able to grasp the front door knob, opening it I pushed Leeper outside.

I asked, "What bullshit concerns are you talking about?"

Standing on the stoop buttoning his coat Lovey said, "Men should be assiduously attentive to their wives' needs. Some men are just interested in satisfying themselves." Obviously I was in that 'some' group.

As I glared at Lovey, Paris slipping past me, bounced down to the street yelling, "Remember, I'm free day or night and it's all free."

Slamming the door I marched to the kitchen but not before filling my hand with three fingers. It was justified, it was needed, and sufficiently inebriated I wanted another stiff one to elevate an angry mind to higher levels of justifiable outrage.

Entering, I found Woody and Pam sitting at the kitchen table coffee and cake between them enjoying a tete a tete. Feeling besieged in my own home, initially I yelled at Pam, "What the hell have you been saying to those two ridiculous fools?"

Pam looked shocked.

Protectively Woody said, "Mac, get a grip on yourself. Pam has been crying."

My fury took a brief intermission to note Pam's eyes were red and Woody was acting like an obnoxious interloper. From a sense of 'who the hell' is he, to defend my wife and defend her from me, am I not the master here, I yelled, "Woody, I want you out of my house right now."

The bastard turned to Pam for her to issue the supreme court pronouncement as to what he should do. Intuitively grasping my mood she told him it would be best if he left.

"Well Pam, if you want me to leave I will. Are you sure you'll be alright?"

I was just a finger or two away from getting physical with Woody and in the time it takes to swallow those fingers Woody was in the living room on the way out of the house. His precipitous departure said he was well aware of my intentions after my two fingers oral fortification.

Ignoring my manifest temper, my threatening stance, Pam informed me of my drunken state.

A little high, possibly tight, definitely feeling no pain, I resented the drunken adjective. Before I could launch into my justified outrage Pam, placing a plate of chicken and rice soup on the table tearfully complained how she made this soup especially for me and now it was cold. Still, if I wanted to eat it, it was there.

There's a line in drinking. On one side of the line it enhances the appetite, passing over the line one finds food irrelevant if not a dead weight to your spiritual elevation and drink is all that is desired and needed. Bypassing the soup I again demanded to know what she said to Star and Leeper, not to find out what she said but why she said it and further what she meant in saying it. Did she actually feel unsatisfied, unappreciated, put upon, all of which I knew, although completely unwarranted I did have a sense of guilt. About to bring Woody into my anger litany I was forestalled when she answered with her counter complaint I was only interested in my own selfish concerns, no one mattered but me. She felt she really meant nothing to me and I didn't care about her and our son. They weren't an important part of my life. How long in marital arguments does it take the wife to drag forth the children; does the wife protect the child or does the child protect the wife. She concluded saying Drs. Paris and Lovey, professional psychologists agreed with her.

My mind befuddled with drink couldn't capture words to explain, to defend, to assuage, to attack, leaving me with the only available response, tossing the soup in the sink and returning to the living room to see how many fingers remained in the bottle.

CHAPTER 17

Another Visit

Unlike my usual waking moods, this morning I felt good. Despite the aggravation of the previous evening and the two hands swallowed, I was better than good, hell was great, so great that on reaching the kitchen, eyeing the watery oatmeal breakfast thinking I felt better than oatmeal, I lied telling Pam I wasn't hungry.

At my favorite diner, over a life affirming breakfast of three eggs over easy, home fries, toast, bacon, OJ and coffee, my thoughts went backward and then forward. Backward in that there was something in yesterday's events, something said, seen, done, which bothered me. Despite taking a respite between the second egg and the fourth bacon strip, I came up with nothing, except puzzlement over Ronni's last minute snow job: could I believe she really liked me, could it have been a frivolous feminine sexual mind game, could it have been some twisted Machiavellian overtures related to job promotions and office politics I know nothing of, could it have been sincere and she respected me. My high self opinion of my desirability to women arm wrestled with my realistic low opinion of her machinating character during OJ sipping ended with her character winning.

Looking forward, feeling energetic despite the heavy breakfast I decided lover boy, Paul Palante was due a visit. Given the order in which Ronni's officialdom's view of most likely targets, Palante would be last on their list and so today he was first on my list. Besides, school janitors, working after school hours, most likely he would be home in the morning.

The address I had for him put him just a few streets from my home and surprisingly living in a house a few bucks better. I forgot he was a city union janitor; can't economize with children's education, can't learn with a dirty bathroom. At ten I rang the bell and was cordially greeted and invited into their pleasant tastefully furnished living room by Paul's wife, Dottie. While she was politely offering refreshments with surprising sincerity, her husband yelled down from the second floor, "Dot, who is it?"

With the upper and lower stomach levels busy taking care of the eggs and all their accouterments, I refused pastry, saying 'yes' to the coffee. As I refused the pastry she yelled up to Paul, "It's the detective who was at your table at the banquet."

We heard a toilet flush and, "I'll be right down."

Giving me a nice, slightly apologetic smile she explained, "Paul just got up. Working from two to ten at the junior high school, he gets his sleep in the morning."

She had a comfortable face and figure, neither so attractive to make you intense, trying to impress her, nor so unattractive as to create a visual barrier to seeing and talking to her. Looking at her as she tried to make polite chit chat while Paul got dressed, I could see it would take a lot of dates to fall in love with her and it would be a slow, unconscious descent into a feather bed, or was it an ascent to a cloud of heavenly repose.

Knowing when Paul eventually came down I'd have no chance to talk with Dottie I plunged right in on her husband's fixation with women. "In the hospital, I couldn't help noticing Paul had a problem with the female staff."

She laughed, took a quick glance at the stairs and leaning forward with an indication of wifely concern confided, "My husband believes he is irresistible to women, and we both know, he isn't." Then she continued, "You look surprised. You men never realize a wife's main interest is the study and understanding of her husband. I know what my husband believes, thinks, needs, does. Paul doesn't know himself as well as I do. I've seen long ago what you recently observed and may have proceeded to jump to the erroneous conclusion that he's a philanderer."

Suspecting I characterized her all wrong, I indiscreetly blurted out, "Why do you support him in his boorish even outrageous behavior?"

Giving a kindly, bordering on motherly smile, she glanced at the stairs before explaining, "You're a detective, in a position of authority, a position receiving respect from others, a position allowing you to encounter interesting situations in going from one investigation to another, a position from which you can reasonably hope to advance to higher positions of even greater authority, respect, prestige. From your position please don't judge Paul too harshly. We all try to live the best we can. Women need love and after love, appreciation and security, but men need unfailing respect and only after respect, appreciation, support and love. If respect in his life is not forthcoming, adjustments must be made. Some men drink, some fight, some cheat on their wives, some steal. My Paul, creating his own world of self respect has devised a harmless defense against his cruel reality."

I told her I still didn't understand her role in participating in her husband's game.

In answer she asked me, "What if you were a janitor in a junior high school with no avenues to excel, and condemned to push brooms and mops for the rest of your life, knowing all your money must be spent on your home and children. We have three, 2, 5, and Paul Jr. 10.""

She had me there and I gave myself fervent thanks I wasn't walking in Paul Palante's shoes, pushing his mop. As far as I was concerned, if he enjoyed living in a fantasy world, let him and best of luck.

Hearing heavy steps on the stairs she whispered, "I'm sure what I said will remain just between us."

I gave her a "yes" and got up to shake Palante's hand as he came in buttoning a plaid woolen shirt. At least for the moment he had my respect.

With a smile ten times brighter than his wife's and ten times less sincere he announced, "Well, we made it buddy, and it's great to be alive."

As we seated ourselves, Dottie went to get us coffee and take care of her two-year-old. Sitting there facing each other, coffee cups in hand, we waited for one of us to speak. Knowing Paul's type, he couldn't outwait an excited six-year-old girl with a secret, and within five seconds, he said it was a dirty shame the Scott fellow died; said it with a face showing neither shame nor dirt.

I responded to his face's communication, "Yeah, though better him than us."

His face lit up. My answer reflected his own attitude and served as a key to opening his real thoughts. Truthfully the lock was not half as secure as the one keeping private a ten-year old girl's diary.

After enthusiastically agreeing with me, he proceeded to justify his lack of sympathy for the departed by mentioning he didn't really care that much for Scott.

My, "Me too," encouragement allowed him to move to specifics.

"Take the problems with Coach Tom Applegate. I really couldn't see why Scott was so steamed up about how Applegate was running the team. Shit, so they lost every game. Hell man, let's face it, the team stunk." Laughing as if he uncovered hidden humor in how bad the team was, and in how woefully ineffectual were our sons, he expanded on the theme. "Those kids couldn't beat a six year old girl's soccer team."

Watching him place an empty coffee cup down and yelling into the kitchen for his wife to bring another, I reflected, *well, very nicely done;* divorces himself from the team and his kid's inept sports performance so it doesn't reflect on him while simultaneously enjoying a sense of superiority of being a sophistically correct adult who is not upset by the team's failures. Intelligent enough to see the big picture, not lost in the moment, he is able to place the moment in its correct context; a man above the petty minutia of caring for a child's sports performance which enmesh common loutish men. He's obeying a Hollywood and TV dictum.

Unfortunately, not being so elevated I commented, "The team didn't score once and the defense, it's best season's performance was holding the opposition to two touchdowns."

With his 'correct' attitude Palante blithely waved aside the facts, the scores, the defeats saying, "It's just a game. Can't take it seriously."

All life is a game. To live, to survive, to prosper, is all about playing the game. It's all games with both society and nature promulgating their own rules and parameters often contradicting each other ending in disaster.

Defending those fathers who were upset, I mentioned how hard it was to go home after watching your son and his team being soundly trounced again and again.

He answered, "Didn't bother the kids too much. They didn't seem to be too down after the games."

"Maybe it's because after losing and expecting to lose, mentally stepping out of the game their hearts weren't in it, which then contributes to their wretched performance."

My leaving pleasant generalities, dropping into uncomfortable particulars, upset, Paul argued, "Wrong there. I never felt the kids gave up. I know mine didn't."

Reminding myself of my purpose for being here I backtracked and got the topic back to the murder and poison. "Applegate certainly was mad at Jim Scott circulating the petition."

"Can you imagine that … a petition to the Pop Warner Organization to remove the coach. Asked me to sign the petition. After the fourth loss Scott came at me waving the petition and pen at me, furious I wouldn't sign. Kept saying I should sign. Should help the kids get decent coaches? That I should stand with the rest of the fathers. Hey, I say a person should stand up for himself and not allow himself to be bamboozled, and being a Civil Service worker I've got to be very careful of what I sign."

Since I was one of the bamboozled and had signed, I could have taken exception to the characterization, but letting it go, continued searching for enemies Palante might have, reminding him of a couple of arguments he had at the games.

"Sure, that guy, what the hell is his name, when I was at the refreshment stand he was screaming and ranting over my trying to make it with his wife."

"Tony Geroni worked the refreshment stand."

"Huh, oh yeah, Tony Geroni was one loud vulgar bastard and I should have told him so. Should have told him he shouldn't blame me if his wife came on to me. Do you remember an early October game, it was Indian summer hot and I was at the refreshment stand standing by myself when she came over and stood real close. She had this long tight split to the thigh denim skirt and a man's shirt tied tight just under her boobs showing a great bare waist. I complimented her on looking great, you know, being courteous. In return she's asked me if I liked her outfit.

Was it too revealing, which it was, and how her husband unreasonably doesn't like her wearing outfits that show her figure to advantage. After telling her he was narrow minded, jealous of his beautiful wife, she goes touchy-feeling slapping my arm saying I was bad, like she couldn't wait to get me in bed. Her asking me to pick out a soda for her caused her husband, this Geroni in the refreshment stand to start yelling at her and me. Good thing he was working inside the stand, or things might have gotten physical. As it was my wife Dot also working at the refreshment stand was able to calm us down.

"Man, I didn't need all that hassle, and told him his wife came on to me. If he's got a problem, it's with her, not with me. Told him to put a leash on her if he didn't want any problems. Needless to say I didn't get the stupid broad any soda and watched the game from the other end of the field."

With all of Palante's conversations one had to not only vigorously shake the verbal of slush through a filter of common sense but exercise judicious judgment of what falls down.

"Dottie came in with a tray of pound cake slices. He asked her, "Honey, remember the fight I had with that Geroni character over his wife? Didn't she come on to me?"

Turning to me, offering me pound cake, she said, "Geroni's wife Babs is a terrible flirt. I'm sure she flirted with every father at the game."

To keep our current game going I confirmed Babs also flirted with me. The confirmation didn't sit too well with Palante. Letting it slide he did pick up on the obvious implication of my presence. "Say, you're a detective. Do you think Tony felt so threatened by me he'd try to poison me? Say he had a grudge against all of us at the table. Remember, Babs, his wife, after coming on to me, and failing to generate interest probably came on to everything in pants. The guy could be jealous, and remember, not showing up at the table, not at the banquet, he didn't eat any of the poison."

"Maybe," I granted.

Looking over at Dottie trying to picture her poisoning table 12 just to get rid of this obnoxious gas bag was a difficult effort. Not that annoying Palante wasn't beyond consideration for poison, it was Dottie's personality that emphatically denied the possibility. Yet was the personality true? Or was I witnessing public sweetness and acceptance that didn't exist in fact. Was it a facet of her life's game.

Taking a slice of cake I started planning to extricate myself from their strange marriage saying, "Well, guess I best get going." Simultaneously taking bear size bites of the pound cake and solid gulps of coffee, both excellent; I started moving my butt to the chair's edge preliminary to getting up.

With Dottie's leaving, Palante, not wanting to end the conversation asked what's the rush. Putting my cake plate and cup down and just as I was about to push down on the easy chair arms to raise myself, Palante told me he had been undecided as to whether he should have attended the banquet. "Hell, I work evenings, you know, school maintenance engineer, and I had to take a personal day to go to the banquet. Bad decision, but I felt you've got to support your kid. You know, I spent a lot of time dodging the rich snobby guy's mistress at the banquet. In a really hot red dress, hitting on me, I had to get rude to get rid of her."

We got up but he refused to let the topic go, "Girls today are really tramps. At work, you'd be surprised, at what I find written and drawn in the girls' bathrooms. It would turn your stomach. Filth you couldn't believe from twelve year old girls."

To end our conversation, mumbling I had to leave I turned and left, but not before yelling a goodbye to Dottie in the kitchen. I'd sure hate to find out she's the poisoner.

CHAPTER 18

The Man Who Didn't Come to Dinner

Standing in front of Palante's house, thinking his wife Dotti deserved better, thinking after last night I deserved better, reluctantly led me to think of returning home. However if my breakfast of oatmeal was any indication, last night's marital ice had not thawed. Enumerating my day's options I found none, save every man's default course, to go home.

My reverie was interrupted by a 'hello' from a girl in her early twenties passing me on her way to Palante's front door. Well dressed, sufficiently well dressed to make me notice, and in noticing noted the material shouted the skirt and jacket expensive. She was a looker, a cheerful smiling looker who had stared at me yesterday over Ronni's car. Before I could reclaim my mind from its numbing surprise she was at the door knocking. My delayed 'who are you?' was issued just as Dottie opened the door to usher in the mysterious attractive 'she.'. Thinking 'who the hell was that' and I'd certainly like to better know who she was, noting her 'hello' was not a polite stranger to stranger casual 'hello', more a 'hello' you extend to a person you know and enjoy talking to. Possessing the beauty which if she responded to your overtures would make you feel special, better than your own current estimation of

149

yourself. She'd force you to search your memory for that prior meeting, a meeting if it occurred wouldn't have been forgotten. My search was in vain leading to the question, never having met her before, why the smile, the hello, the eye contact, all brief meaningfully personal. My ego wanted to say 'Mac, you're a dog, you're a babe magnet.' My common sense neutered the dog with what the hell is this about.

My confused ruminations were interrupted by a red sports car's siren beep and Ronni Deutch waving a finger at me to come, doglike to her. Responding I felt I pissed some testosterone in the gutter in going.

She accused, "You've just been seeing the Palantes," followed by rubbing in a pinch of salt, "Woody won't like that. All the agencies want their investigations to be unencumbered by interfering outsiders. They'll be angry at anyone who isn't official, freelancing."

My "so what" was answered with a Ronni lecture. "There has been much confusion as to each agency's particular areas of investigative responsibility. Currently there are four separation oversight committees meeting to construct the definitive overall schematic delineation of areas of responsibility for the numerous different investigative entities.

"Unfortunately the meetings couldn't reach a consensus, in fact ended acrimoniously." Giving a gentle social laugh at the last bit showed she possessed sufficient common sense to see modern life's absurdities.

She then asked, "Who was that entering the Palantes house? She seems to know you."

The later was more an accusation tinged with a hint of sexual suspicions.

My honest "never saw her before' she dropped in the gutter along with my testes. "I thought we were working together, we had a connection."

That was a dirty lie but I didn't throw it away; despite the dirt,, I liked it.

Relentlessly she continued, "Is she Homeland Security? No, she's too hot, too expensive. Those threads if off the rack, the rack was at Lord and Taylors. She's from the White House. What do you think? And why is she seeing the Palantes?"

Announcing, "Look Ronni, I'm getting cold standing here," I move her from my mystery woman.

Covering my hand gripping the door's edge with her hand I remained silent in the cold waiting to discover the purpose of her finger wave. Given the smile, the hand touching, the intimate feel of her confidences, suspecting they were all manufactured for a specific purpose. The question remained for what purpose, and was there only one purpose to steal what I knew!

Nodding to Palante's house, she asked if I discovered anything new. Seeing the purpose exposed, I played psychologist, telling her Palante is nuts and his wife is his keeper.

With her hand still keeping mine company she divulged the factoid Palante had made a play for Courtney, Ray Brothers' girlfriend. It certainly could give Dotti a motive. Ronni shared this as if it was a nuclear secret.

I couldn't resist, "On that same theme I have firm counter information Courtney made a play for Palante and was rebuffed." To my factious factoid I told Ronni, "Being rejected by Palante, Courtney could have reason to poison table 12 to get even with Palante," allowed us to enjoy the risible idea. I added froth to the Starbucks we were brewing telling Ronni, Geroni's wife made a play for Palante and he and Geroni almost came to blows over it."

"Mac, you've got it wrong. Palante came on to Babs and Courtney. My gosh, he's like Clinton, only not as successful."

Her grip on my hand going from gentle to firm, announcing it was there as if there as if there was any way I wasn't aware, Ronni angrily related how Palante had complained to Woody that she had suggested an intimate evening interview with Palante at her apartment. She then laughed at its absurdity. I just felt sad either at Palante's complaint or if never made, at Ronni's manufacturing it out of whole cloth. Finally she produced her constructed end product of her finger wave. "I'm planning to interview Geroni and his wife Babs. Want to come along?" She sweetened up the manipulation suggesting after we could have lunch together. The 'lunch together' was delivered as if saying, your place or mine. She didn't realize how I wanted to walk where she wanted me to go, and cold had worked its way up to the thighs numbing everything below.

Cognizant of my option's void, acquiescing to her manipulation, I got into her car, both feeling we won: she feeling her feminist power was once more validated, I feeling my sexual and intellectual attraction was the basis for her manipulation.

Employing the usual gymnastics of getting into her car I wondered if by analyzing too much, like politicians and TV pundits, I was losing touch with reality.

At Geroni's front door we met Homeland Security Agents Damian Donaldson, and Flower Weiser leaving. They stared at us as if seeing Republicans at the Oscars. My returning glare was suggestive of discovering environmental green people secretly drilling in the Arctic for black gold over the bodies of dead polar bears. Chubby Donaldson demanded to know why we were there. Heavy weight Flower demanded to know what the hell we were doing there.

Possessing a goodly share of testosterone, Ronni growling as if facing down a pair of Dollar Store shoplifters shot back, "New York Police Detectives." Pushing her way to the door she advised them to check the latest schematic of agency protocols at the chief Senior Oversight Meeting last night outlined on plate A17 addressing just this situation.

We ignored Donaldson's complaining Homeland had preference in terrorist attacks and never saw the chief's SOS Memo. Flower adding a further clarification haughtily said, "The White House Oversight Committee in memo 47/K has unequivocally delineated terrorist attacks as falling within our exclusive domain."

As we maneuvered, Flower yelled they had already obtaining all pertinent information and in duplicating their work we were wasting our investigative time and our duplication will cause confusion in their ongoing investigation, giving aid and comfort to the terrorists. Donaldson threatened to tell the White House's Emergency Task Force 7Z14 dealing with worldwide threats of cockroach poisoning about our interference and intransigence.

Struggling on the small stoop, pushing aside the two, I managed to get my nose to the front door as Ronni, badge in hand, knocked with authority.

Geroni's wife Babs led us into a living room showing a lot of living, little cleaning. Babs sufficiently young at thirtyish, not to be so callous as to be inured at her house's disarray, apologized for its state. Making our zig zag way past articles of clothing, papers, movie magazines and yes, miscellaneous undergarments, to a couch cushion, Babs continued her lame excuses for sloppiness, "What with the tragedy, the horrible death, how it could have been her Tony dead, or heaven forbid little Anthony, I hadn't been able to do any real housework. In fact I've been so upset I had to take sick days at the clothes cleaners."

Ronni said she understood but didn't amplify what she understood. I, eyeing some suspicious couch crumbs mumbled forgiveness, thinking given her Tony wasn't even at the banquet you had to wonder if each day of her life was filled with drama so intense she was perpetually precluded from any cleaning. After mentally condemning her as a lazy housewife, I wondered at Tony allowing his home to sink into trash.

Still feeling guilt at her dereliction of wifely duties Babs lamented on how hard it was given the long hours she worked at the neighborhood dry cleaners, quickly adding working as a cashier, not as a cleaner, to remove any misapprehension.

Dressed in a checkered skirt sufficiently short to make crossing legs a gross view, with a man's white shirt top three buttons open giving evidence of no bra, she suggested a school girl porn movie. The porn imagery was all mine.

With Ronni and Babs exchanging pleasantries while evaluating each other's sexual appeal as exhibited in choice of clothing, I had time to classify the character Babs and her living room illustrated. Some social TV pundits maintain you can't judge a book by its cover as if it's possible to actually read the book. Of course they firmly believe they can read, interpret, dissect your book; a book only God can read and understand .

Babs explained, Tony, out on an emergency call, left her to go to the banquet all alone. Was she putting out a gratuitous 'all alone' for sympathy or as a complaint. Probably both.

Eyeing the exercise mat in front of the TV, noting the absence of books, seeing the proliferation of women's fashion and Hollywood gossip magazines sitting with me on the couch and at my feet, I felt this was living in a feminist basement, an unhappy career mother without a career above doing wifely domestic chores. Amplifying on Tony's absence, Babs said she was getting dressed when the emergency call came and Tony being a conscientious plumber went out to answer it. Yes she fully expected him to go to the banquet when he was finished, and wasn't it lucky he didn't come.

Busy pushing back a shock of naughty blonde hair dropping across her left eye Babs didn't grasp the import of the admission.

To Ronni's 'what did the Homeland Agents want?' a frowning Babs in a quarrelsome voice complained the intrusive twosome asked if she had relatives in North Africa. She was white, one hundred percent Welsh, and proud of it. Suddenly aware of the implication of her statement's political incorrectness she qualified, "Of course North African people are just as good." With the politically correct addition in place, she was back to her outrage.

"Weren't the Homeland Agents terribly fat? Shouldn't an important Federal Agency have better looking people representing the government? Er, I mean projecting healthy eating habits. Obesity is such a critical health problem. Anyway, they weren't as bad as the CIA Investigators. Can you imagine, one wore sun glasses in my house and it's November. And nosey – do we have foreign bank accounts? What about off shore accounts? Where do we take vacations? In Switzerland, Dubai, hell you'd think we can bank the type of money politicians, rap singers and Hollywood stars do." Leaning to Ronni, Babs complained, "Honey, after the honeymoon, it's all just stay at home.

"Say, can I get you two anything?"

We quickly declined. For me, the easily observable surface dirt and grease, the miscellany papers, magazines, and clothing filling all surfaces and tumbling down to the floor suggested a kitchen serving problematic food.

Getting up, sociably Babs suggested some wine. To justify our quick refusal she told us and herself, she understood being on the job we couldn't drink. Her commiseration suggested her belief if our job chains were broken, we'd run to the nearest bar.

After a few moments she returned with a full glass of wine. Explaining she never drank so early in the afternoon but the devastation and shock of the past few days in destroying her nerves, a little wine with lunch helped her regain equilibrium. To buttress the equilibrium she added how a glass of wine was very healthy. She heard it on *The View* and Dr. Phil recommends a glass each day.

Her equilibrium and the aids to health were easily penetrated covers to herself and others. I suspected the wine was the lunch and her days were filled with tragic occurrences necessitating a daily nip or two around noon to be followed every other hour.

Taking a sip, trying to make it polite and delicate, it was sufficiently deep to half the glass. She returned to vacations, an obvious sore point. "When I say Tony and I didn't take any vacations I mean we've never been outside the country. Tony likes to gamble and I confess a preference for the slots, so we make Atlantic City every year or so." In memory of AC and the disappearing money the rest of the wine vanished and in respect for its absence it became a period to Babs' conversation.

To jump start Babs, Ronni asserted her belief that the CIA had no right to intrude into citizen's personal life.

Staring at her empty glass, I related to her struggle on how to refill without looking like a problem drinker. Babs decided to talk. "The FBI was the politest, well mannered, tastefully dressed, very respectful. They were extremely professional."

Suspiciously looking left, then right, to the front door, back to the kitchen, suggesting the living room was a conduit serving government spies interested in her life, Babs confided to Ronni she thought one of the agents, the young one, was interested in her. If she wasn't married, well who knows? Of course, she'd discourage any disrespectful inappropriate behavior, after all she was a married woman. In the pause while she again brushed back that clump of blonde hair masking her left eye, I suspected if he jumped her, the only yells and complaints would be the day after the violation when he didn't call back. The sexual fantasy brought to her mind Palante as proof of her virtue. She complained how he bumped into her at the boys' football game and then accused her of deliberately making physical contact. To Ronni she asked, "You saw him, a school janitor for heaven's sake, and he kept telling me he had no interest in me and I shouldn't touch him. Me, him, I couldn't believe it. Tony heard him and treating it as a joke made nothing of it.

"Detective Deutch, do I look like I need to bump into men to get attention? Not in this world, not in this life, not me, not him, not a school janitor. It's so ridiculous it's laughable."

Listening to her rant, foot pushing aside several 'Easy way to lose ten pounds in ten days and have fun doing it' magazines on the floor, I thought if Tiger Woods or Obama jostled her, she'd stick like glue.

Babs' outrage at Palante's bump drove her to the kitchen seeking wine fortification. Back with a half filled glass, the top half probably downed in the kitchen, Babs again tried to seduce us into drinking with her. Sin can't stand on its own two legs. Have to confess, watching her deep sips slipping energy into her, I felt if a couple of fingers were nearby I'd be tempted.

Girl to girl Ronni asked Babs how her marriage was.

Babs' first reflex usual answer was, "Oh wonderful. We have a loving relationship," stayed in the room long enough for a sip before the wine said, "of course we have our problems," followed by an ego bandage, "but all couples have their ups and downs."

"Currently is it up or down," I asked.

If gossipy Ronni girl to girl gossipy asked, we might have heard some truth. Being a man, outside women's perspective all I got was a cold stare from both and a sip from Babs.

Satisfied I was put in my place Babs earnestly asked Ronni if she knew a Sonia Major. Babs gave the Major a Spanish twist, Ma hoar.

Having heard of her Ronni said, "She's a lawyer."

"Yes, but how good is she?"

"Has she been in touch with you, your family?"

"Wants us to hire her, to sue for the damages we suffered."

I interrupted saying, "You didn't suffer any damage. Tony wasn't even there."

That got a finishing sip, a perplexed look at the glass, a hard dart at me, and an offer to get Ronni some refreshment.

Ronni refused.

Suspecting the interview would last as long as the wine and Babs needing an out so her third kitchen trip wouldn't signify wine problems I gallantly said, "I could use a little wine on this cold November day." It gave her the excuse to go to the kitchen and return with glasses of wine. Her's filled, I had three empty inches down from the rim.

After a chaste taste sip as if she never saw a Gallo gallon jug she continued, "This Sonia Major came yesterday with papers for us to sign, you know, contingency papers. It was terribly awkward when O'Malley, another lawyer came when she was leaving. He also had lots of legal papers for us to sign."

Ronni asked if they signed any papers yet.

"Hell no. Tony and I argued which law firm to go with. I liked the Spanish Major because we were poisoned with salsa and Sonia said Goya had the deep pockets we wanted to get our hands into." She giggled, "I mean to get money."

I hadn't realized the sexual innuendo 'til, like a TV laugh track she pointed it out.

Babs took a sip.

Eyeing my less than clean glass, not wishing to risk Montezuma's revenge I stood firm in abstinence's virtue and let Gallo just sit there. I told her it made sense, a Spanish lawyer going after a Spanish firm.

"That's what I said, but Tony likes O'Malley. He says it with all the affirmative bullshit, er, excuse my language, anyway he maintains her law degree was probably awarded due to mandated affirmative shit, ops, excuse me, anyway for all we know she could be totally incompetent. You can't judge minority's confidence with all the minority affirmative crap."

With her sex advantages and being Woody's ideological friend and partner, Ronni couldn't hope for promotions if she let such a politically incorrect statement escape unchallenged. Correcting, "Of course we shouldn't judge people by their ethnicity. It's very discriminatory and hurtful." She didn't indicate how it hurt and who it hurt.

Continuing Ronni said she couldn't possibly comment on which lawyer they should hire.

Out of politeness, to forward the interviewing process, I took a sip of wine hoping the alcohol content was sufficient to cleanse the glass of whatever and was punished. Every outraged taste bud instantly decried to my mouth, 'how can you drink this cheap pis,' 'Mac, how could you toss this wine urine down at us?'

I told Babs, "You know O'Malley certainly hasn't had any affirmative advantage." Feeling I now had a sufficient read on Babs' character, putting the wine glass down on an end table, I rose.

Babs, a little tipsy, a little sleepy, needing another glass of wine preparatory for a nap, getting up forced Ronni to rise. We left with relief to be out of Geroni's house.

Standing next to her car Ronni asked what I thought.

I said it was a very sad house.

Ronni harshly commented, "Never seen such a pig sty, and her drinking, she's a lush."

"Do you feel she's capable of murder?" I asked.

"Certainly, what's your opinion?"

With intended ambiguity I emphatically said, "I'd certainly never eat salsa at her house."

Getting into her car, no invite for me, I was left standing in the cold. Obviously our 'lunch together' disappeared into the space's ether never to be seen, never to be mentioned, never to be eaten. Justifying her abrupt departure Ronni saying she needed to get back to headquarters told me Woody and the Brass, heavy Brass, are having important meetings all day to evaluate and collate mountains of informational bits they're getting. She and her red sports car left me to decide where to go, and what to do. At that moment I felt as lonely as Babs.

CHAPTER 19

The Plumber

I walked the cold damp six blocks to Tony Geroni's plumbing establishment, ten foot wide squeezed between a Dollar Store and a Bodega. Inside Tony was at the end of a twenty foot corridor constructed of miscellaneous tubs, toilets, sinks and numerous undeterminable plumbing supplies. Looking up from a desk serving as a home for unwashed coffee cups, a hodge podge of paper scraps, a dog eared desk calendar, he asked,"

Yeah." There was a hint of surprise at a customer approaching him. To determine whether I was here by chance or for some plumbing purpose he asked what he could do for me. The glimmer of hope for employment was stillborn as I identified myself as the detective who was poisoned at the banquet.

With employment disappointment his, "Shit, tough luck," was given without a trace of empathy. His lack of empathy was capitalized with his continuation, "Better you than me," which I thought, impolitic given our dynamics, police to plumber.

I said, "Yeah, you were lucky in not attending the banquet. Why was that?"

"Huh, yeah, well as I said a hundred times, I had a nasty joke played on me. Some guy calls up saying he's got an emergency leak flooding his kitchen. Being a good guy I didn't tell him tough shit but promised I'd be right over. After all, it's double time, labor and material. You know what I'm saying."

He gave a smile, the standard union overtime grin.

My complicity in overtime pay extending to a nodding acknowledgement allowed him to continue. "Anyway, I got to the address and it was a vacant lot. I was pissed. If I could get my hands on the bastard, well, he'd never pull that stunt again, you know what I'm saying."

"Still, you could have made the banquet."

"Yeah, well so angry I dropped into a neighborhood bar to let off some steam and drown my anger and frustration. You know what I'm saying, anyway, that's the reason I didn't go to my kid's banquet."

My saying nothing I inferred my criticism of his action, feeling he hadn't sufficiently justified not going to the kid's banquet and remain a good father, he added, "Being so filled with anger I'd only spoil the kid's time. You know what I'm saying."

My asking for the phony emergency address confused him, "Huh? No one wanted it, why do you?"

In interview techniques you never answer a suspect's questions. It only gets you off the subject and you lose focus. "Can I have the address."

"To be honest, irritated, when I saw the vacant lot, just threw it away, you know what I'm saying."

"You're saying you don't have it."

"Why? Is it important?"

His taking a sip of cold coffee enabled me to digest the significance of no information. "Look Tony, you have a favorite bar, a bar you visit when happy, sad or angry. What bar did you go to and did you see anyone there?"

Employing bluster Tony challenged, "Look, I wasn't at the damn banquet, so why all the questions? You know what I'm saying."

"Tony, know what I'm saying. Someone poisoned table 12, the table you were supposed to be at, and to everyone's surprise you weren't there, and offer a snow job of an excuse. Did you have prior knowledge of the poisoning and murder?"

"Not on my kid's life, no. What are you trying to say?"

"What I'm saying, not trying, is either you are the poisoner or knew about it. In either case it's a murder charge. That's what I'm saying."

He stared at me, remained silent though his mouth had dropped open. For him time didn't pass, it stood still, whether from the fear of guilt or the shock of innocence being accused.

To jog him from his momentary trance I advised him it was best to come clean adding to my lie, "If what you say isn't important to the case it will remain between the two of us."

Faced with the danger of daylight, some shadowy characters hunker down, diving deep into sullen silence, others desperately seek a lifeline no matter how irrational hoping for survival. Tony was the later personality, plaintively asking, "Babs my wife doesn't need to know."

I thought, ah, now comes the real dirt. Thinking the worse of people, you'll seldom be disappointed is a universal truism. His requesting my compliance in his nefarious misdeeds was an indication of his fear. A ridiculous request. Of course I swore his wife will not be told, and knew I was lying, and so did he, but he needed to trust me. "I was at the Golden Times Bar. When things at work or at home get too much I occasionally drop in to unwind with a beer, you know what I'm saying."

The last addition, an appeal for sympathetic 'we're comrades in arms' connected possibly too well with me. Still from experience, professional as well as personal knew no one shoved all the dirt at once. Hoping to sell half truths they show only dust. I knew there had to be nasty trash in his life by looking at the thirtyish something, still in good shape if one overlooked a small deforming pot and a growing forehead, I didn't see him in the Golden Times Bar drinking alone. "What's her name?" I stated as if I had the name written in my notebook.

He tried a pathetic version of innocence, "Who?"

His voice, his head bobs, his eyes staring at an old toilet leaning against a rusty sink confirmed by bluff, "Look, your wife won't find out but I need the name to alibi you. It's just between the two of us."

"Shit man, she's just a friend. We see each other once in a while for a drink, you know what I'm saying."

Lying I told him I knew it was all innocent and friendly and could be subject to misinterpretation. Guys can have a friendly drink with buddies but drinks with a dame were as innocent as Eve's apple. "Look Tony, the name of your friend."

"Just between the two of us?"

"Certainly."

"Zoe Bernstein."

"Zoe!"

"Yeah, hell, I didn't name her. Anyway she's a respected practitioner of cosmetology."

Mishearing, smiling I repeated, "Cosmetology?"

"Sort of. She's head of the Cosmetology Department at Sears. Look, do you need to talk to her?"

Still confused I asked, "She's located at Chicago's Sears Headquarters?"

"Er, what headquarters? She works at the Sears in the Westchester Mall."

My mind cursed itself for its innocence. First I had her studying dark holes then I had her in a lab coat peering in a microscope surrounded by test tubes, and she was a makeup woman at a mall cosmetic counter.

I've got to stop watching politically correct TV drama shows portraying politically correct women scientists and generals.

"She'll alibi you?"

"Certainly. Look, if you've got to talk to her, she thinks I'm separated, sort of living with my wife but not sleeping with her. You know what I'm saying."

"She believes you!"

"Yeah, and she thinks I'm a top executive with Kohler Plumbing Corporation, sort of head of the NY branch. There's not need to disabuse her.'

"She believes you!"

"Can I have your word you won't screw me up with Zoe."

With sincerity, worthy of a hand on the bible, man to man told him I appreciate and sympathize with his difficulty and wouldn't disillusion her.

He was reluctant to give up her address and phone number but realizing I could easily get it, gave it up.

Apropos of nothing, sadly he confided business was slow this time of the year. Seated at a messy strewed desk, at the dark end of a plumbing disarrayed ally, I figured this time of the year lasted all year and sincerely felt for him, at least at that moment. "Do you think your wife suspects your relationship with Zoe?"

"Hell, I hope not. I think she doesn't. Hasn't said anything to me. Did she say anything to you?"

Thinking of the wine and the mess I told him, "She didn't say anything but she struck me as a woman who suspects all life will turn out bad for her, so she very well may suspect you."

"Damn it, hope you're wrong."

Believing I'm never really wrong, I told him I was probably wrong. It was a kindness to give him what he needed. I asked if Zoe had an ex husband or boyfriend, who hating you would try to poison you.

Tony had trouble grasping the concept of people trying to hurt him. People are of three types: one views himself as a beautiful flower expecting all mankind to love, admire but never pick up, the other individual sees himself as a beautiful flower constantly picked on by people jealous of his specialness. A third type sees himself as a stink weeds expecting everyone is determined to pick on them. Tony saw himself as a special flower which inexplicably, out of jealousy, the world and fate conspire against. "Well Zoe has an abusive ex husband as well as a recent jealous ex boyfriend. I really can't see how either could get poison salsa on my table. Though Zoe told me her ex husband fought against the divorce and still stalks her, the ex boyfriend was so upset at the breakup he threatened her life."

Seeing some doubt gripping my face, Tony continued, "Guy to guy, if you knew how fantastic Zoe is in bed you'd understand the anger of the exes."

To get us out of this soap opera sleaze I asked about lawyers. He said O'Malley was his man and they are planning a class action civil suit against Goya, the caterer and the city. "You know I could have been poisoned and suffer irreparable physical and emotional damage. Because of this poisoning mentality I may be too fearful to go out on emergency plumbing call at night. Even now I'm afraid to go out at night for a beer. O'Malley brought my hidden fears to the surface. You joining the O'Malley class action?"

"As a member of the police department, don't think I will."

"You're missing out on millions. O'Malley's talking about millions, not each family but each member of the family could get their million."

My repeated refusal had him shaking his head at my foolishness. "You know, the more in a class action the more money, the better chance of success, and remember this is free money. You don't have to do a thing, but give a statement as to your injuries. Remember, if you don't sue with us, the jury may have doubts about the extent of our injuries."

Telling him about his wife's preference of Sonia Major as her lawyer brought an angry, "That Mexican broad knows shit, knows less than my wife, and the only bar she passes is a bar. Hell, the only thing worthwhile coming out of Mexico is jalapenos."

"Can you think of any of the wives of table 12 having any issues with you including Coach Applegate's or Zapp's ex wife?"

"Can you believe how inept that coach was? I could have made that team a winner. Signed someone's petition, but it was a useless gesture. Had my kid playing guard when with his power could be a devastating fullback. And the plays Applegate called, remember the time we had the ball on ---"

"Tony, did you hear about the big memorial affair they're going to have. Were you invited?"

"Yeah, was invited but don't know if I'll go."

"Because you weren't at the banquet and weren't poisoned?"

"What are you talking about? No, it's them having me and Babs sitting in the audience. Being part of table 12, I feel we should be on the stage with everyone else. O'Malley says he'll fight to get us on stage as it helps with the class action if we have an impressive presence for the media. My wife is shopping for a tasteful black dress and I have my navy blue suit. Say, you know O'Malley is planning a stage rehearsal for his class action members."

"You're kidding."

"It's true. O'Malley wants Babs and my son to stand with all the other wives and kids on a stage. He's planning to arrange where everyone stands, who should cry, who should break down, who should speak, and what should be said. This O'Malley is going all out to get us money and being free money, it smells sweet, you know what I'm saying. He says women with children are golden in media presentations, maintaining it's all about visual appeal. The guys will form a backdrop looking angry at the injustice and hurt inflicted on our families."

I said O'Malley hasn't actually talked to me, and I won't attend any of his rehearsals and won't attend the memorial.

Passing all his plumbing junk on my way out he yelled a reminder to me to tell Zoe he was separated and a Kohler executive.

CHAPTER 20

Mall Chats

Planning to kill two chicks with one visit I drove to Westchester Mall where Sears's cosmetologist Zoe worked and Courtney's Dress Boutique was located. Sears was the mall's right arm, Target its left, and an upscale Macy's was the waist to lend prestige to the cheap arms. Little suspecting Zoe as the poisoner of table 12 I decided to interview her first and quickly eliminate her. I planned to tackle Courtney, who did have a financial motive to say goodbye to Ray; millions in insurance combined with the fear she may never become Mrs. Ray. However if Zoe was angry for some reason, one reason could be his lack of interest in divorcing wife one in order to take on wife two, she could be a suspect except that he was with her and not eating salsa, and the men's wives, in particular Babs, never ate the poisoned salsa. To be honest with myself, which I often am, I didn't have anything better to do. Home currently not a pleasant option and it was lunchtime and there was a food court to give sustenance to all the mall rats running through the maze of stores.

At the Sears cosmetic counter devoted to hiding reality's ugly face, I found Zoe working with the intensity of a neurosurgeon, powder puffing the nose of a fifty year old trying to find her forties. Standing aside, waiting for the end of all Zoe's cosmetic applications she employed to hide and lie about a woman's face, I gave myself a short shot of men's free cologne. I wasn't buying it, but smelling nice for free, I couldn't resist. When she was free I approached Zoe, badge discretely palmed. Staring down she jumped wide eyed as if I unzipped my fly, crying with a politicians' questions, 'I did nothing, know nothing.' What do you want? What the hell did I do?

Telling her it was about the cockroach poisoning, her smiling with relief led one to wonder at her initial reaction and be suspicions; what the hell was in her past? With heavily applied pancake, blush, mascara, glistening lipstick, inch long violet eyelashes and plucked eyebrows filled in with black arches you had to know a face laid beneath but was as undecipherable as if she lay in a sarcophagus. Possibly late twenties, fearfully peering at early thirties lurking just around the corner had her scared. Her lacquered jet black hair contrasting with her white face powder creating such an artificial look it was intriguingly attractive. The marring element was a nose bending down, a chin looking up trying to touch the nose, squeezing a receding mouth as if aghast at all the falsity around it, Mentioning we couldn't talk at her cosmetic station I suggested coffee at the food court. Looking at her watch, imitation gold with a pink face, she said she could take a break.

She had a sticky bun with her coffee. I had pork lo mien with mine. Disregarding chopsticks I persevered using plastic spoon and fork fighting to transfer the lo mien to its destination, as the slippery and shy noodles with all the oil, or was it grease, struggled for life. As far as the pork, one pig could have kept the outlet supplied for a year and never fear for his life. With Zoe's difficulty with the sticky bun staining her fingers and my struggle to capture elusive noodles and search for invisible pork, conversation was delayed.

When Zoe returned from washing her hands in the ladies' room and I ended the last noodles' life struggle, we got to talk with me asking.

"Were you with Tony on the cockroach night?" (The night had become so infamous its cockroach nomenclature sufficed for identification.)

Suspicious she asked if our meeting was about the cockroach night or was it about something else.

Reassuring her, I wondered about the 'something else.' Was she hiding something besides her face, possibly her character? After reassuring her it was about cockroach night and her being with Tony, she was at pains to legitimize her relationship with Tony; to remove it from cheap sex into a TV scenario of tragic love beset by past entanglements just a few courageous steps away from eternal bliss, an epic worthy of Shakespeare.

"You know Tony is separated from his wife and is planning a divorce."

My "really" with a question mark tone said 'not really.'

"They don't sleep together, though living in the same house he sleeps in separate bedroom."

My "you don't say" said I didn't believe what she said.

"He can't get a divorce 'til he straightens out his financial affairs, you know child support, alimony. It's all so tangled up with lawyers. Currently he's talking with some lawyer called O'Malley and his wife is talking to her lawyer Major. Have you heard of them?"

After saying I had, I decided to lie and be generous to an obviously needy woman, telling her O'Malley and Major were excellent divorce lawyers.

She announced with the firmness of someone who needs to believe, "Tony's a great father to his son and he's hoping to get full custody, and then his wife would have to pay child support."

Lest I think of the money angle she inadvertently brought up she subtracted money from our conversation. "We're not thinking of money, only what's best for the child. You know, his wife has a drinking problem and doesn't take proper care of Tony, Jr. nor their home."

Relieved to be able to give an honest response, I told her I've seen Babs drinking.

Zoe didn't respond with similar truth. "My heart goes out to the poor boy, having a drunk for a mother. You know I have two of my own, a boy ten and a precious three year old girl."

"I didn't know. Does Tony know?"

She didn't need to go to Disney Land to visit her Fantasy Land and she was living in Tomorrow Land. "Of course Tony knows. He's met them and loves them and they simply adore Tony. When his divorce is finalized he's going to request the Kohler Corporation to relocate us its California Headquarters in Malibu.. Our plans are to marry and raise our children as a blended family."

I expected that dream would come true the day after people acknowledge I'm always right.

Asking about her ex husband she answered with defiant pride, she was a single mother as if claiming to be a recipient of the Congressional Medal of Honor.

My simple stated fact, "You weren't married," she treated as a pebble tossed against her glass world with the inferred condemnation of having two bastards.

Defensively she countered with how she takes good care of her children. They lack for nothing.

I refrained from mentioning, except for a father.

After sips of coffee, in strained silence we continued our conversation with her telling me she loved Tony and he loved her.

"And you were with him on cockroach night at the Goodtime Bar?"

"Tavern," she corrected, and yes, he met her at 7:30.

My, "And you stayed there?" question caused slight hesitation 'til she confessed they did spend some time at her home. Lest I get the wrong idea, she added the baby sitter having to leave early, she was worried about the children and Tony wanted to see the children and say goodnight to them.

"What time did he leave your place?"

"Oh, about 9:30, 10."

My saying 'that's very early' in tones heavy with doubt said neither I nor the man in the moon believed her.

To convince the moon she added an hour. "It could have been around 11."

I coached, "Could it have been later?"

"My time with Tony, er the time we spend together is too precious to clock watch. It may have been near midnight but certainly not later. Why? Is it important? Is that damn wife of his making trouble?"

"No, I don't think so. She may not know about you."

Not relieving her, my lie annoyed her. "She knows. Tony told her all about us and how we love each other." She was right on the 'knows,' wrong on the 'telling.'

On the way back to the counter and the tools necessary to create fantasy, I asked about her kid's father. Did he know about Tony and their plans to relocate across the country? Could he resent being supplanted in his children's life?

"They have different fathers," escaped from Zoe. The anger she harbored over past evaporated dreams flashed out. She growled out to the world, "Men are such bastards," as if revealing a cosmic big bang truth. "They aren't interested in their children. The bastards, as soon as child support is mentioned, they disappear. Dead beat dads, I could kill all of them."

"So you don't think either would want to kill Tony."

"You're kidding. Those bums. My marriage to Tony where he adopts my children will relieve them of the child support they never pay." After a pause, a retraction, "You know either father could have done it. In fact, so angry at my leaving them they would do anything to destroy my happiness. Want their names?"

Her offering their names given with her hopeful expectation I'd be able to screw them, couldn't be refused. To make up for all my questions and the real sorrow and pity I felt for her, I told her I'd certainly check up on the two.

"They hang out at the Good Time Tavern. Tony and I often go there to show them I'm getting on with my life."

Thinking 'getting on with the third in a series' I told her it was Tony's favorite bar.

"Tavern," she corrected.

We were interrupted by a stick figure of a woman looking forty, was probably thirty, wanting to discuss serious eye lash issues.

Leaving Zoe to give her professional diagnosis of the stick's eyebrow dilemma, I grabbed an additional few quick squirts of Canoe, waving my arms past my nose to sample it.

Going out of Sears, passing a few lost souls wandering up and down its aisles, sadly looking for something on sale, I turned to check on an underwear sale, a package of three briefs, half off. Looking up from the price I spotted a new searcher for beauty and youth. On a high chair, she was intensely talking to Zoe as if a cancer cure was the topic. Tossing the bargain underwear away I was startled. The woman was the same well dressed babe who gave me the eye at Palante's. This time, not getting eye contact, deciding to forget her; still I wondered, was I being stalked by an attractive woman? An unsettling but pleasurable thought as I made my way to Courtney's boutique.

CHAPTER 21

Sadness in Courtney's Boutique

The incongruity of Courtney's upscale dress store's location, between a sneaker outlet and a video game store dealing in used games, struck me as sad. On the positive side, opposite Courtney's boutique was a Victoria Secrets store selling bits of see through gauze guaranteed to reveal any and all woman's secrets in the soft porn manner.

Walking into Courtney's tastefully decorated store I passed mannequins with sly smiles or intense faraway stares suggesting past intrigues and promises of an exciting future, looking better than real women. The store's expensively attired haughty looking mannequins said the life they live was superior in every way to yours. Dress like them and possibly you could approach their sharp distain for people like you. In the aggregate, the subdued atmosphere said high class, and not belonging, I was an illegal alien.

Courtney tried to create a patrician establishment with lots of space, hidden racks, and dainty tables holding gaudy babbles to attract the eye and confuse thinking. Designed to cater to hot sophisticate career women married to successful men, the only clientele were two teenage girls, looking eighteen, acting twelve, wearing jeans barely hiding their ass crack and t-shirts outlining perky nonsagging breasts. Didn't repress my looking at their perkiness, and certainly not my momentary salacious enjoyment, however, one bending from the waist revealing a substantial part of her ass didn't do it for me. Not being an ass man, virtuously I looked away with disdain.

Approaching me with a stately gait and subdued smile as if I stood at an altar ready to say 'I do,' Courtney asked if she could be of assistance.

Before I could answer she cast a disapproving glance at the giggling nubile teens definitely touching, looking, picking up but certainly not buying. Turning to me, adjusting a colorful silk scarf around her neck, she appeared distracted by the teens.

Courtney managed to look sexually attractive, yet all business. Her lips, moist and sparkling as if they sweated flakes of diamonds, along with false eyelashes, dark purple eye lids, blond shoulder length hair laying with dormant uniformity, all looking false, suggested she purchased her face in the same place Zoe works. Dressed in a white silk blouse, modest two buttons undone, and blue wool skirt, the outfit sufficiently subdued to suggest business, not funny business; she certainly suggested expensive business.

It took Courtney a few moments to lose her initial hope of a customer, and to recognize me as the cop who interviewed her and Ray. She repeated her offers of help, but now without the eager subservient hope a bona fide customer receives.

I told her that since I was in the mall I decided to drop in and see her dress shop. She corrected, "Boutique," and after staring the two 'wanna be' sex toys out of the store she commented, "They don't have the fashion sense to appreciate my boutique's apparel. You have to have a sense of style to shop here."

Looking at me without much hope of a sale, she again offered to help me. "Can I interest you in a new cocktail dress with spaghetti straps in a deep red flaring silk, short but not too short," adding, "showing cleavage sufficient to evoke interest but subtly not blatantly. Your wife will look fantastic in it."

Curious, I asked the price as if interested in buying it.

"Six hundred. On Fifth Avenue it would cost five times as much."

Able to afford a hundred, expecting two hundred, the six showed how far the distance between us. Trying a nonchalant look suggesting six hundred was well within my comfort zone, my blasé stance wasn't as effective as I hoped.

In weak expectation of success, Courtney opening the celebrity door and out popped, "Cher wore the Gucci original at a Waldorf banquet to accept a lifetime accomplishment award for her work in feeding the world's starving children."

My eyes glazed over in confusion at Gucci's inclusion with starving children, and my only picture of Cher was her ever displayed belly button dripping jewelry.

Courtney decided to double down, tossing out that Beyonce wore an exact copy of this Oscar de la Renta original when receiving the UN Humanitarian Award at the Four Seasons. In full steam, ignoring her audience of one, pulling out another dress from a mirrored closet and holding it up, she mentioned this Givenchy dress was on Oprah and the girls on *The View* absolutely fell in love with it when it was modeled on the show. "Do you know Oprah has donated one hundred exact copies to poor black girls to wear at their prom."

I could mentally let 'exact copy' pass by, but poor girls going to a prom struck a discordant note.

On a climatic note, pulling a new outfit from somewhere, she announced this cocktail dress appeared on the back cover of *Vogue,* with the expectation these factoids would close a six hundred dollar purchase.

I gave her a polite, That's very interesting," which said, not very interesting.

She misheard the comment as indicating real interest, but an interest needing to be nursed to robust health and therefore, not giving up on me, Courtney went to the utility pitch: the material's quality, would last at least ten years. She allowed me to do the arithmetic. If I worried about changes in fashion she guaranteed the dress would be in style years after the material gave its last breath.

Lamely I countered my wife and I didn't attend many cocktail parties. I could have said none, but pride forced the equivocation.

She countered, with all the numerous party invites we'd receive if my wife wore the dress they'd become tiresome. It could be worn at weddings, parties of all sorts, even at formal dinners and banquets raising money for the poor and also democratic fund raisers. Having me living a life you only see on women's TV she continued, "Of course, an attractive wife dressing to advantage is a great assist to your professional advancement, and she'd just love getting it as a gift expressing your love and an indication of your appreciation and pride in her appearance. You would make her so happy."

My "Pam doesn't like to dress up," was so lame, it embarrassed both of us.

Desperately Courtney went to the saleswoman last resort. I could charge it and pay it off in convenient monthly payments. Sensing a 'no' was coming, she quickly played the last card in the sales deck, discounts. If I purchased it now, this day, this moment, I could take advantage of a storewide discount of 20%. Lest I stumbled over the arithmetic, she producing a microscopic pink calculator and with sharp two inch purple glittered nails pushing the buttons, she announced I could save $120 and winking, she'd even wave the sales tax.

"To be honest Courtney, I'm not here to buy anything though I'm really impressed with your dress shop."

"A boutique, not a shop."

"Well, you certainly have decorated it with great taste and stocked it with beautiful merchandize."

Modified with my bull, never really expecting a sale, her disappointment was real but not too deep to drown her. She gave a last try saying I should send my wife to her boutique and she'll give her a discount, possibly as much as 50%.

We walked to the back of the store where cash register and charge machine were hidden beneath a counter, not to sullen by commerce the colorful silk scraps tossed with care. In fact, all the store's price tags resided only in Courtney's blond lacquered head. Considerations of high fashion and monetary concerns like the intake and expelling of food must always be kept separate.

I started by asking how business was doing. For me it was not as a question, given I was fairly certain of the actual situation.

Parting moist sparkling full purple lips, she gushed the universal initial expected answer of how great everything was.

Glancing at the pristine expensive expansive deep blue rug void of any past, present, and probably future traffic, I suggested Ray wasn't too confident over the store's prospects.

I irritated a mental scab which she immediately picked at, "Ray has no business sense," then realizing his McDonald's franchises she qualified, "he knows about fast food, but is clueless about the world of women's high fashion."

Tentatively I suggested Ray may be contemplating closing the store.

"Boutique, dam it, it's a boutique, and Ray plans to persevere 'til it's a going concern. People don't realize it takes two, three or more years for a high fashion boutique to show a profit. Women of taste who appreciate quality discover a boutique such as mine mostly by word of mouth."

My disbelief expressed in a long drawn out 'well' kept her on topic.

"You know it's that soon to be ex of his, always complaining, always harping at him wasting money on my boutique."

"Eleanor wants to close you down!" I gasped as if just falling off a cabbage truck and was astounded to find out where baby's come from.

"It's all about money with her. She resents every dollar poor Ray spends as if it was her money and it isn't; he earns it not her. Besides having absolutely no fashion style, she can't appreciate the high end dresses I'm selling. If it's not hanging on a Sears rack it's beyond Eleanor's appreciation."

She was like a cell phone, all buttons, and knowing how to press them I wasn't repressing my sense of power in dialing her up. To get her out of fashion and into meaningful reality, I mentioned Amber and Willie will eventually be old enough to take care of themselves and cease to be a financial burden to Ray and her.

As expected Courtney responded with dirt talk, "Do you know Amber is sleeping with a nig... er black, and I doubt she's using protection. Ray is broken hearted over this, worried she'd pick up an STD or even worse, get pregnant."

To keep her on target I sympathetically murmured, "He doesn't like his daughter sleeping with a black kid?"

Glancing about the empty store, in a lowered voice as if the mannequins were listening and taking notes to send to the PC police, she gave some politically incorrect observations, "Look, what father would like to see his daughter screwing a black, er African American. Would you?"

Truthfully I told her I'd either shoot the black or shoot myself, and certainly would disown the daughter.

"Exactly, that's what I keep telling Ray. Put Amber out of your life. There's nothing you can do, so why kill yourself worrying over her disgusting self destructive behavior."

One down, she started on the second. "And his son Willie is turning into a fat soft momma's boy. Only with full custody can Ray rectify his son's condition. Unfortunately the children being Eleanor's meal ticket, the bitch will never let go of them. What Ray needs to do is start afresh. We could be so happy if he'd divorce and emotionally separate himself from Eleanor and the children. I'm not saying he shouldn't occasionally visit them, that wouldn't be right. You know I'm sure I can make Ray happy."

Somehow I had the feeling it was bedroom happy.

She concluded, "We love each other and left to ourselves could be so happy. We're soul mates. Do you know that?"

With soul mate, with all the love and happiness talk, it demanded the awkward and seldom mentioned question, "When do you think Ray will get the divorce and you two will be able to get married?" I'm sure I kept the cynical doubt out of my question.

Frowning she said, "It's all so complicated, what with getting my boutique on its feet and Ray trying to finance a new franchise, a Wendy"s. Oh, I shouldn't have said that. Please don't say anything. If McDonald's Headquarters knew about Wendy, they could cause Ray financial problems."

She demanded secrecy as if in the financial world, the bulls and bears were desperately anxious to discover Ray Brothers' next business venture.

Promising to keep Wendy from big Mac's ears, I brought up cockroach night and pressed the 'what would happen to her if Ray died' call button.

"I'd die, I'd simply die if anything happened to my Ray."

I pressed the money button asking what would happen to her boutique. Would she have to close it down?

"Close it down! Never." She said it as if I suggested pulling the plug on her youngest child. "If heaven forbid, Ray did die, he has me down as beneficiary of a generous life insurance policy."

I gave her 'generous' a number, "Three and a half million, and if he was poisoned, double indemnity translates to seven"

"That much!" she exclaimed, as if the number dropped from the cabbage truck.

Pressing a red button I asked, "Who gets the franchises?"

"Ray's will leaves everything evenly divided between Amber and Willie, which means that bitch will get it all."

"Certainly with you in his life he'll want to make changes in his will."

"Definitely. Though I'm not interested in my Ray's money, I can't see the greedy bitch getting it. All I want is to make Ray happy and make certain that bitch doesn't hurt him any more. He's so vulnerable financially, er, and with his children's custody."

To effect an escape I repeated her boutique impressed me with its tastefulness. Walking past the haughty mannequins staring above and through me I wordlessly told them Courtney's countless words of love and phrases such as soul mates, suggest deep seated concerns if not fear that love may be fading fast. Repeated talk of the mutual great love you and your lover shared is usually spoken at the departed lover's casket to buy a good cry. After a while talk of great love and its loss wearing thin is discounted, put on the sales rack, pulled out to occasionally buy some sympathy 'til a new love appears, and then the mantra is 'one must get on with your life'.

Making me a compatriot in her love and concern for Ray, she explained how she constantly asks Ray to make a new will, but men don't like to think of the possibility of their future death."

"Aren't you Ray's beneficiary on his life insurance policy?"

"Yes, Ray insisted. I tried to point out his children should be protected, but the dear wouldn't hear about making the change. Of course I promised to look after his children as if they were mine."

Getting tired of pushing her buttons, I once more pressed the last red button. "Courtney, I want you to be perfectly honest. Do you think Eleanor is capable of poisoning Ray?"

Dangling a piece of raw meat in front of a hungry she wolf, she greedily snapped at it, "Do you think she's the poisoner? I suspected her from the start. She'd rather see Ray dead then enjoying life with me. She's just that evil and mean. For her it's all about money. She'd do anything to get all of Ray's money and his three big Macs."

Noticing a speck of spittle on her lips I edged with, "Now honestly, be brutally honest, what about Amber? Do you think she's capable of patricide?"

"Amber, Amber," she repeated. The possibility of Amber being the poisoner was new to her and was a fresh wonderful savory piece of pork. Hesitating as if holding and savoring the idea, Courtney asked, almost pleaded, "Do you think she could do it?" And then in the same breath continued, "Yes, yes, now that you mention it I really believe that little slut could have done it. I'd hate to think she could do such a terrible thing, but with that black boyfriend suggesting with her father dead they would have a lot of money and live a Hollywood life, who knows. Girls in love will do anything. Yes, she's capable of trying to kill poor Ray, especially if that black boyfriend encourages her and promises they could live together.

"And Detective, the black lives in a public housing tenement and cockroaches are cotenants, so roach poison is a familiar article."

Having a good read of Courtney's character, deep and pure as a muddy rain puddle, I promised to tell my wife about her wonderful boutique. Neither of us believed my lie.

Passing through Sears to get to my car, when looking back I noticed the same woman I saw at Sears when I entered now going into Courtney's boutique. I stared; she smiled and gave a little finger wave at me before entering the boutique. Who the hell is she?

CHAPTER 22

Invitation to Celebrate

After my less than uplifting conversations with Zoe and Courtney I had to decide my next move. Actually I didn't control my movements. The man downstairs, my dictatorial stomach still roach sensitive murmuring its unhappiness over my lo mien gift of greasy noodles, demanded no new exertions and to be kept near a clean toilet.

Obedient to my tummy's demands I went straight home. Walking in, the first thing I spotted was a camel hair overcoat tossed across my chair's arm wordlessly telling me Woody was here and my stomach and I growled our displeasure.

Again, Pat and Woody were sitting in the kitchen, coffee and éclairs between them. I suspected I supplied the coffee, Woody the éclairs. Damn it, the guy was moving in. My gruff, "Hi Woody," told Pam of my displeasure. For Woody it meant nothing more than what the words said.

Feeling the need to explain his presence Woody said he came to see me. Pam backed it up saying she told Woody I'd be home soon and invited him to wait. In the following awkward pause, Pam volunteered to get me lunch in the form of a tuna sandwich and was quickly and firmly rejected by the guy residing in the belt neighborhood.

To get Woody out of my kitchen I suggested we talk in the living room. On our way there, the downstairs guy rejected Pam's coffee offer, suggesting tea as a suitable alternate. Woody had the decency to allow me my easy chair, taking possession of the facing couch.

With fresh coffee in hand, a serious look plastered on his face, Woody asked if I discovered anything helpful for 'the' investigation. He left out his normally possessive 'my' investigation. With our past dynamics I knew the possessive 'his' was there, yet now with his self deprecation it was omitted.

Telling him I uncovered no insignificant facts, I asked how his and Ronni's investigation was going. I added Ronni just to annoy him.

Similar to Courtney's and Zoe's dreams filled with expectations of fantastic successes, Woody told how great progress was being made. How the progress was made left unsaid, encouraging you to employ your imagination. My suspicion, his progress if any residing in committee meetings wrestling with deadening trivia, I maliciously asked if he and Ronni were close to an arrest. My 'close to arrest' caused him a degree of unrest, given there wasn't any. However, Woody being a phony, swearing me to secrecy suggested an arrest was imminent but couldn't be more specific. I believe nothing was happening including an arrest, except for the scheduling of more immediate important committee confabs.

Moving from progress not made, Woody complained about me and Ronni working together. The hurt and sense of betrayal in his voice suggested Ronni and I engaging in sordid trysts. "Mac, you know you're not on the case. In fact you've been explicitly forbidden to get involved, and involving Detective Deutsch in your disobedience shows a callous disregard for her future in the NYPD. Your actions can very well derail a career with great potential."

His altruistic façade of concern for Ronni was so selfish I wondered if he was banging her, or still trying. He got personal telling me he should tell Pam to keep me home and discourage my investigating the Roach Case with Ronni.

Damn him, Pam and I were having trouble and here he's suggesting telling Pam I was getting too close to Ronni, possibly inferring I'd like to screw her, which was true but unlikely to happen.

I reacted with defensive anger, "Look Woody, Ronni has been coming to me to get my help, not the reverse."

My hope of pin pricking his ambitions in her direction harmlessly bounced off him. Being Woody, he didn't believe Ronni or any woman he was interested in could betray him. "Let me tell you Mac, being her senior, she tells me everything she's found out in accompanying you."

Given my read of Ronni Deutsch, she was a woman who gave nothing away free. If it didn't help her, you got nothing from her, neither a hello nor goodbye.

Our coming to an impasse recognizing any exchange of information was nil; so we sat silent, both empty gas bags.

Then Woody informed me, Pam and I, and our son had to attend the big gala Memorial Ceremony for the roach victims tomorrow at noon.

My "Don't plan to attend," was greeted with shock.

"Mac, all the bigwigs will be there. You've got to go."

"Don't want to."

"I was sent here expressly to order you to attend."

"Too sick to go."

"Shit, don't give me that crap. You're well enough to tramp over my investigation with Ronni."

Well, the possessive 'my' didn't stay hidden long.

"Relapse. I could get a doctor's note."

"There's going to be TV coverage. You, Pam and Mickey will be on TV. Nationwide TV is covering the Roach Night Memorial Ceremony."

"Not interested."

"Not interested! Mac, you can't be uninterested. Matt Lerner giving insightful commentary will be there along with Heraldo Rivera doing interviews with his usual exuberant flair."

"Still not going. It's just a waste of time."

"This Memorial is telling the world that as a country we refuse to be cowed and frightened by roach terrorists."

"Woody, only one poor bastard died, and it's still doubtful if he was even the target."

"Mac, realize that poisoned salsa could have ended up on the kid's table. Think of the danger the children were in. What if some, if not all of the cheerleaders died."

"They didn't get the poison, didn't get sick. No one died except Jim Scott, and it was his ulcer that did him in."

"You just don't understand how big the Roach Memorial is going to be. Mac, the President will speak at the Memorial."

"In person!"

"No, of course not. The election is over. He'll be on a television feed from the Pebble Beach Club House on a giant 50 foot wide screen."

Ambivalently I said, "Can't get bigger than that."

"Damn right. The only thing bigger is if he came in person, and I've heard the Vice President may actually come in person. Now that's pretty big."

Unimpressed with the VP's bigness I maintained my refusal.

A frustrated Woody asked, "Did I tell you Diane Sawyer will be Mistress of Ceremonies and everyone knows she's the best with teary sad eyes commentary. Not only that but by live TV feed Sean Penn will lead the convocational secular prayer from Nigeria where he's filming a documentary expressing his concerns for starving African children."

"I can live without secular prayers and certainly without multi millionaire Sean Penn or any other celebrity crying over starving children in front of cameras."

With his name dropping gambit weakening against my resolve, he launched his most powerful name telling me Oprah may be there talking to some of the surviving children and their parents. There's a rumor she'll be giving to all attendees a free basket of Oprah's cosmetics, a hard copy of Oprah's inspirational biography, as well as a signed 12x18 glossy suitable for framing of her hugging Obama."

"Pathetic," was my only comment on the largeness of the gifts. Even Woody, after enumerating them, looked sad and defeated.

In the ensuing silence, Pam, coming with my tea and buttered toast reinflated Woody.

In telling Pam I was being obstinate in not going to the Roach Memorial, he asked if she could convince me as it was a once in a lifetime event.

"Oh Woody. Certainly we're going." Turning to me she stated, "Mac, we have to attend the Roach Memorial. It will be a learning occasion for Mickey, and an event all of us will remember forever."

Calmly as possible, given her irritating opposition to me in front of Woody, I answered, "Pam, if at the end of our lives, our attendance at a Roach Memorial is our life's high point, we lived sad lives filled with wasted years."

"Have to argue with you," Woody put in as if he was asked for his two cents, still for him his cents were heavy gold nuggets buying inarguable truth to be accepted without comment. "Mac, you're being selfish in depriving Pam and son the unique opportunity to stand next to America's luminaries and be part of a historic event."

Pam did the usual deceitful womanly trick, fighting behind the children. "Mac, you can't deprive Mickey of experiencing this wonderful event."

More than just a little annoyed at her contentiousness in front of Woody, emphatically I told her, "Let's discuss this later."

Her, "No," came back at me with the shock of a slap. "We have to settle this now. If we're going I have to buy an outfit for myself, and if it's decided the children won't be wearing their uniforms, Mickey will need a new suit."

Woody clarified, "The plans are for the boys to wear their uniforms without shoulder pads, and the girls their cheerleading outfits. They're going to look precious and pitiful. It's still undecided if the girls will lead the audience in a cheer."

Pam seconded Woody, "See Mac, you don't have to spend money on a new suit for Mickey."

Shit, two against one. Pam was beginning to bring my Irish to the surface. Was she arguing I was not going because of cheapness?

Eyeing the teacup my mind wanted to check out my liquor cabinet's hands, but with my stomach starting to churn with all the tension I vetoed the idea, agreeing with my mind's second thoughts that shaking my cabinet's hands in the middle of the afternoon in this juncture of argument would say lack of character and possibly personal problems. "My mind is made up. We're not going and that's final," I stated in the tone of a Roman patriarch.

"Mickey has to attend," was Pam's forceful edict.

Damn it; she's in revolt, and in front of Woody. My skin was red with Irish blood; my growing anger demanded a helping hand from my cabinet but believed taking that hand would shame me and say something nasty to them and myself about my character. In my silent struggle with my anger over Pam's flagrant denial of my authority, Pam told me she would never let little Mickey to go to the Roach Memorial alone, so she was going and she wanted me to complete the family picture.

With a face sad over witnessing a family's struggling dynamics, Woody's eyes said he was enjoying himself. He told me the ceremony would be short. "Less than three hours." He announced it as if he had timed it.

I countered, "The Crucifixion took three hours. This will be double the time. Look, with all the time waiting, by the time meaningless speeches are made, introductions of people as if they were notable for something, it would be astounding if its end occurred before the fifth hour."

"Mac, with the network covering the Memorial Ceremony, it can't run that long. It will make the noon news, will be carried live on cable, and will appear on network evening news, and it could be on reruns for days after."

We both knew it would be edited to say what the editors wanted it to say on the evening news.

Brushing aside time considerations as inconsequential, Pam again went to the child. "Mac, Mickey must be there ... to experience it, to learn from it, to be inspired by it, to find closure through it, to discover how America works, to know, though evil exists in the world it will never overcome America's spirit, to see how good can come from evil, to share with his schoolmates this defining moment in their lives."

Shit, Pam was throwing a hell of a lot of contemporary gibberish at me. What blow words ... experience it, learn from it, be inspired by it, to know evil never triumphs.

Finishing the tea, wishing it contained a little stiffener, I announced ex cathedra in my role of paterfamilias to Woody, "We, Pam, I, and Mickey are definitely not going. And that's final." With my back to the wall I had no choice but draw a line in the sand. Damn it, who's master here.

Woody, a slithering serpent suggesting I was being totally selfish in not considering what my family wants, was inflammatory.

Pam fanned the flames telling me she and Mickey were going no matter what I said.

What could I say? I said it all, and saying it all felt empty, impotent and alone. Needing a friendly hand, my hand and cup were empty. My salvation was standing up and not seeking out a finger or two. Mulishly I repeated my intention not to attend no matter what others decided to do. Felt there was a principal involved though would have difficulty enunciating it.

"Look Mac, let me set you straight," Woody stated. "The big brass, the men residing high about us demand you attend in full uniform to represent the department for fantastic departmental PR. I've been told if you don't attend, a patrol beat in Staten Island was the mildest alternative mentioned. Loss of job and pension for disobedience was definitely on the table."

Job security triumphs principal every time. Lost pension brings strong men to their knees. Imagining the cold hand of joblessness, alone, standing out in the cold, looking at an empty future, Woody scared the hell out of me. Irish blood was churned into whipped cream.

Going to the cabinet, dipping a few fingers into my teacup to accompany my surrender, announced if everyone was determined to go I'll go. I didn't want to ruin Mickey's enjoyment. Damn, was I hiding behind my child? And shit, it was lame, so lame Mickey would be embarrassed hearing his father.

Having won, the victorious left the battlefield. Woody disapprovingly eyeing my tea cup refill left.

Pam, eyeing my tea cup with anxiety, a breath away from saying she disapproved, refrained and going into the kitchen decided one victory was sufficient for the time.

Hating myself, emptying my cup of liquor and sorrow, I debated: upstairs to bed with a full teacup to seek oblivion, or to the kitchen to argue with Pam without Woody's support, or go outside in the cold. My self loathing demanded the argument's continuation on my principal complaint; my self respect was breached. Call it pride, call it self respect, it's what makes a man. Without self respect you lose your sense of self. To bring man down, Satan first destroys his self respect. Without self respect, man can never respect anything; self respect, the bulkhead against depravity is washed away. Listening to Eve and not to his own voice was Adam's destruction.

With a refreshed tea cup I entered the enemy's camp.

Pam, cleaning the coffee and tea cups was inexplicably mad. She won and was dissatisfied. Women can only achieve victory and gain happiness in surrendering. It's their immutable nature.

Eyeing my tea cup, placating she asked, "Do you want anything to eat?"

In high outrage I asked how she could argue against me in front of Woody.

She answered, "The Memorial is only a few days away. We have to decide quickly. Anyway, let's forget about it. It's settled."

Her generosity, victor to defeated, resurrected my Irish. With my draining the tea cup then slamming it down to give symbolic indication of my anger forced her to criticize my drinking. "Mac, lately you're drinking too much."

Not to be deflected I pushed aside my drinking as inconsequential, in fact given current provocations in my home occasionally I needed a little helping hand to cope with all the disrespect I'm getting. "Forget my drinking … the point is you sided with Woody against me."

"You were being very obstinate. There was no reasoning with you."

"I stated clearly to you, I felt we shouldn't go. It's a farcical nonevent and we demean ourselves participating in it."

"We have to go if only for Mickey. Now, do you want something to eat? Given the ordeal your stomach has undergone, drinking is the last thing you should be doing."

Looking down at the tea cup, even without tea leaves, its residue whispered she's right. I punished the cup's insinuations away by picking it up and draining it of its few remaining drops. Putting it in the sink I walked out, and in the living room again had to face options. I had more than enough testosterone to grab hold of an additional few fingers in defiance. Sipping, I thought of the possibility of finding blissful Nirvana in the bedroom or with numbing TV. What else was there to do. Being poor is to have little if any options. Feeling desperate, running from being poor, I decided to continue my haphazard investigation. Possibly, solving the murder I can regain some sense of the masculinity and self respect I felt was lost today,

CHAPTER 23

The Law Arrives

Coat on, hand on the knob, the doorbell rang. Damn it, I'm trying to escape from my house and more irritating visitors trapping me.

I opened the door to face a clean shaved ruddy faced handsome guy, one hand hugging a briefcase, the other extended to grab mine. The fortyish fit body announcing to the world 'I play squash, golf, tennis and jog,' introduced himself, "You must have heard of O'Malley."

Was this happy healthy specimen the lawyer everyone was talking about?

Letting go of my hand, without my realizing how it got there, he replaced it with his business card. Peering down to read the card, he passed me, had his overcoat off, and asked in a loud voice if my wife was at home.

Running after him I dumbly said, "You're O'Malley?"

Putting his briefcase down and opening it on my coffee table he allowed I could say he was O'Malley and not be wrong.

Standing in front of my easy chair to protect it and to keep him standing I stupidly again asked if he was O'Malley.

He said he was a member of the NY Bar.

Pam came in to see the uninvited occupant who invaded our living room.

Going up to Pam, giving her an orthodontic constructed smile he introduced himself as Jerry Moody, partner in the O'Malley Law firm, specializing in obtaining justice for people who crying out for justice have no justice.

Pam, not fully realizing the future difficulty of getting rid of him, invited him to sit down. Now it's going to be a heavy lifting job to get him out of the chair and out the door.

I guess I was scowling, for ignoring me he turned to Pam as more receptive, asking if anyone was representing her and her son adding it was critical for her family's welfare to have representation.

Pam quickly put lawyer and concern for her family together as if they naturally belonged together.

With Pam and Jerry Moody sitting down, I was forced to reluctantly sit down.

The smell of easy greasy money accompanied him and his briefcase into my house and it will take fumigation and the work of several rubbery gloved hands to cleanse the house of the stink.

Asking if he wanted any refreshment Pam caused Moody to struggle: keep his more easily manipulated victim present or get her to go for coffee knowing, armed with a coffee cup it would be that more difficult to get rid of him. The more you can get the sucker to do for you, the more they'll like you and will become more malleable. No man is loved and admired more than by unpaid servants.

"Coffee would be nice," he decided.

Pam asked me what I wanted. I suspect she knew what I wanted and needed, but wasn't going to serve me even a fingernail from the cabinet.

With Pam getting coffee, smiling a shark's smile, Moody going for the kill asked me if I realized how large, how highly reputed, how eminent in the field of law, how successful in getting money for their clients were O'Malley and Moody. He assured me they had the strength, determination and resources to take on the biggest greedy adversarial corporate organizations in our name. They were fearless in defense of their clients' rights.

With Pam returning with the coffee, Moody quickly downsized O'Malley for her, explaining although large enough to strike terror into the heart of the forces of evil, they were sufficiently small to render personal caring attention to their clients. "Our clients aren't just numbers to us. We treat our clients as people, as good people needing a strong advocate to protect their rights."

Deep in his BS we could only wait for his other shoe to drop in the muck. The shark smile temporarily disappeared replaced with earnest concern asking again if we signed with any other law firm regarding the roach poisoning. "I hear some disreputable law firms are seeking to sign up table 12. I'm not inferring the Major firm is in that group. Couldn't do that. Professional ethics. Still I advise any honest person not to employ them as their representative."

Pam, saying we were free from legal snares allowed the Moody smile to resurface.

"You are wise not to sign up with just any law firm. Our firm has a stellar reputation for getting our clients all the money they are entitled." Then leaning to me, winking, he added, "and more." He gave us a few moments to consider the money we're entitled to, and the 'more.'

Finally I told him we were very busy right now and will get in touch with O'Malley in the future. My gambit was so unconvincing I didn't even get up. My negativity was ignored as if I was whispering white noise.

Talking to Pam, Moody went political, delving into the horror and injuries we suffered and how deeply he felt for us, and how our pain was his pain. He told Pam, Mickey may suffer lifelong psychological difficulties from the trauma of roach night.

Putting in another negative I told Moody I doubted Mickey suffered any damage. In fact, he enjoyed all the excitement. Again negativity was ignored as if issued in a foreign tongue.

To Pam, Moody continued, "Being a mother you want to protect your child and see if he suffers any future, heaven forbid, mental or physical damage there will be sufficient resources available to treat any future difficulty."

Having a mother now worried and protective of her son he glided to me and into money. "We, at O'Malley feel the City, the State, and Goya Corporation have been grossly negligent regarding salsa preparation to the tune of three million."

That got me sitting up. Pam wide eyed repeated, "Three million."

"That's only what we're demanding for your son, and of course for his mother undergoing lifelong fear and anxiety for her son's health, at least a million."

Leaning back in my chair I religiously waited for mine to come with the certitude of the 'last coming.'

"As for you Mac, the near death experience, the physical pain, possible future impotence, as well as years of back and stomach trouble, ten million is more than justified." He gave a brief pause for us to enjoy the millions floating and bouncing about in our living room before doing the sum for us. "Fourteen million, let's round it up to fifteen million is the amount we will sue for your family, and we all know you deserve it, if not more, and we won't charge you a cent."

Our not jumping up giving high fives, hugs and wildly boogieing about the room worried him sufficiently to ask, "Is that figure adequate? If you feel you suffered more than that, well at O'Malley the client is always in charge. We're just here to see you get what you deserve, free of an upfront fee."

Somehow between my ten million and the fifteen total, a and sheaf of papers spilling from his briefcase and a Mont Blanc pen slid towards Pam. Dangling the pen as if a fish lure and fat gold fish were swimming about on the paper, Moody, with a smile exuding lifelong friendship for us, told us a signature was all that was needed to receive fifteen million.

To forestall Pam from swallowing the lure I asked as if an innocent, "This is a contingency contract."

"Certainly," Moody answered as if he had been explaining the contract ad nauseam.

With Pam still hungrily eyeing the lure I asked what percentage of the money awarded, O'Malley will get.

The fact of O'Malley receiving money tarnishing his altruistic affectations, took Moody's smile away as he begrudgingly admitted one third of the money recovered would be O'Malley's, but quickly reassured me it was well within the legal amount. In fact, some unscrupulous law firms charge as much as 40%. I hear Major is asking for that and even higher. Additionally he added in the heroic struggle O'Malley will shoulder all expenses incurred now matter how great to secure justice for us.

Pam was looking at me waiting for direction.

Getting up I told Moody with all the sincerity a liar can manufacture, "Pam and I will discuss it together and will let you know our decision."

He must have had a Blackstone Law book as a breastplate. My dismissal arrow bounced off him as he anxiously said, "You have to act fast. Every second of delay is injurious to your claim."

It was like saying no to Pam's new Memorial dress. I repeated we'll think it over.

"Are you aware all of table 12 has joined together to initiate a class action suit under O'Malley s professional guidance. The total three hundred million is the number sitting on the bottom line that O'Malley is seeking for our clients. If you don't join everyone now you may be left out of the huge three hundred million settlement. Time is essential. You must sign now."

Taking the lure, looking at me Pam said, "Mac, we've got to join the others."

Just as I was about to grab the pen from her to keep her from signing, the doorbell sounded. Shit, more people.

Moody mumbled, "Shit," as Pam, answered the door returning with a woman of forty who lost her waist at twenty and at thirty her breasts melded into an ever expanding waist. Modestly dressed and in high heels to add two inches to her five foot frame, smiling, she came in behind Pam. Her warm smile lasted 'til she spotted Moody. Thereupon it froze to a mean grimace. Seeing a pen poised near legal papers she pushed past Pam shouting, "Don't sign anything," as if saying ... the dam burst, run for your lives.

The one thing I was grateful for, her entrance got Moody out of his chair crying, "Too late Major, the McCoppins have agreed in principal to have O'Malley represent them."

With hawk piercing glance taking in the unsigned legal papers strewed about, Mayor asked Pam, "Did you sign anything? You didn't sign anything. Before you sign let me explain, the Sonia Major law firm has a great deal of experience in getting our clients all the money they deserve."

Moody's shark teeth came out ready to take Major's head off in one snap, "Trudy dear, I believe there's an ethical problem here. To interfere with the sacred bond of a lawyer and his client in the vain attempt to gain financial advantage, well, we reputable lawyers are above such conduct I'm afraid the Board of Ethics will have to hear what you are doing. To save embarrassment and possible future professional ethical difficulties, Trudy, I think it best for all concerned you recuse yourself."

Being a lawyer Trudy sneered at law threats. "Shove it Moody. You have no signed commitment on part of the McCoppins to represent them."

Stupidly I interjected, "Excuse me, are you Trudy Major?"

Giving me a warm smile, auntie to beloved nephew, she admitted to being Trudy Chase.

Grabbing the Monte Blanc pen and thrusting it at Pam, Moody pleaded, "Mrs. McCoppin, I believe you were about to sign this."

The 'this' was a tri folded blue bordered document.

"Don't," Trudy yelled, as if poison was about to be drunk. "Before signing anything let me explain the services the Sonia Major law firm offer their clients."

Giving a shoulder bounce to Trudy, Moody, standing in front of Pam explained that as her lawyer he reviewed all the documents he placed in front of her, and found it was perfectly correct for her to sign them and receive fifteen million, and be an integral part of a three hundred million dollar class action suit.

Slapping aside Moody's hand holding the legal papers sufficient to scatter them about on the floor, Trudy told Pam if signing with Major she personally would be by her side throughout the proceedings, and being a woman could relate to her nervous breakdown during the trial. In an undertone she asked Pam if she was having trouble with her ovaries, was she experiencing any reproductive difficulties, as reproductive problems are worth a few million a problem. Infertility was in the hundreds of millions.

A very nervous Moody pulling Pam away from Trudy said O'Malley was famous for getting out of court settlements for his clients. She needn't even go to court, just sign, give a simple disposition and –"

"Don't listen to him. Out of court settlements are notoriously smaller than jury awards. At Major we go to the mat for you. We don't fear any law firm, no matter how big, no matter how corrupt," and staring at Moody added, "or how incompetent and unscrupulous."

Moody and Trudy were now yelling in each other's face; Pam and I, inconsequential observers.

Moody yelled, "Trudy, it takes years to take a jury awarded money through the appeals process. That's why at O'Malley we strive for out of court settlements where a client receives his money in a matter of months, not decades."

Trudy Chase shot back, "What about that vaginal napkin case where you represented Virginia Bots. You lost a feminine hygiene case. It's virtuously impossible to lose them. They're good for at least a million."

"Look Trudy, it wasn't our fault. We were claiming Virginia was made sterile and the checks were about to be signed when she went out and got pregnant."

"At Major we would have made sure she took the pill."

"Yeah, but what about the asbestos class action case Major won. That was such a big settlement the company went bankrupt and except for legal fees, no money was ever awarded."

It was getting so heated Pam suggested we all sit down, have coffee and there were some chocolate chip cookies.

With that offer, both combatants realizing they had an audience took a peace break with Trudy suggesting a co-joint representation and Moody begrudgingly agreeing. This of course demanded fresh documents, papers allocating co-counsel fees and legal obligations for us to sign.

Picking up papers and coats and promising they'll be back like we'll be holding our breath, the outer door slammed as Pam came in with a tray of cookies and coffee.

CHAPTER 24

Pep Boys

It took the cold damp November air to lighten my mind of a few fingers and steady my measured steps. Taking a chance the Pep Boys Auto Parts store would still be open I was in luck by a good half hour. Since Jim Scott was the only murder victim and his buddy Zapp's absence from table 12 was notable, it would be profitable to get more background on both.

The store was large, sufficiently large to support a parts manager, an installation manager, and to round out the trifecta, a store manager. Deciding to go from high to low I broached the store manager, a man of substantial heft, a man hiding a face behind a full black beard, a man controlling twenty thousand square feet, millions in stock, thousands in sales, and twenty people for thirty five hours a week of their lives.

After introducing himself as Joshua Dumont, he told me what we both knew as if he divined it, "You're one of the detectives investigating poor Scott's tragic death. We at Pep Boys still haven't recovered from his death." Whether his lips hidden deep within their hair's lair were sad or not couldn't be ascertained, but his eyes glancing over my shoulder through his open office door at the checkout aisle if saying anything, said Joshua was bearing up admirably.

Picking up a microphone he yelled to the twenty thousand square feet an additional cashier was needed up front. He sighed or at least the exhaled sounds escaping from hidden lips were similar to soulful sighs. He complained over the brisk increase in business at his Pep Boys since Scott's murder was reported with his store featured on the six o'clock news, "Here at Pep Boys we're trying to deal as best we can with poor Scott's death. Sadly customers are buying at Pep Boys, not because of our low prices and caring service, but out of some macabre curiosity of wanting to see where Scott worked, and with Jim's death he's leaving us a man short it's been hard to handle the rush of customers."

Refocusing his eyes on me he complained about all the interviews, re-interviews, follow up interviews, clarification interviews he had undergone by at least fifteen investigating agencies, never mind nosy news people popping up from behind tire stacks asking the most personal questions.

"Still let me say we at Pep Boys are cooperating one hundred percent and corporate headquarters has issued over thirty memos urging all outlets to cooperate."

Pointing to a stack of binders he asked if I wanted to see the memos.

Seeing the thickness of the binders, I didn't doubt the number and guessing each memo had to be over ten pages in length, I passed on his invitation.

Dumont continued his complaints, "Of course all these investigations and the news coverages are playing havoc with our ability to deliver Pep Boy quality service. The number of customers is beyond belief, er excuse me…" Grabbing his mike Dumont roared, "Rolanda, get to your register."

Noting my being taken back by the sudden harsh command, he explained Rolanda's deep mourning for Jim has made it difficult to extract her from the ladies rest room. "All of us here at Pep Boys are working hard in giving honor to Scott's memory. In remembrance for, er .."

"Jim."

"Yes, Jim Scott."

"Either from Zapp or the widow I heard money is being collected for Scott's widow and Jim's kid."

"Huh, oh yeah, nationwide Pep Boy's Corporation and its employees, taking care of their own, have contributed over thirty five hundred dollars. Zapp, being a friend of the family, is in charge of the collections. He set up a can somewhere around here where the guys can drop in a contribution. Should be pretty full by now for er –"

I helped, "Jim."

"Yes, certainly, Jim. Well, his coworkers have dedicated themselves to working even harder for Jim. Scott was a devoted Pep Boy, a conscientious worker willing to put in that extra time if needed, the epitome of the American worker. Do you know, Corporate has decided all Pep Boys stores worldwide have a moment of silence during lunch hour. Not only that, but our store is having a Scott Memorial Tire Sale 'til the end of the month."

My reiteration of 'lunch hour' followed by Memorial Sale accompanied with question marks necessitated a continuation. "Detective, do you know that Corporate has ordered this store to close for four hours to allow all of Scott's coworkers, in nice clean pressed Pep Boys uniforms, the opportunity to attend the Memorial. I'm going to bring a giant wreath in the form of the three Pep Boys waving goodbye to er …"

Taking pride in keeping the sarcasm from my words I told him, "Jim. And I'm sure Jim Scott, wherever he is, will be appreciative."

And that's not all. At the Memorial, Pep Boys is planning to announce a college scholarship for, er .."

I helped him out, "Jeffrey."

"Certainly, Jeffrey," Dumont said as if he didn't need to cheat. "Well anyway, if he, er.. Jeffrey gets into college, Pep Boys will offer him a scholarship. It will be known as the Manny, Moe and Jack scholarship."

I commented, "Universities … Harvard, Princeton cost a lot. Only wealthy students or students receiving the assistance of affirmative action scholarship and loans can afford to go there."

"Huh? Well Pep Boys' Headquarters was thinking along the lines of a neighborhood community college. Anyway, knowing his college costs will be covered will be a strong incentive for Scott's boy, er --"

"Jeffrey."

"Yes, Jeffrey, to finish high school and go on to community college. Hopefully after college, if he passes the rigorous Pep Boy Management Team exams, he may be accepted to the Manny, Moe and Jack team. Let me tell you, there are a hell of a lot of worse jobs than being a Pep Boy manager."

Apparently the joy of his management position necessitated enumerating how quick you can get out of the job. "Retirement in thirty years at half pay, full pay after forty, and with social security, well, you can't beat the benefits. I've almost got nineteen years in and am planning to go for the full forty." He said it like a prisoner talking about his sentence without the possibility of parole.

"Besides the generous retirement pension, every employee has a life insurance policy for a hundred thousand, and you don't contribute towards it, unlike the employee pension and health plans. So Jim's widow, er …"

I gave him, "Joy."

"Of course Joy, his wonderful wife will benefit. Here at my Pep Boys Store we're all family, and feel deeply for her loss. Let me tell you, it's also our personal felt loss."

I told him Jim's murder, for insurance purposes being considered an accidental death, the widow would receive double, two hundred thousand. Mentioning money draws conversation away from warm cozy BS feelings and the comfortable expected murmurs into hard prickly reality.

An amazed Dumont said, "Shit, that much. She's going to do alright for herself." Catching his unsympathetic words he followed up with, "She'll need every penny to raise little .."

In the pause I assisted with Jeffrey.

"Of course, Jeffrey, the one we're putting through community college, a wonderful kid with a great future career at Pep Boys, if he could cut the mustard.

"Er, Detective, did I tell you we're thinking of closing Jim's tire rotation bay out of respect for Jim, 'til he's buried."

Given the 'T' in thinking is way down the alphabet from the 'D' of doing, I had to ask if they were actually doing it.

Begrudgingly Joshua lamented, "Yeah, well we all wanted to do it, were planning to do it, in a memo Corporate permitted us to do it, but the boys, Scott's coworkers felt Scott would have wanted to keep the tires at Pep Boys rotating and balanced, so as a tribute to Scott, his coworkers are keeping his bay open. Being the embodiment of the Pep Boys spirit, always giving his all for the customers, it's what Scott would have wanted, keep installing new tires for customers' safety on the road."

The beard, so full of BS, sitting in his small glass enclosed office, I felt I was drowning in it.

Joshua gave me permission to talk to the service manager, Jim's immediate supervisor and his tire rotation co workers, only requesting I be brief. With Scott's death business was brief, so brisk overtime was in the offering, but only after the four hours spent at the Memorial Ceremony were deducted.

Assuming Zapp was Jim's immediate supervisor, given it was his excuse from moving from table12 to 13, I was surprised he wasn't. A character in stained overalls, three days stubble, steel framed glasses hanging on a suspicious bulbous red veined nose suggestive of a serious problem worthy of Dr. Leeper's six months of analysis, introduced himself as Bobby, tire supervisor.

Wanted to be charitable about the nose, thinking of his fifty something years of age, years working in open bays in all weather, should be considered before pronouncing judgment. After consideration I decided, no, an affectionado of booze in need of Leeper.

Unimpressed, coming face to face with a police detective, supervisor Bobby commented, "Another one of you guys." His characterture, 'you guys are as thick as latrine fleas,' indicated he wasn't a Pep Boy rooter, definitely not a supporter of a safer society, and not interested in contributing to the Police Athletic League.

He brought me to his office, a stool and clipboards struggling for air amid scraps of oil stained paper on a work bench Goodwill would pass up. Asked his opinion of Jim, Bobby issued his brief epitaph, "A good guy and a great bowler."

In surprise, repeating, "Bowler," he elicited more details. "Had a three hundred game once, bowled consistently around a two hundred average, was the team captain."

Fishing behind several thick black binders containing a multitude of discarded tire rotation instructions from Corporate, Bobby extracted a twelve inch trophy topped with a golden bowling ball, finger holes displayed. "This is last year's trophy for the Pep Boy Tire Rotation bowling team. Without Jim we could never have won."

A hollow bowling trophy ... what an epitaph to receive at your game's end. Then again, what will be mine? Will it be any weightier, taller, shinier than Scott's?

Interrupting my morbid considerations and getting us back to the real world Bobby said, "As for work, let me show you our wall of merit."

I couldn't determine if he was pulling my leg or was he serious as he pointed to an Employee of the Month certificate honoring Jim for changing a thousand tires in September.

"Hard worker," I summarized.

"The best. This year he had a lock on Pep Boy Tire Employee of the Year, and I hear that at the Memorial, Corporate is planning to award the widow a special honorary Employee of the Year Plaque, laminated on walnut."

I couldn't tell if his words were dripping with cynicalism or stupid innocence.

I continued, "Heard Jim's co workers are making a collection for the widow."

"Yeah, Zapp is in charge. Heard he's got almost two thousand collected from all the Pep Boy tire rotaters in America."

Two thousand! Could Zapp be dipping into the Corporate three thousand donation. Heaven forbid ... a Pep Boy? Dropping such cynical negativity I said, "Dupont is going to close the store for four hours so everyone could attend the Memorial Ceremony."

"Yeah, crap, one of those four hours is our lunch hour and we've got to show up in clean uniforms."

Bobby's meaning was clear; he viewed the Memorial in the same light as I did.

Looking about I asked for Zapp, saying I wanted to talk to him. We both scanned the bays noting numerous grimy faces without seeing Zapp's face.

Suddenly Zapp appeared coming out of the toilet.

"Shit," Bobby mumbled, then yelled, "Zapp, taking another shit break. You must have the runs for all the time you spend sitting on the bowl."

Not a coward, Zapp yelled back, "I'll take a shit whenever I want."

Joining Zapp at his tire station, talking face to face over a deflated tire limply hanging on a rim, I accused, "Didn't you claim, being Jim's supervisor was your reason for moving from table 12 to 13."

"Not supervisor, superior, given I have three years seniority over Jim. I can retire sooner. I've put in almost twelve years."

Looking at his grease stained overalls, dirt encased face and hands, still looking in pretty good physical condition, I estimated his age at around thirty five. He still had thirty five years to reach the age of actually doing nothing. Physically he formed a good triangle, shoulders to waist, One could say he had a male physique, but being a man it wasn't for me to say.

Coming up to us, Bobby repeated his opinion on Jim's work ethic, "Would have been employee of the year," was more for Zapp than me.

After Bobby left, Zapp commented, "Jim was such a suck up. He kissed Bobby's butt, wiped Dumont's ass." This sudden revealing burst of honesty coming from Jim's best friend, comforter of the widow, demanded Zapp backtrack, "Well, Jim deserved all his awards. I wouldn't begrudge him his Employee of the Year. For me, I don't care for all that stuff."

I couldn't resist, "Given it would never be tended to you, it's always easy to reject and despised what you won't get." Enjoying irritating Zapp I continued, "Jim was the bowling team captain with a bowling score of three hundred."

"Bowling is for losers. That's why I quit the team. Shit, you never hear of anyone famous bowling. For me, I golf."

"Where?"

"Huh, currently I'm taking lessons."

"From who?"

"Haven't decided which golf pro I'll hire."

Deciding to discontinue baiting him, I walked over to a work bench where a coffee tin labeled 'For Jim's Kid' was half filled with singles. I asked how the collection was going.

"Great, just great. Now look, no more questions. I've got a tire to inflate."

With air hose connected to tire's nozzle, the tire was inflated tight to the rim. Leaving, I felt inflated to my rim. Before I could gain the street, store manager Dumont came running up to me shouting for me to wait. "Wow, let me catch my breath.""

After moving his beard in and out for what seemed a long time, well a long time watching his facial hair doing calisthenics, he finally came to the point, "Decided I couldn't let you leave without giving you a mini Manny, Moe and Jack bobble head. We're going to give each child at the Memorial a Pep Boy bobble head figure. What do you think of that?"

"Nice touch," I said.

"It's my idea, sent a memo to Corporate and within a day they okayed the idea and the expense up to two hundred."

"Two hundred!"

"Yeah, well you can get hand painted bobble heads costing forty five a copy, but of course the kids will get the plastic ones."

"It will be nice for Jim's Memorial."

With my bobble head in hand I left a satisfied Joshua walking back to his managerial office.

CHAPTER 25

Diversity. Love it, you paid for it

By the time I stepped out of the oil, grease, noise and dirt of the Pep Boys Service tire bays and onto a street slightly less greasy, it was nearing six. What to do. Damn it, that question again. Should have some plan of action allowing me to go from A to Z in an orderly logical progression. The feeling one isn't in control, not directing one's actions but following impulses is disconcerting and depressing. Should devise a plan and follow it; maybe not all the way to Z, but having a goal should structure the intermediate steps.

In the autumn mist I again faced a night void of options ... home to face stress and silent pressure from Pam concerning my drinking and the stupid Memorial, wasn't even sure of a dinner. My stomach, hearing dinner, woke up and suggested a beef and brew tavern near the precinct. So my A was dinner and drinks, leaving B up in the air, never mind C through Z.

I retreated to Carmichael's Tavern, home of the pig and cow serving delicious roast beef sandwiches and baby back pork ribs accompanied by refreshing frosted steins of beer.

Seated in semi darkness, holding a three inch high rare roast beef, with the Jewish rye struggling to keep the gravy from being squeezed out, I was for the moment content and more importantly, the guy behind the belt buckle was happy. My throat said another stein; the buckle man suggested it would be glad to see another stein. Finishing finger licking clean some of the gravy that escaped the rye, and the second stein now half finished, I considered my alphabet and decided on my goal; solving the damn murder or at least having a go at it.

Going through my list, I visited Ray Brothers, Courtney at her boutique, plumber Tony Geroni, his wine tasting wife Babs, and his mistress Zoe, a Cinderella dreamer, Scott's widow Joy (I was able to size her up as having no joy), and her good friend Zapp, the Pep Boy, without pep. Having no idea as to the actual intended victim, still Ray Brothers, with his millions in life insurance had to top the list, followed by Jim Scott, who actually was murdered, and with his wife and best friend, he deserved consideration. Who was left to interview but Eleanor, Brother's separated wife, and Abdullah and Dagmar, and someone called Jimmy involving drugs and debts, along with Coach Tom Applegate who had bailed out from table 12.

Unfortunately Carmichael's stool had grabbed hold of my ass and didn't want to let go. My stomach was slow dancing with the roast beef to beer music. My arm was doing easy arm curls with my third stein. Third! Did I order another one? Where did the second go? Looking up, the mirror behind the bar didn't say anything nice about my looks. Certainly not James Bond. I blended in with the Carmichael crowd, presently still working, with future doubtful. The six o'clock crowd was mostly hangers on, hanging on to a job, hanging on to a marriage, hanging on to a girlfriend, hanging on to life with hope of something better fading fast, if not having already completely vanished.

Finishing my stein, and without thought, ordered another while looking about the tavern feeling pity for the occupants. Shit I thought, they probably spend Christmas Eve at Carmichaels. Poor bastards. My pity lasted 'til I realized I was nearly one of them, with Pam currently making independent noises. Could my future Christmas Eves be at the cow and pig's home? Playing with the idea of being alone, still not really believing it, I enjoyed feeling sorry for myself.

By seven, having downed my 'nth stein, bored, feeling sorry for myself, again I faced what to do, could see my B, when was C to show itself. Being on sick leave, working was out and with Pam being pissed about something, a something I fully didn't understand and certainly didn't want to deal with, so home was out.

Again, by default, I continued my investigation into who tried to poison me. For the B I decided to visit Eleanor Brothers, Ray's separated wife, the one with the strongest motive, millions in insurance.

The house was a brick three story job with black wrought iron railing protecting a small stoop. The house's narrow width made the three stories look like six. I rang the bell and no one came. I rang again and again. While peering into a first floor window, Amber and Eleanor appeared, staring at me as if I wanted money from them. Rushing to the front door they were inside so quickly and about to close it when blocking it with my shoe, I said, "Detective McCoppin. I'd like a few moments of your time."

Standing inside behind her mother, Amber told me, her mother, and any passerby within a hundred yards they didn't have to say anything to me. She managed to insert the 'F' word between every word. The loud vulgarity caused the mother to hesitate in slamming the door. Having to show her maternal discipline, turning to Amber, she told her to watch her language. To insure I knew she didn't run a disorderly home she added, "Amber, you know I don't allow that kind of language."

Amber answered her mother's admonition with a flippant, "Whatever," and walking away tossed a "screw you," aimed at either her mother, or me, or both.

People with money need the police to protect their money, but only as servants similar to their cleaning women, so I decided to drop, "I'm a police detective." Capitalizing on Eleanor's temporary embarrassment over Amber's mouth, I switched to being a father and a victim of the banquet poisoning, troubled over our children's safety, asking with deep concern how her little Willie was doing and how my son Mickey was having trouble sleeping.

That temporarily saved my five toes from being squeezed into three as she had to reciprocate with similar concerns for my son, but my ass was still in the cold.

Shit, why am I trying the usual gambits when I have at hand Eleanor's Open Sesame. "I've just come from interviewing Courtney at her boutique. I suspect her boutique is failing."

She almost drooled as she let me follow her to the living room, spacious, interior designer furnished so it resembled a room pictured in a glossy magazine, nice to look at but not a room to live in. We stood facing each other. Devouring with relish my boutique failure gambit she stated, "Knew it was a failure. That stupid woman hasn't the fashion sense to run a Good Will stand, never mind a fashion store. I can't understand Ray wasting our money on such a tramp."

To get my ass in a chair I gave an understanding listening to her litany of undeserved woe: with a marriage ending; with Ray being a bum; with her a single mother raising two children on her own; with the psychological trauma they all have suffered being exposed to roach poisoning; with the impact on little Willie's psyche.

I added her litany with my hope Willie and Amber will recover unscarred, and ending my BS with, "I feel your pain and can empathize, having personally endured the poisoning."

Her response was asking me if O'Malley had talked to me, and if so, what was my opinion of his idea of a class action suit. This got my ass into a floral brocade chair.

She continued, "Do you think we should join the others, or sue separately? My divorce lawyer thinks the best course is to go with the group, however, a friend of ours, a well respected corporation lawyer, thinks our best avenue to go down is to travel alone, as a family, given our financial prominence, the loss of Ray's income, never mind Willie's future income and our standard of living. After all one cannot financially compare poor Ray's death with this Pep Boy Scott's. The quality of the men and their life, their money, their social contribution is so totally different. Ray's life is worth much more. The corporation lawyer is so sure of success he's offered to represent us on a contingency basis."

Her conversation was bi-polar; the maniac phase deals with money, the depression phase deals with her divorce. Needing to wedge between the two I asked if she or Amber saw anything suspicious while preparing the food.

She struggled mightily to come up with something against Courtney, no matter how small, but in the end confessed she had nothing. "Like I had to tell all those investigators, Amber and I were working so hard to give the children a wonderful banquet we didn't have time to notice anything, not like that bitch, Courtney who thinks she's too good to help at preparing or serving."

Eleanor rose signaling I was terminated and to be sent on my way. but I still wanted to talk to Amber, find out if she saw anything. Oh what the hell, it was a damp and cold night, and my ass didn't want to leave, even though the living room ambiance was showroom sterile.

To keep my seat I reintroduced Courtney, mentioning she was at the banquet.

"I know. Do you think she's the poisoner?" Eleanor still stood but wasn't making motions towards the door.

With false sincerity I lied, "I hope Ray doesn't find out. Before the banquet started, at the open bar, Courtney came on to me."

"Really! I believe it; I can believe it of the tramp. Courtney will sleep with any man."

Feeling I was better than 'any man' I told her not to tell Ray. It was like telling a do-gooder not to talk about poor blacks, baby polar bears, melting snow, and anything in Africa.

Her first impulse, Ray had to be informed as to the type of woman he left his family for. It was absolutely the right thing to do.

Trying to leash her I asked her to wait for the poisoner to be captured. It was like trying to restrain a do-gooder from spending other people's money on their 'good' causes for your good.

"He must be told. If she was there she could be the poisoner. His life is in danger. I'd never forgive myself if anything happened to poor Ray."

Suddenly becoming a hostess she asked, "Look, can I get you anything ... coffee, a drink?"

To secure my ass to the chair's cushion, I agreed to a whiskey, if she had it. I was prepared to go to Scotch, beer, but not some Chardonnay crappy wine. I still had some masculinity to shun girly booze.

With haste, afraid of missing any Courtney gossip, she disappeared to get my drink.

The doorbell rang and Amber came flying down the stairs yelling, "I'll get it," as if a herd of people were racing to open the door before her.

I rang many bells in my life and no one ever ran to the door yelling, I'll get it.

Who was this guest? A father, brother, girl friend, a rap singer? Of course not. It was her lover. She ran to admit him, fearful if delayed a moment at the door, out of pique he would disappear, never to reappear.

The man, (to call him a boy would subtract at least ten years of age) was a tall, thin black with shoulder length dreadlocks, each braid tipped in gold.

She hugged and kissed him with such intensity I was fearful she'd go down on him right in the foyer. Was there ever a time in my past to receive such uninhibited sexual greeting? If there was such a unique occurrence it escaped my memory.

The recipient of such sexual frenzy was blasé, a statue allowing an adoring groupie to press her breasts against his unresponsive breast. Looking into the living room he asked, "Who's that?" but 'th' requiring too much tongue effort came out 'dat'. The possessive 's' was also omitted in the interest of brevity, so I got 'who dat'.

Dismissively Amber answering, "A detective. He's nothing," then immediately pleaded, "Let's go upstairs."

His, "What's the detective here for?"

The 's' was omitted and the 'th' metamorphosed into 'da', detective came out 'dick'.

Amber had him hard by the hand pulling him to the stairs. Obviously the delights awaiting upstairs were not very unique to him because resisting her, he stared at me. Out of curiosity, fear, or anger was subject to interpretation. With his attention riveted on me Amber had him stumbling over the stair's first step.

Eleanor returned, cut crystal glass showing less amber than Amber did with her cleavage.

If one would expect maternal shock over a prurient daughter dragging a black man up to her room, you'd be disappointed, sad but in today's elevated cultural acceptance, not surprised. Eleanor smiled at the two lovers as if her daughter was clutching Prince Harry as he was lovingly carrying her to the altar.

Peering at me as I watched the foyer tableau, Eleanor introduced the black guy as Amber's boyfriend, Ali Bay Mohammad, as if it was his actual baptismal name, and not Derek. Ali Bay, not particularly pleased with the boyfriend identification, certainly considerably less than Amber's gratification at the boyfriend identification, gave me some hard eye, intending to show I was face to face with a proud black man who's proud he's black and not white. The surface message of her daughter's need, graphically sexually expressed in her daughter's attempts to drag Ali Bay to her bedroom in front of a stranger forced Eleanor to grab Amber by her hand and lead the reluctant twosome into the living room. Once in the living room, standing legs apart, Ali Bay, aka Derek, with hard stare still in place, had Amber holding on to him for dear life; a teen girl clutching a strong man for security.

Eleanor again introduced me as a detective who was poisoned at the banquet.

"Detective," Ali Bay spit out, to show he wasn't a black man to be trifled with. "What you here for?" It was said as if my sole raison d'état was to harass him and if I valued my life, take care, his hard stare was devastating.

Eleanor explained I was telling her about Courtney.

"Wasn't at the banquet," Ali Bay growled, as if anyone asked. "Had to work."

Amber, fearful of her identification as his girlfriend was weakening, jumped in with, "But Ali dearest, you dropped me off and we were going out after the food was served. You had to be there."

"Shut that fat mouth of yours before I close it."

Eleanor protesting said, "Derek, excuse me, Ali, if I thought you meant it I'd forbid Amber to see you. I will not tolerate any physical abuse in my home."

The threat of separation left Ali unfazed but scared Amber into crying out, "Oh mom, he doesn't mean it. He just likes to say stupid things like that."

Wow. Everyone, white and black in the living room realized the gross social faux pas in covertly suggesting a black man may be stupid.

With Amber clutched Ali's arm as if it was gold, Eleanor chastised her daughter explaining how Amber didn't actually mean how it sounded, and the couple should go upstairs and talk.

With my believing it was a true description of Ali, I tossed at him an inquiry as to his job.

"Screw you," was hit back at me.

What I caught was unemployed. No big surprise there.

Eleanor, feeling Ali's employment or lack of, needed to be excused. "Oh Derek, excuse me, Ali, has been looking hard for a job, but times are hard."

What I mentally added, not as hard as to get Ali Bay boy to actually do some work.

Amber, intent on getting Ali Bay into her room, into her bed, and into her, clutching him kept plaintively repeating, "Honey, let's go upstairs."

Eleanor, still fearing stigmatization as a racist from a black, moved to give her blessings to the couple muttering how happy she was with Amber finding such a nice boy for a boyfriend.

Boy! Had to be kidding, and if he had spent half the time in braiding his hair in working, and the money squandered on gold chains, ersatz diamonds in ears, lips, tongue and nose, he could afford an education.

Seeing I was unimpressed with his gold, BS diamonds, and most of all his hard challenging stare, he asked if I had a problem, an oblique reference to his dating a white underage girl.

I felt Ray's pain and he had my fullest sympathy.

My not answering Ali, aka Derek, suggesting I had a problem, both women sensing an angry exchange being a hard stare or a hard word away, quickly moved to defuse the situation with Amber suggesting they go out to dinner. Eleanor taking the clue emphatically seconding the suggestion, pushed both out the door. Hearing the mother whisper to Amber did she had enough money, I easily translated Ali and Amber's financial dynamics.

Eleanor, sitting down, eyeing my empty glass asked if I needed a refill.

Shit, I needed something, but said no to the booze.

Sensing my grasp of her daughter's situation, she defended saying some ignorant racists have difficulty with a white girl dating a black boy. Unfortunately Ray experienced some difficulty with the race thing

What could I say? Disapprove and be cast into the deepest hell reserved for racists, or agree Amber's courageous choice of a partner was made out of pure love. I felt either comment was impolitic and my remaining silent forced Eleanor to fill in the gaps, "We're not racists, we believe everyone is equal and skin color makes no difference." She said that as if it provided impeccable saintly bona fides to being immaculate on race. Strange, those most pure always see and talk about the grievous sin of others of less purity.

My remaining silence forced her to continue, "The most important consideration between two people in a relationship is, do they love each other. Don't you agree?"

The direct question necessitated an answer. "There is compatibility in interest, in background, in education, in values to be considered among many other areas."

Not liking my focusing on things outside love's embrace, maintaining her position, she reiterated love was the most important factor in a relationship.

It's behind the shield of love women find protection from all their foolishness, for all their errors in judgment, for all their lies, sins and crimes. Their universal mea culpa is: I loved too much to change, love blinded me, in love I could choose nothing else, my love manipulated me, my love makes me weak or strong as the situation demands. In a woman's surface world it's romance, love and sex; money is hidden in fiery furnaces beneath the surface.

Given this, against my best interests pursuing her acceptance of her sixteen year old sleeping with a twenty eight year old unemployed black man, I asked when Ali Bay Mohammed changed his name.

"Just recently. He found his true self and adopted a name which better reflects where he's now at."

"Has he legally changed it?"

The question frazzled Eleanor's thought process. "Legally, legally, what do you mean. Of course it's his name. He's Ali now, not Derek."

"Still, is it legally changed?"

"Of course it is. It must be, it's his name. Why would he assume a pseudonym? It makes no sense."

"To us, no. But must make sense to him and to me as a detective, it might be an alias."

"Well if it isn't his real name, Mr. Detective, what is it?"

"Don't know. Was hoping either you or Amber would know it. You should know the name of the man your daughter is dating."

"You shouldn't suggest ridiculous things without proof. We know his name is Ali Bay. He wouldn't lie about his name."

I almost said, yeah, you've got his word for it, however with Eleanor's heels dug in, but with the seed of doubt planted, I moved to another topic dear to a mother's heart, employment. By inquiring what is Ali Bay's profession. Yes I deliberately used 'profession' just to be nasty as well as drive home a point.

"Ali is going to college."

"He's at least twenty eight, a little old for college. Is he going for advanced degrees?" The last was me just being sarcastic and a bit nasty but after all, Eleanor was annoyingly stupid.

"You don't understand. With his deprived background, no father as a role model, stuck in an underfunded educational system, it's perfectly understandable it took time for Ali to mature, and after earning his GED, he entered college with a scholarship."

She pushed scholarship as if it was an award for high academic excellence. I correctly interpreted it to mean he's not paying, I am, and I'm paying because he's black.

Deep in my irritation at the stupid woman, to prick her I asked his major.

"He told Amber he's majoring in Black History and after graduation is planning to work for the betterment of the black community."

Knowing I was sloshing through a lot of crap I couldn't resist opening the sluice gates a little more by continuing, "How long has Ali Bay been going to college?"

The seven years answer didn't surprise me; on a scholarship with a living expense allowance, Ali Bay will be pursuing his education 'til he graduates to social security.

With raised eyebrows I repeated, "Seven years?" followed by "Is he near graduation?" Yeah, I get very nasty sometimes.

"He's going into his sophomore year. You know, with his deprived background you can't expect him to finish college in just four years, even for a bright student like Ali, it's asking too much."

Feeling a comment was unnecessary I remained silent.

Believing I wasn't yet converted she said Ali and Amber were planning to go to Africa to teach children over the coming summer.

Deep down, Eleanor was so needy, charitably I granted her a simple 'that's nice'.

"To help finance their trip Amber is going to get a part time job after school and Ali is hoping for a grant." She said it in the same desperate fervor a modern liberal Anglican on his death bed avers his belief in the Almighty.

My saying of course Ray and you would make up any shortfall brought Courtney to the fore with her complaint how Ray, being shortsighted in not realizing this wonderful once in a lifetime educational opportunity for Amber and how it would look on her university admissions application. "It's all that bitch's fault. She wants to separate Amber and Willie from their father."

"Does Ray like Ali Bay?"

Eleanor struggled with Ray's character portrayal; an accepting liberal father, or a bigoted bastard who divorced his wife. A colorblind Ray finally emerged, a liberal Ray who, ecstatic about Ali, didn't see any difficulties in Amber dating a black man, in fact when Ali's name is brought up Ray is continually surprised anyone could even see Ali's color, never mind mentioning it.

To get back to the business at hand I said, "So Ali Bay was at the banquet."

"Yes, I guess so. Ali is so in love with Amber it's to be expected he'd want to be near her."

"Ray has a considerable life insurance policy with Amber and Willie as beneficiaries."

With money mentioned Eleanor quickly leaving fantasy land landed hard on reality. "Are you suggesting Amber or Ali would poison her father? Detective McCoppin, I think you should leave, and I suspect you're a racist. I'm half inclined to report your racism to your superiors."

Shit, that's all I need, what with Woody convinced I am, and the past reprimand for using the 'n' word in my jacket, it could mean my job.

Hastily standing up and following Eleanor to the front door I kept apologizing for any comments that seemed in bad taste. I even sank so low to mention voting for Obama and giving donations to the NAACP. Damn it, PC cost a man a lot of self respect.

Opening the door, standing on the stoop, we came face to face with the strange woman who was always staring and smiling at me. She was about to ring. "We meet again Mr. McCoppin"

"You're name is?" I asked.

Before she could answer Eleanor whisked her inside. The strangers' only words as the door slammed were, "I'll be seeing you soon."

CHAPTER 26

No Eggs Dropping

A little past eight, exhausted and depressed talking to depressing people about nothing, going nowhere, leading me no nearer to solving the roach murder, I entered my home where a warm drink and my ass to my easy chair made me mentally dumb susceptible to TV's perpetual laugh tracks' ministrations, hopefully chasing the shadows lurking in my mind. My enigmatic greeting from Pam wasn't loving, not even welcoming. Apparently my sin was a sin of omission, of being absent from the house when I was urgently needed. Anxiously Pam explained they were in Mickey's bedroom examining him, and I should have been here supporting son and wife.

"Is he hurt?" were my fearful first words.

"No, physically Mickey is in good health," Pam reassured me.

"Then who the hell is examining him and what is the trouble?"

"Well if you were home you'd know," then inexplicably Pam added, "Had to throw out your dinner."

Before she could add a third sin, in rapid succession I asked: what was going on, who was examining Mickey, what were they examining him for, and why the hell were they upstairs in his bedroom and not here in the living room, and why did you give permission for them to intrude so far into my home. My voice raised to shouting forced Pam to nervously pat the air signaling for a lower volume, explaining in hushed reverential tones employed at wakes that Drs. Paris Start and Lovey Leper were back accompanied by Ms. Harriet Bursome, a child social worker.

Running to the stairs I yelled, "Shit, I want them out right now."

Screaming as if seeing a mouse size cocker roach, Pam pleaded, "Mac, don't go upstairs. You're going to cause trouble. They explicitly requested for you not to interfere."

"Why the hell not. He's my son, this is my house."

"It's your negativity. They feel it will interfere with securing a free exchange with Mickey. He'll pick up on your negativity and not cooperating with their examinations, delaying our son's healing process."

Pushing Pam aside I ran up the stairs with her following close behind, whining about my not doing anything to hurt her child. Irate as I was, the 'her child' registered, fueling my intention to exert control over 'my' child and 'my' home. At that moment for me there wasn't 'my wife.'

Entering the bedroom I saw Mickey sitting on the floor clutching his favorite action hero figure, listening to child care worker Ms. Harriet Bursome, middle weight, at a woman's age where eggs haven't been dropping for at least five years. She was asking Mickey if he ever wet his bed.

The question, freezing the nine year old, shocked me into demanding who the hell was she, what was she doing in my home and in my child's bedroom.

In their world of saving children by virtue of saving children, Harriet, Lovey and Paris, as prosecutors and judges were immune to answering questions. They alone asked the important relevant questions and delivered the final judgment. Any questions critical of them were treated as symptoms of mental disease needing not be answered but in turn to be examined, analyzed and categorized by them against you.

Paris Start, sitting on Mickey's bed next to Lovey Leaper told Ms. Harriet Bursome I was the father. The 'father' was put forth as here comes male ignorant interference which must with fortitude be tolerated. Bending down Lovey whispered something into a mini recorder. Sitting at Mickey's desk, Bursome, if her facial expression was any indication, wrote something disagreeable in a leather spiral notebook. As a seer high on a mount constructed of several college courses, Miss Bursome patiently explained to a pathetic short sighted mole that they were here to ascertain if Mickey needed further psychological help, given the trauma he's experienced and as an addendum she quickly added her services were free.

Ignoring the 'free' tossed at me I reasonably told them my son was perfectly healthy and not needing their help and requested they leave my house.

"Ah, Mr. McCoppin, we can't leave 'til we're sure the child's mental health is satisfactory," came from Paris.

"We're here for the child, to insure he's getting proper care," Bursome pronounced, as if sitting on the Supreme Court delivering the unanimous opinion.

Pam backed her up stating if I couldn't stay quiet and listen to the experts I should leave.

Expecting Pam's support, her traitorous words reignited my Irish. I told her, Bursome's credentials consisting of a few courses in child development and sociology, courses, in the world of curriculum being considered shallow in depth and high in pretentions, attract only the marginally intelligent.

Turning to my enemies I attacked saying I suspected Ms. Bursome was a childless spinster living a mother's life vicariously through other mothers with the surety, thanks to her matriculation in a few college courses, she could raise their children better. If her advice was universally adopted, childhood problems would disappear, forgotten in the joy of a happy future, all thanks to her ministrations.

That got everyone up yelling, "I couldn't say that," though I just did. "Being childless has no relations to child raising qualifications." (As opposed to the experience of being the child's mother.) "I was ignorant, fearful of people better educated," as if policing the city's streets gave no insight into human nature, certainly not as deep as they had gained from their text books. "I was being hurtful," as if truth didn't hurt, and I'm sure I heard the abhorrent label 'sexist' as if there were no sex differences.

Poking a stick into a beehive they fluttered about trying to sting me: with words without facts, with feelings without evidence, with intuition without reality, with learned nostrums from learned authorities who learn from other authorities all without ever leaving the sterile protected campus environment.

I yelled back to them their ad hominine hysteria showed their emptiness. Deliberately using 'ad hominine' I had the satisfaction of hearing shouts of horror, "He's homophobic."

In the confusion, Mickey took the opportunity to escape the bedlam and seeing him scoot away, was proud of him to recognize fools; to flee fools and all their BS was the first critical step in attaining true knowledge. With the subject of their inquisition absent, with difficulty, I was able to sheppard them out of my child's bedroom, but only to have to endure the bleating of threatening bureaucratic retribution: a child was in mortal danger of mental scarring; reports will be written; people of authority will be informed; this is not the end; they will return; a child's life being at stake, they vow to save him.

To sheppard them I had to play the sheep dog, running to keep Paris from going into the master bedroom to look for Mickey, and head off Lovey who was heading for the kitchen.

Paris howling I hit her which quickly evolved into wife abuser accusations. Collecting Lovey and Paris together, I desperately searched for Bursome, fearful she had gone back upstairs. Found her in the downstairs bathroom apparently confused and disappointed in not finding Mickey cowering behind the toilet, wetting himself.

Finally, with a firm push which I'm sure will be in someone's report, I got the herd out and the front door closed. Returning to the kitchen I found Mickey enjoying ice cream with Pam fluttering about, constantly asking if he was alright, was he frightened, did he want to sleep with mommy tonight. Crap, the kid was nine, for heaven's sake. Also, the son sleeping with mother left open the question of where dad will roost. Telling Pam, Mickey was alright, he seconded my diagnosis with a "Yeah mom, I'm okay."

Pam couldn't let it be. It was as if she couldn't let go of the drama, asking Mickey if he was sure he was alright. "Don't let your father influence you." (If not the father, who is to influence the son?) "Is there anything I can do to make you feel better and more secure?"

With all her offers of 'her' ministrations, not 'our' ministrations, not 'mine,' Mickey's father was apparently absent in Pam's mind.

I told her, "The kid's eating ice cream … he's alright. Mickey, when you're finished, go to bed, and Pam, you should air out his bedroom."

After again asking if the nine year old needed to sleep with his mother, after again, in front of Mickey, complaining of my conduct, after again referring to the dinner tossed, she vowed there wouldn't be a replacement dinner.

Good thing I stopped at Carmichael's and apparently by default I'll be allowed to sleep in my own bed. Shit, where are all of these defaults coming from. To reassure Pam I again asked Mickey if he was alright and hopefully his, "Yeah dad, I'm okay," gave relief to Pam.

It didn't. She didn't believe everything was alright. Didn't want to believe, wanted the night's drama to continue, especially when Mickey went up to his bedroom.

Coming downstairs from saying goodnight to my son I sensed the tension as dinner plates were being slammed about. Now I was pissed, and not needing all the tension, and again left without a goodbye.

CHAPTER 27

The Fourth Man
in the Queue

Wanting, possibly needing the comfort and comradeship of Carmichael's as a sign of weakness, I resisted going there and decided to visit Tom Applegate, my son's coach. Could there be a more sinister motive for his bailing out of table 12, other than the desire to connect with his players. With sadness, stupidity and greed all about me, I needed to continue my investigation, to do something, particularly after Mickey's bedroom confrontation. I hoped Applegate could give me a substantial start on my investigation. It would be good to find something firm, a hard fact to point to the 'who' or the 'why' of the roach murder.

Applegate's front door was opened by a teenage boy showing a rainbow tattoo on his forearm, and a ring hanging from his nose to accessorize the large medallion size earrings cut into his earlobes, all creating a quaint faux African look. His dismissive, 'Yeah what do you want," showed a gold tongue ball in case you missed all the prior subtle character messages.

Requesting to see his father I got, "He's not my freaking father," quickly followed by, "he's not here."

Confused as to who was the absent 'he', Applegate or the father, I guessed Applegate was the absent 'he'.

The only thing stopping the door being slammed in my face was a woman yelling, "Pierce, who's there?"

"Some guy looking for Tom."

Pushing aside the Aborigine 'wanna be,' his mother challenged, "Who are you?" quickly followed by "Why do you want to see Tom?"

"Ed McCoppin, I was one of those poisoned at the banquet."

My identification quickly brought a determined, "We're going to sue," as if I wanted to challenge her wisdom in suing. "Sonia Mayor is our lawyer," was stated as an irrefutable fact, as if I wanted to strenuously debate her choice. "She doesn't want us to talk about the poisoning without her present," as if I planned to destroy her lawsuit and rob her of wealth with my conversation.

Wondering how O'Malley missed this family I quickly assured her my purpose was to thank Tom for all he's done coaching the boys.

Her repeating, "He's not here," one couldn't tell if she was glad or sad over the fact.

With satisfaction, the boy behind her said, "Mom, I told you he wanted to see Tom." Such is the petty everyday victories of life's defeated.

My 'when will he be home' brought from the wife a simple uninterested, "Don't know."

The boy, bored, a state I felt he should learn to live with and enjoy, left.

His place was taken by a well developed teen age girl wearing the heavy makeup often seen on fading fifty year old 'has been' actresses pimping on TV for pills, health food, or exercise equipment for a percentage of each sale. Her clothes, tight and revealing, had to be a ten year old's outgrown rejects she picked up at the Salvation Army. In case anyone missed one of the more interesting and endearing physiological attributes, from a bare midriff she exposed her belly button's inserted dangling three inch gold chain. Apparently she felt her umbilicus so noteworthy it needed a white canvas four inches above and four inches below to give it and its gold chain sufficient background. Here is the modern teenage girl, a pre modern woman not easily led being her own person.

I wondered if Tom and her mother were enchanted by the persona son and daughter projected. If they weren't satisfied, why did they permit the teenagers to play the fool? If they were satisfied, what was wrong with the foolish parents?

The mother's and daughter's exchanges concerning my presence consisting of 'who is he?' and 'what does he want?' were made as if I had left.

"Really would like to thank Tom for coaching my son. Will he be returning soon?" I asked again.

Trying to look the cheap tart and being successful, the daughter dismissively told me, "Tom is at some bar."

The wife, feeling 'bar' was demeaning either to herself or Tom, added, "He's at a tavern, Carmichael's Tavern," as if, except for the prices there was a real difference.

Having an unexpected fortuitous excuse to visit my restful oasis, I quickly left, escaping having the door slammed in my face.

He was sitting at the far end of the horseshoe bar, a beer before him.

Approaching I gave him a, "Hi Tom."

Looking at me, staring, he focused, did a memory search and didn't recognize me.

To help him out I said Mickey McCoppin was my son.

It didn't help as he mumbled, Mickey McCoppin?

My mentioning he played tackle offense/defense, and with the aid of a beer sip he eventually registered me and looked quizzically at me, possibly fearing an attack on his handling of the team and my son.

I attacked his reticence with, "The name is Mac and I want to congratulate you and thank you for all the work you put in coaching the team. Can I join you? Let me get you a refill."

Cautiously, waving his hand he granted me the adjacent stool, followed by a more vigorous wave to the bartender.

I took a whiskey highball; Applegate had a shot with a beer chaser. Hadn't noticed the shot glass. Boilermaker! Obviously I'm sitting next to a serious drinker and recognition of that fact it made me comfortable with Tom Applegate.

At the bar he looked different. Coaching the kids he was always in ratty old jeans, with a denim shirt just as ragged and an incongruous conspicuous straw cowboy hat with a red feather in the hat band; the epitome of a weirdo. Now eyeing him through the bar mirror, in a suit, dress shirt, tieless, instead of the football weirdo I was drinking with a compatriot and felt a growing friendship. He was tall, thin, hair showing white, a nine at night beard stubble, a red veined nose I now discounted as being a wound earned coaching boys in cold windy autumn weather. You could guess mid forties; the mention of fifty wouldn't be a total surprise, however, saying under forty would be out of place.

To get things off to an amicable start I told him my son and I appreciated his coaching the team. My verbally extending a hand in friendship got a shrug accompanied by a beer sip. I waited and it took a good ten seconds for him to recognize to respond to my overture saying, 'thanks' followed by complaining how hard a job it was coaching a Pop Warner football team.

Fearful I didn't recognize the travails it entailed, he directly told the mirror he faced and obliquely me, the hours spent weekday nights running practices, the numerous league meetings for coaches, the aggravation of fund raising, and the reward, boys that wouldn't listen, a team that lost, and parents losing control, berating him even to threatening physical violence.

"Say," he asked, "were you one of the parents who signed that guy Scott's petition against me?"

Since I was one of the signers, politically I ignored the question, answering it with a non sequitur how I was totally shocked at the violence against him. With a tone of disbelief of such conduct I asked who could be so outrageous to threaten a coach.

"Don't like to say."

"Was it Jim Scott, the guy with the petition?"

"Actually he was alright, apologized for initiating the petition. Felt it was something he should do for his son, feeling the kid wasn't being treated right. Of course, he was totally wrong. The kid was a blob of fat who still couldn't fill the holes in the line. Scott was nice about it and I felt the wife and Zapp instigated him to organize the petition. Still, the petition was absolutely wrong and very hurtful."

Hoisting the shot glass, throwing it down his throat, slamming the glass hard on the bar, then taking a relieving beer sip, he complained, "That bastard Tony Geroni, the guy was totally out of control at the games, hysterical. You heard his language. And then the guy didn't even show up for his kid's banquet. Would like to see him try to coach his kid's team. Hell, NFL coaches don't have half the pressure or the aggravation midget football coaches endure."

Turning to me for the first time he asked if he could buy a round.

My highball being shallow, I quickly cleaned up the shallows telling him, "Yeah, thanks," and in the interlude while out drinks were being constructed and laid before us, I said, "Geroni wasn't the only 'no show' at table 12."

"I heard," Applegate said, "that character, Zapp, Scott's friend, bailed from the poison table. If you ask me he's one strange guy, cheering for Scott's kid more than his own. Don't know what's going on with that."

Suspecting I knew, I asked Tom if anyone was aware of his intentions of leaving table 12 to eat with the kids.

Eyeing the whiskey level, to be assured the level was even with the shot glass rim, he complained, "Whoever set up the seating arrangement had to be an idiot leaving those boys sit and eat by themselves. There'd be an Animal House food fight before dessert was served. Besides, they were my boys, at least for the season, and I wanted to be with them for the last team meeting".

"Yeah, understand," I gave him. Giving a good tug at my drink I continued, "So no one knew you were going to change your table."

"Don't think so. All along I thought I'd be sitting with the boys. With the mothers arranging everything I was dumbfounded to see I wasn't. Anyway just took my seat at the center of the team's head table."

"Your wife, your kids didn't know before hand?"

"No," then turning to me said, "don't get me started on them." After that warning he started on them. "You know, people think I'm my wife's second husband and know the older kids aren't mine. But let me tell you," and shouting he told me, "the older boy and girl are shits. Got hope for the little kid." He emphatically slammed the bar as if I was going to argue the point and he'd have to get physical. "Have nothing to do with the little shits but support them and get no respect in return."

"Their father doesn't support them?" I naively asked.

"Three different fathers ... all are bastards, even the youngest. Both kids and their fathers. Haven't seen nor gotten a dime from Robin's past boyfriends. If I was actually their father I'd slap the snotty attitude out of them before you could say 'slap them again.'"

"What about Matt? I thought he was your son?"

"No. Matt's father is the one Robin seldom talks about. The first two, she constantly evokes words like 'no good' 'drunk' deadbeat' 'loser' but the youngest kid's father isn't mentioned, not even to be cursed. Makes you think. Anyway, trying my best with him, but given all the chaos going on in the home, don't know if I can make a difference. If you're not the biological father, if the kid's father is there, but is invisible, living in the past, still always present, mystically without speaking able to contradict, to deny your authority, it's hard to assume his role."

In sympathy we sipped.

"You know, just between us I never married Robin. Tried to sell me a bill of goods." In memory of the sale's pitch he downed half a beer, then cutting the shot glass in half continued, "Told me, married the first guy in her teens, didn't know what she was doing, thinking she was in love. Both being too young for marriage, she found him cheating several times. Could she stay with a cheating husband?"

"Certainly not," I said sensing he needed a little certitude at the moment.

Turning away from the shot and towards me he pleaded, "You can understand my believing her about the first one." He didn't wait for the compulsory drinker's agreement before continuing, "She said the second marriage was a rebound romance, her search for stability and security for her and her child after the first deserted her.

"Doesn't that sound plausible? You see it on TV a thousand times. You know, after a disastrous teenage marriage the girl, older, wiser falls in love with a guy who says he cares about her and promises to take care of her and her child.

"Shit!" he suddenly exclaimed, "we need another round."

Finishing his beer, Tom raised the empty up then down to the bartender, as if blessing him. With Tom's attention on sanctifying the bartender I didn't need to give my agreement or express my thoughts. He was one pathetic needy guy.

Cold beer in hand, eye on the shot, Tom continued his ruminations mostly to himself, a soliloquy I suspected he's held numerous times. "To tell the truth I believed it when she said the second often abused her, often in front of the children. Well, er, yeah ..."

"Mac," I prompted.

"Yeah Mac. She couldn't stay married to a wife beater, now could she? You see it a thousand times on TV, in movies and on talk shows."

As I said, "Certainly not," Tom bowed down to the rim filled shot glass to carefully sip and lower the whiskey level.

I thought, was the guy a lush? Still he was drinking in my bar, fitted in with the guys drinking at my bar, and feeling comfortable talking with him' what did it all say about me?

Reassuring myself, I may be among them but am not one of them, Tom continued to husband three. "Escaping the wife beater, needing stability in her life and more importantly in Pierce's and Myanmar's lives."

"Myanmar!" I repeated as if not hearing him right.

"Yeah, the daughter originally had the cute name of Burma, but when Robin found out about the country's name change she officially changed it to Myanmar. Stupid."

"Yeah, sounds stupid."

"Anyway, she got rid of wife beater number two and married number three, an elderly gentleman who she believed would take care of her and her children and give her love, security, a sense of being a worthwhile woman, a whole woman, an independent woman, a free of manipulation woman, you see it on TV a thousand times."

"Whole woman!" I commented.

"Look, it's what she said. Didn't understand it but at the time it sounded reasonable. Of course, you've got to know we were at the most intimate stage in our relationship, so everything from her lips sounded gospel, before bed, in bed and out of bed. You can understand that."

Halving my highball I commiserated, "Been there, done that, heard that, regretted that."

"Well, er –"

"Mac."

"Well Mac she told me about husband three, an old guy, maybe not so old, she had her youngest with him. After they were married he wanted her to do degenerate disgusting sexual things in the bedroom, even wanting her to consent to threesomes. His being absolutely sexually corrupt, she had to leave him. His sexual demands were so horrific there was no way she could stay married to him and keep her sanity, and there was the danger to Myanmar. According to Robin, his perversions and depravity extended to underage girls. You see it on TV a thousand times,"

He took a beer sip before continuing, "Tell me, er ... Mac, what could she do but leave him. Anyway, I swallowed husband one, husband two, and even husband three, but I have to admit the third was a hard swallow, still, seeing it on TV a thousand times, and –"

Suddenly, looking at my half empty glass, he asked if I was alright.

Saying yes, finishing my drink, I did the up/down ritual in sanctifying the bartender. The way we were going, sainthood was a surety for him, don't know about us.

"Now, er, it's Mac, right?"

"Right."

"Now Mac, here's the kicker. I'm number four in the bedroom sequence, and she wants me to marry her and officially adopt the kids. If you saw the oldest two you would understand, no way in heaven or hell would I adopt them. As for the youngest ... maybe. Anyway, to get out of the adoption talk and still look good, I told her if I adopted them they'll lose any chance of child support they'll never get from her past husbands.

"That's when, in the bedroom, wearing a hot pink teddy, falling on her knees sobbing, tears falling in such profusion they converted her pink teddy into a wet tee shirt, she clutched me as if I was the only one standing between her and a black bottomless pit. Dragging me into bed she slowly dropped the story on me. Apparently her first marriage was a very romantic affair done in a friend's finished cellar game room. With drinks and scented candles they exchanged vows of eternal love witnessed by good friends. In her innocence, in her youth she felt by exchanging vows among friends created a true lasting marriage, a deep spiritual bond stronger than the old fashioned paper kind. When I told her 'you believed that shit' she cried on my shoulder. She was so young ... she had no one to advise her and she had seen it on TV hundreds of times. Anyway, the net result, kid one was a bastard, father long gone."

Tom continued his lamentations, "After a couple of ear blows and ear cleaning kisses which with marriage and adoption in bed with us were wasted on me. She went to husband two, the abuser. Apparently according to her, with a child, being alone, having no one, husband number two was a master manipulator. She was unable to resist his cunning, his strength, as he forced her to marry him. Before she knew it they were on a beach in Jamaica exchanging vows of eternal love before Johnny Walker, the resort's Event Director. Number two had brainwashed her into believing, in Jamaica, Event Directors could perform legal marriages. She was totally destroyed when finally finding the strength to escape his manipulation and overcoming her fear of physical abuse, leaving him she found the romantic beach wedding wasn't official. Actually the Event Director was some unemployed bum her husband met at the bar, who did the marriage for a bottle of Johnny Walker.

"At the end of the second husband's recital, she got more intense, groping my privates along with tongue cleaning my ear better than a Q-tip. Again, it did nothing for me as I was still on the beach with number two and Johnny Walker, the Event Director.

"I asked Robin about husband three, the old sexual pervert. Certainly out of three one marriage would be legit.

"Mac, throwing a foot over me, she confessed number three promised marriage, vowed to marry her, would absolutely marry her once his divorce was final, once he was free they'd marry. He and she would move to Hollywood so he could sell his TV scripts in person rather than having to go through an agent.

"He told her he wrote scripts for *Sex in the City* and *Two and a Half Men*, and to prove it they watched several episodes of the shows. As the credits rolled he pointed out all the pseudonyms he used. He couldn't use his name because if it became too well known he'd be pestered by 'would be' no talent writers wanting him to read their scripts. He said he'd love to help talented new writers but he was too busy writing new scripts.

"With her children needing a father figure, and he being so successful, he'd be able to give them the needed financial stability. So when pregnant with Matthew, Robin pressed him for a commitment to at least leave his wife and move in with her, she was surprised to find out he was already divorced and it was his second divorce. There were four children he didn't support, and no TV scripts. He worked part time as a roofer. She thought his great tan was from trips to and from LA. All their bizarre sex with others and his videoing them wasn't his attempt to get her into films. It was his attempt to use her to get himself into the porn business.

"Ed, it's Ed ..."

"No, still Mac."

"Between licking my lips, with both legs now tossed over me, hands industriously working to purpose, she told me if per chance I saw her films with number three and some other people on the Internet or on some video rental I must believe it was made when she was drunk and disoriented by some drug substance given to her to make her unaware of the other people in bed with her, or even that a video was being made. Unconscious she woke up to be horrified at all the cameras, lights, and people standing around. It was a date rape."

With a sigh Tom confessed he didn't believe her, even though he had seen it on TV a thousand times.

"So all the kids are bastards," I commented.

"Hey, PC, not bastards, fatherless. Anyway, I was sold a bill of goods, shoddy, dirty goods, and here I am. Did I tell you about the STDs number three gave her and passed them on to me?" He didn't wait for an answer asking if I was alright drink wise.

Didn't get a chance to say yea or nay. With concern for my spiritual well being, he again blessed the bartender.

"So you haven't adopted the kids."

"No way. I'm not going to be financially responsible for the little bastards, er, excuse me, fatherless children."

We both sipped and smirked at the 'fatherless.'

Then I asked if he planned to marry Robin.

"Don't know, haven't decided, but being number four it's unlikely. Our living together is a farce and sex is now a problem. It's hard to enjoy it knowing you're the fourth in the queue. Hell, fourth, shit the damn queue could run around the block several times for all I know. Being in bed with a battalion of ghosts certainly makes her 'it's special' one stupid joke."

"The longer you stay with her the greater the support claim. Letting her and the kids stay in your house, the more difficult it will be to get them out."

"There is that," he admitted.

"Is there a lot of life insurance?" I asked feeling after the boilermakers he wouldn't take offense at any personal bluntness.

"Well, there's the City policy for a couple of hundred thousand. You know I'm a Senior Clerk at Building Permits. However my bank accounts are in my name. Robin has been bugging me about us becoming closer through joint accounts, joint credit cards and checking accounts. For some reason I've been reluctant. Could be her bedroom confession. Probably had the best sex that night. She brought her 'A' game to bed. It's the sequences that are piss poor."

"Does she know you're contemplating tossing her out?"

"Well … a few weeks ago I did tell her she and her kids could go to hell for all I care, but that was in anger. Didn't mean it."

"You didn't mean it?"

"Hell, yes I did mean it, say let's have a last one. I've got to go home to Robin, Pierce, Myanmar, and poor young Matt.." He said it as if he had to go to a homeless shelter.

I said, "Yeah, I've also got to get home ." Was feeling sorry for the bastard living in a house of bastards, when I realized, currently my home was not all that welcoming.

Just to be nasty I told him, "You know, if you were poisoned Robin may think she'd collect double and she'd probably be able to get at her hands on your bank and IRA accounts through common law marriage."

"Really! Shit, yes. Maybe it was lucky I switched tables. What do you think?"

"Could you see Robin or her two oldest kids poisoning you, particularly if they felt money, not marriage was in the air?"

He said no, but I'm sure he thought yes, yes his ass was in danger, and he'd better be careful, get rid of her and in safety, being her ex number four, pity her number five.

CHAPTER 28

He's Coming

Came home to a dead, dark, silent house. Mickey was asleep, and since it was nearing eleven, Pam was in bed, quiet. From interviewing Applegate at Carmichael's, carrying a considerable buzz, I made for the kitchen for what I couldn't say except I didn't want to face Pam in bed, knowing my greeting would be at best problematic, certainly not loving. In the kitchen, feeling the emptiness made starker by the cleanliness, all surfaces stripped of any miscellany, no odd cup or plate, no cake in sight creating a warm homey feeling, searching to find some warmth I decided on coffee and a piece of toast. Hell, the remembrance of Carmichael's with its colored neon's gaily welcoming you, different shaped and color liquor bottles smiling at you, the noise, the conversation, the fellowship all served to underline the soullessness of the kitchen.

Alone, making coffee and toast brought home how alone you stand in life, and in such a stance is frightening as death. Didn't need the toast, but to sit in a silent house, all rooms dark save the florescent kitchen light with a single cup of coffee was unforgivingly depressing. The coffee needed a companion.

I spotted a note next to the sink, short of words, terse of sentences, brief of length, all reinforcing my kitchen isolation. Pam wrote Woody dropped by and I needed to call him at once. The measure of my deep sense of loneliness can be measured by my calling him, if only to distract a mind desperately not wanting to be alone.

He answered right away telling me he was in his Jag driving to a meeting with the mayor's task force. Before he went into what else he was doing, going to do, had done, I quietly steered the conversation from him to us asking what was his urgent message.

"Wait a minute Mac, I'm picking up Ronni at the Federal, State, City Coordinating Committee where she's an assistant chair woman for some ad hoc committee."

"Woody, what do you want to talk to me about?"

"Over here Ronni," and conversation ceased as he waited for her to climb into his Jag while informing her, "I've got Mac on the line."

Ronni ordered, "Make it short Woody. I've got some fantastic information."

"What information," I yelled into the phone.

"Should Mac hear it," Woody asked more as a fact than a question.

"Woody, why did you call me?"

"That can wait. I've got to find out what Ronni's got."

"Woody, turn off your dam cell," came from Ronni, the last words heard as dark silence came out of my phone.

Mumbling 'shit,' I went to my liquor cabinet for a couple of fingers to massage away my annoyance. Half my annoyance was my evaluation that their information was totally nonsensical at worse, trivial at best, and I'd waste time listening to their mindless blather. The annoyed other half was because sometimes they have information important to me. The last half consisted of being an outsider, an inferior who will be told or not, will be told just enough and not anymore, and told in an annoying manner as they, between themselves decide what to tell and not tell me.

I had bitten one of the fingers off when the phone rang. Pride said forget it. Let them ride to nowhere in the Jag. I'm not going to let them play me. Damn it, there was self respect to consider.

Self respect stood strong 'til the sixth ring, then I answered. "Yes Woody."

"Shit Mac, you're in hot shit."

With that opening a man with respect would hang up after replying 'screw you.' Having lost self respect at the sixth ring I demanded clarification.

My demanding placed me in a power position, forcing Woody to maintain his domination by indirectly refusing my demand and changing the subject.

"First Mac, let me tell you, he's coming."

"Who?"

"Who? You ask who? It's the Vice President. Do you realize what that could mean?"

"It means the Vice President is coming."

"No, don't be so dense," Ronni yelled into Woody's phone.

"Damn it Ronni, let me explain. After all it's my phone."

"Explain it then, you talk too much, to no real purpose, and watch the road," Ronni complained.

Woody proceeded to explain, teacher to special ed student. "Mac, they say it's the Vice President, to justify making security arrangements robust. Now who does the Vice President stand in for?"

I didn't deign to answer, so after a few moments of dead silence an exasperated Woody shouted, "It's not really the Vice President. The word is the President himself will be coming to the Memorial. Mac, it's the President himself."

In an emotional outburst Ronni shouted, "Can you just imagine, the President himself is coming."

Couldn't care less. Didn't vote for him, didn't respect him, and he doesn't care for people like me. My opinion, if you're not white he cares. If you're white, screw you.

I proceeded to tell them, "Hell, you two are like overage groupies, ecstatic over seeing a ninety year old no voice rapper singing no talent songs made hits through advertising. Now, is that all"" Finishing the last finger I was ready to hang up.

"Woody, watch your driving," Ronni cautioned.

Woody, sounding wounded by my lack of appropriate jubilation at his coming said he was only calling up to tell me the Memorial Celebration will be held day after tomorrow because it's the best time for Him.

Sarcastically I asked if he was sure He was coming, actually in person.

Blind to the sarcasm Woody shouted, "Certainly he's coming, to make an important speech to reassure a troubled public."

Ronni yelled at me, "The theme of the Memorial Celebration is America, Yes We Can."

It was probably one of the fingers that made me do it. I had to ask, "Can do what?"

Again, missing the sarcastic message Woody explained, "We can overcome this tragedy and learning from it grow even stronger."

Ronni, being more perceptive complained, "Mac, your attitude is not very helpful in this time of national crisis."

Woody explained, "Would the President be coming if the situation wasn't a national crisis? We need him to calm a troubled people."

While Ronni and Woody were busy educating me and reassuring themselves they had the truth, I took a walk to the bottle, still having six fingers left. I took two from it. Swirling the fingers around the glass I asked, "Is that all?"

Woody wouldn't let me get off the phone, telling me the Memorial will start at eleven and I had to be there in uniform, with Pam and Mickey, at least three hours earlier, so everyone will be in position when He comes and the cameras are running.

"Shit, three hours? You can't be serious. I'm not standing around for three hours so I can spend three more hours listening to Him and his BS."

An offended Woody told me to show respect for Him and his office. Ronni explained the three hours were necessary for the stage arrangement committee, one of the more important sub committees of the Memorial planning committee to complete their arrangements. Also the time was needed for both the Floral and Flag sub committees to complete their preparations.

Woody added, "Yeah Mac, you think this inspirational Memorial celebration just happens. Hell, it takes a lot of planning, a lot of money and the work of many dedicated people to make it a success."

To justify the effort mentioned, Ronni said, "Well, with Him there, all the TV media cameras will be there." She continued, "The Apparel subcommittee, after a turbulent all night struggle has announced the boys will wear their uniform shirts, no shoulder pads, blue pants and white socks and sneakers. The girls will wear their complete cheerleader outfits."

Breaking into Ronni's speech, Woody vowed it will look absolutely fabulous, especially when the girls deliver cheers not only for the departed but in cheering America on.

Having lost most of my self respect at the sixth ring, respect the fingers couldn't resuscitate, I promised to attend at the time ordered dressed as required with Pam and Mickey in tow.

They couldn't let go of being excited, repetitiously shouting, "Can you believe it's going to be on TV. It's to be carried live, it's to be seen by billions the world over."

Suddenly Ronni screamed, "Damn it Woody, watch where you're going. You almost hit that car."

"Shit Ronni, I know how to drive. We weren't even close to that car and it was drifting over to us."

Before being forced to be an audio witness to their shouting complaints at each other or even worse Woody driving his Jag up a tree, hoping to end Woody and Ronni's orgasms over Him coming, and clean my glass of its last finger, out of politeness I foolishly asked if there was anything else before hanging up on them.

"Shit, yes," Woody said, as Ronni shouted her urgent demands he let her drive.

"Shit, no," Woody yelled. I deduced it was at Ronni as he began telling me, with all the sorrow friends express while relishing your trouble as they are going to tell you all about it. Usually they can barely hide their joy. Knew he was smiling when he said, "Mac, hate to tell you, but you're in deep trouble with headquarters."

Screaming Ronni was heard, "Either you let me drive or let me tell him about it. You can't do both. Oh my gosh, look out, you just went through a red light."

Not answering her, Ronni started to tell me but stopped and said, "As my partner and good friend of the family, it was best I hear about it from Woody."

Knowing when best friends out of kindness want to be the first to tell you, you can guess the lab tests came back malignant. I sidled over to my liquor expecting I'll need a helping hand, if gauging the seriousness of the bad news was measured by their eagerness to share.

"Ronni, get your damn hand off the steering wheel. You'll get us killed."

"If you don't stop you're going to have an accident. Stop being a fool and let me drive."

I asked, "Woody, I'm tired. I'm just going to bed. Can this news wait 'til tomorrow?"

"You've got to know," Woody yelled over Ronni's screaming.

Taking a single spiritual thumb I asked what was the difficulty.

"Charges have been leveled against you," came from Woody.

Ronni was able to shout, "Mac, serious charges."

Asking, "What charges?" I sucked my thumb dry.

Ronni yelled into Woody's cell phone, "Mac, you're charged with ... watch out Woody, you almost leveled that kid on the bike."

"How can I drive with you shouting in my ear. The damn kid was too far into the road; should stop and give him a citation for irresponsible riding."

Ronni criticized, "Yes, stop. You don't know how to drive. Let me."

"Look, this is a Jag, a high performance car needing an experienced driver, not some hysterical woman."

Interrupting Ronni's screams accusing Woody of sexism, I asked Woody what was the problem headquarters had with me. Didn't feel particularly threatened, so I felt only a pinky was now needed to follow the thumb.

"Homophobic," shouted Woody.

"Gay basher," Ronni put in, in case the problem wasn't sufficiently delineated.

Where did this come from I asked pinky, Not answering I sent him away and poured the bottle's remaining fingers. "Who's accusing me of homophobia? I may not be a homophile like the rest of you because I don't fear homos."

I stopped there. The thumb and pinky almost had me confessing that the mental picture of two men engaged in sodomy was nauseating.

Ronni informed me, "Both Drs. Start and Leeper heard you use homosexual in a disrespectful manner."

Woody instructed me, you can insult anyone, any institution, belief, custom, if it's white, male and Western European. All deviations from that norm must always be spoken of with respect and reverence. It's how we progressives evolved into diversity.

As was her proclivity, Ronni corrected Woody. "The exception is children. They're sacred and Mac, a Miss Burnsome has reported you for child abuse."

Shit. I've got to have another bottle around here. Thinking maybe some cooking wine was about, indicated how these serious charges shocked my system. My privates ran up to my throat, my solar plexus registered a seismic seven. "Where is this coming from?"

"Burnsome has made a report to Child Welfare and you'll have to answer to them," Ronni continued.

Woody jumped in, "Yeah, you'll have to prove you're a fit father."

"What possibly could be the charges of being an unfit father?"

"Ronni, let me explain this to Mac and stop your back seat driving. Mac, the first charge is you refused child welfare investigators Start, Leeper and Burnsome to interview Mickey so they can assess any psychological damage due to the roach murder. They're sure your kid has suffered serious mental trauma needing to be identified and treated."

"Screw them," I shouted, as I discovered a bottle of cooking sherry. It was lady fingers but damn it I need help.

Ronni took me up on my "Screw them," scolding me, saying they only have the child's welfare at heart and once you pass their investigation you can continue being Mickey's father.

Woody solemnly informed me these were professional doctors, learned experts in child raising, and I should respect them, listen to them and follow their advice.

"They're idiots, experts only in digesting words of other like minded idiots," I argued. "Education doesn't translate to real knowledge. In fact, it's an impediment. If you wish to find the really gullible, go to a university's dorm. The more prestigious, the more gullible the inhabitants."

Ronni criticized me as talking foolishness.

My stomach turned macho, rejecting the lady fingers. I argued, "State college students are dumb, but at Ivy League and Seven Sisters is where they not only live in the Land of Oz, but being true believers in Oz, swear outside Oz live not only the benighted but, is filled with the East and West witches frightening the inhabitants of Oz."

Woody accused me of sounding drunk.

Ronni reminded me how serious the charges were. "You'll have to report to the Department of Sensitivity tomorrow at one to answer the charges."

Woody warned if I didn't answer the charges I couldn't participate in the Memorial Celebration.

"You and Pam could lose custody of Mickey," was Ronni's message as I hung up and emptied the wine into the sink. Damn lousy girly mouthwash.

CHAPTER 29

Lying to Health

Next day, at 1 o'clock on the dot, I sat like an errant child on a bench in front of Sensitivity and Diversity Department's offices referred by all outside the department as SAD. In my pressed uniform, miscellaneous ribbons bouncing on one breast, my badge shining to a glare on the other, shaved twice over, and despite four aspirins still suffering from yesterday's booze, I suspected it was the cooking wine; you can't drink that girly shit with the hard stuff.

With no one else here I deduced lunch 'hour' did not apply to city employees. At twenty past, the secretaries and lower functionaries arrived allowing me into a wooden reception area chair enabling me to be a spectator to watch the comings and goings: small talk, touching up of make-up, sipping of soda cans, 'til the second bureaucratic tier arrived at one thirty. The junior executives flowed deeper into SAD's office complex dragging me with them. Now seated in an upholstered chair, feet resting on a plush rug, I watched them watch me. My stare disturbed no one. Their stares were unnerving me.

Finally a minute before two, so no one could accuse them of enjoying a two hour lunch, three masters of the universe, in pressed uniforms festooned with brass medals and ribbons entered. Observing their prevailing good humor and sleek looks, their lunch must have been bountiful, leisurely and enjoyable. None glanced at me as the triumvirate quickly entered SAD's sanctum sanctorum conference room. Silence came from the holy of holies for at least another twenty minutes. Charitably they were engaged in such topics as war or peace, life or death, the salvation of mankind. More likely they were settling their asses in chairs, commenting about the roast beef's preparation, or on the freshness of the lobster salad, or the wine's temperature.

At 2:17, I was allowed into the conference room to find the three facing me across a polished walnut interview table the length of a Vegas Casino's check-in desk. As I stood looking down at the seated triumvirate, they gave me the looks judgment pedophiles can expect on the last day.

Politically incorrect, Commander Hillary, a steel gray, short haired, mid forties female sat on the left.

To make up for the sex slight, a black was firmly ensconced in the middle, shiny bald, no Afro here, (but then does anyone know where all the Afros went,) with an expansive waist saying his lunches were bountiful as well as delicious. His name plate announced he was a commander.

The white guy on the right, his nose deep in papers spread out in front of him, had passed through his twenties with thirty five coming up fast in his rear view mirror. A believer in politically correct doctrine, white guy was driving in the fast track, passing me as if I wasn't moving, then again, was I really moving or just shuffling my feet.

The black, indicating a single paper, pushed it with his finger tip towards me as if it was contaminated, saying, "Detective McCoppin, serious charges are brought against you," saying it in a great sounding deep baritone he could use doing voice overs on TV. He gave me a few moments to digest his statement, as if my stomach, after last night, needed or wanted anything in it.

After I spent a few moments giving the paper a bleary eyed stare, reading nothing, comprehending nothing, seeing nothing, sliding it back to him I gave him a yes, to get them started. The fast track white informing me I was accused of being a homophobic and using hate speech.

"In front of your child," Steel Gray added, glad to be able to pile it on.

"What is your defense?" the deep black baritone in the middle gave out from his diaphragm. "Now, before you say anything let me inform you, those bringing these horrific charges against you are highly respected."

"Learned," the upward mobile white inserted.

An annoyed at being last to put in her penny thought, Steel Gray continued, "We cannot reveal who has charged you, but needless to say they must have sound evidence to support their charges."

While I was trying to swallow her last heavy chestnut, Whitey went to specifics, "Detective McCoppin, the first charge is that you have hate in your heart against homosexuals."

Deep Baritone added, "And you gave expressions of your hate aloud."

Always last, Steel Gray ended with, "You're teaching your son to hate, hate homosexuals, and probably to hate people of color, and all people who are different from you. You are accused of teaching hate to your son." With vicious vehemence she snarled, "By perpetuating your hate, your child is in danger of acquiring your attitudes of hate that will stay with him a lifetime. Don't you feel ashamed and guilty of such reprehensible conduct against your son?"

Black Baritone, going for the brass ring in this carnival merry-go-round, told me, "If a person is a homophobic, he's a hater and most surely will also be a racist. Tell this panel, did you ever say the 'n' word?" (Like he didn't know I said it, from my file.)

Steel Gray asked if I ever used the 'n' word in front of my son.

Fast track Whitey adding, "Tell us if you ever thought of the 'n' word," before summing up, "A person who hates one group will hate all groups. It's a sign of ignorance. We're here to stamp out ignorance and educate the ignorant to the bright new world of sensitivity, diversity and acceptance."

"Amen to that," came from Baritone.

While they spoke I had the feeling of participating in a Salem witch trial and the righteous three preachers were placing tinder under my feet.

Steel Gray asked what my feelings would be of her if she told me she was a lesbian, would I hate her for her sexual preference.

Crap, thinking, *if she told me, I wouldn't be surprised and currently couldn't think any lower of her,* before saying, "I've only the highest respect for you and your position in the Sensitivity and Diversity Department."

There went my self respect again. To hold on to a paycheck I continually sell myself as often as a twenty dollar hooker and accomplish and give less gratification.

Believing she was special, hearing my soul destroying statement, Steel Gray liked my saying it, just didn't believe I believed it, despite her belief everyone believed and should believe what she believed. I believe I was getting nauseous.

Getting bored with verbally beating me up, Whitey finally gave me my opening, asking how I could defend myself against such charges, repeating they were initiated by learned independent highly respected professionals whose words were beyond impeachment.

Seeing how things stood, I dropped as futile my initial plan of denying all charges by giving them the reasonable explanation of how my ad hominen comment was understandably misunderstood. I had planned to defend myself with earnest smiles embedded in a sincere face while maintaining I welcomed the child psychiatrist's intrusion only believed the boy's small bedroom was not the most appropriate place for interviewing the little lad.

Unfortunately their preliminary harsh comments, suggesting my ass had been basted and needed only to be sliced for it to be served to the PC crowd, any calm rational discussion among these irrationals would avail me of nothing. Looking at the sensitive and diverse three hanging judges, in their eyes I saw my pension, seniority and job swirling around the SAD toilet bowl about to be flushed down the sewer.

When cornered and desperate, some fools believing there is a basis for rational discourse, logically argue their defense up to the knife falling on their neck; some believe by acquiescence, by giving numerous mea cuppas, by crass crawling hope to escape as if the pretense of penance fostered by fear of imminent punishment can still the blade's fall. Some desperately plead for mercy expecting none and getting none. Some, inspired by latent genius agitated to life by desperation, rescue themselves by a bold stroke, as I did.

To their expected faces waiting for what would be my pitiful explanation, my plea for forgiveness, my begging for mercy before my death sentence is delivered, I quietly whispered, "Lady and gentlemen, I've got a secret, a shameful one I really can't confess. It's too painful to speak of it aloud."

In unison they sat up straight hoping to hear something to excite their interest, to justify their bedrock hate of people thinking differently from themselves, a juicy morsel of PC sin to titillate them and reassure them, their belief world is filled with hate and only they, out of deep love, compassion and wisdom, are able to crush the life out of those sinners convicted of being PC haters. Abject confessions of mortal sins against the PC commandments wouldn't save me but will make the SAD happy. To fight against bias and discrimination and hate there necessarily must exist bias, hate and discrimination which can only exist in people, so they firmly need to believe outside their world, bias, hate and discrimination run riot in mankind's soul.

"What is it?" Steel Gray coached. "Is it something to do with my suggesting I may be a lesbian, though of course I'm not saying I am? Do you feel threatened by a strong woman?"

Black Baritone told me, "What happens in the Sensitivity and Diversity Department's hearings never leaves the conference room."

Fast track Whitey, encouraging me to be painfully truthful maintained having heard all man's insensitive depravity to fellow man, there was nothing I could confess that would shock the heads of the Sensitivity and Diversity Department.

Finally, almost as a choir, they whispered an encouraging expective, "Well,"

Where it came from I couldn't say, as I heard it for the first time as they did when I said, "I'm gay."

Three mouths dropped; Steel Gray's mouth had falsies, Black Baritone had some serious teeth gold, Whitey had an orthodontic constructed masterpiece. I kept my mouth shut fearing a stomach trying to come to grips with last night's cooking sherry would toss it across the shiny walnut table.

"Yes," I told them, "standing here, listening to the Committee and your courageous acceptance of diversity, I feel confident to finally say aloud for the first time, I'm gay."

"Gay!" gasped Blackey.

"You're not," gasped Whitey.

"You can't say that," Steel Gray challenged.

Surprised at my inspiration and enjoying myself I continued, "Want to thank the Sensitivity and Diversity Department for giving me the courage to finally say it. Damn it, I'm coming out of the closet, and now feel so liberated."

Looking at their puzzled faces as the trio tried to come to grips with my bold brilliant counter ploy, I complimented myself giving myself mental high fives for my stroke of genius.

The group struggled to absorb this new idea. My ousting their previous preconceived position of an enjoyable self satisfying need to punish a stereo typical homophobic cop caused the trio to lean forward.

Still puzzled, Whitey again asked if I really meant homosexual and wasn't happy when I answered, "Gay as a Hollywood hairstylist."

Black challenged, "You can't be gay, you were charged with being a homophobic."

Steel Gray stated, "I know gay people. I live with gay people, love gay people, and looking at you I know you're not gay, just as I may not be."

I shouted, "You want proof? You need evidence? You seek confirmation? Well –"and addressing Blackey shouted, "I'm going over to you and give you one big wet kiss with lots of tongue."

The whites of his eyes almost fell on the table as he shrieked, "Hell, no. You stay where you are."

Telling him I found him very attractive as soon as I came into the room he jumped up and backing away from the table threatening, "If you come over to this side of the table I'll charge you with sexual assault."

In my turn I challenged him to come to grips with his own sexuality. "One gay man can recognize another."

"Shit, I'm not gay," he yelled and swore to Steel Gray and Whitey's open mouths how straight he was.

"Can I give all of you a big hug?" I asked joyfully. Damn it, I was having a ball.

In unison they screamed, "Hell no."

Walking to the window and staring at police plaza traffic I started waxing poetically in my new role, telling them, "It's dark in the closet, where only furtive whispers of love can be heard. Now, thanks to you, the door is thrown open. I see the light of freedom, freedom to be who I am, free from the shackles of sexual lies, free to show honest interest in hot beefcake guys and not have to feign interest in hot babes. I can't wait to get to my locker and rip down those disgusting Hustler pictures of naked girls and put up some Playgirl's hot pictures of guys, muscles bulging, wearing only a brief stuffed with a sock. The hell with what all the guys in the locker room will think."

Turning to them, sitting so close together it could be classified as a huddle, I cried, my life was lived in midnight shadows, my soul was corrupted by the false life I was forced to live, my world was a dark world, but now I've found the sun's warmth, and in the light can take my first steps out of the closet into a world of honesty.

Blackey timidly asked if I was sure I was gay.

"Come over here and get a kiss you'll never forget."

"I'm sure I'll never forget it, but keep your distance. I'm straight, got three children, a wife, and a mistress."

"Yes," Steel Gray jumped in. "Detective McCoppin, you have a child you abuse and probably your wife is a victim of your sadistic violence."

For a moment I thought, *shit, the old bag's got me.* Then again realizing the best defense is offense I challenged; did she believe homosexual men couldn't be just as good parents as straight men, believing gay men physically abuse their wives. Was she casting stones at my child rearing just because I'm gay.

Retreating she cried, "Good heavens, I'm not saying that."

The other two went to her defense explaining she was just articulating the charges reported to the S.D.C.

I debated with myself, should I continue. Was I going over the top, risking exposing my lies with unbelievable exaggerations and metaphors? Shit, never. With sensitive girly liberals, there is no top, there's never too much, there's only more and more feeling, so pile it on and enjoy yourself.

Having them on the defense, joyfully I pressed on, "The reason I was a tad short with Start, Leeper and Burnsome was my fear they, with their education, experience and degrees would see what I had denied for all these years to myself and others, my true sexuality. It was not to keep them from my son; it was to keep them from discovering my sexuality. Certainly the Sensitivity and Diversity Committee, with its deep knowledge of gay dynamics could sympathize with my shameful defensive behavior."

Whitey, with the look of one getting ready to stand up preparatory to going for a hug, repeating what I just said as if I hadn't said it and he just discovered it, said to all, "I can see the social dynamics of the situation. Detective er –"

"Ed McCoppin."

"Thank you. Mr. McCoppin, concealing his true sexuality from the world particularly from the malignant machismo code of the police department, adapted the camouflage of marriage and a child, as is often seen, and is now in torment living a lie and denying his true self."

Feeling charitable I gave him an astonished, "Yes, you're right. I never fully knew my predicament 'til now."

I had Whitey in my pocket and Blackey was going soft, especially with threats of tongue hanging in the air. Steel Gray was still hanging tough possibly because she had difficulty going against her preconceived prejudices. It meant admitting she was wrong in this instance, and therefore being fallible was not who she believed she was. Why she hated men in authority, police, military, I could make a guess but everyone knows what my unsaid guess is because they guess the same, and everyone's right.

Steel Gray attacked, "What proof can you show to prove you're gay?"

Blackey and Whitey were listening for my proof.

"I could list gay bars where I'm well known, the bath houses I've visited, the parks at night I've walked alone, loveless, but I won't, it's too painful. I went there, not to engage in any lovemaking, only to despise those men who habituated such places."

Whitey, confident in his wisdom repeated, "You hated homosexuals, but it was really yourself that you hated."

The man was totally mine. "Yes, you're so right," I said as if he explained the secrets of what was happening before the big bang. "Now that you pointed it out I see it all."

Blackey murmured, "It all makes sense to me." Blackey was a mental weather vane and though Whitey was blowing my way, it still was only a summer breeze.

Steel Gray was the north western perfect storm. Without her on board the vote would be two to one against me.

Speaking directly to her I announced, I did have proof, proof I couldn't divulge as it involved another person.

"Who?" Blackey asked.

Steel Gray eagerly asked, "You've got to give us a name."

With sensitivity, Whitey told the other two they couldn't expect me to drag someone out of the closet who wishes to remain in the closet.

Blackey told Whitey he was right, but suggested the Committee certainly could open the door a crack and peek in.

Steel Gray said she didn't believe there was anyone in my closet, didn't believe I was gay, in fact still thought I was a gay basher. It was the uniform. She couldn't get over the uniform and its visual masculine authority. Had to play to her bias and give a name. There was a tinge of conscious guilt but it quickly vaporized when, deciding on a name I asked Steel Gray directly, "Do I have your assurance that what is said in this department meeting is treated as a sacred confidence similar to the confessional."

Whitey amplified, "More than confidential, legally bound to withhold all committee discussions and any information shared in unbreakable confidence."

"Who?" prompted Blackey, eager to discover a closeted gay.

"Who?" demanded Steel Gray doubting I could come up with a name.

"Don't say who," sensitive Whitey advised, "if you feel your conscience won't allow you to say the name."

Conscience, he had to be joking. Wearing a solemn troubled expression melting into a sad, near tear face was hard for me to generate as internally I was slyly smiling at my cleverness, and yes, meanness, even though feeling I was getting mine back.

Whispering so softly, Steel Gray asked me to speak louder, I mumbled, "A few years back Woody and I had a brief liaison."

"Woody?" Blackey asked.

Clarifying I told them, "Detective Woodriff Biden. It was a brief encounter lasting a scant few weeks. Happened when we were investigating the Indian Hoboken Case. Have to say we both were ashamed of our love and though still remaining investigative partners in the police department we never again dared to be partners in love."

Needing to give a little more feeling I told them we remained friends and viewed our brief affair as one of the most wonderful loving experience of our lives.

Smiling at me indicating, 'you have my vote,' Whitey mentioned my situation paralleled the movie *Brokeback Mountain* he had seen several times.

Blackey was trying to figure out how to react.

Frowning, Steel Gray was writing Woody's name down.

Yes, now there was a crack in her bias against me and my uniform.

I continued, "Now I beg you not to question Detective Biden about his sexuality. Ashamed, he hasn't come to grips with his true sexual self, and still living in the closet's darkness is currently hiding his sexuality by showing interest in Ronni Deutsch, an attractive detective, currently working with him on the Roach Murder."

Steel Gray exclaimed, "Ronni Deutsch? I know her. I have my eye on her ... feel she'll go far, er, in the Department."

"Well Woody may have his eye on her but his mind is on me," I said.

Blackey, to show he was still relevant, popping his head up from a paper filled folder to announce with appropriate horror, "I see the mention of the 'n' word in McCoppin's file."

Ouch, the 'n' word, the most hated word the world's ears have ever heard. I was in danger of losing him. The word that could destroy careers if even whispered to a confessor, the word above all others when spoken condemns the speaker to the civil, economic, and social netherworld. Other than stripping myself to the buff, whipping myself with barbed wire, how could I possibly redeem myself? In fact, only by tying myself to a stake atop a ton of kindling and lighting myself up, could I hope for some marginal forgiveness for committing the mortal sin worthy of eternal damnation for those saying the 'n' word.

About to tearfully confess while writhing on the floor screaming for forgiveness, I stopped myself. Such conduct never works; best to attack. "You see from my confidential personal file my accuser is my past lover, Woodriff Biden. He could never get over my breaking up with him. In a jealous fit he flung the hateful accusation at me. To defend myself from such malice I'd have to expose his sexuality and of course mine. Just couldn't do it. Now, thanks to the SAD, er ... the Sensitivity and

Diversity Committee I found the strength to be free and walk in the light of self honesty."

I directed my emotion with all the honesty my dishonesty could manufacture to Steel Gray. "I particularly owe my sexual salvation to you. My wife and son will be so happy to know I've finally come to terms with my sexuality and we will celebrate as a family my being a gay man."

I made a reach for Steel Gray's hand saying, you saved my family.

Pulling her hand away, not in a quick jerk, more a sliding out of reach, indicating she liked the idea of her saving people. Sensitive people are all about saving people, creating happiness, destroying sadness, poverty and hate. The idea of my remaining with wife and son was the reason for the slide denying my touch. Married women with husbands weren't her idea of what should be.

To end her hand slide I confessed,"Now out of the closet I don't know if I could live with my wife. It would be such a lie. Most probably I'll find my true love and marry him. My wife and I will share custody, and my soul mate, my new male wife will love my son as deeply as I and my soon to be ex wife do. I hope to pay alimony and child support once we've settled our diverse living arrangements."

Blackey liked the idea of supporting the mother and child.

Whitey expressed his opinion of me as being one hell of a sensitive open person who is a credit to the police department.

Steel Gray liked the idea of me leaving my wife and child.

In connection with that motif she asked if Detective Ronni Deutsch had shown any interest in Detective Biden. You know, relationship interest. If she did, it would be necessary for the Committee to warn Ronni of Biden's sexual orientation before she broke her heart by falling in love with a gay man.

The sentence ending 'with a gay man' brought the SAD investigation of my misconduct to an end with a resounding reaffirmation of my being a detective with great sensitivity for and love of diversity and a credit to the department.

Meaning so much to him, Blackey couldn't get over the 'n' word commenting aloud, <u>"So if this Biden accused this detective of the 'n' word, he must have written it in his report, said it to himself, even thought of the 'n' word in his racist soul and an investigation is certainly in order."</u>

They all took turns shaking my hand expressing admiration for my courage followed by hugs showing their love for me now that I'm out of the closet. Baritone, a little leery stayed on the other side of the table giving me a shitty grin, a weak nod, and a flabby 'right on' fist. Whitey's hug was uncomfortably long and I felt a pat that could be characterized as inappropriate.

Now sure her fire hydrant formed body was safe from heterosexual inappropriate touching Steel Gray came up to me and gave me the last hug. Coming up to my chest I could easily look over the Steel Gray to observe Whitey and Blackey smiling at the sensitive caring tabloid. With her letting me go, the SAD Committee decided to let me go with the admonition I must welcome the professionals who know, care, and love children to interview my son.

I readily agreed. Was that more self respect dropping from me? Not much left. Sadness drains the normal.

Leaving with such resounding confirmation, I heard Steel Gray asking for Ronni's file and Whitey suggesting he should meet in conference with Woodriff Biden to assist him in finding his true self. Demanding they look at Woody's file Blackey was asking if Sensitivity and Diversity Committee hadn't uncovered another example of racism prevailing in every aspect of America.

CHAPTER 30

Walking on the Dark Side

My spirit, so helium pumped I almost danced out of SAD's office, although didn't. It would be too gay and I couldn't dance if my life depended on my doing a Fred Astaire. I had learned a lot in the land of Sensitivity and Diversity; being different is where it's at, normal gets you nothing. Thanking heaven the idiots didn't ask me to do a few disco shoe shuffles, I raced home to change out of my best uniform.

Just after three, I was hurrying to interview Rufus and Dagmar at dinnertime knowing they were hard wired racists with suspicions of, if not hatred for police, and I needed to soften my image. Making use of their low income prejudices, swearing all whites are unfairly economically above them with money stolen from them, I put on my best suit. You may hate the wealthy, but on meeting the rich you automatically show respect. After all, the rich are where you dream of going and never arriving.

Who did I find waiting for me in my kitchen, sandwich and coffee in hand? Woody. Shouldn't be surprised, after all who but a best friend will be the most eager to hear about your sorrows, and offer sympathy. Telling him I escaped unscathed from the SAD Committee, Woody's face dropped faster and lower then your 401K after one of the bubbles burst. I burst his bubble saying my meeting went beautifully.

Hating to hear my escaping unscathed, pressing me to give some tidbit of wretchedness to buoy up his spirit, he continued, "Are you sure you're alright? Not trying to hide your troubles from Pam?"

Topping off Woody's coffee, Pam said Woody had informed her about my SAD meeting that was to determine if I should be dismissed from the Force.

Other than losing her first born, a wife is never so tormented as suspecting the husband's paycheck is in jeopardy.

"Honey, I'm golden. You should have seen me at the meeting. At the end they were singing my praise, fighting to be the first to kiss my ass."

Meaningfully glancing at Woody, I told her I'd give her all the details when we're alone. You'd think Woody, Mr. Sensitive himself would take the hint and leave.

Woody, glued to the kitchen chair I habitually sit in, was having a difficult time giving up his joy at my 'hoped for' sorrow, again asked if I was sure my meeting was a success.

My honest hosannas, my smile at his disappointment, my repetitive reassurances deflated him.

Pam, picking up on Woody's disbelief asked if I knew the Committee's decision, I must tell her the truth.

Damn it, belief never follows good news happening to you; instant belief invariably follows bad news.

In desperation, Woody seconded Pam, voicing his estimation of her being a strong woman, she would be able to withstand the meeting's results no matter how unendurable. Getting up he went to her side telling me she needed to hear the truth, and as my wife, she deserves the truth, and as a mother she had to know the truth.

Shit, he was almost on his knees begging for some scrap of bad news. I reiterated, "I'm telling you both, the meeting was fantastic, and Woody, I even wiped away the 'n' word stigma you reported against me."

Seemingly reluctant to cross over from the dead street to the street of life, Pam asked, was it for the third time, am I telling the truth. She couldn't bear it if I lied to her.

Looking with hard unambiguous meaning at Woody I told her, with Woody's departure, when alone, I'll tell her all about my successful interview then added, "Pam, I'm telling you, your husband was brilliant at the conference. Facing annihilation, real men rise to the occasion and I did just that with an inspired defense deliver with panache. Never was I so proud of myself. Now if Woody would leave, I'll explain all that happened at the SAD meeting."

A reluctant Woody, by fits and starts eventually made his way out, aided by no small measure, by my persistent expressions of good humor, and not a few chest bumps.

Upstairs looking askance at me hurriedly changing clothes, Pam wanted to know where I was going and what happened at the SAD meeting.

"Got to do one last interview, probably the most difficult of all, and will need a great deal of finesse to pull it off."

She questioned the good clothes saying I'll need them for the non denomination, non sectarian, totally secular memorial evening prayer service.

Evening? Prayer service! Pray to who, certainly not to a personal God. Pray to no one to help make everyone more saintly.

"Look," I told her, "I've got to wear my uniform at the Memorial celebration. And the evening secular prayer service sounds totally bogus, and we're not going."

"About your interview, Ronny Deutsch called asking how it went. Ed what happened at the SAD offices?"

Ronny, another friend inquiring whether the patient is beyond hope, and is it time to send flowers and condolences.

"If she calls again, tell her everything went great. Now Pam, I had to agree, the psychologists and Burnsome can have another go at Mike, so don't get upset if the trio shows up. Our son is sufficiently strong and resilient to stand against their help's damage. In fact, at his age he probably has the maturity to see them for what they are. Once he's in college he'll become blinded.

"One more thing, you might hear some strange sex rumors about me, which are totally untrue and laughable. It's part of my defense to keep my job and keep Mickey out of the State's clutches."

It's a mistake to give an inch and not to expect your foot to be demanded to follow that inch.

Worried Pam asked, "Mac, what untruth? What sex rumors?"

"Damn it Pam, trust me. I'm in a rush. There's a lot to do before I do my last interview so I can't go into details. Just remember, it's all false."

"Is it true about the SAD outcome? Was it really successful? Mac, tell me. Tell me right now. Is that what's false?"

Shit, now I'm getting demands from the little woman. Saying with determination, "I'll tell you when I tell you" tautology, I escaped Pam, her demand for explanations, her plea for inclusion, and some tentative coat grabbing in getting out to the street.

If I hoped to get Rufus, the reborn Muslim Abdullah, and Dagmar Miller, the pragmatic, together at home willing to talk to me I had to arrive at dinnertime. In addition, given their attitudes and prejudices, a key was needed to get inside the door and in addition I needed a face they'd talk to, and I had my key and knew exactly where to find my face.

Cruising the mean streets, passing professional girls working their way through college, or feeding their starving children by jumping in and out of cars, I found black Clarence in the midst of one the corner groups. A diverse study group of working girls standing around were loudly engaged in a strenuous critique of Elizabethan poets.

Parking next to the corner I beeped my horn. Instead of Clarence, I attracted a flock of studious co-eds who, with high expectations slow hip walked to my car exuding boundless love and an infinite well of good friendship. The love, along with the promised friendship dissolved into finger gestures and hurtful gay hate speech when I told them I was only interested in Clarence.

Before anyone wonders or starts to suspect, he was my confidential informer, my CI, and nothing else. He was able to give me an arrest whenever I needed a small time shoplifter or drug dealer to fatten my monthly reports.

A connoisseur of street drugs, living rough for years on the mean streets, Clarence was a carrier of all the city's contaminants. To keep him from my car's interior, knowing if he got his ass inside I'd have to get a complete detailing job along with a couple of economy size Lysol spray cans, I jumped out and pulling him aside asked if he'd like to earn a quick forty.

The suspense of his reply lasted as long as it takes one of the nearby war painted co-eds to unzip your fly. And just as coyly, he asked what he'd have to do,

I told him he merely had to accompany me as I interviewed a couple.

Of course, the forty was a mistake. Too much, causing Clarence to get excited and smell more.

Looking a dying fifty from a thirty year old perch, the missing twenty years he had sold for what he sniffs, swallows, inhales, injects, the uppers, the downers flowing from spoon to vein to aerosol can to huff, searching to escape who he is, a loser, Clarence became a druggy, who he detests; a circle if you will, does drugs because he hates himself, and hates himself because he does drugs. How could he stop? If he lost his loser and drug user persona what would be left of him. He would be annihilated, soul less, sent into the terrible void.

Waving a twenty got Clarence's attention as well as the co-eds and brought forth a benevolent forty year old college freshman offering to introduce a gay man into a world of straight delights.

Telling her to move away, Clarence turned to me saying, "Detective McCoppin, I've not scored for over three days and I'm hurting." Not sensing any flow of sympathy he introduced a new script, "Haven't eaten for the past week, need money for food, can you see your way to adding an extra twenty to that forty. Once I score and get straight I'll spend the rest on food, healthy food." He added a humorous exit line saying then he would be in condition to look for work.

Hurtfully, the insensitive co-eds laughed at his unintended joke as I did and even Clarence had to enjoy his jest with a smile. If I acquiesce to the added twenty, another twenty would immediately be requested, and all our time would be spent arguing over a couple of bucks.

"The forty is firm," I said.

After shuffling around and squinting at the two twenties I waved under his nose, he reluctantly closed the negotiations announcing he was my man, was willing to do anything I needed him to do.

Hoping he would draw the line at murder but wouldn't like to put his conscience to the test, and certain it would cost at least a hundred I told him, "Clarence, I want you to accompany me for a few hours while I interrogate a couple."

With his widening eyes showing yellow he grunted a 'huh'. A 'huh' filled with equal measures of disbelief and anxiety. "Do you want me to be your muscle? If so, got to tell you I'm not in the best condition, still if I could do a couple of lines and carry some heavy heat, I'm your backup man."

Hell, he'd do the line and pawn the heat.

"I'm planning to interview a nice black couple, and having your color with me will make them more comfortable talking to a white guy."

"Shit, no way will I turn in a bro. It's a line I won't cross. Still, if sixty was placed over the line I may be tempted, but only for a righteous crime."

"Clarence, there is no question of incrimination, no arrests will be made, just an informal friendly conversation, and where the hell is this bro shit coming from. You gave me at least a dozen just this year."

We were again interrupted by a black blond haired co-ed eyeing the twenties I was waving about. Seeing me as a potential philanthropist interested in helping her reach her educational goals, generously she indicated, seeing how I was good looking she'd discount the cost of her company by half and see me right for forty..

Clarence yelled back at her, "Precious, he's talking to me. Take that big fat ass away and don't bother us."

With her hands akimbo, throwing in one hell of a mean stare, packing at least one fifty, not all fat, Clarence was risking his life.

Fortunately for Clarence the study group, hearing Precious threatening to destabilize the corner price structure attacked her with loud curses, vigorous pushes and many disparaging remarks about her age, her weight and her attractiveness with some even suggesting she wasn't really a blond. To me, a complaining Clarence confided how the whores continually interfering with his business.

Knowing his current street corner business was small drug exchanges with heavy self testing of his product I took a good look at him. With our current brief exchange optimistically I hoped Clarence still held some watered down stock in the ability to think rationality. Unfortunately the future would prove me totally wrong. He was physically shaky, so shaky I knew he'd never last through the interview. Hoping my read was erroneous I asked if he was okay. It was stupid to ask. What junky is ever okay, is not in need of a fix to hide behind.

"Okay! okay!" Clarence repeated, then added, "I'm okay. You don't have to worry about me." His wobbling legs almost forcing a fall said not okay, said probably a line was needed to brace up his legs. He continued, "Been clean for two weeks, going to rehab, but for you and this job I'll need a line, just one line. It'll cost about twenty to get me healthy."

Seeing he was in no shape to face down Rufus, never mind Dagmar, I gave him ten, the cost of two lines, gave him Dagmar's address saying sixty would be waiting for him and he'd better be there in a half hour. I took a chance, he could become lost in a land of lines, but with only ten if he doesn't collapse, the prospect of an additional sixty will drag his ass to Dagmar's. Suddenly I thought, hell, if does heroin or some downer he'll be nodding asleep in some dumpster. Happily he did cocaine or some equivalent upper which enabled him to meet me at Rufus' door only twenty minutes late.

CHAPTER 31

Last Interview

Standing on the sidewalk in front of black Dagmar's house I spotted Clarence approaching, so high he couldn't help tap dancing down the street. Shit, wanted him conscious but not so totally jazzed. He was bouncing while continually snapping his fingers.

"Man, I'm good. I'm feeling no pain. In fact, trust me. Right now I could do anything. Just name it."

"Clarence, what the hell did you take?"

"Don't ask, don't tell, like gays say in the Army," he said laughing as he jumped off the curb into the street.

Correcting him I informed him you can now ask and they'll definitely tell you and you better say that's great for you, wish I was.

After a few moments Clarence discovered he was in the street and giggling jumped up saying, "Hey man, did you say sixty? Where's my sixty? You promised sixty if I show up and here I am, ready to go."

Firmly I said, "You'll get the money after I interview Dagmar Miller and her live-in Abdullah Malcolm. Won't take long."

"Interview? No one said anything about work. I'm disabled ... get a check every month because I have a substance addiction."

"Listen you idiot. All you need to do is stay by my side and nod yes whenever I ask you something. You can nod."

"Nod. I spent my life nodding. Trust me Detective McCoppin, I can nod, and nod, and nod and –"

"Enough nodding. You're to say nothing, don't look surprised at anything I say, and for heaven's sake, and forget I'm a detective. Don't, absolutely don't refer to me as a detective."

"But you are, aren't you?"

"Yes, but you're not to refer to me as a detective."

"Hell Detective McCoppin … I've got you … I'm with you … we're under cover and I'm your back-up."

"Clarence, listen, you're not my back-up. Just stay next to me and nod."

"If I'm to stay with you as your protection I need heat, some heavy mind blowing heat."

Began to reevaluate downward my estimation of how watered down was his stock in rationality. I again repeated his instructions, "There's no heat, just stay next to me and if I say 'isn't that right' you nod yes. Don't say it, just nod."

"What if I want to say no? What do I do?"

"Clarence, there will be no nos, but if the occasion demands it just shake your head."

"If we're not detectives and not carrying heat, who are we?"

"We're going to be friends of Jimmy."

"Who's Jimmy?"

"Just nod, never mind who Jimmy is."

"Is he a detective? Thought we weren't going to be cops."

In frustration I shouted, "Damn it Clarence, just shut your damn mouth and nod, and the sixty is yours. Can you understand that?"

Suddenly the door opened and Dagmar Miller in all her fearsome bulk stood glaring down at us demanding who the hell we were, why we were making a racket on her stoop, and to get the hell away before she starts getting mad and we didn't want to see her mad.

Clarence smiled, nodded and snapped his fingers while doing some jumping exercises.

Out of her muddy face Dagmar growled, "Fool, are you high?"

Clarence answered, "High on life," between vigorous nods then asked me if he could have his sixty and go home.

He was the black face I needed but should have given him only five dollars to stiffen him and cure him from the shakes. The ten created a cartoon character.

With my black face vigorously nodding at the mountain of mud, I yelled loud enough to penetrate the house's interior, "We're from Jimmy and need to see Rufus." That succeeded in rousing Rufus. From inside the house we hear a scream, "Jimmy's here? Shit Dagmar, let the brother in."

Dagmar yelled back to the interior, "Fool, it's not Jimmy ... it's two idiots."

She received back, "Damn it Dagmar, don't leave Jimmy waiting in the cold. Tell him I'm glad he dropped by."

Disgusted Dagmar waddled away leaving the door open as a disgruntled invitation.

I walked in, Clarence bounced in and we headed to the kitchen at the back of the house. A plate of spaghetti in front of him with a couple of strings dangling from his lips, looking at Clarence a surprised Abdullah Mohammad, aka Rufus announced, "You ain't Jimmy," as if none of us knew Jimmy wasn't in the room. "Who the hell are you?"

I growled, "We're from Jimmy, about your IOUs."

Standing at the stove Dagmar continued ladling meatballs and sauce into a gallon size plastic bowl. Without turning she told us where we could go and take Rufus with us.

Now nervous Abdullah told her to keep quiet, his name is now Abdullah, and let him handle the situation. To us, in a whiny voice he told us Jimmy will be paid in full after the lawsuit.

"What lawsuit!" popped out of Clarence, my back-up.

"Clarence," I said, "keep quiet. Remember Jimmy told me to do all the talking."

He nodded on cue.

Seeing the question, "Who's Jimmy," forming in his bright unblinking eyes, in a gruff voice I quickly told Mohammad, "Jimmy wants the money you owe him for the drugs he advanced you, as well as paying your gambling debts."

Suddenly Clarence's eyes stared in recognition as he shouted, "Jimmy, I know Jimmy. Jimmy, isn't he –"

"Clarence, we work for Jimmy, right?"

Nodding vigorously he was about to speak when I preempted him asking Dagmar if Abdullah died, would she pay his debt to Jimmy.

Her smashing a meatball with a two foot long steel ladle I took as a no.

"Look, suppose Abdullah here dies from roach poison, Jimmy would like to know if you'd be interested in taking over your husband's business and work for Jimmy."

Getting very animated Clarence told Dagmar he could steer her to the best corners to sell drugs, even could set her up with good customers and –

"He's referring to college kids," I said to put a period to his drug ramblings, "Right Clarence."

He nodded, he smiled, nodded again, then asked Abdullah if he was carrying. Did he have anything around the house.

"Clarence," I shouted, "we're here about money owed Jimmy and not concerned about drugs."

Nodding he asked Abdullah if he could introduce him to Jimmy saying he knew about Jimmy but only had dealings with his street people.

Abdullah, busy with sucking up a few strands of spaghetti didn't answer.

I did. "Clarence, you know Jimmy doesn't want you talking about his business."

He gave me a dozen rapid nods before mentioning his hope of working the wholesale side of the business and getting some deep serious discounts.

"Clarence damn it, we work for Jimmy. We're his collection men. Right?"

More nods as he repeated his request for some heat. "How can I do collections without some heat?"

"Clarence, Jimmy said we're not to do any rough stuff this time. Right?"

He nodded, then started to concentrate on sniffing the air.

Abdullah, a meatball in each cheek, complaining with all the media attention on the survivors of table 12, he couldn't drive his cab and service his customers, and would Jimmy wait a while..

"What cab? Where do you drive? Do you pass under the 36 Street Bridge?" an eager Clarence asked, before adding, "I sometimes crash there."

"Forget the cab," I told Clarence, and nodding he stuck his head out the kitchen door sniffing at the living room; a bloodhound trying to pick up a scent.

Dagmar, insulted over all his sniffling demanded to know what he was sniffing at and there were no sniffable odors in her home, and if he didn't stop sniffing he'd lose his sniffer. Backing up the threat she waved her steel ladle dripping sauce in front of her formidable bosom.

Eyeing her, Clarence nodding, taking a sly last sniff before coming back next to me, whispered just sufficiently loud for all to hear, "You should have given me some heat to carry. She's dangerous."

"Quiet," I told him and nodding he nervously watched Dagmar spooning meatballs with angry emphasis as if they were misbehaving 'Head Start' children.

"Look Dagmar, what about you taking over Abdullah's route if he was killed," I repeated.

Turning from meatballs to me, steel ladle in the air dripping blood red sauce on the linoleum, she said, "Fool. Do you think I could fit in that damn car? Think I'd want to ride all day squeezed into that compact wreck of a car? You're a fool if you or Jimmy thinks I'm going to take my fool's cab job."

Up to that point Abdullah was content to munch meatballs, sop up sauce with bread and struggle keeping strands of dancing spaghetti in his mouth. Now he proclaimed, "Hey, my rich chocolate pudding, as long as I'm alive you'll never have to work." To Clarence he said, "Tell Jimmy I've got a lawyer, a black lawyer who says I'm going to get at least three mil for all my pain and suffering."

"Three mil!" Clarence gasped in wide eyed astonishment.

"What lawyer?" I asked.

"Sharif Shalom," Abdullah answered. "Works for O'Malley and he's black."

Clarence shouted, "Shit, I never heard of this O'Malley. How good is his product. Look can anyone connect me up with this Sharif guy. How long has he been working the hood?"

Ignoring Clarence Dagmar quickly corrected, "O'Malley is really Goldstein. He confessed to being Jewish when I told him I'd only deal with a Jewish lawyer. He then came clean and showed his skull cap."

A bewildered Clarence exclaimed, "Wow, the Jews are moving into the hood. Will they be discounting for good customers?"

Turning to Rufus I asked if he was suing. He ignored me telling Clarence to forget O'Malley, and Goldstein. Sherif was their lawyer. He was staying with a Muslim brother."

"Hey, those Middle East guys have some fantastic product."

I punched Clarence in the arm and put a shoulder into it. With his mind doing chemical calisthenics he felt nothing, just smiled asking if we were going to make arrests and seize some products.

Dagmar, peering at Clarence, then me, over the two foot high meatball pot asked, "Say whitey, don't I recognize you? You sure look familiar."

"Working for Jimmy I get around. Right Clarence?"

Nodding Clarence proudly told Dagmar, "I know Jimmy. Heard about him, a great guy. Can you introduce me to him?"

"Clarence, remember we work for him."

Shaking his head I had to remind him, "Damn it Clarence, nod."

I got a nod.

After another long sniff at the living room, snapping his fingers Clarence announced, "There's definitely a smell, trust me, definitely a smell."

Dagmar threatened waving a dripping ladle overhead as if leading a band at halftime. Dagmar threatened, There's no smells in my home. One more nose comment and you'll be a noseless fool. Am I clear enough for you?"

My, "Let's stay focused here Clarence," got a series of nods. Turning to Abdullah I reminded him we were there to collect Jimmy's money.

Still staring at me Dagmar asked Abdullah if I didn't look familiar.

Hand pulling mischievous spaghetti strings dangling off his chin, Abdullah told her all white guys look the same, then after telling us to leave, he said we were to tell Jimmy, Abdullah is rich, lawyer rich.

A nodding Clarence pointing to the living room asked if Abdullah could help a brother who's hurting.

Ignoring Clarence's importuning, Abdullah announced he'll be selling his gypsy cab and buying the biggest Mercedes as soon as his man Sharif gets him his money.

Nudging me Clarence whispered he needed his sixty, saying he'd like to talk alone with Abdullah in the living room.

I told him no.

Turning to Abdullah, nodding, loudly sniffing, Clarence asked him besides grass, what else he sells.

"Clarence," I shouted, "shut your damn mouth."

Answering with generous number of nods, deep sniffs, and shifting from one leg to the other accompanying his nods to me, Clarence told Abdullah not to be uptight because a detective was present. I was cool and he had sixty bucks to buy whatever they're selling.

"Detective," yelled Abdullah. "Hell, a white detective."

Dagmar turning from the stove so quickly we were all sprayed red with sauce from her formidable ladle, "What are you two doing in my house?" said as if two cockroaches slipped in under the door.

Attempting to salvage the situation I mentioned Jimmy has many good friends on the force and we have an arrangement with him.

"Screw Jimmy, the force, and you two. Get the hell out right now," Dagmar shouted, and shaking her ladle, more sauce was thrown about and damn it, stupidly I had to wear my best suit.

"My midnight delight, I recognize the white guy. He's no detective. He was one of the guys at table 12. His son plays on Winslow's team. They're no detectives," Abdullah announced.

"And not from Jimmy," added Dagmar. "They're trying to get in on our law suit. They know, as the only black poisoned victim we'll get better treatment and more money. I put calls in for Al Sharpton, Jesse Jackson and Goldstein, our lawyer. They'll see justice is done for a poor black family."

Abdullah, springing up from the table braced Clarence with being an Oreo, a traitor to the brothers, and nothing was lower than a black playing at being white.

Vigorously nodding Clarence asked what he was carrying.

Calling Rufus a fool, Dagmar tossed a meatball at Clarence, splattering on his Salvation Army coat.

Abdullah belly pushing Clarence demanded he should become a Muslim, talk to his Imam at his masque and stop trying to be white, be Muslim and leave the police force and as a righteous Muslim go to Mecca.

"Mecca, yeah, Mecca, I heard about this Mecca place" pounced a nodding Clarence. "They've got some serious hashish there. If you could front me some money I could make us a fortune." Then peering into the living room he asked who Rufus was. Was he hiding in the living room, and what was he carrying.

Dagmar, staring at us as if we were insane stated, "These two fools have lost their minds."

Abdullah, trying to make a convert said, "You're black. You shouldn't let whitey corrupt you. You wouldn't be interested in drugs if it weren't for white people keeping you economically down. Imam Caliph could explain –"

Suddenly Dagmar shouted, "I know exactly why they're here. These slimy eels want to use us to get close to Toni Brite. Well forget it. She's ours and no one else's."

Before I could ask who the hell is this Toni Brite, Abdullah complained about her being white. "Imam Caliph says we should stay away from white contamination."

"Who's this Eman?" a startled Clarence asked. "A dealer who supplies Jimmy? You've got to introduce me. I'm ready to handle the wholesale part of –"

Abdullah angrily yelled, "You insult my religious beliefs. He's a holy man, a righteous street organizer currently working to free a black man from –"

A meat ball hitting Clarence hard in the ear couldn't be ignored, and backing up, nodding his head up to the ceiling and down to his bony breast he made his way to the sidewalk where I quickly joined him. Trying not to stare at his meat stuffed ear painted red with sauce I gave Clarence his sixty while complaining he didn't do what I asked him to do.

After concentrating on counting the three twenties three times because he kept losing his place, he complained if only I gave him heat we could have searched the place and found their hashish stash and everyone knows where hashish grows, harder goodies are always nearby.

Tired I told Clarence let's call it a day.

Nodding vigorously, snapping fingers, Clarence asked if that Abdullah guy was serious about sending him to Mecca along with some Eman to buy tons of hashish, and would this fellow Rufus who's hiding it in the living room come along.

Due to ear meat, not hearing my hysterical laughter, he started to go back into the house when I stopped him mentioning Dagmar was in there yielding a steel ladle like a war club.

"Shit, yes, thanks. Almost forgot. Got to get in touch with Abdullah when he's alone. Do you think this Toni Brite is a working girl? I've never seen her working any of the corners. Say, Detective McCoppin, do you know if Abdullah and this Rufus guy are they working for the Eman or for Jimmy like we are. If I'm to work under cover and meet these guys shouldn't I have some heat and serious upfront money?"

Busy shaking my head in bewilderment before I knew it Clarence was in my car's passenger seat expecting to be chauffeured. Vigorously cursing, telling him I didn't want him in my car yet knowing the futile struggle to extract him, I eventually resigned to drive him to his corner.

Ignoring my continuous bitching about him he asked if I didn't think he did a great job, certainly worth a bonus of at least another twenty. Telling him no to the twenty, no to the good job, in fact he talked and didn't just nod.

After a blessed few moments of silence save for continuous annoying finger snapping, Clarence asked if this Brite broad was a professional girl and did I think he could be her pimp. For Clarence and others of his irk, the pinnacle of masculine success was to have a stable of professional white girls supporting him.

I told him, "Don't know who the hell this Brite girl is."

He continued, "You know, those corner girls are mean and nasty, especially if you've got no money, not carrying, and are hurting."

Nodding he told me, "Hey, hear what you're saying, but still I did uncover a drug house, a plan to ship drugs in from this Mexican town, Mecca by Eman and Rufus for Jimmy. All that should be worth something, say an extra ten."

Arriving at his corner, the professional co-eds, bending, peering into my car, disappointed at seeing Clarence cursed and spit, hopefully not hitting my car, then returned to resume their literary discussions.

Still high, Clarence asked if I could introduce him to Jimmy, or Eman or Rufus. He'd like to be a friend of Rufus, sell for Jimmy, and be a fellow importer with the Eman, maybe he could be Jimmy's muscle and get deadbeats to pay up.

"Clarence, I don't know Jimmy."

"That Abdullah guy does. Maybe when I arrange to go to Mecca with the Eman and Rufus I'll meet Jimmy there."

"Clarence, do you know where Mecca is?"

"Certainly, it's in Mexico, probably a suburb of Tijuana."

Mumbling "Shit," I told Clarence it's in Arabia.

"Hell, I'm not going to Africa. Don't care how much hashish they have there. I'm desperate but not that desperate."

Jumping out of the car, smelling of $60, the co-eds pounced on him on him trying to strip him bare in desperate attempts to get tuition money. Last seen, he was running down the street with my forty year old gaining on him, yelling she'd love him for twenty,

CHAPTER 32

A Diverse House is
Not a Home

Home, changing out of my sauce stained suit, but before I could complain about the stain, Pam spotted the red and brought it up asking, "What are those stains on your coat? You even have red dots sprinkled on your shirt collar."

Innocent, feeling defensive, believing she suspected lipstick, appearing the fool if not downright stupid, I told her it was spaghetti sauce a suspect in the Roach Case threw at me. Only after minutely eyeballing each stain, and doing a sniff test at the shirt's spaghetti sauce confirming its origination, was her interest satisfied.

Balancing with one foot paused high to plunge into a pants leg, I started to explain, the purpose of my interviewing Dagmar was the hope of discovering if she had cause to poison her boyfriend. Before the period after boyfriend was dropped I realized my mistake.

"Dagmar!" Pam asked. "Who's this Dagmar? You never mentioned her before."

"She's that fat black woman at Mickey's football games, yelling so loud obliterating the cheerleaders' best efforts."

Still uncertain, in half question, half statement, Pam told herself, "She's Dagmar? Never knew her name. So coarse and vulgar – oh my gosh Mac, I didn't mean she's coarse because she's African American."

Hell, political correctness is not just running amuck out there, it's slithered its way into my bedroom and unless vigilant, will soon be in my mind.

While bending to pull up my pants, Pam continued my inquisition. "The spaghetti sauce, how did you get it? Did you have dinner there?"

With her next question, 'who else were you eating with' a breath away, I quickly explained that vitriolic Dagmar, taking exception to one of my question tossed the sauce at me.

"So did you have spaghetti for dinner?"

Buttoning my shirt I told her, "Crap Pam, hell no. My stomach is so sore and I'm feeling so low, a stiff drink accompanying some quiet time is all I need right now."

Feeling she misjudged me on the sauce, attempting reconciliation, Pam mentioned cheese ravioli currently resting at their ease on the stove could be quickly warmed up.

Images of Rufus sucking up spaghetti strings, and Clarence with ear meat, definitely prohibited ravioli and the accompanying sauce.

Relaxing in the living room, lights dim, shoes off, drink in hand, ass resting snuggly in my recliner, I was content. I was about to give the case some reflection, or maybe if audacious I could approach the dangerous edge of the black hole evoked when you reflect seriously on your life. Then again I could be merely entering sleep's night. The doorbell's harsh sound woke me to the present. "Damn it Pam, can you get it."

"I'm putting the ravioli away."

Cursing, drink in hand, raising myself with effort I answered the door. I recognized her as the woman I've recently seen hopping up on the peripheral of my life. She hand waved me as Ronni and I left Scott's widow, and followed me to the mall and to Courtney's boutique. At the door she gave my scowl a bright smile.

Answering my, "What do you want?" with a happy face, she said, "I've soooo wanted to talk to you and Mrs. McCoppin."

I returned her 'sooo' in an abridged addition, "So."

Cheerfully she quasi asked, "Can I come in," as if no one could deny her: a girl possessing glistening green eyes, glittering red lips, purple eye accents, a face made smooth with sufficient powder to fill in any wrinkle and bury any pimple, and with cosmetic installed symmetric red cheeks. The sudden apparition of cheerfulness, self assurance, and beauty, in stepping towards me pushed me back a step or two. With her hand gently resting on, not shaking my extended hand, she maneuvered herself into the living room making any invitation on my part superfluous. Tossing off her gray wool coat, adjusting a garish bright green and deep blue silk scarf hanging artistically over her right shoulder, she introduced herself as Toni Brite. Sitting on the couch, her suggesting I'd be more comfortable sitting, she easily transformed herself to hostess, me to a guest.

Except for Dagmar's mentioning her name it meant nothing, told me nothing. as she continued enthusiastically complimenting me on the living room.

Given the room wasn't very special, in truth looked tired and a little disheveled especially as a background for all her expensive perky newness, I put the compliment down as polite grease normally utilized to sell something.

Standing, mouth open, I recovered sufficiently to ask her to sit down. Already sitting, graciously thanking me she ignored my malapropos.

I watched her make a production of crossing her legs, shifting and angling her tight butt to give me a full side view, thigh to ankle, in case I missed seeing or hadn't fully appreciate the legs.

Sitting on the edge of my recliner, finishing my drink and holding the empty glass between us, I asked if she wanted a drink. Wouldn't have been surprised if this expensively made up and dressed hot babe asked for champagne, but she only requested wine.

Getting up and making myself a stiff one, I justified it to myself: girls like Toni Brite deserve guys holding stiff ones inside and outside. Hell, I needed a stiff one to face down this hot, very assured Brite, whoever she was. Yelling into the kitchen for Pam to bring out a glass of wine, I hoped Brite's constitution could handle cooking sherry better than mine.

Crouching on the edge of the recliner, feeling like a horny cat, I finally asked what she wanted, hoping she'd say me.

Interrupting my Brite concentration, Pam came rushing in ladle in hand, asking who was at the door. Reminding Pam about the wine, and seeing the expensively turned out twenty something Brite artfully arranged on the couch, Pam ran in and out the kitchen. Between the in and the out she lost the ladle and apron and picked up some wine.

Smiling bright even teeth, she introduced herself to Pam as Toni Brite, a representative of Madison, Adamson, and Donaldson Inc. Along with the words two business cards magically materialized and found homes in our open hands. With just a slight rotation of her firm round rump. she extracted sheaves of legal papers tucked into an embossed soft leather folder from her oversized purser. A quick glance at the business card gave no illumination, as it averred in golden raised lettering Toni Brite was an agent for MAD Inc. whose numerous worldwide abbreviated city locations extending over two lines.

Hating to disappoint a young person, more so if she's a girl, even more so if she just left her college dorm possessing looks you could fall in love with, still I regretfully told her we weren't interested in any legal representation.

She laughed, more a giggled, more a wiggle of her soft red lips, allowing a peek at her pink tongue darting in and out and again a glimpse at her straight teeth so white they suggested never having been used, and whose cost of orthodontic treatment could feed a Nigerian village for a year. She said, "Heavens, you think I'm a lawyer." Turning to Pam trying to establish a girls against silly boys union she repeated, "Mrs. McCoppin, er, if I may, Pam, your husband thinks I'm a lawyer."

Face to face, hot babe to a housewife cooking ravioli, Pam wasn't having any 'we girls' moment. Instead, in icy politeness Pam repeated my questions, who was she and what did she want.

Surprised, opening wide deep green eyes suggesting we had a go signal to travel with her, she explained she was here to represent us in a literary sense. "My dear Pam, I'm visiting you to insure the millions of dollars standing just outside your door will be yours."

Skeptical but interested Pam asked, "What millions?"

Was this turning into a girls' NOW moment? Could have interjected myself as master of the house, but eyeing Toni's tush while taking a quantity from my glass, well I was distracted.

In answering Pam's 'what million,' smiling sophisticate to innocent, Toni asked Pam if she had knowledge of book deals, of film rights, of TV interviews.

Pam's dumb look said ignorance of deals, rights and interviews.

Asking if Pam would consider TV interviews, Toni said, "We at MAD Inc. could arrange to have you talking on TV all Sunday morning from nine to one for considerable remuneration."

Talk, TV. Pam's interest being provoked prompted Toni to amplify, "Besides news interview programs, it's absolutely certain I can get you and your son on *The View*. Can you imagine the thrill for your son to get a hug from Barbara Walters, never mind you being the recipient of

Woopie's cheek kiss, and keep in mind you'll be paid handsomely for your appearance."

Whether it was Walter's hug or Woopie's kiss, Pam was definitely nibbling at Brite's bait.

To allow Pam a few seconds to imagine being hugged by Walters on TV's *View*, Toni took a sip of wine. The cooking sherry definitely wasn't up to her pallet's standard. Hesitating between spitting it out or swallowing, she, like me last night, feeling the moment was worth the sacrifice, swallowed with a grimace.

An expensive hot babe talking to you, concentrating and showing interest in you, easily purchased a reciprocal exhibition of appreciation and interest. An expensive hot babe ignoring you, dissing you, suffices to elicit feelings of nastiness, a desire to repudiate your initial interest. It's in the later mental context I asked Toni how is the wine, suggesting she drink up, mentioning we had several bottles, one of which was currently decorked and breathing heavily in the kitchen alone with the ravioli.

Pam, about to ruin my play with some truth with what was actually in the kitchen was forestalled by a frightened Toni desperately saying she was fine, didn't need any more wine, was satisfied and complimented me on my wine's bouquet. Continuing venting my ire at my exclusion of their tete a tete, getting up telling her the wine was a perfect conduit for conversation, I made motions of reaching for her glass, inviting her to drink up and enjoy a second glass. Wrinkling her nose, shifting her rump so her legs blocked my approach, she was adamant about not having more wine.

Again, Pam almost gave the game away mentioning she used it often in the kitchen.

"Yes," Toni answered. "I often enjoy a glass while cooking."

Shit, the glass was true, the cooking was total bullshit. Fifth Avenue hot young literary agent babes, probably from Vassar, are far above cooking. They inhabit a world where housewives are pitiful alien creatures.

I said, "Look Ms. Brite," the Ms. was a deliberate barb, a separation from Miss which suggests youth and desirability, and the Mrs. suggesting a woman who has succeeded in the marriage game left Ms. Brite neutered and in limbo, "I can't see how my being poisoned can translate into millions," was not for information but to refute her.

She took it both ways, answering my doubt and supplying irrefutable evidence those millions were just outside my door ringing the bell, banging on the wood, begging for admission, and Toni Brite and MAD Inc. held the key to opening the door and allowing the millions showering me with happiness forever.

Moving her round tight ass to its initial pose, Toni waited for me to get seated with a new stiff one in hand before explaining, "We have excellent ghosts, one of whom will be assigned to you."

"Ghosts!" Pam interrupted.

"Ghost writers," I amplified.

"Yes, today, no one whose name is on the dust jacket actually writes the book. The ghosts do the writing, you get all the credit and most importantly all the money."

Interrupting her flow, looking for a resting place for the wine's remains, Toni settled for an undignified stretching to reach the cocktail table.

Summarizing, Pam stated, "You want us to write a book?"

"No, you don't write it, you only get the money. Of course you'll have to have a few conversations with the ghost so he'll have some fact hangers to drape the seventy thousand words over.

"Now Pam, once the book is written, will you be willing to appear on Letterman and talk about your book and your family's horrific ordeal?"

Being definitely pushed out of Toni's conversational loop, I stubbornly asked what my role will be in promoting the book.

Free of the wine glass, back into the teasing side view of thigh to ankle, and the bust in silhouette definitely on display, Brite told me, "You misunderstand, you're not irrelevant, it's just that in today's current marketing procedure you're invisible. With the advent of PC and the promotion of diversity's advantages, Pam, you and your son will be on TV appealing to the public who love to empathize with those who are in pain. The story will be of a wife and mother who has faced the pain of almost losing a child and husband, and how the wife, conquering her fears became a strong independent woman.

"Tell me Pam, what work do you do? Do you have a profession?"

Apologetically Pam confessed, "Toni, I'm a stay at home mom."

To defend and justify Pam, I put in, "And my wife, who has an extremely hard job and does it great." Somehow the stiff one didn't say exactly what I meant to say.

Within the context of their exchange, my comments were easily excluded by silence.

Toni Brite continued, "Pam, it's a shame you haven't a career. It would lend an important dimension to your story, your difficulties balancing your work along with raising your child. It's what women have come to expect, suggesting either you're a strong woman struggling to keep your family together by working at a low paying job, or having a career you could be portrayed as a successful woman who has it all, career, children, and a husband."

Somehow I felt Toni had the sequence's importance backwards.

Still apologetic over being a housewife but with a core of defensive irritation Pam again confessed to being a stay at home mother.

Brite lamented Pam's missed opportunities, "We could have your fellow workers give antidotal stories of your courage, cheerfulness in the face of overwhelming devastating disasters occurring in your life. I don't suppose we could get you a job before the book is written and in time for your TV interviews."

The two women sat silently reflecting on how to get Pam a career or at least a job. For my part, killing the second stiff one I felt another one may be needed sooner rather than later despite my two previous stiffs resting on an empty stomach started to massage my mind into a happy glow, or was it an angry burn.

With finality, deciding to limit myself to the two, Brite burst forth, "Pam, the greatest idea … we can get you into some charity doing selfless volunteer work."

With both women getting excited, with 'oh yes's repeatedly flipped between the two of them, accompanied by joyful clapping of hands, getting up I retrieved a third stiff one vowing it would be the night's last one, suspecting I was a liar.

Enthusiastically Pam came up with the suggestion of her reading in a library or in a classroom to a group of diverse children, like Presidents' wives do.

Since it wasn't her idea, after some begrudging thought to the suggestion Brite allowed, "We could have a picture of you sitting on a carpet surrounded by say ten diverse smiling cherubs as you tell the camera how volunteering to read to children is a wonderful life fulfilling experience for you. The privilege you have seeing the joy of young minds emerged in the exciting world of books, knowing how with this experience you're giving them they'll read for the rest of their lives."

Again a moment of silence as each pictured the 'feel good' scene; Pam loving it, was framing it; not being her picture, Brite was tearing it up.

"No Pam, it's not the powerful picture we want to present to the public of you and your volunteer work. Every politician's wife has planted herself in some library or classroom reading to or teaching children. We need more powerful volunteer work, one that will have the women suffering heart palpitations picturing your heroic sacrifice placed in front of an enhancing background of sympathy evoking sufferers."

Hating to let go of the library, Pam suggested a cute furry dog could be added to the mix with maybe cookies and milk being served to the kiddies.

I started to say I really don't like the charity idea as it was so much bull when Brite excitedly waving her hands reminiscent of a teen rap concert fan announced, "Pam darling, I've got the perfect venue for your charity work. A woman's homeless shelter, a place where sexually and physically abused women go for safety. We could place you in the midst of a diverse group of these woebegone women and their wretched children where, between hugs and soup you can praise them for their courage in leaving an abusive relationship and simultaneously offer advice on ways strong women can support themselves and their children. You could hand out college brochures suggesting careers in medicine: physical therapy, practical nursing, pediatrics, billing. It connects with TV conditioned women believing TV's never ending messages of strong confident women looking to a happy future despite living on welfare in a pathetic homeless community shelter."

Two prior stiff ones and half the third had me tossing out, "Don't know if Pam, a stay at home mother giving career advice would be appreciated, besides Hollywood's contrite DUIs and drug addicted stars have a monopoly on serving food, advice and love to the homeless."

It's debatable if my splash of cold water caused the silence, though Brite did murmur, "It's true."

Suddenly again with excited hand waving Brite gleefully shouted, "Cancer, children suffering from cancer. That's where we can go. Pam, you could be visiting the children's ward bringing toys to the little tots along with sympathetic words of love and encouragement to the children and their parents."

Pam suggesting it may be a little too sad elicited Brite's, "Nonsense, on TV no child dies, it would kill ratings. All survive through the courageous efforts of third world female doctors working for free. Just imagine the grabbing power of the video; we pick up a few dozen cute teddy bears, wholesale, for you to give to each bald child. In fact, if we mention the manufacturer there could be an appreciable financial gratuity."

Did I see a nano second flick of a pink tongue licking a Brite lip?

Pam, struggling to get comfortable using suffering children as a ploy to sell a book stuttered, "Toni, I really don't know," was countered with Toni's verbal pictorial. "You could be looking sad, standing over the crib of a bald girl of say five, and as she smiles up at you, you hand her a teddy bear."

"What if the child doesn't want it?" my nasty two and three quarter stiff ones said.

Not turning to me Brite answered Pam, "We'd video a dozen bear giving scenarios. It's just a matter of time 'til we get the perfect picture of a bald girl hugging the bear smiling gratefully up at you. There could be a follow-up picture of you, hand in hand with the child dragging her intravenous stand walking down the corridor, the foreground in shadows with you walking to a bright light at the end of the corridor."

That last picture killed my third stiff one, and in its whiskey death throws I yelled, "Crap. That's sordid."

Pam agreed, "Toni, I don't think that's very nice."

My stiff trio and I were silenced out of existence as Brite continued, "Remember Pam, there are movie rights. To be honest with you I don't think we have a theatre product, but definitely a TV movie. Of course there is the problem of your husband."

Getting up at that, on my way to make a fourth one, only not as stiff as its predecessors, for appearance sake I asked how I was a problem.

Again tet-a-tet with Pam, Brite mentioned he's police, as if saying 'exposes himself.' "The only way to soften that threatening male macho image is to show your husband helping diverse at-risk teenage boys trying to keep them out of trouble and advising them on how getting a college education leads to careers in medicine or law where they can give back to their improvised communities."

Hearing her as I was pouring a light one, I couldn't stop pouring 'til I held a stiff one.

Pam's addition, "We could have my husband dressed like Santa Claus carrying a bag of cute stuffed bears. After all, Christmas is only a few weeks away and men in uniform giving Toys for Tots is a traditional feel good –" was interrupted by the door bell sounding the end of a hard fought round.

Fourth one in hand I went to the door as a way to escape them. Besides, it was obvious Pam was glued to Brite, and Brite wasn't getting up.

CHAPTER 33

The Closet Door Opens

Woody and Ronni were standing there, Woody's panic was writ large by his messed up hair, his pale face, and his disheveled clothes. As he charged past me he tossed back in his wake, "Mac, I've got to talk to you." He went by so fast I almost spilled my drink.

Ronni had a Cheshire cat's smile of a puss holding a quart of cream in her stomach. She followed Woody and by the time I closed the door and regained the living room Ronni occupying the couch's other end with a quick glance evaluating Toni Brite: her age to the month, the last time dye was applied to her hair to the day, her weight to the ounce, the clothes' cost to the cent, and the layer of face makeup to the milliliter.

So agitated, pacing up and down, Woody didn't even steal my recliner. Couldn't remember when I had last seen Woody stripped of his superior sense of self importance and self entitlement.

Staring at Brite, Woody discourteously asked, "Who the hell are you?"

"I'm an agent representing Madison, Addison, and Donaldson and I'm in serious consultation with Pam McCoppin."

Ronni gasping, "MAD! I know the MAD agency. You rejected my manuscript depicting my struggles in solving crimes in a male dominated police department."

Patiently Toni Brite explained, "You need to solve a high profile murder, or be sexually ravished by fellow officers, maybe be gang raped in a locker room with higher-ups engaged in a cover up of your abuse, in order to be seriously considered worthy of a reading."

Ronni told Brite she was the principal detective in the Roach Terrorist Murder.

Passing her card to Ronni an excited Toni told her, "Darling, resubmit your manuscript directly to me after you solve the terrorist attack and I'll see it gets serious attention."

Woody, still pacing shouted, "Hell, everybody, I'm in serious trouble here."

Hearing that come out of Woody, I knew he wouldn't say no to the stiff one I was offering to him.

Accepting the offer of my cheap undiluted whiskey at twenty dollars a liter, said Woody had definitely lost his aplomb.

"Mac, I've been approached by GAP. They want me to join them. They promised to protect me. I don't know where this is coming from. I need you to back me up."

"GAP? I repeated. What the hell is that?"

Ronni, unable to hide her amusement explained, "Gay Alliance of Police."

Woody shrieked, "They think I'm gay. Mac, can you believe it? GAP is after me to join."

I told the three stiff ones currently doing a tango with my mind, I knew where it came from, and had to enjoy my role while wondering about how serious was the Committee's commitment to confessional secrecy.

Handing him his stiff drink, impishly I told Woody that although I'm surprised to find out he was gay he shouldn't be ashamed of being gay; it's where it's at in America.

Enjoying herself, Ronni added that she thought Woody was interested in her, "Shows how mistaken a person could be."

I agreed with Ronni, complimenting Woody on how successful his subterfuge had been, and didn't think any less of him and promised to continue fearlessly riding next to him in the squad car.

An excited Brite interrupted Ronni's and my playful acceptance of Woody's gayness, "A gay detective solving the Roach Murders, I see an incredible literary work that will sell fantastic in the gay community."

From somewhere, Toni placed a business card in Woody's hand, stating if he got in touch with her, she could get a gay ghost writer who would be able to write a sympathetic and sensitive account of the difficulties he's experiencing in his coming out in a homophobic police department.

Woody cried, "Mac, damn it, tell them I'm not gay." So agitated he spilled some of my whiskey and tossed Brite's card back at her.

With three, and working on a forth stiff one, I couldn't resist, "Don't be ashamed Woody, be proud. I'll still have the same opinion of you, just don't try hugging me any more."

Slipping her card in Woody's jacket, Toni said, "Detective, now out of the closet, are you involved in any charitable work, visiting terminally ill AIDS patients, courageously mouth kissing them."

Woody yelled, "Screw AIDS. I tell you I'm definitely not gay, and Ronni, if you come over to my place I'll show –"

Aghast, Ronni denied herself the pleasure of proving Woody straight, telling him she'd be afraid of how devastated he'd feel when he couldn't perform.

Brite, the bit in her even white teeth asked if Woody suffered mental abuse from his fellow cops, was he denied promotion for his sexuality, was he gang raped in the shower room, was he the butt of inappropriate jokes.

Emptying the glass with one swift swallow Woody groaned, "Mac, you've got to help me."

Brite blithefully continued her pictorial theme, "We could arrange for you, in uniform, to be Grand Marshall of some gay parade. Wait, no, that's no good. In uniform you could be mistaken for one of the village people."

"Ronni, you know I'm straight. Remember the session we had in my car."

"You didn't go all the way."

"Damn it Ronni. There wasn't room, and I wanted to go to your place and you refused."

"Lucky I did, otherwise when you couldn't do it, I'd lose confidence in my femininity thinking it was my fault, wasn't attractive enough to excite you, wasn't sufficiently experienced to assist you in performing. That could be psychologically devastating for a woman."

Taking a sip, I mentally enjoyed her unintended joke, not experienced. Hell she could give my corner college co-eds advanced courses.

"You are attractive. Damn it Ronni, let's leave and have a drink together at your place, or my place. Hell, any place.

"And Mac, you've got to tell everyone in the department you know I'm not gay. Do you realize this evening walking into the precinct's crowded locker room after opening my locker and turning around, the room was empty. Do they think I'm interested in them in that way?"

Brite asked if he had a significant other. Was he married to his boyfriend? If not, the marriage could create a feel-good chapter and a picture of him in his uniform walking out of the church hand in hand with his husband, and with rice being thrown would make a fantastic dust cover picture.

Poor Woody, I poured a couple of stiff ones for us.

While Woody was expostulating over not planning any stupid marriage, not interested in children, didn't have a lover, my doorbell rang, signifying the end of another spectator entertaining round. With all speech and animation momentarily suspended, with no offering to answer the bell, as master of my home, yet feeling I was playing the butler, I went.

A trio of caring faces stood looking sympathetically at me. Given the day's conference I should have expected the return of Paris Start and Lovey Leeper, but not so soon. I was totally surprised and not a little nonplus. A third woman accompanied them, so butch she had to be a democratic activist of the true believer stripe, hitting five ten in flat heels, short black duck back hair, the reincarnation of teen age boys in the fifties, she looked stern even censorious, even pissed off at me.

With my mouth wide open in shock at their arrival, Paris went for a cheek kiss whispering, "I understand all now."

Lovey got a hug in, mumbling something about brotherhood.

Should have slammed the door on them but with the shock of seeing the three, along with Woody, Ronni and Brite inside the house occupying my mind, the uninvited trio walked past me as if believing what was mine was theirs.

Once inside, taking off coats, they seized chairs: Paris on the couch between Ronni and Brite, Lovey in my easy chair, and the third invader grabbing the last straight back chair. Woody was still walking a hundred yard dash in circles looking bewildered at the newcomers and drinking his new stiff one. I was annoyed and sipped my drink, skipped introductions and dragged a kitchen chair into the living room for myself.

Positioning myself on the peripheral, planning to enjoy a new show, Paris and Lovey announced sans drum role they were psychiatrists sent here to administer to a family in pain. The dike announced she was the

City Coordinator for GLASS. What was GLASS? She remained silent on what GLASS was in the full expectation we all knew.

Misinterpreting the puzzled looks generated by GLASS she didn't clarify but announced, "I'm Babs Hoch."

Pam, barely holding on to mistress of the house role asked about GLASS.

"GLASS," Babs Hoch explained, "is the gay and lesbian agency for safety and security, a government agency initiated recently by our democratic governor in reaction to the spurt of the assaults on lesbians and gays from ignorant and hate filled men."

Stopping in front of her a perplexed Woody asked what the hell she was doing here. He didn't need her, was able to look after himself.

Babs Hoch, pulling out a notepad from her pants pocket asked Woody if he was experiencing any persecution, any threats to his life since he came out.

"Holy shit," he screamed, "I just heard the rumor barely two hours ago, and it's already spread to GLASS."

Prefacing her advice with, 'as a psychiatrist,' a concerned Paris told Woody he should be open and honest about his sexuality.

A sympathetic Lovey, from deep in my easy chair, mentioned, as a psychiatrist he read that in a San Francisco study, at least ten percent of the population was gay.

Paris corrected, "No Dr. Leper, I've read in the *Village Voice* it's over 25%."

"Ridiculous," spat Babs Hoch, "everyone knows it's over 50%, with most of them cowardly hiding in the closet afraid of physical assaults. If only everyone would courageously come out of the closet we would have a wonderful diverse democratic loving world." When saying that, for some reason Babs gave Ronni, who was wearing a pants suit a suggestive stare.

"Well," Lovey said, "as doctors of psychiatry we've been sent to help a wife and her family deal with a husband who has recently walked out of the closet."

Babs got up, and standing over Ronni asked if she had any sexual difficulties, adding as an expert and coordinator of GLASS she could lend sympathetic encouragement and knew the names of women who could offer counseling and a safe place to live, if her sexually ignorant husband abused her over her confused sexuality.

Never saw Ronni Deutsch lose her overcoat of superiority 'til then. Emphatically stating she was normal, wasn't married nor living with Woody, and didn't need any help from a _"

Woody stopped her, "Ronni, don't be hurtful and judgmental. Mrs. Hoch has made a simple honest mistake. Crap, no one's noticed your severe pant suit, no one is making judgment, no one is judgmental, but admit it. your outfit presents a masculine persona."

The 'honest mistake' had Ronni struggling to get out of the couch, but pinned by Paris' bulk she gave up and settled for shouting, "I dress the way I want and it's nobody's business, and Woody, just because I haven't slept with you doesn't mean I'm a lesbian. Shit, the gall of men."

Ronni looked ready to say a lot more when Babs Hoch, taking umbrage at Woody referring to her as Mrs. attacked him. "It's Ms. Hoch, and being gay is not a mistake. Lesbians aren't mistakes and I'm going to submit a report to GLASS about your Neanderthal abusive, even threatening attitude about diverse people."

Paris put in, "In my professional opinion as a psychiatrist, he's in desperate need of our help. The poor man thinks he can go back into the closet."

From my recliner Lovey seconded it, "Certainly, the closet door is closed."

Babs complained, "I came here to give professional support to the wife and child of a recently ousted gay man, only to find myself in the midst of cowardly deniers and haters. From what is transpiring here, I feel a serious intervention by the full GLASS membership is absolutely and critically needed and needed immediately for all of you."

Looking down at her tablet and scrolling, she asked the room how was a week from tomorrow.

Desperately Woody begged, "I'm not married, not gay, but I swear, if I was gay, far from being ashamed, I'd be marching down Fifth Avenue leading the next gay demonstration in a tutu. I'd be proud to be gay, shouting it from the rooftops, kissing men in public, going on TV telling the world how great it was to be gay, but unfortunately I'm not gay. Regretting it I'm constantly melancholy of this personality flaw."

Babs' hand quickly pulled a form from her severe 'take no prisoner' pant suit worn often by political women. Looking at Woody she pronounced, "Detective McCoppin, you admitted your homosexuality to the SAD Committee just this day. and at this moment everyone at headquarters is applauding and supporting your courage."

Wide eyed Woody exclaimed, "I'm not McCoppin." Then turning to me the rat pointed, "That's McCoppin."

"More denial," lamented Babs and quietly told Woody an emergency intervention by GLASS could be held in two days to help him discover his true self.

Ronni, pointing to me, now standing next to the liquor cabinet, drink in hand, gleefully tried to correct the misunderstanding. She announced, "Yes, he's McCoppin, and you've been talking to Woody Biden, who's also reported to be gay."

A joyful Babs exclaimed, "Two gays! Are you two living together? Are you planning to get married? Adopt a colored child?"

Paris and Lovey begged Pam to go into the kitchen and discuss with them how difficult it is to deal with the disastrous discovery of who your husband actually is, and then come face to face with his lover.

Sitting on the conversational edge, a dangerous two feet from the kitchen's entrance, Pam stated, "My husband's not gay."

Was I sensing a tonal undercurrent of doubt in her voice? I wasn't all that satisfied with the tone of her confidence in my masculinity.

Going up to her I whispered, "Pam, I'll explain it all to you later. Just play along."

She really floored me. Looking up at me she quietly asked me if it was true. Was I gay?

"Shit, Pam, just have confidence in me. I know what I'm doing," but that was the stiff ones talking. Deep down I had serious doubts.

Turning to the room I confessed to being gay, but also was sexually interested in women.

Woody screamed, "Mac, what are you saying? We're not gay."

If crudely, Leeper succinctly expressed his appreciation of the situation. "He's AC/DC."

An excited Paris asked the room if they thought transvestite would be the appropriate descriptive word.

Babs demanded Pam and my son make an appointment for counseling. Scrolling through her tablet she thought three days from today would be good for her, but if Pam thought her situation was an emergency and needed immediate counseling, there was a support group of women whose husbands turned out to be gay. They met at Babs' house every Friday and Saturday night to find healing, to discover their own true sexual selves and gain confidence in their sexual attractiveness.

Pam gave the invite a definite no.

As an enticement Babs added drinks and finger food would be available.

Ronni, no slouch to TV humor, laughed at the finger food. She and I were the only ones to get it. Damn her, I know she was planning to have fun with my gay confession, when the door bell rang.

Desperate to escape a room nearing chaos, rushing to answer the bell, I came face to face with child services' Gestapo agent Harriet Bursome. Far from her prior antagonistic, if not belligerent attitude towards me, now she embraced me with a full press, whispering she understood. Topping off the assault, she delivered a cheek kiss accompanied by how she respected me. Disconcerted, I could only stare at her as she marched into my home, fast becoming a house of bedlam.

The crowded living room brought her up short. Traversing the loud crowd Bursome yelled her announcement, "I'm from child services." She let the announcement hang for a few seconds expecting trumpets and hosannas. The actual reaction was as varied as unexpected.

Totally befuddled, Woody announced for the 'n'th time he wasn't gay, had no children, wasn't interested in having children, then made for my liquor cabinet.

Brite, standing up, placing a stack of business cards next to her barely tasted wine glass, announced anyone interested in making millions and appearing on Letterman should take one of her cards and contact her. She had hundreds of erudite ghosts ready, ghosts who help politicians, Hollywood stars, and athletes, alive and dead tell the public about their exciting, fabulous lives.

Making for Brite's vacated couch seat, Bursome came into hard staring conflict with standing Brite, accompanied by words getting very personal over whose seat it was. The struggle for seating rights was interrupted as Babs Hoch, jumping out of her chair made an unexpected attempt to hug Bursome, screaming, "Harriet, is it you? I'm Babs Hoch. You attend my Saturday night sexual awareness meetings at my home."

Eyeing Babs' vacated chair, Bursome made a fast end around move and was sitting down leaving Babs hugging empty space and puckered up for an air kiss.

In this game of musical chairs I offered to get everyone a drink with the evil purposes of serving glasses of cooking sherry. Babs got my vacated chair and asked for a Rob Roy. Several asked for assorted drinks: a Cosmopolitan, a Vodka and Lime tonic, as well as a Shirley Temple. Leeper had the Shirley Temple.

Edging aside Woody, who was holding a tumbler half full, I made myself a stiff one. Seeing my chair taken by Babs, I positioned myself near the front door, ready to do exit honors for all those wishing to leave.

Forgetting my liquor cabinet wasn't supplied as his was at his condo, Woody tried to make some of the requested concoctions. With one hand holding fast his drink with life and death urgency, the other hand was ineffectual, and my liquor cabinet holding only whiskey, he gave up making the drink orders, much to the room's disappointment. Taking his position in the center of the room, he explained quietly, very rationally, he supported the gay agenda one hundred percent including makeup and wearing dresses in the workplace.

Mishearing Woody, Babs shouted, "So you finally admit you're gay. I'm so proud of you. Can I expect you at my house this Friday?"

Laughing so hard, Ronni had to cross her legs tight not to pee.

Desperately stretching, Drs. Start and Lovey struggled to give Woody their cards while keep possession of their chairs.

Bursome also gave her card promising child services is anxious to help a single gay man adopt a child. "In fact," she shouted, "I've got a perfect twelve year old Hispanic boy just released from juvenile detention that for some reason is hard to place."

Unthinking, Woody put all the cards in his pocket.

Brite, afraid her card was possibly lost in the card deck he was accumulating, gave him another.

Totally muddled, Woody was reduced to mumbling about how he loved children of color; they were the best, just needed love, encouragement and guidance to become neurosurgeons.

With Bursome fishing out a picture of some sinister looking kid making finger gestures, I signaled Ronni to take Woody out before he's forced to adopt a gang of nasty kids. Unable to handle my cheap booze, not used to taking it straight, he was losing it big time.

Ronni got my head shaking message and steered Woody to the door while he was alternately hugging a mean teen ager's picture to his breast, and lovingly staring at it murmuring, "I could change his life. His entire life would be different thanks to me." His eyes were glazed over as he left humming, *We Are the World,*.

With them gone the struggle over chairs subsided and the noise level dropped, thanks to people giving up celebrating Woody's gayness.

Next to leave were Babs Hoch, Paris and Lovey, each in turn telling Pam and me how they realize we are good parents, given they now possess real information about me. Babs Hoch summarized the parting comments saying she couldn't possibly conceive of a gay man being a poor parent. That would be just so hateful. Then added the proviso I must be open to my son, explaining to him in a sensitive way how gay is not inherited and he may not be gay. The last sounded more like, and he may not be bright.

Running after the trio, Bursome said she'll report to child services how courageous Mickey's parents are, then shouted, "Babs, wait for me. I've got some great topics and video tapes for Friday night."

Toni Brite gathering up her papers and miscellaneous business cards scattered about, plaintively told everyone as they were leaving to call her.

She knew there were millions in book and movie deals, and MAD was more than stacked with hovering ghosts just an opportunity's knock away. So pitiful was her plea, I promised we would get in touch with her. Leaving, she took her perkiness with her, leaving an untouched wine glass behind.

Immediately starting to straighten up, Pam commented on how much I drank. I denied the justice of her comment. Unfortunately, immediately after my denial I stumbled into the liquor cabinet. Her observation, "You're drunk," elicited my denial, admitting to only being a little high, and when she comes up to bed she'll see how gay I can be. Waiting for her, I fell asleep. I'm sure she deliberately delayed coming up. It was her loss. Felt frisky for the five minutes before I fell asleep.

CHAPTER 34

Freedom, the Power to do Nothing and Say Anything

If the massive hangover I suffered in the morning was any gauge, I was blind drunk the previous night. With my head sensitive to any sudden movement, my angry stomach asked if more roach poison got tossed into it last night, I carefully put on my uniform one thread at a time. Finally dressed, like a ninety year old after hip surgery, I made my way downstairs, one cautious step at a time. In the kitchen, desperate to quench my thirst, I downed a quart of orange juice out of the carton accompanied by four or was it five aspirins, anyway, a handful. Pam looked at me with pity, or was it disgust, I couldn't determine which and at that moment of pain couldn't care which.

Splashing cold water on my face and in the process wetting my shirt and jacket, I mumbled, "Shit," and with slow measured steps made the Herculean journey to my easy chair with the satisfaction of one achieving the Arctic Pole on January 1st. Lowering my body with the care, crane operators position steel girders, I sat, I sighed, I cursed myself, cursed the world, and made several solemn AA vows.

Pam, by her very exertions in getting herself and Mickey dressed, with her busy talk about how much she had to do, how wonderful the ceremonies will be, how exciting it will be to be on TV, how a neighbor promised to record it, how appropriate or not was her dress for the occasion, how will her dress appear on TV, how handsome Mickey looked in his football jersey, how -, well crap, she didn't run out of 'hows', but if she did, she'd start over, varying only the sequential order.

All this talk, this to and fro movement around a man who now knows how hospice inmates feel on visiting days, was inhuman torture, torture I suspect she was inflicting at least in part, deliberately in wifely retribution.

At last with Pam dressed and Mickey washed, dressed, looking cute in his football jersey, Pam turned to me. My turn consisted of her cajoling me to get up, accompanied by numerous aggravating offers to help getting me up. The only thing that got me up was her eventually resorting to yelling at me to get up, yelling at a man whose mind shrieks with pain if it heard a rain drop landing.

Standing, and after at few moments achieving balance, I checked the body: stomach queasy but not threatening to toss ugly things out; head still aching, but I could move it without brains crashing against the skull; and as an incentive harboring hopeful thoughts of crisp fall November air supplying a needed anodyne to a suffering body got me to open the front door.

The needed sun, the needed crispness, the needed invigorated air were not waiting outside. Nature was conspiring to continue my punishment. In its place was a cold damp New York November day where moisture hanging in the air, forcing cars to resort to windshield wipers, and coats becoming damp without a drop falling.

Seriously debated taking the car but the up/down of getting in and out versus walking a cautious straight line was a no brainer, and so we walked the five blocks to the Memorial Celebration banquet hall.

To Pam's complaints of hair, coat and shoe damp damage I gruffly answered we'd never get a parking spot, which turned out to be true.

The initial police barricades were set up three blocks from the Memorial hall. Traffic was prohibited; pedestrians were questioned as to their purpose in approaching the hall, with only the most trustworthy justifications allowed to pass through the barrier.

The second barrier around the hall was two blocks away where suits with ear pieces, accompanied by uniforms interrogated and asked for picture identification.

Between the first and second barricades were tangles of tables selling everything, and selling aggressively. We had to fight off t-shirts with aphorisms only incidental to roach poisoning such as 'Jobs not War' (couldn't argue with that), silk screen shirts with pictures of salsa dishes, along with shirts demanding 'Hate the Poison, Not the Salsa' under a picture of a rat and a bowl of salsa. Pam wanted me to buy a sweatshirt proclaiming 'I survived the roach' and to get Mickey one announcing 'I was at the roach murder' with graphic pictures of roaches. Despite Pam's and Mickey's pleading I kept my money and kept moving them. The last challenge to my authority was when we encountered a table selling bottles of salsa proclaiming it was the actual salsa used at the banquet.

At the third and last barricade, one street away from the hall, were the purse peekers of the women and gentle pat downers of the men. Hell, to pass through Heaven's pearly gates would be easier and with far less personal scrutiny and interrogation.

A few energetic individuals somehow escaping all the searching, questioning, and pat downs, were hawking memorial tickets, rear seats, only ten dollars, front row discounted to fifty with only a sparse few available

Other than these obnoxious vexing scalpers, the only vehicles and personnel accorded preferential treatment other than luminary's limousines were the media trucks and buses. Parked, they circled the hall with dishes pointing to the heavens ready to electronically thrust out into the universe the breathless doings here on earth.

On the street adjacent to the hall were numerous brightly lit tents under which sat two or three communicators discretely wearing microphones to enable their words to reach the heavens, always a man and a woman, always a white and a black. On the edge of these circus side-show tents stood worried groups of people: several peering under large shrouded TV cameras, others with clipboards scurrying about as if the parachutes being issued were one short. With make-up kits in hand, several nervous functionaries darted in and out of the tents, one dabbing a powder puff to the nose of a seated one, another with a cotton ball running to absorb the hint of sweat forming on the brow of one going to talk to the expanding universe.

At one tent, rushing about like a harried general, a man strode up and down alternately shouting to the seen, and through his face mike to the unseen, while continually peering down yelling orders at the handlers of several monitors arranged in the dark.

Off to one side, a bald spectacled man sat in front of a computer typing messages to be printed on monitors draped above the cameras. He had a bored look, but a quick peek at what nonsense he was typing into the monitors said his look was in sync with his output.

Almost passing the Eye logo tent, a harried young man rushed up to us asking our names.

Innocently feeling it was merely another procedural security request I foolishly identified myself as Edward McCuppin, wife Pam and son Michael..

With a name badge under the Eye logo indicating I was talking to Chet, Interview Coordinator Assistant, the young man frantically rummaged through a loose-leaf book two inches thick 'til suddenly looking up cried, "Shit man, I can't find you. Who are you again?"

I told him, "Ed McCoppin."

"Never mind that, what's your connection with this Memorial? Are you a speaker? Are you – say, your son is wearing a football jersey. Was he at the roach dinner?"

"Well," I started to say, and it was all I was able to get out as Chet screamed to the head mike and ear man, "I've got one."

"Who?," was returned.

"One of the football players, with his mother."

"Fantastic. Makeup, get off your asses and do something to them."

Powder puffs and cotton balls attacked Pam to her pleasure, to Mickey, much to his discomfort.

Finally they were seated at the brightly lit table, but seated skewed in relation to the interviewers, Shirley and Teddy, so neither couple actually faced the other but appeared to do so from the center camera's perspective. The arrangement enabled the left side camera to have an unobstructed full face view of Pam and Mickey, the opposite side camera would likewise, without any obstructions, allow viewers to enjoy popular Shirley and Teddy plucked straight from the 12 o'clock news.

After introducing Pam as the mother of a child who escaped being poisoned, a heartbroken Shirley, close to tears, looking straight past Pam's shoulder with believable TV's sincerity asked how she felt learning how near her son came to being killed.

Pam said she was happy at her son's escape.

To myself, *as opposed to being sad her son escaped.*

A shouted 'cut' from the mike and ear man stopped everyone. Going up to Pam, with patience dipped in sarcasm, he asked if Pam knew this was a Memorial service. Without pausing for Pam to answer he continued, "There are no happy people at a Memorial, only sad, devastated people who after washing themselves in sorrow can be allowed to courageously express hope for a happier future. Forbidden at a TV Memorial are smiles, glad words and happy faces. Understand?"

With Pam nodding 'yes' he told her she had to be sad if she wanted to be part of TV news' coverage of the Memorial. Asking Pam, "Do you want to be on TV?" He allowed Pam to say "Yes, and now I feel terrible."

Again Shirley, close to tears, repeated the question, how Pam felt learning how near her son came to being killed.

After saying she felt terrible for all the children especially for poor Mrs. Scott and her son, Pam smiled at the camera and almost gave a little wave.

A shouted "cut" from an exasperated ear and mike man who, rushing over to Pam told her, "Honey, this is a visual media. Pictures convey the news, not the words, so Pam dear, if you feel terrible you've got to 'look' your feelings so the viewers, who have no feelings, seeing your feelings will be able to share your feelings. Remember, if you don't look sad, people won't recognize it's a sad story, or worse, with your video feelings out of sync with your audio words, the viewers will convict you of being a lying hypocrite. People must believe in their TV news. What's left to believe in if not in TV news. Now, for the viewer's gratification, can you cry? I'm not asking for a rain storm, just a mist sufficiently damp to require you to dab at your eyes. Can you do it?"

Pam promised to give it a try, but apologetically mentioned she didn't feel sad, felt excited being on TV.

"Okay, time is short. I've heard the wife of the dead guy is around here, and we're hunting for the black family and there's a rumor a gay cop is somewhere, so this is what we'll do. Make-up will give you a big shot of eye moisturizer so appearing teary on camera will allow your feelings expressed in words to resonate with our viewers. They want to feel for you, feel your pain. Remember, all they want is to feel for you.

Feeling is all they expect from TV news. Feeling is the only way they can participate in an ongoing drama. Now let's start over. Shirley, take it at the first question, then Teddy, you take question two and you'll alternate."

Hiding her coffee cup, Shirley again arranged her face to look with teary concern as if the question of world peace rested on her shoulders. Slyly looking past Pam's shoulder at a scrolling monitor just above the camera Shirley asked how Pam felt, as a mother learning how close her child came to experiencing a horrible, painful death.

Now with glistening eyes Pam told Shirley how she was so frightened for her son's life.

I mentally commented, *as opposed to being not frightened.* (It's a contra comment, *a* CC which lately has become a reflexive mental habit. It consists of negating trivial statements obviously true or more likely blatantly banal expressions of white noise.)

Out of camera range, the mike and ear person pushed Mickey into Pam, who instinctively put a protective arm around him.

A worried Teddy, staring hard at the scrolling monitor asked Pam if she was happy her son wasn't poisoned.

Dabbing at her watery eye Pam, although saying she was very happy Mickey was safe, was so sad for the man who died.

I counter commented, *as opposed to being unhappy her son was safe and glad Scott died.* (These CC thoughts are irritations to the mind.)

Shirley, still ready to cry at any moment, reading over Pam's shoulder, asked the next question, "Did your son suffer psychological trauma from his horrible experience?"

A fearful Pam said it was too soon to tell, with a face telling she expected the worse, but the counseling he's receiving is helping Mickey to get over any mental damage done to him.

"So glad to hear it," courageously Teddy extemporized.

Counter comment, *as opposed to not being glad to hear it.*

Teddy read his next question off the monitor with the face your doctor would wear when saying it's malignant. "Pam, I know this is a trying time for you, but can you tell us how you feel going to this solemn Memorial event."

Poor Pam, knowing there was an expected answer and wanting to say the expected, to gain time to think of the expected answer dabbed an eye, hugged Mickey before finally saying what was expected, "I feel so humble and grateful over everyone's loving responses to my son's near escape."

Counter comment (CC), *as opposed to being excited with being the center of all this attention.*

Shirley was back reading what had just been typed on the monitor, "What will you say to the widow of the murdered man when you meet her?"

Clutching Mickey tight as he was starting to get restless and curious about all that was goings on out of sight of millions of eyes, Pam gave an "Oh," and again had to dab and hug Mickey to gain thinking time, "I'll express my profound sorrow over her loss and hugging her will offer her my love and all the support I can give her at this tragic time in her life."

CC, *as opposed to being happy it's you, not me, and everyone knows the offer stops short at any real money and time, still the expected words are always there for the asking.*

Teddy, reading over Pam's shoulder asked, "If you came face to face with the murderer, and your son was the victim, what would you say to him?" And to give her a clue to the expected answer, he hopefully continued, "Would you extend forgiveness to him?"

Still slow in the uptake Pam did another dab, left eye then right eye before she came up with the correct answer, "Oh, I'd forgive him.

Being a Christian I couldn't hold a grievance against him. Punishing him won't bring my son back."

CC, *as opposed to I'd like to ram roach food down his throat and see him in hell.*

Shirley, getting rotating hand motions from the mike man to hurry, quickly validated Pam's statement, "It's very hard to forgive, but you are a strong woman."

CC, *as opposed to being easy to forgive, and she's a weak woman.*

Shirley, turning to the camera, excitedly read, "We have just heard that the Governor has arrived and *The News at Noon* will try to get him to speak to us."

"To commercial," was shouted.

Shirley and Teddy sipped coffee from their hidden cups as Powder Puff and Cotton Ball rushed up to them to repair the ravages of doing a live interview on tape.

Clip Board came up to me saying, "Officer, you can escort Mrs. McCoppin and her son to the hall, and please move quickly. I've heard the Peacock has people looking for the widow, and ABC, the Alphabet, has some black agents looking for the black victims, and we're trying to confirm the gay cop rumor, but we, the Eye, want to capture them first. Now officer, if you happen to see the widow, the blacks, or the gay cop, send them over to the Eye we'll give you a generous finder's fee."

Taking Pam by the arm, I had to exert some force to get her away from the tent. Obviously she had a lot more to say and wanted to say it and now felt she knew what to say, how to say it, and knew she could say it with teary conviction without any more intervening dabs nor eye moisteners.

Walking past the ABC alphabet, I heard an O'Malley representative demanding at least ten thousand for a ten minute interview with Dagmar and as an added incentive Dagmar promised she'll hold Winslow on her lap and give him judicious pinches on his ass when the Alphabet requested tears.

Behind the O'Malley rep was hot Brite, correcting O'Malley's generosity, arguing MAD has been given the copyrights to all interviews with anyone in the Dagmar family and no interview can be given unless MAD's copyrights are preserved and such preservation would cost thousands payable to MAD.

An outraged Alphabet representative stoutly maintained the Alphabet never pays for news stories, never has, never will, then the rep whispered they would consider an honorarium of five thousand, contingent on a poignant tearful interview.

Hearing five thousand, Dagmar hoisting up Winslow shouted, "For five thousand I'll throw in my remaining five children."

Brite, pushing forward, looking all business, and her business was looking hot, said, "Mrs. Mohammed cannot say a word as MAD has all the rights to hers, to her husband's and to her children's words. Any print, picture or video of her words without MAD's permission is forbidden. In fact, if you try to video her, MAD will sue for contractual infringement. However, I'm authorized by MAD to grant a waiver for ten minutes for a thousand, but that doesn't cover any replaying of the interview, or any part of the interview."

Brite reminded Dagmar, the contract she signed giving MAD sole authority over her words and pictures, she can only speak to the media with MAD's approval. "Dagmar, if you talk, MAD, getting mad will have to sue you and the Alphabet for contractual bad faith."

Once again the Alphabet agent stoutly reiterated the Alphabet's policy of never paying for a news story but certainly extending a few thousand to cover an interviewee's expenses is definitely appropriate.

The O'Malley representative felt MAD was going too far in the ownership of Dagmar reminding all standing around, that by signed contract, O'Malley is the sole authorized legal Dagmar representative, and in protection of their authority has the legal right to vet any venue, negotiate any remuneration, and any abrogation of O'Malley's legal binding contractual arrangement with Dagmar will be robustly pursued in civil court.

"Shit," Dagmar complained, "I can't talk, I can't go anywhere. This is slavery, it's not right."

Hearing the 'slave' word from a black, brought a collective gasp from ten or so throats standing nearby. O'Malley countered, "My dear, and you are dear to O'Malley and Associates, you must know, as everyone knows, if it's legal it can never be wrong, it must always be right. If it's not legal it can never be right, it must always be wrong."

An irate Dagmar shouted, "I'm being robbed of thousands. This is a hate crime. O'Malley is really O'Reilly. The FOX should be killed and MAD is the front for the KKK."

Suddenly Al Sharp, a man reported to have actually been seen marching with King, with barely fifty people separating him from being arm in arm with the man, came running up shouting, "Did I hear race? Did I hear hate? Did I hear O'Reilly? Is the FOX slinking around? Have no fear, Al Sharp is here to uncover racism, to attack racism, to shake my fist in racisms' face, to fight mano a mano racism to the death." Turning to his personal photographer Al ordered, "Get this," and hugged a surprised Dagmar. Pictures were snapped to capture the poignant moment. Then picking up Winslow, Al rewarded the frightened boy with a kiss. Holding the kiss he moved in a tight circle so various news agencies could capture the wonderful moment from several perspectives. That done, Al dropped the boy and turning to the head Alphabet representative said, "Five minutes, usual rates?"

The Alphabet man hesitating forced Al to promise, "I'm hot with outrage at this hate crime. A black child was almost killed because he's black. I'm so outraged I'll skin and castrate that damn Fox."

"Okay Al, can give you three minutes at the usual rate, but your spiel better be jammed with foaming and frothing anger, and we'll expect some spittle."

Pam and I left, and coming up to a couple of cops, since I was in uniform, they comradely stopped me asking if I heard the news. With Pam walking ahead I asked what was up. One cop said he won't be coming, we're only getting the chief of internal security, the Pimentos broad. The second amplified, "Yeah, the reason is the damp cloudy weather is forcing him to stay in San Diego."

Answering my, "Who's he?" the first cop said, "The President, he's in conference with Bill Clinton about some Haiti crisis.

Smirking the second cop added, "Yeah, they're having the conference at the Pebble Beach Golf Course. Shit, it's tee time in California. teeing off at the first hole they've got to be deep into wrestling with the problem of saving millions of Haitian children, living waterless, sewerless, homeless, foodless, healthcare less lives. What's the bet, after playing the 18 holes, in the clubhouse over cold highballs and jumbo shrimp, they'll solve the Haitian crisis and the solution will cost only a few billions of your money."

I commented, "Starving, homeless, educationally deprived black children like the tide obedient to the electionary moon, come in when needed, recede when not needed."

"Yeah, you're right there," said the first cop adding, "anyway we won't be seeing him."

Neither cop expressed disappointment over the President's absence, nor showed any confidence in the resolution of the Haitian problems despite your money. They added that the governor is also going to be a no-show . He's addressing a few hundred contributors at a Waldorf banquet to discuss inner city poverty.

The reason for the scarcity of big political office holders, a cynic could point to the elections just being over and won, and exhausted from running, all need rest and recuperation. One cop jokingly said, "Don't be in despair. The VP is going to talk via a video hook0up." Leaving them laughing disrespectfully at the VP, I warned of SAD being about.

Hurrying to catch up with Pam and Mickey I saw a line of people waiting their turn to be interviewed at the Peacock tent. Some I recognized, most I didn't. Later I discovered most were friends, far and close, relatives, far and close, neighbors, far and close, of the families involved in the roach poisoning. All were anxiously waiting to tell how terrible they felt such a terrible tragedy could happen in America, how hopeful they were it will not happen again while simultaneously expressing disbelief it actually did happen in America. Mostly women were in the queue, some sobbing, some crying, most excitedly talking to each other. For some inexplicable reason, women with their eye faucets running wide open were quickly moved to the head of the line much to the anger of the dry eyed, who being taught an important TV lesson began to wail, flail hands and enjoy histrionics.

I was about to pass through the tearing flow when I spotted Paris Start squeezed between TV's Dr. Ozzie and Dr. Philly. Being interviewed by the Peacock, all expressed their expert psychological agreement this was a terrible crime, (CC, *as opposed to a nice crime*) with Ozzie suggesting a remedy consisting of renewed national interest in exercise and a strenuous non fat diet regimen. For the viewer's enlightenment he casually mentioned his diet which will add ten years to your life is outlined in his book *Lose A Pound a Day Without Dieting* available on Amazon. He also recommended his cauliflower diet supplement pills available on Dr. Ozzie's website with his personal guarantee that taken four times a day for a year will make you look ten years younger.

Dr. Philly was into having the affected families meeting with his people where free expert guidance and counseling were readily available, leading to mental health. Looking deep into TV's eye he told you a happy life was the answer to pain. If the suffering could meet with his people, faithfully watching Dr. Philly's TV programs filled with deep insights into troubled families, accompanied by deeper profundities it would create joyful families. In creating a happy and joyous family, the most important factor was the diligent reading of his books and newsletters published by his son and available through his website.

Against such intellectual experienced TV heavyweights giving TV look of deep concern over everyone's problems and the curative power of their learned precepts, Dr. Paris struggled to hold her own. Slipping a word, a phrase, occasionally as much as a sentence as their profundities squeezed her hard, I did hear her reference of a father discovering his gay sexuality. As a result of her counseling she can discover in any tragedy some good health can be found.. The discovered gay was greeted with joy, Ozzie applauding the man's courage; Philly suggested the man in question contact his people for a possible spot on his show. The interviewer, female, and of course, blonde, pancake thick, trim, proud perky breasts hinted at with a three undone button exposure, positioned sideways to enable the invisible millions the pleasure of viewing her leg, mid thigh to ankle possessed a face having the ability to contort itself worthy of a world class mime as she expressed her desire to hug and applaud the man.

A nervous long haired man with a clipboard running up and down the queue continuously pleading, "Is there a gay guy here. If you're a gay man, go immediately to the head of the line."

Several tear stained women waved their hands shouting they were gay, their husbands were gay, and given sufficient time they could find and bring their husbands and their gay children to the Peacock tent.

Thank goodness, seeing the line's length, Pam passed it by. Passing the MSNBC tent I saw several angry faces shouting into the camera their sure belief the Republicans supporting racism, sexism, tax cutting, government reducing madness were absolutely responsible for this poison tragedy. Just as angrily they growled how they and only they loved little children, the poor, the minorities, and Al Sharp will shortly be with them to share his profound insight on this tragedy.

In passing I managed to hear their rote learned solutions: calls for funding for new safeguards, new regulations, and new programs to save and guard America's poor and minority children.

What attracted my attention was Woody, in uniform, in deep conversation with an ugly broad clutching a clipboard and an ear and mike guy, whose hair went down the back to his belt, and with a beard down his chest to his buckle. The broad's pepper and salt hair was shorter than mine.

Jessie Jack was currently on camera wearing a Rainbow Coalition sweater and standing in front of a sign requesting your donations and support for the Rainbow Coalition to help rainbow people and save America. He was rhythmically sing songing some rapper lyrics about racism being all about us, every color but white was beautiful and for you to support his ground roots program to build a rainbow of love.

Would have loved to linger at the Fox's tent as it was overflowing with fantastic hot babes, mostly blondes, seasoned with an occasional midnight brunette, all jabbering at each other, mostly in agreement except for two who were hard staring stilettos at each other. Waiting to be interviewed were well dressed prosperous looking men, not a beard nor hair beneath the collar. Don't know what they'll be saying, but feeling they're my people they must be saying and standing for my ideals, and thereby couldn't say anything wrong.

Finally reaching the banquet hall's entrance we endured another pat down, an identity interrogation, and a suspicious stare by an officious man with a phone hanging from each ear, a gold badge hanging down on a silver chain, and a plastic encased identification card pinned to his suit coat pocket announcing Hedja Hussan, Head of Federal Internal Security.

CHAPTER 35

All TV is a Stage
Showing Nothing

Immediately on entering the banquet hall, Pam, Mickey and I were separated and directed to make-up tables. I fought hard but they were too quick, and the results achieved gave me the pallor of a film zombie with a hint of pink lips. Upon seeing a guy, a guy only in the broadest anatomical sense of the word, approach me holding aloft as sacred relics: comb, scissors and eyebrow pencil, in horror I, pushing him away and escaped any more of their ministrations to create a TV me.

All the actors in this televised memorial drama appeared present. The girls in their cheerleader uniforms were queued up waiting for their turn for makeup touches. Appraising the girls, at most eight present at any football game, had now grown to eighteen, with several sufficiently mature to jiggle with braless abandonment. The boys in their football jerseys were constantly having hair combed and lacquer sprayed. The mothers dressed for Easter, and the fathers in pressed if not new suits were unrecognizable from the men at the games wearing assorted jeans and sport shirts.

A harried Ray Brothers, bumping into me exclaimed, "Sorry," then recognizing me despite my uniform continued, "Shit, all of them are here and it's the devil's work keeping them separate. Courtney is over there arguing with one of the organizers on why she should be on the stage standing next to me. On the opposite side Eleanor is fighting with an organizing official, haven't a clue about what, as I'm trying to keep out of sight. Don't know where Amber and that Derek are, just hope they stay out of sight. Then there's Desiree standing at the rear waiting for me to wave her down to sit next to me. Shit Mac, three McDonald's are tough to manage but nothing to juggling three broads."

I asked if he knew how the event was to be organized.

"Damn if I know, but you better go over to the registration table and get your coded name sticker so they'll know where to put you."

At the foot of the stage was a long table surrounded by an officious agitated crowd gesturing, shouting to and at each other. Getting into the midst of them I heard, "He's not coming." From another, "Is it definite?" A third added, "Yeah, the weather is too dangerous for Air Force One." Some black woman hearing this bit of information started to cry. The first speaker inquired, "Who's going to stand in for the President?"

"Will the Vice President, what's his name, deliver the main address?"

Another disrespectful person added, "Shit, not that dead head. He'll have the hall sleeping within five minutes, and everyone knows he can't shut up 'til he's shoveled his BS spiel for at least an hour."

Another informed personage with authority told the table the VP will be giving an address by video hookup from a UN Conference on Poverty he's attending.

Suddenly the hall's back door was flung open and a herd of uniformed florist delivery men came running in, each holding a floral arrangement.

An officious person detaching herself from the table's crowd screamed, "Finally, my flowers have arrived," and began to order the placements of the floral arrangements about the stage with great authority.

Quickly inserting myself into the space she vacated at the table, I requested a name tag from a grandmotherly type, not the matronly House on the Prairie type, but the scary Haunted House on Elm Street type.

I suspected her grim accusatory greeting, "You're late," was her normal attitude. Looking down at numerous scattered papers she sternly announced, "McCoppin's wife Pam, and son Mickey are registered," as if from her papers they had been given life. I barely escaped being thrown into the nether land of the paperless when she found me alive on a huge ream of orange papers.

Resisting the initial impulse to apologize for my tardiness, I demanded my name tag. Begrudgingly accepting my presence she gave me an orange coded tag, as if selling me a hundred million dollar winning lotto ticket. She added, "Keep it prominently exposed at all times, and your color is orange." Not being blind I already suspected my color. I was ordered to put it on my left breast pocket, definitely not the right one, and again ordered to never take it off 'til told to do so,

This done, pointing to a man standing at the stage's podium she continued, "See him." Done with me her head solemnly bowed down reverently to her papers. I noted she was shy of hair at her head's top

Looking about to gather Pam and Mickey, Hedja Hussan, head of Federal Internal Security ran up to me ordering, "Officer, you've got to stop the fight. It's ruining the atmospheric healing harmony we're striving to create at this memorial service." Now he fronted a tri colored plastic tag along with all his other identifying tokens.

Following him to the rear of the stage I came up short seeing Eleanor facing off with Courtney, both surrounded by a blood thirsty fight crowd hoping to see gore and blood splashed about. The two circling each other were throwing vicious word punches, working themselves up to hair pulling. I gave Eleanor a definite weight advantage, and with younger Courtney's quicker feet, the contest was fair. So far no blows were struck, but throwing hard hurtful words were landing with affect. It was only their natural concern for expensive coiffeurs and dresses that inhibited hair pull urges; still with growing volubility, the danger to hair may soon be in play. A brunette, whose mammaries were sufficiently abundant to insight thoughts of plastic, was alternatively egging the combatants on and yelling for her MacMuffin.

Knowing my current sex sensitive world, despite Hedja Hussan, head of FIS demanding I get involved, I hesitated, believing a woman cop would be more appropriate. Unfortunately, wearing a uniform suggesting a duty that couldn't be ignored, I was saved when Amber and Derek materialized. Despite the daughter's current anger at her mother, family blood coming to the surface had Amber joining her mother in the verbal fighting ring. Not only making the war of words unfair, Amber was looking as if she'd risk her hair to have a go at Courtney's, especially being goaded on by Derek, aka Ali, who seemed to be enjoying himself. The busty brunette, yelling to all fight spectators she was here as Ray's personal guest, and the two combatants should be thrown out. They definitely were not Ray's guests.

Sighing, knowing no good would come to me, I started to separate the fighters when a scream as loud as an echoing gunshot poured ice cold water on the combatants.

The shriek came from an excited functionary holding a clip board and wearing ear and mike attachments as he screamed, "Interracial." All looked about as if someone shouted, "He's got a gun." All eyes turning to Derek brought Amber to Derek's side. Grabbing his hand so there could be no doubt as to who was the interracial girlfriend, she announced to no one's question, "I love Ali."

The clip board screamer hurrying up to the couple excitedly asked if they would like to be interviewed on TV. "The Alphabet is now set up at the hall's rear and would love to devote as much as twenty minutes talking about your love. The great Diana Saw is there, already misted up, dying to hear about your loving relationship."

Would Amber like to be interviewed! Amber's eyes lit up as if Justin Timberlake just consented to sleep with her. Derek's inflated chest suggested he was well worth being the subject of a Saw interview. In fact in his mind, damn it, it was about time.

Pulling the loving couple aside, Clipboard asked if they'd like to meet Oprah.

"Better than meeting Jesus," Amber shouted.

Derek told everyone standing around it was better than meeting and rhyming with Jessie Jackson.

Promising a visit to misty Saw at the Alphabet after they gave an Oprah interview, the interracial couple was quickly ushered over to OWN's setup.

As a preface to their interview Oprah gave bountiful TV hugs and kisses enabling her viewers to know the couple were good people. Without any preliminaries Oprah quickly asked the couples' reaction to the poison attempt, and did they think the poison was racially inspired because of their interracial love. After allowing their response, 'it must have been done by evil people frightened by their love,' time to breathe, Oprah asked if the attack had affected their relationship. The couple, not being too intelligent and not wise to Oprah's TV in-depth interviews, Oprah had to quickly hint, "Do you think it made your relationship stronger?"

Amber being more alert to questions of love quickly gave Oprah the expected answer accompanied with an eye roll, "Oh this tragedy has made our love sooooo much stronger." Seeing Oprah's purse of lips, her leaning forward, her holding her hand, Amber felt empowered to continue relating how she felt so protected and safe with Derek by her side. Looking like she was an Oprah hug away, Amber hugged herself with happiness.

In Derek's turn he vowed he'd die before he'd let anything happen to Amber.

As the lovers snuggled together Oprah gave a full five seconds of air time to allow her TV acolytes to appreciate the modern diverse Romeo and Juliet moment before asking her next question. With the concerned sad near weeping face of a woman putting a dying child to bed, Oprah repeated, did they feel the roach poisoning was racially motivated.

Reflexively each tossed back the sweet bun Oprah and her TV minions wanted to eat. "Yes, so many people are against us just because we love each other," from Amber.

Derek replied, "They hate me cause I'm a strong black man."

To show people out there, the love the viewers saw and heard and now must learn to believe in was true, Amber gave Derek a mouthful of tongue. The interracial kiss in TV's current context was acceptable if edgy. However, the tongue, being for sit-coms, not for Oprah's serious interviews, made Oprah uncomfortable.

Facing the camera, eyes glistening with sorrow, Oprah told how when growing up such love would have resulted in a sure lynching from ignorant racists. "I've seen such hatred in my youth." was her sighing conclusion. If you could wash your mind of her billions you could feel her pain as completely as did millions of women. It was the sad look which generated those billions, and developing it to high perfection she once again magically gave it through the cameras personally to you in your home. Can't get more real than that. You actually hear and see it with your own ears and eyes.

Turning to Derek who with difficulty eventually was able to toss Amber's tongue from his mouth, Oprah, with the sorrow she had a valuable TV patent on asked if he had been subjected to discrimination. Suffering from being tongue licked on TV and seeing the larger than life Oprah in the flesh, Ali had to be cajoled. "Do people follow you 'cause you're black? They do me and I even had trouble buying a purse."

"Oh yes Oprah, all the time, even in the bathtub I feel eyes watching me."

"When shopping, do you feel people don't trust you? Think you're going to steal?"

"Yeah, and those petty theft convictions were bogus ... and I just want you to know, I just forgot to pay and cause I'm black, I'm always arrested."

Oprah, not wishing to parse that particular aspect of Derek's past, with glistening eyes only a centimeter from overflowing with emotional tears, leaning forward, she asked in her throaty voice if he and Amber were refused service cause they were an interracial couple.

Amber jumped on that invitation with complaints of hundreds of people staring at them. "Oprah, don't you hate it when you're the center of attention." Enthusiastically she once again related an example of blatant racism she experienced, "Do you know going through Wendy's drive in a mistake was deliberately made in our order. The fries we asked for weren't in the bag, just cause I'm with a black man."

"Yeah," Derek added, "and don't forget the napkins. Oprah, they deliberately didn't give us napkins with our order, just cause I'm black."

A wide eyed Oprah gasped to the camera. "I can relate to your pain with my purse experience. In fact I'm sure all Afro Americans have experienced hundred of racial slights." Still full face to the camera she dropped that particular aspect of her outrage to ask Amber if her parents objected to her dating an African American.

As if Oprah pressed Amber's button she angrily lamented to Oprah and the millions of worshippers sitting and watching over Oprah's shoulder how her father was racist cause he objected to their dating and she hated her father and loved Ali.

"And your mother, I'm sure she's more supportive of your relationship."

Amber, about to give a holy water splash to her mother as being supportive and therefore not being racist was saintly, when interrupted by Derek's complaining that Amber's mother did not give Amber sufficient allowance out of the racist reason; her mother was afraid he, a proud black man, was after Amber's money.

After giving Derek a cold stern eye bitch slap as a warning, Oprah quickly turning misty and concerned and asked, "Ali, I'm sure your parents are supportive of your dating Amber."

Chastised for his misstep though he wasn't sure where his foot went wrong, sensing what was expected of his parents, he told Oprah they love Amber as much as if she was black, in fact seeing her as black and not white. Being accepted as being like black was a great achievement for Amber, and he was proud of her.

Oprah started to move on but Derek had inadvertently pressed Amber's button. "Ali honey, remember when your mother refused to include me in your family's Labor Day barbecue and how, anyway when I showed up, everyone was so rude, not talking to me. It was as if I didn't belong there, it was as if I didn't exist, and you didn't speak up for me, nor _"

A frustrated Oprah sensing these two were totally incompetent to play the Oprah TV game, told her TV herd of jersey heifers how Ali's mother, being a victim of a lifetime of discrimination, was understandably protective of her son. Then leaning over, motherly gripping Derek's hand with both of hers she told him and the TV herd contentedly chewing on her words how just a few years ago if he dared look at a white girl he'd be lynched by the KKK. "I think this is the fear your mother has for you, worrying about you dating Amber will lead to your being lynched."

Having her name moved to objective status rather than the sentence's subject, unasked, Amber said that although her father told Derek he was a bum and loser who would never be successful in life, she defended Derek to her father and proudly denounced her father as a racist.

Amber inadvertently pressed an Oprah button, and she had many. Oprah retorted, "Black men are successful. If not, they would be, it's only racism that keeps them from succeeding, and people who watch TV and the movies know that. Derek, which university are you attending?"

Caught unawares innocently he said it's a college.

Disappointed Oprah still managed to generate glistening joyful eyes, "That's wonderful, what college is it?"

"Well, it's actually a community college."

You needn't spend hours of TV with Oprah to read the downward flash of disappointment in her expression. Picking up her face, like the true professional TV interviewer she was, Oprah suggested it was because his parents are poor he couldn't pay for a four year college. To her TV cow herd and to the camera, Oprah, with her mouth downturned as if she ate something sour evoked with great world weary sadness one of her profound axioms, "Due to poverty, due to the lack of encouragement black minds thwarted by racism were not being utilized much to America's loss.

"Now, I'm so proud of you Derek. You've graduated from high school and despite all your handicaps are perusing your education."

"Yeah Oprah, I'm working on my GED while attending the community college under a minority scholarship program."

Amber enthused how she's helping him with his GED studies. "I'm so proud of Derek."

Given Amber was a high school sophomore, and Ali had at least six years on her, Oprah ignored asking Ali what he was planning to do after college.

Gun-shy from Derek's prior not suitable answers for TV and her loyal herd's ears, and fearing the herd may be getting restless, Oprah quickly answered for Derek, "You're probably planning to be a doctor, lawyer or educator and working in the minority community to help save at risk youths, and by your example give them encouragement to escape their poverty and overcome racism."

Liking the picture Oprah painted for him and for her unseen millions resting in pastures, he bought the picture with an emphatic, "I feel it only right to give back to the community."

You could almost imagine the sighs of contentment emanating from Oprah's cows.

After pumping helium into Derek's future, Oprah felt it was time to continue damning Amber's racist's father by asking what he does.

"Oh, he owns _"

"Amber, shut your damn mouth," shouted Amber's mother from the sidelines.

Eleanor, accompanied by O'Malley and MAD representatives, dragged Amber unceremoniously from Oprah's tent. Outside in the dark away from the herd's gaze, Eleanor whispered with a voice of steel, "Dad's franchises are our money, and after calling him a racist, identifying his McDonald's would ruin his business. Remember with that slut Courtney having her claws into him, our money is in danger."

An ambivalent MAD representative wondered if the exposé of the father and big Mac could be a great jump start for Eleanor's 'tell all' book and documentary film. "Just think Eleanor, you were married to an abusive racist, who sells unhealthy fatty food to obese poor black children. Narrating your family's pain, and despite your children's sufferings from the abuse delivered by their racist father, you've be able to teach them: to love everybody who's different, to be understanding of everything except exclusion, to support and accept diversity, to be able to express deep feelings of empathy with all the world's suffering, and to love and protect the environment while simultaneously protecting your children from an insane racist degenerate who now cavorts with disreputable women. Can you feel it Eleanor? The love people will have for you seeing how good you are in the secular accepted way, and listen to this, your husband, Ray could write a 'tell all' book detailing how he was a racist member of the Arian brotherhood and was a food polluter who through your love seeing the error of his ways is now an accepted member of the NAACP as well as a fighter against obesity and an Fib informer against racists. Definitely a TV movie here, possibly a movie in the multiplex realm exploring a family's struggle to find love and tolerance in racist obese America."

The O'Malley representative chastised, "MAD, what are you saying? There are civil lawsuits with millions sure to be awarded and would be put at risk if Ray is portrayed as a racist. No matter how justified our claims, blacks, Hispanics and white women on juries being horrified and disgusted by racist Ray will feel the need to be moral and certainly not be in the mood to award us a penny. And it's not only about Ray, his racism affects all our clients. Unscrupulous lawyers representing the corporate money side would complain, where you expose one racist like a single cockroach, invisible millions are crawling beneath the surface"

Both O'Malley's agent and Eleanor, in agreement, physically kept a crying Dagmar from running back to Oprah to expose Amber's father's McDonald's.

Derek wasn't leaving, waxing thick to Oprah's inner joy and horrified face, on the psychological damage he suffered as a black man when he was followed and watched in a Dollar Store. That revelation almost lifted a yelling outraged Oprah from her chair, "I feel your pain, I suffered the same discrimination over a thirty eight thousand dollar purse, however thank goodness the publicity didn't hurt the reviews of my new movie, especially in the Afro American neighborhoods."

CHAPTER 36

Talking the Dead to Death

Being told by all respected TV news readers, serious and profound TV news commentators, and late night comics, the Memorial service was not only an important event but also highly successful in healing the country, the people could do nothing less than believe what they were told.

The substratum underpinning the massive belief was populated by numerous vacuous feelings: feelings of enjoyment in satisfying your needs to empathize for the victim; feeling by proxy the victims' pain was sufficiently alleviated by the service; feeling the service brought a national sense of harmonious togetherness; feeling the service, in having addressed and condemned evil has made everyone a better person; feelings of a renewed optimistic attitude for society's continued happiness and success; feelings that with the service's end, closure having been achieved, roach poisoning is now placed as a forgettable historic event; feelings the viewers and country did a righteous thing in having a Memorial service, and the most important overarching feeling, the feeling of love, caring and the sense of common humanity are real because it had been seen, heard and reported as real on TV .

With the country awash with such feelings nurtured and encouraged by TV only a cynical reprobate, a person who pisses on good feelings, an outsider who repudiates a society he's not invited to participate in, only such a person could resist being blown away by all the blow, and Detective Ed McCoppin was such a man not only to think it but to say it's all just BS and frighten people.

The theatrical presentation of the Memorial service for the victims of roach poisoning couldn't be faulted if its purpose was to dazzle, entertain and touch the feelings of the TV viewers without engaging anyone's mental thought. At the stage's foot the profusion of flowers stretching out six feet into the first rows' feet was reminiscent of a politician's or film star's funeral. It was impressive, as was the gigantic spotlighted American flag hanging across the stage's back. To start the proceedings the lights were lowered, leaving only the podium spotlighted on a film star singing *Amazing Grace.* Her voice came through hidden speakers and she looked as if she was at the foot of the cross. (Only a cynic would suspect her presence was due to her film about to be released to three thousand movie theatres where single handed she destroys an army of robots. Hopefully you have sufficient faith to believe in public people's goodness and not to succumb to suspicions that would separate you from them.) Couldn't fault her singing 'cause it was never there. She was bad, sufficiently bad to drag only a pitying sporadic applause across the stage. The dragged applause was adequate to induce several bows, waves and air kisses tossed with love at the cameras and through the cameras to you, the viewer sitting at home, hopefully feeling a little closer to a star, and knowing her you had to love her.

The music turned to *America the Beautiful* accompanying the cheerleading team in red skirts and blue blouses armed with blue and red pompons parading down the center aisle followed by the boys in their blue and red jerseys. A few of the girls forgetting the solemnity of the occasion gave smiling waves to friends in the audience. Must admit, a couple of the more mature never seen at our midget games, braless cheerleaders got my attention. (Yeah, a dirty old man, but if shown dirt, having it shoved into your face, you can expect to get dirty stares.)

Mounting the stage the girls and boys formed a line behind the spotlighted podium. From the wings came the fathers from table 12. We were accompanied by our wives, who, with inappropriate smiles at the audience, appeared to be a slight gesture of encouragement away from starting to wave to the nation.

All in position, another star whose TV sitcom was perilously near dying in ratings murdered *The Star Spangled Banner*. If the purpose of the occasion wasn't sad enough, her rendition was sufficiently pathetic to double the hall's atmospheric sorrow. Listening to her maul the lyrics made everyone squirm uncomfortably. Out of patriotism, getting applause not boos, she rewarded the audience with waves, blown kisses, before humbly bowing. The Chief of Federal Internal Security, Hedja Hussan, the FIS guy, dangling more identification badges from his chest came out to escort, more resembling dragging, the TV star from the podium.

Although the service was to be secular, FIS Hussan introduced an Imam in full robed regalia to lead all in prayer because one of the intended victims was Muslim, and diverse feelings must be respected. The victim, Rufus, aka Mohammed, coming to stage front, waved, put down a prayer rug and on all fours was about to accompany the Imam in prayer. The Imam, chubby, with a fuzzy beard long enough to beg for a good pull to be delivered by an infidel, chanted sing-song some utterly incomprehensible prayers accompanied with bows here, hands raised there. All the while Rufus had his head down to the rug as if he was suffering from the dry heaves. The rug resembled Dagmar's hall rug.

Not to be left out, Dagmar approached the podium wearing a garish silk scarf about her head, and an equally colorful sarong so tightly wound, her figure resembled a mountain range undergoing a series of earthquakes, with each step rumbling ten on the Richter scale. With her sarong wound so tight she was forced to take two- year-olds baby steps. Those respectful of diversity commented her swaying, hip rolling was in the prayerful Muslim way, although she had the pork to endanger anyone standing nearby. Well, after the entire religious convocation performance at this secular Memorial ended with rousing applause, the Imam waddled off the stage almost tripping over his robe. Rufus picked up the hall rug and with Dagmar swinging and swaying in the Muslim way went back to the rest of the parents.

The FIS guy, Hedja Hussan introduced the next performer who was going to cleanse the hall of evil spirits. Most of the audience was confused 'til a guy dressed up as a B movie Indian, hopping up and down as if treading on red hot coals came dancing out, headdress feathers so high and hanging long down his back he kept struggling mightily to keep from losing his chapeau. His open buck skin jacket revealed a hairy chest, skin sun lamped pink. Despite all this, it was his buckskin briefs hiding what no person would like to see, combined with all his dance gyrations you had to hope a Haines brief was somewhere present. He tried to do some expect and accepted Indian jumping up and down cultural looking dances, but packing sufficient Sumo Wrestling weight, resembling a walrus climbing out from the ocean, he was a failure.

After a few embarrassing jumps, out of breath, in pigeon English he announced he was a Shaman Medicine Man, Eagle Who Flies the Sky, here to purify the hall of all evil spirits. Pulling out a large wet sponge attached to a feather bedecked stick he splashed all four corners of the hall. Getting some of the boys and girls wet brought out giggles and screams causing disorder to the lines. After the symbolic washing, raising arms and eyes to the ceiling in pigeon English, he loudly proclaimed the hall cleansed of all evil spirits. He exited to the thunderous applause from the newly baptized, who believing in nothing, having nothing to believe in, believed all they're told.

With diversity satisfied, Hedja Hussan, the FIS host ran to the podium to introduce Diane Saw, who with misty eyes told the audience the President couldn't attend due to an emergency Haitian crisis. The crowd as one groaned. Expectations of the show's star being unable to tread the boards, the crowd gave voice to their disappointment; women in their misery cried and wailed; men shouted in disbelief into each other's face, 'Is it true he's not coming.'

However, upbeat dried eyed Saw smiling teased her audience, "We have the unexpected privilege to hear," she paused to heighten the anticipation before exclaiming, "the Vice President and war hero Heinz Kerry." She announced it as if expecting Heinz Kerry would bring the walls down with joy. The resounding silence greeting the mention of VP Heinz Kerry momentary dragged Saw's mouth down, and her glistening eyes suggested tears just behind the glitter. Having Heinz Kerry as a very special personal friend, she was disappointed in her audience's lack of appreciation. Fortunately being an experienced news reader she pulled her mouth up and like mayo, spread it into a smile announcing to the ignorant mean spirited audience, VP Kerry will talk via video hookup from Paris. Given Paris suggested fun and gayety, she quickly added, "VP Kerry Heinz is attending a conference to end world hunger." Her ending with 'world hunger' received less applause and enthusiasm than what greeted Chief Eagle Who Flies in the Sky.

Feeling disappointed but putting on a brave front she announced, "Here's our VP, Heinz Kerry," and behind her a huge TV screen was lowered. The disbelief at the lack of cheering, in fact the obvious silence, left Saw wondering how such Neanderthals ever got into the Memorial service. *Where the hell were the Park Avenue party faithful? Should have gotten some Columbia and City College students to achieve a proper reception. Should have held the damn service in Beverly Hills.*

The lowered monitor obscuring the flag, the table 12 occupants, the cheerleaders, and the football players, forced us to crowd at the stage's fringe to view the TV.

Viewers at home being fed directly lost the sense of watching a TV show on a TV show sent to their TV sets and innocently felt the VP was in their living rooms addressing them directly. Given the time differential, the VP was in a tux about to go into a working dinner being held in the main dining room of the Ritz to discuss ending world hunger. Standing in the Ritz foyer, with sincerity you had to believe, he told you it was an important conference in solving the problem of world hunger. Using several paragraphs, he told those who bothered to listen he and the conferee's had issued a white paper stating world hunger is bad and world hunger should end, and in addition all wealthy nations had signed an agreement binding the signatories to fight world hunger. He was joyful and expected you to be joyful when he announced a report will soon be issued stating all conference attendees, being firmly against world hunger were determined to rid the world of hunger by the year 2099.

Suddenly a wave of waiters carrying platters of blood red lobsters each packing three pounds of white meat in their skeletons walked behind Heinz and entered the dining room. In the brief time the double doors were open you could see a vast array of linen draped tables supporting crystal and china surrounded by bountiful number of stuffed tuxes and lavish gowns sipping champagne, while protecting the crystal and china and eyeing the lobster's entrance.

So intent in fighting hunger, the VP, not noticing the army of lobsters passing behind him continued with outrage only politicians running for office can achieve. "Little innocent children are dying in the gutters of Calcutta and starving to death in the slums of the Congo's Kinshasa. We can't stand by and do nothing any longer, the situation is too dire for complacence."

So touched of the poor's plight, almost in hysterical tear mode, Saw, stepping to the podium tried to get Heinz back on point asking him if he had anything to say about America's concern for possible threats of widespread roach poisoning.

Always the politician, an open question such as 'do you have anything to say' was the template of rhetorical BS. Heinz announcing firmly, "People, children dying of roach poisoning is totally unacceptable," was expected to make you feel better. (CC. *People being poisoned is acceptable.*) "I've been in constant communication with the President and we're committed to insure it will never happen again." (*CC. As committed to having it happen again.*)

The dining room doors behind the VP opened, and several impeccably dressed waiters pushing serving carts loaded with empty champagne bottles ran into carts carrying full bottles going in. From the quantity of corks having been spent, and those still to be shot, mass dehydration at the banquet conference was dangerously prevalent. The commotion of clashing carts getting VP's attention, Heinz ordered the dining room doors to remain closed while he makes an important speech to anxious troubled people.

Picking up on his previous train of thought Heinz mentioned hundred billions of dollars were being promised at the conference to fight world hunger. It was announced with some petulance probably derived from his embarrassment at the paltry sum.

Seeing Kerry stroll again off topic prompting Saw to ask his view of people scared of salsa poisoning who were not buying salsa and boycotting all Mexican food. In tone and expression telling you, you were definitely not one of the ignorant masses, Saw told of people (not you) believing Mexican drug terrorists may be behind the roach poisoning and this roach poison incident may be only the first terrorist strike against America's children. Frightened, (but not you) the misinformed were demanding retaliation. Since no one had even an inkling of such thoughts, all viewers could feel pity for those holding such unsophisticated beliefs. With Saw saying disbelief in Mexican terrorist was the sophisticate position, viewers adapting her view could consider themselves politically deep.

"Mexican food is safe," Heinz heroically answered without a prompter. "In fact, just last night at the working world conference dinner we enjoyed hot tamales covered with salsa.

"Diane, to believe Mexican food is unsafe is racism at its worse. There is absolutely no truth in the common misconception there exists something called Montezuma's Revenge. Whenever Mrs. Heinz and I visit the wonderful people of Mexico we enjoy eating al fresco, chicken and beef tamales from street vendors stands as we promenade down quaint narrow native streets greeting all the wondrous ordinary Mexicans who love Americans."

Two waiters, unmindful of the VP, the camera and millions hanging on his words, moved into view struggling mightily to carry between them a huge fifteen tiered cake supporting on top a three foot chocolate replica of the Eiffel Tower. A disembodied hand materialized to roughly pull waiters, cake, and quivering tower out of sight.

Saw, feeling Heinz needed a little prompting as now he constantly tossed hungry longing glances at the closed double doors asked, "Mr. Vice President, what have you and the President planned to make America feel it's safe to again eat salsa."

Inadvertently she waved a red flag at Heinz with her oblique inference; under the present administration salsa food had become unsafe. He emphatically told her and you, "Since we've taken office, no effort, no difficulty has been spared to insure America's food is safe. That may not have been true of the previous administration. Since taking office, the President and I have been tireless in safeguarding

America's food supply. And, Diane, not only that, but with the help of the President's wife we're committed to make America's food nutritious and not lead to dangerous childhood obesity, and the attendant lifelong bad eating habits, The President, with the first lady are at war with sugar, fats, and fried foods. They are the enemy we're fighting to the death, and organic vegetables, non fat milk are our weapons, and slim bodies and healthy happy people are our goal."

Now in full stride he announced the President has appointed him to head a blue ribbon panel to investigate salsa and no later than six months to make a comprehensive report to be followed up with recommendations within a year. "In fact, the Goya people and the Mexican government have promised their full support. The commission certainly will have to visit Rio de Janerio to fully examine salsa from its cultivation to the American family's table. Now Diane, right after this conference to cure world hunger, I have to fly to Vienna to seriously investigate the causes of a worldwide epidemic of rape and ways to protect women. Then it's immediately on to Squaw Valley to set up the Salsa Investigation Committee, the SIC panel to start our in-depth investigation and determine how dangerous is roach poisoning and does it pose a public health danger. Then it's on to Rio's beach to trace salsa from the harvested vegetable to America's kitchen table. Once SIC is finished with its tireless investigation at Rio, SIC will be ready to deliver its recommends to stop roach poisoning's health threats to the American public at its Hawaii Conference.

"Now Diane Saw, and the good people viewing this important Memorial Service, I've got to leave and get back to the conference as we're near a breakthrough on curing the problem of world hunger."

Walking backwards, waving to the camera, a smiling Kerry almost knocked over a melting Eiffel Tower and its foundation as it was running to the door before it turned into a lump of mud. The screen went gray black and lifted out of sight.

CHAPTER 37

Tears and Cheers

Coming from the wings the FIS man pushed the Saw aside, ordering the stage children and parents to return to their assigned places. Not used to standing aside for anyone, after all Saw read the news on TV for the yahoos who couldn't read, she promptly made a serious attack on the podium. Hedja Hussan, with both hands gripping the podium achieving the high ground, left Saw with the choice: get physical or gracefully retreat. Eyes glistening with fury, Saw went into the darkness vowing a quick return.

Turning to the cheerleader coach, FIS Hussan asked if her cheerleaders could entertain everyone with renditions of their cheers. He didn't have to beg. Stage center, the girls danced, wiggled, waved, yelled before the audience. They were shaking pom-poms up, down, left, right, feet doing jumping jacks, knees flying to their chins, voices screaming something about fighting and winning. They were jumping over each other's backs, standing on each other's shoulders, some did hand stands, most just tried. The mature girls jiggling so hard had you wondering how strong were their maraca's attached to their chests. Out of scientific interest, I intensely watched, hoping none would injury themselves. The girls, their gymnastics and maracas got sufficient applause to warrant an encore, which unselfishly they obliged.

From somewhere in the dark wings Hussan emerged with stacked cardboard buckets signaling the girls, much to their disappointment, to stop. Handing each girl a bucket he told the audience a collection was to be made for all the victims of roach poisoning in America, and adequately fund research into roach poisoning. To encourage the people to be generous, Hedja Hussan announced roach poisoning, a serious health problem, was desperately underfunded and a thousand victims needlessly die each year.

As the girls descended into the audience, Hedja looked straight at the camera, and somberly, conversationally as if sitting in your living room reminded you, you were caring, giving he was confident you'd donate generously. To move the viewers from their recliners to the phone, pleadingly he reminded you, this very night hundreds, thousands of children may be suffering and dying of roach poison. In case some viewers were hard hearted, Hedja tossed in pets, lamenting puppies, and kittens and baby hamsters in their natural innocence accidentally eating roach poison are suffering horrible deaths. He ended with eyeballs filling the camera asking how the viewer would feel if their beloved pet was wracked with unbelievable pain caused by roach poisoning.

While the girls ran up and down the rows of chairs, to distract the audience from the pain of giving, and for those at home time to call, he gave out phone numbers and information where to send their checks: Hedja Hussan, PO Box 6252, New Mexico. Hussan then requested the boys give a scrimmage performance. Obviously this part of the Memorial Service program, being unplanned, he had to announce Tom Applegate, their selfless coach, is going to put the boys through some of their plays.

Standing next to me Tom mumbled, "Oh shit, what the crap is this," before gathering his boys into a huddle. The boys, waist high around him appeared as unruly puppies confused but anxious to please and play.

With a play called, Applegate still had to move each boy into his designated place. Finally with the team in position Applegate yelled, "One, two, three, hup." Nothing happened save they all looked quizzingly at Tom. Rushing to the center of the line, coach whispered to his left, to his right, to his back 'til finally satisfied understanding had been achieved he retreated once again to the side shouting, "One, two, three, hup."

In slow motion the boys milled about as the designated quarterback tripped backing up, and the running back stood staring at him 'til a frantic Tom yelled, "Run through the four hole."

The boy walking to the milling crowd tried pushing his way through. It was painfully obvious why the team not only failed to win a game, but lost by such wide margins despite the opposition's third string playing most of the games.

For some unknown reason the running back, after eventually making his way through the milling line continued jutting and jugging past an invisible defense crossed the stage to disappear in the dark wings. With someone crying, 'where's he going?' four men in the audience, concerned for the boy's safety, rose yelling, "I'm his father, I'll get him back.' running out the banquet hall never to return.

On stage I hit myself for not thinking as fast as the four fathers.

With the entire celebration's attention on the sudden drama at the stage's back, Saw experienced in dealing with studio emergencies as well as fast breaking news stories, quickly regained the podium from the bewildered Hussan. With eyes glistening fearlessly she ordered everyone to be calm and remain seated. Given no one had yet raised their seat, all obliged, but now were becoming definitely restless. As a courageous and highly respected serious news reader, she told all, particularly those absent and reclining in their homes, she would not leave the podium (as if anyone thought she would) 'til the missing boy was found.

Seeing this fast breaking news story was not creating the concern and news interest Saw's announcement deserved, she came out with, "A precious child is missing, possibly abducted." This statement was made with a face ready to collapse with fear as if she saw Mephistopheles coming down the center aisle to collect her soul, a soul sold for ratings.

With this sudden exciting TV drama beginning to unfold, and may absorb a lot of TV time, people reclining pulled down the footrest and hurried to the kitchen to grab a quick snack. While FIS tried to regain the podium and camera, Saw holding the podium with a dead man's grip asked everyone to hope (not pray) for the child's safety.

Shoving his head between Saw and the camera's eye, Hedja Hussan announced, "As head of FIS I can tell you FIS is fully involved in finding the missing child and is committed to returning him to his family.'

Saw, with a good hip hit assisted by several out of camera aids pulling FIS away, half turning to me asked if the police could give a worried nation an update on this fast developing tragedy. To be so referenced out of my anonymity, in fright, my crotch going female was an understatement: testes vaporized and the penis became attached to the left kidney. Fervently praying 'shit not me' Saw, grabbing my eyes was a moment's word from picking me when FIS announced, "I have here a decorated policeman who is a major investigator in the roach poison tragedies." Out came Woody resplendent in a made to order uniform bemetaled from left shoulder to waist followed by Ronni Deutsch, looking hot in her uniform but hard hot. By her hauteur she easily suggested to the recliners Woody was merely her precursor. Employing uniformed Woody as a battering ram Hedja Hussan was able to supplant Saw with his surrogates.

Woody, a today's man, gripping the podium and eyeing the camera grandly announced to recliners returning with their quick snacks he was Captain Woodruff Biden, head of the NYPD GLT task force to protect gay, lesbians, transgenders from hate and harm inflicted by ignorant people who hate people different than themselves.

Ronni, giving him an unseen hurtful ankle kick prompted him to introduce her as Lieutenant Ronni Deutsch of the GLT Task Force. If Woody's podium grip wavered no matter how slightly, Ronni would have quickly supplanted him and given her report. With white knuckles Woody held on, telling the audience that the entire resources of GLT Task Force were currently investigating the missing boy and are hopeful for his safe recovery.

Being a highly paid news reader, Saw was sufficiently prescient to know the correct question the recliners wanted her to ask. "Do you think the child is unharmed?"

Bending into Woody's camera space, Ronni told everyone all dedicated GLT officers hope so.

Woody told everyone his time was urgently needed to head the GLT investigation as the more time passes the more dangerous the situation for recovering the boy alive .

The audience giving a gasp of shock was sufficient to bring tardy snackers back to their recliners, asking, "What did he say?"

Despite the urgency of time Woody still remained gripping the podium as if it was about to fly to the ceiling to reverse gravity's dictum and destroy all science. Of the group surrounding the podium, Hussan, furthest removed from the camera's eye pushed his head between Saw and Ronni, asking what the public could do to help locate the missing boy.

Woody, ready for such a question answered, "The public, without profiling, should be alert for a suspicious man dragging a small boy to a car or to the woods."

Almost banging heads with Woody, Ronni reminded the public not to try to stop the man but call the police.

"Yes, Lt. Deutsch," Woody seconded her, while shouldering her out of the camera's eye. "This man or men could be armed and should be considered dangerous, however, even more important the public should not engage in any vigilantism."

At the 'not engage in vigilantism' phrase, Saw, Hussan, Ronni, even the camera in unison nodded up and down.

Saw, getting desperate at both her lack of air time and being out of the camera's eye pinched Woody's ass. When turning to see the person guilty of this sex crime, Saw slid past Woody as he was angrily threatening Hedja Hussan of being a sexual deviant.

Saw asked Ronni, "In GLT Task Force's opinion, was this a terrorist attack on children, or a sex hate crime perpetrated by a white man. Did it have any connection with the roach poisoning."

After threatening Hussan with sex crime arrest, Woody, glanced at Ronni, suspecting or more accurately hoping she was the pinching culprit.

Oblivious of Woody's smile and sly glance, Ronni promised Saw, the audience, the city and the world that GLT is foremost in battling hate crime against diverse people especially sexually diverse.

Earning a smile and nod from Saw, the recliners knew Ronni's statement was worthy of their agreement.

Hanging on Woody's arm, not to pull him closer but to stiff arm him to keep him from the camera, Ronni said to you and me and everyone else listening, "GLT was investigating the roach poison as a crime motivated by gay hating terrorists groups, given one of the victims was a gay policeman."

Shit, standing on stage, the only one in uniform, I tried to duck behind Brothers who, wrongly suspecting my attentions, moved his behind three fathers down the line.

Woody, feeling out of camera, out of words, forcibly interjected, "Yes, Lieutenant Ronni is referring to me. I've announced my sexuality and I'm proud to be a homosexual. It's liberating to proudly announce I'm gay and am actively involved in making the New York City police department more sensitive, and through GLT efforts, a city safer for gays."

Saw, hoping to stand near and be supportive of Woody's courageous announcement was internally torn between an in-depth interview with Woody's difficulties in being gay in the police department, or the immediacy of the fast breaking missing boy story. Being a seasoned hard hitting news reader Saw combined all in one question, "Captain Biden, is it true there exists an Arian gay hating terrorist army located in the Catskills who, besides kidnapping young boys to indoctrinate into their hate, are also planning to attack Greenwich Village gays hoping to institute a gay blood bath, as well as poison everyone in the city?"

Hedja Hussan, leaning his head between Saw's and Woody's, revealed to the world FIS is planning an all out assault next week not only on the Catskills but the entire Adirondacks.

Just as Ronni was about to ask Hussan who the hell was he, the remaining podium group as one began demanding more government money, new government agencies, and form new agencies to stop roach poisonings, child abductions, and protect gays.

It was then, when a scream from the audience froze the talking at the podium. A woman in the audience suddenly realized the missing boy was hers. Being excited at all the stage drama, needing to text friends to keep them abreast of her feelings about the unfolding podium events and send phone pictures of the stage luminaries to neighbors, she didn't notice her son was not on the stage. When becoming aware, natural maternal horror gripped her, stood her up, and pointing at the stage she yelled, "Where's my Peter? He's not there." Running out to the center aisle moving in frantic circles looking for her son she hysterically cried for her Peter.

Saw peering past the stage lights and the wall of flowers, seeing a woman crying for her missing son ran over to her flunkies in the wings ordering, "Get that mother to me. Gold! Those tears are TV gold. We can't have her waste them. America needs to see them to be able to shed their dry tears with her and by empathizing, enjoy feeling sorrow for her pain. Now move fast. I see Alphabet people approaching her to harvest all that gold for themselves and the Eye has its eye on her."

The poor woman was quickly surrounded by solicitous media personnel each trying to pull or push her to their cameras to answer sympathetic questions concerning her feelings.

With the aid of two burly assistant producers and a Vassar intern, Saw was able to whisk the hysterical woman up to the stage allowing her TV audience to personally experience the excitement of a woman enduring the pain of a lost son along with the Saw's legendary TV love and expressions of caring concern. On the way to the podium, with strong assistance, the woman's feet occasionally were allowed to touch the floor in a dragging motion.

With moist eyes under drooping eyelids, Saw asked how the mother felt learning her child was missing.

Copiously weeping, the woman pleaded, "Oh I hope he isn't hurt."

As proxy for millions, the brilliant news reader asked a follow-up question, "How would you feel if he is hurt?"

Gasping for breath, tissue drying the deepest face puddles, the woman moaned, "All I ask is he to be returned unharmed."

Redundant answers being boring, Saw took a new tact asking how the mother would feel towards the child's abductor.

Now gaining breath, conscious of the camera, cognizant she was talking to the famous Saw, dumbly she repeated her desire for her son's return unharmed.

Sufficiently TV wise not to directly ask the mother how she'd feel if her child was molested or killed, Saw settled for asking the mother what she'd like to say to her son if he could hear her.

To no one's surprise and to everyone's expectation she said she'd tell her son she loved him and only wanted to hold him safely in her arms.

You could almost hear the caring murmurs from TV land, 'that sounds so nice, it's so sad, I feel for the poor woman, I hope the little boy is safe, but if he's not I want to hear about his tragedy and am prepared to feel sad about it and not to enjoy the exciting drama too much.'

Woody and Ronni, nearby, in uniform, joined the Saw and the mother, vowing the entire GLT Task Force has immediately engaged in finding her son. However, if the abductor is a sexual predator, everyone should know he was not a homosexual. Even thinking a predator attacking little boys is gay is hate thought leading to hurtful profiling.

Head bobbing up and down like a duck on stormy sea, Saw agreed hate thought was totally unacceptable, then asked the dynamic duo if they had any progress to report to her, the mother, to a worried nation sitting in their recliners.

With the mien of a Tibetan wise man, Woody announced the GLT was following up important confidential leads, but due to the sensitive stage of the investigation couldn't reveal them. Ronni Deutsch added the snippet of how revealing them could endanger a poor child's life.

Continuing to press for more information Saw asked, "Was the FBI involved? Did the President know, and was he involved?"

"FIS is on top of this abduction," shouted Hedja Hussan. "FIS is in touch with the President as he's playing the eleventh hole. Am happy to report he's very worried, wants to be kept informed, and is currently two under par. In addition, VP Heinz is so upset he's left the banquet without eating any part of the chocolate Eiffel Tower. I can tell America FIS agents and investigators are currently sweeping the East Coast with heavy investigative assets concentrating in the Catskills."

"What!," Ronni exclaimed, "The Catskill action is the sole responsibility of GLT, and who the hell are you?"

Pointing to his badges, waving plastic encased ID, Hedja Hussan told her he was head of FIS and outranking her she should know her place.

"Know her place! She should know her place!" Woody shouted. "Is GLT hearing sex hate speech?"

Ronni told Woody GLT's hearing was perfect.

Pushing Hedja Hussan back on his heels with such powerful sexist accusations he tried to proclaim his asexuality with avows of being a neuter, when a gasp came from the audience. People stood up, people shouted 'look' into nearby strangers' faces, people pointed at the stage's rear, as the group in front of the camera's eye turning, saw the missing boy calmly walking back to join his team as he licked an ice cream, and looking smugly at his teammates.

FIS was the first to recover yelling, "FIS agents have recovered the boy. Unfortunately, out of fear of jeopardizing future prosecution, I will not say anything about how he was recovered, nor any of the details of his horrifying ordeal."

The same two beefy Peacock assistant producers and the Vassar intern now quickly escorted the lad to his mother and incidentally to Saw, who with the mother was crying for joy. As Saw and the mother tearfully asked the boy if he was hurt, Woody challenged Hedja Hussan for claiming the credit for saving the child.

Although the podium area was congested, Drs. Ozzie and Philly rushed out from the dark wings, one hoping to place healing hands and love on the boy, the other, hands and love on his mother, both telling the camera and you they were prepared to bring back to normal mental health these poor souls teetering on the jaggered edge of poor mental adjustment, and their treatment is free. Dr. Philly mentioned his army of sensitive mysterious unknown experts were ready to spring to life, prepared to heal the mother. Dr. Ozzie offered at no cost a visit to his health spa for mother and child where they could eat healthy and healing vegetables and possibly enjoy some acupuncture.

In her simplistic concern, the mother asked the boy where did he go.

"Heard bells from an ice cream truck and went to get a pop."

Hearing an unauthorized vendor in the sanitized corridor around the Memorial selling ice cream to children for who knows what evil purpose, Woody ordered Ronni to go out and arrest the alleged pervert. Lieutenant Ronni didn't move but looked at me. For my part I stared at the ceiling, shaking my head as if lamenting over the piece of gum stuck there by an unsanitary felon .

The mother and son were able to affect a bodily exit from the hall as the two Peacock assistant producers and Vassar intern entered the stage with an ice cream vendor between them, also miraculously walking on air. Approaching her and her live camera, Saw had to mentally decide between a simple ice cream vendor who rescued a missing child, a definite feel good approach, or go exciting and frightening with the vendor being a sinister seducer of guileless children, tempting the dears into the living hell of lifelong obesity as well as the debauchery of children's innocence with delicious empty calories, milk fats. and sugar.

In TV, denouncing sin trumps praising virtue, so as the hapless air walking vendor, ten feet away was closing fast, Saw condemned the man before the world as a corrupter of children's health.

As Saw exposed the vendor as the lowest of the low, out of TV ignorance, the vendor refused to play his role. With idiotic smiles at the camera, with a finger wave and his, "Hi Trudi … it's me … I'm on TV" creating a disconnect with Saw's manufactured righteous anger it caused viewer confusion. In interviews, evil men do not smile, wave and send greetings to girlfriends. They are expected to look furtive, snarl, beg for mercy, hide heads under coats or ineffectually proclaim innocence. With the vendor refusing to respond as her accusations demanded, Saw tossed him into oblivion and turned her and your attention to Hedja Hussan who is leading some people to her, her camera and her audience.

CHAPTER 38

The Widow Joy

Missing out on laying hands on the boy and arresting the ice cream seller, FIS agent Hedja Hussan fearing he and his agency were being marginalized into TV's irrelevant obscurity decided to play the memorial ace before anyone else. Rushing to the wings he brought forth Joy, the Roach widow, desperately leaning for support on Zapp's arm, with Jeffrey walking behind them like a ring bearer. Leaving Saw, the camera followed the widow's progress from darkness to light. Her legs continually giving way forced Zapp, in his pressed Pep Boy uniform, to hoist her up moments before her bottom bottomed out. Her progress was so slow Jeffrey had time to stop, pick his nose, inspect the results before wiping it on his new jacket. Like bluebottles rushing to a dead body, the podium crowd flying about the widow required Saw's assistant producers and Vassar intern to clear a path to Saw at the podium so through the camera all could enjoy the dramatic scene.

Getting to Saw, a collapsing Joy almost disappeared behind the podium but not quite, being able to self resurrect, and to the camera, unasked, courageously inform all she had loved her husband. Shouldering between a salivating Ozzie and a concerned Paris, Saw asked how the widow felt with her husband being murdered.

With such a question, Joy could do nothing less than respond between a profusion of tears how totally destroyed and absolutely lost she felt.

Dr. Philly pulling Dr. Paris away, grabbed her place to announce with the wisdom of Solomon, "With her husband killed, it's natural for a wife and mother to feel crushed and alone, and my people will cure -"

Before his people could get any further out of his mouth and into people's minds, Dr, Paris Start popped up from underneath Zapp's arm telling Joy she should try to get on with her life for her son's sake.

Here everyone frantically searched about for the boy hoping to see him in tears. Discovering him talking and joking with his teammates, Jeffrey had to be ignored as being unworthy of TV drama. Paris, being squeezed between Ozzie and Philly, advised Joy, for her son's psychological health, mother and son should seek professional counseling. In giving this hackneyed advice, Paris tried to hand Joy and Zapp her business cards.

In the continuous rough and tumble jockeying for camera position, the falling cards were trampled underfoot as Paris Start, attacked by several stiff shoulders was pushed into irrelevance.

Woody, vigorously pushed from behind by Ronni, making it between Hedja Hussan and Saw, was able to tell Joy and more importantly you, GLT was expecting a quick arrest in her husband's murder. Ronni, diving under Woody's arm, asked the widow if Jim had any homosexual lovers, or was a member of a man/boy love organization, or was he involved in fighting against terrorist groups, or was a member of a gay hating religious fanatical Catskill group.

The questions' surprising absurdity dried the widow's tears, which up to now were a raging tempest. Her, "What the hell are you saying? My husband was all man, a great husband, a fantastic father who working hard at Pep Boys and had nothing to do with terrorists or gays."

Angry at all these interruptions serving only to keep the widow off message, Saw asked, "Joy dear, how do you feel seeing such a national outpouring of love for you and concern for your future?"

Her tears for her departed husband switching to tears for her and her son's bleak future, Joy confessed she didn't know how she could cope without her Jim, didn't know how to explain to her son his father was gone, didn't know how they would be able to survive, didn't know how -.

Sensing the 'didn't know hows' would go on 'til midnight, Saw interrupted, "A nation feels your despair and I'm sure will respond generously."

With eyes flicking with hope, Joy turned to the camera expressing her belief in America having a generous heart and she proceeded to give an online address where a caring America could show their love and generosity.

Zapp, being primed and rehearsed by corporate Pep Boy's headquarters joyfully announced to the widow, the Pep Boy organization, er - then remembering his scripted lines corrected, "Pep Boys' highly trained employees have made a collection to help you and Jeffrey and here it is."

Two fantastically looking males hired from a male modeling agency entered carrying a check the size of a highway billboard. The men were dressed in impeccable Pep Boy uniforms and carried their billboard to the podium. With everyone easily giving way fearing it could topple at any time, the check was placed just behind the widow.

A business suit popping up next to Joy announced to her, to Saw, and to the eavesdropping TV public, " The Pep Boy Corporation is proud of our loyal professional employees who, out of love for Jim Scott, collected this money, and I'm now proud to present this check for one thousand three hundred forty five dollars and sixty nine cents.

The money was collected from Pep Boy employees working in eight thousand Pep Boy stores. In addition corporate Pep Boys, to honor one of our highly esteemed employees will augment Pep Boy employee generosity by doubling the amount."

Zapp hugged Joy for her good fortune. She tried mightily to show America her gratitude and happiness for the Pep Boy gift but there was an occasional look of 'is that all' sliding between smiles.

After this example of employee and corporate generosity, the suit felt obliged to introduce himself as Moe Pep, grandson of one of the original Pep Boy founders who was proud to be Vice President of Pep Boy's East Coast network of outlets. Moe Pep, turning to the stage's wing waved someone to stage center and announced Pep Boys East Coast network of outlets supplying driving America is happy to present each child on the stage with a gift.

Carrying a large carton, bearded Joshua Dumont walked to the podium announcing from his beard that Pep Boys was proud to give each child a bobble head of Manny, Moe and Jack. If such generosity was not enough, he announced parents will receive ceramic Pep Boy Manny, Moe and Jack collector dolls only available at Pep Boy stores.

Dumont and grandson Moe were about to present each child a bobble head as if giving out Congressional Medals of Honor, when Saw stopped them as she told Moe and you the bobble heads would be cherished by the children. The audience rose as one, giving cheers for Manny, Moe and Jack's unheard of generosity. Recliners at home mumbled to themselves how it was such a nice generous gesture. Before Moe and Dumont could start to give the children their gifts, Saw again intervened.

Some free TV publicity is permitted, but with Moe going for an hour's Infomercial on Pep Boys, Saw knew no one cared about the bobble heads after the minute's feel good passed with the viewers' good feelings for the widow, so at her signal two burly assistant producers and Vassar intern helpfully assisting Moe, Dumont, the bobble heads and the two beefcake model agency check carriers off stage. The stage cleared of Pep Boys, Saw was able to ask Joy how she felt receiving such a tribute from her husband's fellow workers.

Through tight lips the widow told you she was overwhelmed at the love Jim's fellow Pep Boys were showing her.

Taking advantage of the Pep Boy's motley crowd's departure, Hedja Hussan, grabbing camera space somberly commented, "FIS and I applaud this act of generosity, but with the dire worldwide threat of global warming, corporations dedicated to keeping cars on the road shouldn't be supported by people who seriously care about the environment."

People at home may experience some mental confusion from feeling both sad and happy for the widow of a beloved Pep Boy who was so loved and are now expected to feel fear, sad for her loss, and for the world coming to a catastrophic end cause by Pep Boy stores.

However, with Saw's environmental button being pressed, she reflexively encouraged Hussan, "Yes, FIS agent Hedja Hussan, we must never forget the loss of Arctic ice. We're losing an iceberg a day."

Encouraged by finding one of many dire rating busting topics Saw loved, Hedja Hussan continued. Even though handcuffed he somehow pulled out a 6x8 picture of a cute polar bear cub and holding it so the camera could zoom in, with a voice cracking with emotion, tears just a melting snowflake away, he told reclining America, "Little Snow Flake here is going to die if you drive your car."

Possibly it was of interest to the audience who, feeling TV evoked sadness and caring for a mythical Snow Flakes' health were able to confirm their ultra compassionate nature as opposed to those who didn't give a damn about Snow Flake. Proving their sophisticated understanding it reinforced their high estimation of their sense of sensitivity versus those who can't empathize with Snow Flake and so are unfeeling. It strengthened their membership in the seriously informed elite as exemplified by Dina Saw and her ilk opposed to those not sharing compassion for Snow Flake and his cute friends. Only such people as they are superior: in mind, in compassion, in understanding, in sophistication, who on being fed oft repeated clichés are able to eat with pleasure and easily digest cotton candy can proclaim, it's the rarest of rare beef

For those standing on the stage, fatigued feet in agreement with bored minds found it easy to shuffle to the stage's wings as if random chance placed them there before disappearing into the dark to seek fresh air, cold and damp as it was. Half the cheerleaders and the entire football team had somehow disappeared. Out of the fathers of table 12, save for Ray Brothers in his blazer showing a Golden Arch embroidered on his chest pocket, I stood alone. Constantly fiddled with papers, sweating profusely, Ray continually started to the podium before retreating as a new drama unfolded.

For those at home, the camera's restricted close-ups veiled the slow erosion of stage's players, but the hall's audience was continuously surprised. Every time they looked beyond the cameras, a few more actors somehow disappeared.

"Shit," Ray whispered, "can't leave 'til I make an announcement."

I told him, "Just go up there and push the pack aside."

Agreeing, saying, "Damn I can't take it anymore," Ray rushed the podium. Pushing his way in as only the rich can, physically parting the group, he bumped Lieutenant Ronni Deutsch back to me.

Expecting Ronni to counter attack to regain podium possession, to my surprise she stayed with me. My legs and mind now reenergized by her standing next to me, together we watched Ray grab Joy by the hand

and announce to the bored recliners, "Being a victim of roach poisoning myself, I'm proud to represent the McDonald's Corporation's billions of employees working in a million McDonald's stores worldwide who wish to present you, the widow of Jim Scott, a check for five hundred thousand."

As he searched his pants pockets for the check, Joy, the excited widow, grabbing his golden Arch crest, in haste, turning the lapel out ripped it as she was suggesting the check could be in the breast pocket. She was about to stick a hand down his back pocket to facilitate the search when Ray produced the check. So emotionally touched by McDonald's thoughtfulness, in the chaos of nervous and anxious hands giving and receiving the check, the check floated to the floor. Zapp went for it, but it was a diving Joy who caught it a mere six inches from the floor. Resurfacing, Joy shouted she was overwhelmed by Mickey D's generosity and promised, now as a single mother she'd eat numerous happy nutritious dollar meals at Mickey Ds.

Looking down at his cheat sheet, Ray announced McDonald's burritos and tamales were one hundred percent healthy and in honor of the deceased, Jim Scott, McDonald's will be putting the burritos and tamales on their dollar menu, for a limited time.

Inexplicably the audience rose as one and cheered, possibly using the dollar menu meal as an excuse to get up and stretch legs.

Wiping his face, Ray waved to all, especially to those reclining who, listening to the Memorial audience's responsive uproar felt something wonderful happened, and possibly they'd have Mexican for dinner, maybe at McDonald's.

CHAPTER 39

Right On

While this self promoting McDonald's theater was being performed, Ronni, with miraculous smiling facial contortions told me out of the comer of her mouth, "Ed, what do you think of all of this?"

From her tone, suspecting what she wanted back from me, but conscious of saying anything good or bad will be used as a club against me, I tossed it back to her, "What do you think Lieutenant.?"

She picked up on the Lieutenant arguing, "Once Woody was declared gay and made Captain of the GLT Task Force, he invited me to become his second in command. Couldn't refuse, even though at the promotion hearing I had to French kiss the dyke chairwoman to validate my correct sexuality."

Treating my 'whatever' response as antagonistic, Ronni defended herself by criticizing me, "Look Mac, you're down as gay, like Woody. You should try to make it work for you. Gay is the new 'open Sesame'."

Fatuously I asked if she was sure of Woody's sexuality.

Her emphatic response, "Don't worry, he's definitely heterosexual," suggested first hand irrefutable knowledge and French kissing a dyke wasn't the only payment she made for her bars.

Since previously entertaining hope, though faint, in her direction, now out of disappointment I mentioned that with Woody being

Captain, he'd never allow her to pass him in rank. My observation, being a cinder in her eye, changed the subject asking what I thought of the Memorial Ceremony.

Ronni wasn't stupid, and it was clear she had suspicions that, what was going on wasn't totally wonderful.

"It's all bullshit," I told her, but suspected she knew that.

Cynically she answered, "So what. Life's all bullshit. What's new about that?"

Despite speaking everyday trite, her retort hit me as a putdown like I didn't realize life was BS. For some irrational reason wanting to recover her good opinion I gave her something she didn't know. "Using my cell phone I checked with the government directory of federal agencies and found FIS, the Federal Internal Security Agency doesn't exist." I stopped there. Let her come to me.

Playing hardball with my ego, Ronni suggested it was a secret agency.

"There are no secret federal agencies, the only secret is what they do."

Still not wanting me to stand above her, she mentioned it could be a recently created agency..

"The first thing a new government agency does is advertise itself and the great things they're doing and going to do for you and the country to increase future funding."

Still combative, hating to say the most difficult words in English, 'you're right' Ronni said FIS had to be real as Hedja Hussan was there talking to the podium and to anyone who'd listen. "Mac, he has the credentials proving he's head of FIS, so FIS has to be real. You can't be the head of a nonexistent entity."

Sarcastically I told her Hussan's credentials are as real as FIS.

Frowning and dropping her adversarial ego role, Ronni picked up and employed the usual putdown ploy, slow announcing to you what you just said as if you never said it, "If FIS is BS so Hedja Hussan is BS." She said it as if I never thought it, and I should be amazed at her insight.

"Yeah, it's all BS," I said.

"Then who the hell is this Hedja Hussan?" she asked in genuine doubt.

"Ronni, if FIS doesn't exist, if Hedja Hussan and all his ID doesn't exist, who the hell is he and what he wants is the real mystery."

"What should we do? We've got to do something."

What I suspected was her wanting me to risk doing something in order for her to gain promotion. Shit on that. Woody's banging her, not me.

Egging her on I suggested, "You should expose the imposter as possibly some terrorist suicide bomber. Saving Saw and everyone's life on real TV time certainly would result in a promotion. Your national reputation as a courageous female cop will generate books and movies of your life, talk show interviews leading to the possibility of your own syndicated TV show."

Wide eyed with girly Hollywood dreams about to pull up anchor, she checked once more with me before going full sail.

To her, 'what if we're wrong' I shrugged as I was definitely not part of her 'we'.

She rode her mind elevator up, yes she should do it, to down, no she shouldn't do it, to up, then down for several minutes. The elevator stopped on 'up'. It wasn't the gold bars. What tipped the balance was the excitement of being famous, arresting Hedja Hussan on national TV in front of Saw.

As I slowly did a sly side shuffle to the stage's wing, Lieutenant Ronni Deutsch, whipping out her police special ran to FIS Hedja Hussan ordering him to drop. A dumbfounded Hedja stood staring wide eyed at Ronni while she patted him down, shouted to the camera, Saw, audience and recliners he might be wearing an exploding terrorist vest.

A frightened Woody did a backward fade, whether because of the vest or Ronni's bold risky action. He knew one of them could blow up.

Saw, the professional, never before at a loss for words looked stupefied, while behind her Ozzie, Philly and, Paris forming a tight circle searched each other's faces for psychological meaning of this unexpected development, and how to treat it.

Zapp, close to the widow and her check, jumped in front of Joy to protect her and her check from gunshots, while she frantically was tucking Ray's check deep into her bra.

Finally, Ronni, with the aid of two assistant Peacock producers and the Vassar intern got Hedja Hussan prone on the ground, With high heeled foot firmly on Hedja Hussan's back reminiscent of a big game hunter, Ronni announced she had arrested a dangerous imposter, probably a terrorists connected with a roach poison group operating out of the Catskill Mountains.

Stunned, turning to the camera and the recliners Saw could only shout, "It's live! It's coming to you live!"

Reaching down, tearing Hedja Hussan's back pants pocket, Ronni extracting his wallet and announced Hedja Hussan's real name was Bernie Fuchs, employed as a pastry chef at a Queens, Long Island all night Belize diner specializing in exotic Belize cuisine.

Saw got down on her knees and putting a mike in front of Bernie Fuchs' face asked how did he feel being arrested, being exposed by a woman.

Again the assistance of the two Peacock assistant producers was needed to help Ronni drag Bernie to his feet so she could interrogate him for the camera. Saw stood on one side, Ronni on the other, Bernie Fuchs in the middle, camera in front, so you could be the fourth and not left out of the drama.

Fuchs was determined not to play his preordained role for TV recliners, neither as an abject sorrowful confessor nor a degenerate imposture refusing to admit guilt. Standing tall and straight he defended himself to the recliners stating he was a member of Green Peace, Save the Whales, Peace Corps, the Sierra Club, and Mother Jones.

Saw was taken back. He was claiming membership in all her holy of holy groups; could one with such a membership list be guilty of any crime? Was he a villain or a hero? She and her producers had to decide quickly for ambiguity is the kiss of death for TV ratings.

Such mental indecision was not Ronni's problem. Having arrested the darkest of the dark villans she was committed to his evilness. Unfortunately for Ronni it was difficult to pillory Bernie while he was beginning to make heart melting pleas to save the whales, the walruses, and especially Snow Flake.

Lieutenant Ronni told Saw, and anyone eavesdropping on them in TV land, how despicable terrorists join numerous wonderful organizations to camouflage their cowardly terrorists attacks on America's children.

Still undecided, Saw was wondering where the hell was her producer and director when needed, was she interviewing a hero or villain. Shit, she really needed a production meeting.

Committed to a single course of action, Lieutenant Ronni had no choice but to announce Bernie Fuchs, aka Hedja Hussan, was a Muslim and he was being arrested as an imposter posing as an official representative of a nonexistent government agency. Feeling there may exist a little confusion with all the nonexistent names, Ronni, deciding to nail something down by adding Bernie was being arrested on suspicion of being the roach poisoner.

To gain time to hear from her producers who were in a tight huddle high in the Peacock's nest, Saw again asked Hedja or Bernie how he felt being arrested.

Eschewing tearful pleas of innocence, or snarling growls of guilt for the satisfaction of Saw and her audience, Bernie continued with his own script. Raising his eyes to the ceiling as a preface, then lowering them straight to the camera he got to his corpus, "If I can save one whale, help a walrus, save a polar cub such as Snow Flake, I'm able to rejoice in my persecution from greedy corporations." Again from somewhere on his person out came a 6x8 photo of a polar bear cub he presented directly to the camera saying here was Snow Flake at four months of age.

Falling in love ... whales, walruses, Snow Flake, Saw, giving her mind to Bernie, allowed him to respond to Ronni's accusations. Asking him if he was the roach poisoner, Saw nodding up and down in agreement with him as Bernie astonished no one in proclaiming his innocence. To bolster his claim Bernie mentioned he, respecting all life especially whales and cute bears was psychologically incapable of committing terrorist attacks.

Behind the trio, on camera, Ozzie, Philly and Paris, nodding their agreement with Bernie's psychologically based innocence tried to gain camera time. However, with Saw, Bernie and Ronni firmly established, they were forced to fall back to argue among themselves. Dr. Ozzie stated membership in appropriate respected organizations reflected a well adjusted personality and only needed a professional planned diet and exercise regimen to be forever happy.

Dr. Philly vehemently argued that respected organization membership indicated a serious dysfunctional personality who, by such membership was desperately trying to hide serious psychological problems from himself and his mother. However, if the person would submit himself to his professional people, happiness would be his.

Dr. Paris suggested a lengthy cure comprising a one on one consultation with a trained psychologist could eventually determine if his membership in these organizations was healthy or a symptom of serious disorders.

Saw, still lacking any guidance from her Peacock master control booth repeated, "So Hedja er Bernie, you maintain you're not the roach poisoner." to which he reiterated his complete innocence, and as evidential proof restating his commitment to environmental goodness.

Shit, Lieutenant Ronni Deutsch thought. I've got to stop this character before he starts saving the Amazon rainforest and African elephants. To Bernie, to Saw, but mostly to the recliners, Ronni said she had firm information that Bernie's Belize Diner stores quart jars of salsa, and on premise has quantities of roach poison as well as even more lethal types of rat poison.

Still without direction, Saw showed her news professionalism by shoving a mike up Bernie's left nostril and ordering him to answer such damning evidential findings at his Belize diner.

Bernie, temporarily tossed off message, could only guiltily mumble he guessed the salsa and poison was true, but as a committed member of Mother Jones he was against poisoning anyone, even roaches and rats.

Being on Mother Jones' Board of Directors, Saw had to defend the Mother. "Certainly Mother Jones has no knowledge of your access to salsa and roach poison. You shouldn't try to besmirch my beloved Mother Jones' reputation."

Sensing the Saw tide was rising in her favor, Ronni tried to make it a full moon tide by stating as if revealing to Saw and eavesdropping recliners the secret to the universe. "Did you know this mythical organization FIS is an alleged underground terrorist group located in the Catskills. FIS stands for Fury in Salsa."

"Really?" Saw said in amazement. She was unsure about the information, or how anyone could believe it, though she half believed it because she wanted to believe it.

Lieutenant Ronni, trying to drag Bernie off stage shouted to the camera, "It may be too soon to say the roach terrorist organization is completely destroyed. America should be alert for suspicious people carrying containers of roach poison, or buying large quantities of salsa, but remember, don't profile anyone.."

Bernie, having a few pounds and some muscles over Ronni, was able to hold his own and lean into the camera announcing, "If anyone wants more information about me and my good work in saving the world, I'm on Facebook, Twitter, and you can reach me at HedjaHussan. Walrus saver. com, HH crime fighter, or Bernie Fuchs.Snow Flake protector.com."

Saw interrupted Bernie asking him what the female audience wanted to know: Was he married? Was there someone special in his life?

"No Dina Saw, I'm married to the creatures of the world. I love all living things."

Saw's follow-up question, Did he have any children? had the response of, 'Yes Dina, currently, the whale, the walrus, are my children. Want to see Snow Flake's picture again? It's pasted on my web site, as well as on my refrigerator."

With the voice of the producer still absent, Saw went to her usual insightful questions: what were his plans for the future, was he planning to marry, was he going to continue his heroic fight to save Snow Flake, did he have future plans for having children?

The last gave Bernie his greatest opening and shaking free the arm Ronni had held with a dog like death grip, "Yes Dina, I'm planning to adopt orphan children."

Ronni pulling hard mumbled, "Shit, can I get some help here?"

Dina, a true TV interviewer knew the necessity of repeating for the dozing recliners, "Hoping to adopt children!"

"Yes Dina, ten orphan children."

An amazed Dina said, "Ten orphan children!"

"All are special needs children."

"Special needs children!" The eyes misting up in wonderment, she had to give it another repeat. "Ten orphan special needs children, how wonderful."

A desperate Ronni, looking at me, wagged her head for me to come, reminiscent of a dog's tail desperate for a walk. Her plea for my masculine help in extracting Bernie wasn't going to happen. Woody was getting her 'it,' not me, so she wasn't getting any of my 'it.'

Building a sweet confectionary sundae for Saw and the recliners, Bernie sprinkled chocolate chips, "The orphans are all black."

"Black! Ten black special needs orphans! I can't believe you. You're the most caring man I even interviewed."

Bernie added a cherry by casually mentioning the ten were all girls.

"All girls! Oh, that's absolutely fabulous."

On a roll, Bernie added some chocolate syrup to the sundae telling Dina and you, "These ten black special needs orphan girls are from crime riddled, garbage spewed, disease filled slums of the Congo."

Unable to contain herself, giving Bernie a hug, Dina Saw conferred sainthood on him.

Still hanging on to Bernie, a desperate Ronni, turning towards me lipped, "Please help me. I'll do anything, anything you want."

Not having gotten anything from her and knowing her type, the 'I'll do anything' holds only 'til it's time for her to do her 'everything,' then it turns into a legal, 'I didn't say explicitly that, and certainly didn't mean that,' 'How could you even think that?' So to her desperate plea I returned a smile, a girly finger wave and nothing more.

During Ronni's active begging for help, an ecstatic Saw repeated, "All girls!" before asking their ages.

"Tabatha, the youngest, is four months; Rachida, the oldest, is fourteen years;, and all are in immediate danger of being gang raped and sold into prostitution."

Dina gasped, "Ten black special needs orphan girls living in poverty saved from rape! Saved from a life of prostitution!"

I was sure Dina just wetted herself.

In recliner land they experienced wonderment in discovering how caring Bernie was and by extension, weren't they, because they felt he was a good loving man.

Bernie sighing, "Of course with all their special needs Ill have difficulty raising them all alone," nudging Dina to ask what were the children's physical disabilities.

With a deep prolonged sigh, Bernie mentioned seven year old Basheba was without legs, allowing Saw and the hall's audience to give out with the appropriate, 'ohhhhh so sad.'

Desperate for help, a begging Ronni turned to Woody standing one step from vanishing into the wings. Woody took a step, unfortunately backwards, to disappear forever. Knowing she was in severe difficulties with her gold bar hanging precariously on her shoulder, surreptitiously Lieutenant Ronni undid Bernie's handcuffs and turning plaintively to me once again promised her everything, only to receive my warm smile.

With hands free, a gesturing Bernie told a melting Saw and recliners, one child had no arms, "Poor Amadia has compensated wonderfully with her toes. Then there's the beautiful teen age girl with facial hair."

"No!" exclaimed Saw.

"Yes, actually a beard of dark coarse hair. It will take years of expensive painful electrolysis to bring out her natural beauty."

Having the viscosity of mercury, Saw gave Bernie an unheard of second hug with a double cheek kiss. They only separated when Saw suddenly jumped back. In the future, 'til his death, with pride, Bernie claimed he had been privileged to pinch Dina Saw's ass.

Fearful of another special needs child making her appearance Ronni told Bernie he was free to go, but not to leave New York without telling the police.

With Bernie's self proclaimed goodness, enthusiastically endorsed by Saw, Ronni quickly backed away and joined me while whispering, "Mac, you bastard. I shouldn't have listened to you."

Sarcastically I said, "Man, Hedja Hussan, aka Bernie Fuchs, is one hell of a great guy."

The last scene on TV screens was Bernie again showing Snow Flake's picture and telling you if you want to save Snow Flake, help shave the bearded girl, give prosthesis to the legless and armless girls, you can find out how by going to BernieFuchs.com or write to Hedja Hussan, care of the Belize Family Diner specializing in delicious healthy exotic Belize pastries and deserts located on Queens Boulevard.

What happened next I couldn't first hand report, as exiting I planned to meet Pam and go home.

I left the stage unobserved due to the chaos at the podium as numerous hugs and air kisses were given and received. Moe Pep and Dumont rushed out to personally hand out the collector bobble heads and get on TV.

I pondered an interesting conundrum. How could Bernie be arrested for impersonating the chief of FIS if FIS itself was nonexistent? Wasn't the agency impersonating a federal agency and should be charged. Unfortunately it didn't exist, so couldn't be charged and how could Bernie be arrested for impersonating a nonexistent person running a nonexistent agency. Of course, all exists on paper, or in air, badges, credentials, words, all his creatures and no one else's.

CHAPTER 40

A Gay and Hopeful Ending

With the banquet hall's rear exits crowded, I went out one of the stage exits only to bump into Hedja Hussan being mobbed by autograph hunters. Most were teenage girls and college co-eds who kept screaming, waving and jumping up and down as if they were auditioning for *Dancing with the Stars*.

A smiling Bernie, signing any scrap of paper shoved in front of his face, kept asking the eager hunters which name they wanted him to use. Some pleaded for Hedja Hussan, others were desperate for Bernie, most were ecstatic when he signed both.

A group wearing Columbia sweatshirts were begging Bernie to address their sorority in his efforts to save Snow Flake. To overcome his reluctance the girls mentioned a ten thousand dollar honorarium. In a now eager voice he asked, "Who do you want to show up, Hedja or Bernie?" The sorority group yelled for Snow Flake.

Several nubile co-eds, college and high school, were forcing him to take strips of paper containing telephone numbers and addresses with pleas for him to call. Surreptitiously he put them in his coat pocket, the bulge of which indicated his coat pockets were overflowing with eager worshippers at Bernie's altar.

Tempted to pick up one of his overflow, I'm proud to admit I abstained. The crush around Bernie was such, I had to manhandle several girls to gain the sidewalk, only to have a gold and blue balloon thrust in my hand by an officious matronly woman.

"Here's yours. We're all going to the park to release balloons in memory of the world's children killed by roach poison."

The damn string escaped my grasp and drunkenly floated up and away.

"Don't worry," she said, as if I was worried. Running over to a group of children and mothers, fists filled with gold and blue balloons, she took one and returned, trying to hand it to me. Keeping hands in my pockets I told her I was a little too old for balloons.

"Oh, it's not for you. We're going over to the park where Heraldo Rivera will interview the children, and FOX News will video the children and parents releasing the balloons to heaven as a memorial for all the victims of roach poison."

A little girl tugged at her mother's coat crying everyone is leaving and they may miss the fun.

Impatiently, she shoved a damn balloon at me. I had to take the damn balloon and watch the mother and child march away with about forty of so mothers and children and balloons. They were a brave band but no tears were shed, no cries of lamentation were heard, only smiles and excited laughter and talk.

I gave my balloon to a co-ed wearing a City College jacket. Looking lovingly at a piece of paper Bernie had signed, she was at first stunned suspecting evil purposes. With my explanation of the balloons ultimate purpose, profuse with gratitude, she ran to catch up to the gold and blue balloon army marching towards the FOX and Heraldo.

All this time I looked for Pam and Mickey among the mass of stupefied people running out of the banquet hall as if it contained a contagious plague. Once outside, the groups milled about. Having recently escaped prison, they hadn't devised future plans of action.

Walking between such groups I heard comments: 'I can't believe they wanted to arrest that saint,' 'it's a shame more people aren't like him,' ' the widow's dress was a little too tight,' 'I cried, actually cried for Snow Flake,' 'I feel so sorry for the little children who were poisoned.'

The last series of overheard comments were most telling. To a question 'who died' another answered 'I think it was someone called Snow Flake, but I'm not sure.' Another passerby corrected they were being ridiculous, the murdered man was someone called Mickey Dee who works in some city on Long Island called Belize.

Finally, the last of the audience disappearing into the mist, I walked in circles about the building getting wet, feeling cold, becoming incrementally angry. Where the hell were Pam and Mickey. Damn it I hope they weren't in balloon land, still with Pam and Mickey on their own, they well might be there.

On my fourth or fifth circuit I ran into Ronni Deutsch, more correctly she ran up to me to vent her anger. "You damn bastard," was her greeting, followed by "that's the last time I'll listen to you, you ass hole," quickly followed by the complaint, "why didn't you help me?"

My, "Thought you could handle it by yourself, thought you were doing great," got, "Bullshit." thrown at me.

"That bastard with those damn kids, shit, I don't know how he could keep on pulling them out his ass."

"Ronni, it was easy cause they weren't real. They had the same substantive reality of everyone's dreams of 'I want to do,' 'I plan to do,' 'In the future I will do, or try to do.' All the 'to do's are mental fictions, so Bernie's talk of plans to adopt was just so much air."

"Never! Mac, do you really believe a person could lie about legless orphans and bearded girls?"

Ronni saying out loud 'bearded girl' suddenly brought the absurdity of it all to her. It was a slap of reality. She employed the usual ego ploy of stating what you said as if you never said it, never thought it. "Mac, it was all BS, can you believe it?"

Only people conditioned to believe what TV reports to be real can believe. If you believe in what your monitor tells you, you believe in Hollywood and show biz and they make money attracting viewers, so the monitor will say what is necessary to seduce the recliners.

It took time for Ronni, herself a phony, to realize the used car salesmen lie. "Mac," she vowed, "I'm going to get that phony Hedja Hussan, or whatever his name is if it takes ten years."

Thinking so much for the much touted women's forgiving nature, I asked if she saw Pam and my son.

She said, "Them," as if they didn't matter. "Woody took Pam and the kid home." She then added as if trying to be helpful, "Your wife is angry at you." Being angry herself she transmitted Pam's anger so I will get angry and keep her company.

She was successful as I angrily thought, *Here I'm waiting for her, walking in circles, getting wet, feeling the cold, and she leaves without waiting for me, and she's mad, and goes home with Woody, what the hell is all that about.*

Ronni, finding some solace in causing my anger and pain left, and alone I stood uncertain as what to do, where to go. Home? In my current temper it would only lead to arguments, and being tired just wasn't up for the shouting.

The stage door opened and Joy, Zapp and Jeffrey peered out fearing a crowd interested in them would pounce. With no one in sight save me, they exited. Joy, doing a quick walk, shouted back to Zapp and Jeffrey they had to hurry to get to the bank.

Toni Brite burst out after them yelling, "Are you sure you don't want to join the MAD Literary Group? Think about it."

After Joy and her entourage passed by me, Toni, giving up on them stopped to give me a warm smile, asking if I decided which literary agency I was going to join.

Even muffled up in the cold, damn it, if she wasn't hot. Looking up at me, cheeks red with cold, hope in blue eyes, innocence of a child hoping for a special present, and I being adrift, decided to prolong the conversation and feed her false hope. I said I was undecided. She took undecided as, not as good as decided to go with MAD, but liking it enough to suggest we go to my home to discuss MAD's pros and cons, and my becoming rich and famous.

Looking down at her moist wet face I could envision taking her, but certainly not home. In fact, I couldn't see taking myself home, and what may await me. I suggested a brandy to warm up, and I happen to know Cavanaugh's was nearby.

In a rear booth at Cavanaugh's she had some white wine, I a highball. We stared at each other, stared at our drinks, back at each other, off towards the bar, then again at each other.

Asking if I came here often I confessed it was my home away from home. Since the bartender greeted me by name, asking if I wanted the usual, I wasn't revealing hidden personal foibles. Her telling me it was a nice place to sit and get out of the cold, smoothed over my fear she harbored any thoughts of me having a drinking problem. Hopefully such thoughts didn't find rest in her mind, but for a moment coming to rest in my mind did unsettle me.

Starting hard on MAD being my literary agent sales talk caused me to take back her youthful innocence, but after throwing off her coat she was still physically attractive especially in her tight sweater, two buttons undone hinting at what was breathing beneath the third and fourth buttons.

To get her off message I ventured, "Look, I'm famished after that Memorial ordeal. Can I buy you something to eat? I can vouch for their hot roast beef sandwiches accompanied by steak fries. It goes great with an ice cold beer."

"Sounds great," she agreed, then asked if I wasn't planning to eat at home. Her checking on my home life suggested she might have left business mode and was entering the same garden I was in.

My, "No, I'm not eating at home," was said with emphasis suggesting I never ate there.

While getting the waiter's attention, I appreciated how her bra was nicely filled. Waiting for him to come over I noted her black hair falling to her shoulders, shining with moisture. She had bangs touching her eyebrows framing a very attractive face, deep red soft lips didn't hurt the picture. In her youth, just out of her teens, she projecting innocence, and with her build she was sexually desirable.

Before the food arrived she talked about MAD's advantages. Feeling this was a performa business conversation I adopted an equally insincere interest in MAD's advantages. During the biting, the masticating, the swallowing and the sipping we ate our way to first names, mutual jokes over the entire Memorial fiasco, with most of her biting witticisms devoted to Joy, Saw, and Ronni. For me, I poked fun at the phony hypocrisy of the entire affair including balloons released to heaven, of course bobble heads had us in tears.

With after dinner drinks ordered I excused myself and quickly emptied a bladder, combed hair, ignored 'wash your hands' imperious signs. If I was going dirty I'd go all the way.

Returning she took the opportunity to go to the doe room, Carmichael's cutesy reference to women's toilets.

While she was away, downing my drink I quickly ordered another. Women tend to count and I hoped to slip one by her. Returning, I'm sure her lips were revitalized, hair combed, and I was able to sniff an enticing aroma over the beer and beef smells. Most important were the buttons. I could swear, before the doe, two were undone. Now three were unattached. The question I asked myself was the new button a sales ploy to sell MAD to me, or was it to sell herself to me. My mind was put to rest, my ego engaged, my id awakened in the booth's soft light by our easy conversation concerning exposing our mutual likes and dislikes for each other's admiration, revealing past backgrounds to each other, disclosing hopes and plans for the future to each other, for each other's approval.

It was touching nine, the bar bill passing two hundred two hours ago, and now feeling good, no feeling great, being at the top, looking confidently at a vague glorious future our evening ended. Toni Brite under the guise of business next day putting on her coat covering up three buttons, extended her business card. Before I could grab it she took it back saying, "Let me give you my home number and address in case you change your mind about signing up with MAD, and you can't get me at the office." Leaning over to hand it to me she and her three free buttons said I could call her any time if I had any questions about the agency. My only question was when would I make the call.

CHAPTER 41

At Cavanaugh's Again

Should have escorted Brite home; she had more than enough liquor to need assistance, possibly sufficient to befuddle her, enabling my managing her into bed. Should have at least escorted her to her door, but when you've consumed a liquor bill like I did, you tend to stay in place with a salacious smile on top of a numbed and quiescent body. Having achieved mellowness, hating to disrupt it, I was sanguine over our future together. Had her card, had her four buttons, had heard her secret dreams and ambitions, and having her past and her future I felt I had her, yet sufficiently sober to realize I may have had a lot of feminist bullshit.

Sitting there feeling secure in my belief I was one hell of an attractive guy when I spotted Tony Geroni hunched over the bar staring at his drink trying to read his future in the spirits. Having achieved a love for one's brother oft spoke of in Sunday's sermons and ad nauseum on talk shows, waving a welcoming glass high I yelled to him to join me. The waving glass got the waiter's attention but not Geroni's, who looked forlorn.

Shit, waiting for the waiter to come, to go, to come again, and sitting by myself looking at the empty opposite bench I got up with surprising ease, and except for the last two steps walked straight to

Geroni. Greeting him with a comradely slap on the back, he turned and stared hard as if I was touching him up for a drink. To remove such demeaning thoughts I reminded him I was Mac. Given I was up and he obviously down made my up so much more up, I asked if he had attended the Memorial as I don't remember seeing him on stage.

"Yeah, was there, but not on the stage. Since I wasn't actually at the banquet, some guy called Hussan told me where to go." Showing some life, giving a broad smile he said, "When one of the kids went missing I got up yelling I'll look for him."

Showing either deep insight, shallowness, or was it where Brite left my mind, I asked if he visited Zoe Bernstein's place.

"Screw her," he said, not as an accomplishment but as a crude dismissal.

I needn't have prodded him with why as he continued, "She saw me at the Memorial on TV when I went out to search for the kid. See, telling her I'd be in San Francisco attending a toilet convention to see the new, soft, self warming seat models, I had to spend at least three hours trying to convince her it wasn't me who raced out of the hall looking for the kid and another three hours to talk her into believing I just returned from Frisco checking for Kohler what was new about European toilets."

"How did it go?"

"I was stuck at that stupid Memorial."

"No, no, I mean did Zoe buy your story?"

"Of course not, pretended she did, but the cost of her pretention to believe me was for me to move in with her."

With our drinks arriving I saw he was in a serious drunken mood, no PC light beer, but a highball to mate with mine. He gave a curt 'thanks' for the drink then mentioned the McDonald's guy is here as well as that Palante character.

Looking about I asked, "Where?"

"The john. Didn't expect to meet anyone when I came to Cavanaugh's."

"I was here with Toni Brite."

"Yeah, she's a looker, offered her my story but she wasn't interested. Hell, no one's interested."

Remembering Babs Geroni and her afternoon wine braced in a house that showed numerous afternoon braces, I couldn't resist, I'm that despicable and I know it. With all innocence I said certainly his wife Babs is interested in his life.

"Screw her."

"Who, Brite?"

"No, screw them all."

Mischievously I said, "I interviewed your wife. I was impressed with her concern over you. You've got a great wife there."

Looking hard at me, Geroni tried to determine if I was putting him on. Since I was, I looked about the bar letting him digest my insincerity with a highball swallow.

In all honesty I really didn't like Geroni and under good fellowship pretense I asked if business was slack, knowing it was and Geroni was tight enough to be truthful.

'It sucks, don't know what to do. Zoe is demanding more commitment, and to be perfectly frank I don't really like her, a stupid empty woman, all powder and perfume. If it wasn't for the sex I'd drop her in a minute."

"Are you getting any?" I indelicately asked, but liquor permits such liberties.

"Nothing any more 'til I move in with her. Shit she actually suggested I may not be so high up in the Kohler organization. Know what the sneaky bitch did? Called Kohler headquarters asking for me.

Let me tell you, a woman suspecting your crap is okay ... it's when she bothers to check and make a stink about it, that's when you know it's coming down to put up or shut up time. Spent six hours arguing with her trying to get into her pants. Shit, how sad is that?"

Shit, I thought, spent a good four hours jollying Brite and a hell of a lot of money and got nothing but promises, and besides, how good am I doing, sitting next to this loser.

Ray Brothers and Paul Palante, both down at the mouth, joined us to form a semi circle with the bar as the diameter. Ray was downing Martinis, Paul downed diet beer. I was the only happy face sipping possibly one too many highballs. It was obvious all three were midway between stand up sober and falling down drunk. Congenial among themselves, not boisterous, but deep into serious bar contemplation, with a Martini in hand Ray cursed women in the abstract, Tony vehemently agreed and even lady's man Paul Palante didn't object to the proposition.

Paul, surprising me, I couldn't resist maliciously pouncing on him, asking how he could curse women seeing how successful he was with them.

As an indication to how many diet beers Paul had, he admitted he wasn't as successful as people may think, but not drunk enough to leave the quasi admission alone. He added, "I still got more than my share of broads coming on to me and hell, I'm even wearing my wedding ring."

Low calorie beers, wedding rings, what a girly man.

Paul concluded with a profound, "All women want one thing," and left the 'one thing' undefined. I suspect the 'one thing' was himself.

After taking a taste of his drink, to assure it was alcoholic, Tony agreed saying the one thing is marriage. "Shit, I've got something on the side and she's giving me ultimatums. Shit, she's good but not that good, and she doesn't believe me."

Munching on his Martini olive, ex cathedra Ray announced, "Money, that's the core of a woman's heart. I've got a little money (being condescendingly modest) but if I listen to my wife, daughter and mistress I'd end up eating at my restaurants, not owning them."

Erroneously feeling I was the sober one of the group, assuming the chair, I illogically summarizing, "So the one thing women want is a man, marriage and money." A trivial conclusion but at that time, with the drinks consumed, we felt we were original thinkers uncovering eternal truths about women.

To Ray, the richest, with false sympathy, I suggested Courtney may be putting the screws on for marriage.

With a spark of anger at me or Courtney, he complained, "I've given her money, moved out of my home, backed her stupid boutique that's bleeding money, my money, and she's not satisfied. Wants me to divorce my wife and marry her."

"Will you marry her?" Paul asked.

"Never! Damn it, never. I'm tired of buying sex from her and for what she's selling, she's damn expensive, even overpriced, and I'm being shortchanged."

I asked, "Did you ever suspect your wife or Courtney of trying to poison you? Both have big financial motives, your wife getting the restaurants and your insurance, and Courtney thinks she's the beneficiary of your insurance. Remember, it's in the millions especially with double indemnity."

"Mac, I had to cash in the policy. Let me tell you, keeping up two expensive homes, two children, two expensive women drains not only you but your bank account. Still I can't see either trying to kill the golden goose, given each still has the hope I'll end up with her."

"What about your daughter and her black boyfriend? They looked capable of spicing the salsa."

"Oh shit. A nigger humping my daughter. My biggest fear is black grandchildren. Tell me, what white man wants black grandchildren?"

Tony interjected his confirmation, "Shit, you see all these black bums dating white girls and if you object you're a racist.'

Paul added he would never date blacks, though he had lots of opportunities, and there was a beauty who could pass for white with a deep suntan who was annoying him.

I continued, "So do you see the mixed couple either singularly or as a couple trying to put you down like an annoying dog?"

That was nasty, out of bounds for our convivial group, so I quickly amended, "Still Ray, Amber can come to her senses and with both Eleanor and Courtney still hoping to win you, they may not have resorted to extremes."

Tony picked up the theme, "Yeah, you're right. My stupid broads, Zoe and my drunken wife treat me as a shuttle cock to be banged back and forth between them."

Ignoring Toni's drunken comment I told Ray, "But you're the referee of the game, standing outside their machinations, deciding who scores points. You see the game their playing and you decide who's the winner or even if there is to be a winner.'

Draining his diet beer Paul said, 'Yeah, I think I got what you're saying. With all the women coming on to me I feel I'm just an object to them."

Felt the poor bastard was right on target with 'just an object'. I feared it applied to all of us.

Ignoring Paul as if he was an object not relevant to the group, Tony stated, 'Yeah, I feel my broad Zoe is hitting me hard with moving in with her. At least my wine tasting wife Babs doesn't know about Zoe."

I let that fool's gold pass and ordered another round. Drunk enough to do the grand gesture, I was sufficiently sober to count the credit card cost. My money was saved as Ray said it was on him. Tony and I fought Ray over the honor but quickly succumbing, mumbled the next round was on us. From Tony's and Paul's expressions, I felt Ray often won with the two quickly throwing in the towel.

With the round settled Tony picked up his theme, "If the wife knows, she also knows Zoe is a passing phase of the moon. Wife, children, home is where I belong. Hell, I'm through with Zoe. She's such a needy desperate broad. Twenty three going on thirty three, and I'm not her first, and if you're not the first, your queue position is completely indeterminate somewhere between second and a hundred. With my Babs, damn it, I was the first and that says a lot about her and her love for me, and I owe he, but I can tell you, she's running up a severe wine bill that could eventually split us."

Silently we toasted Babs' honor, a rare honor, too rare.

Paul, feeling a conversational tide was passing him by jumped into our liquid world with a rejoiner, "I'm sure of Dorothy. She's my rock"

On his rock we halved our drinks, all considering Paul a barnacle attached to his rock. In fact he was a barnacle to our group.

Such was our boozy fellowship again we toasted Dorothy as the greatest. Our tolerance was severely tested with Paul's next statement, "You guys know how successful I'm with broads. They come on to me like flies to beefsteak."

Tony and Ray passed looks and before cruel laughs and words issued forth I quickly said, "Yes Paul. I met Dorothy and I'm telling you I was impressed."

"Still a looker," he said.

"Yes, certainly, but I was speaking of her personality, so feminine, so wise and pleasing, can't see her poisoning table 12."

"Dot poisoning me? Ridiculous. She loves me, I love her, and despite many chances, I've been faithful to our love."

Seeking to find some similarity between Paul and himself, Ray asked Paul if he had any money, insurance, property.

"Money! Crap, I'm only - I work for the Board of Education and you know how poorly they pay teachers and the school staff."

Tony asked if Paul was getting anything on the side.

Given Paul's proclivity to see women jumping out of ambush lusting over him the question could have been a sarcastic comment or a literal inquiry. I suspected the former.

Taking it straight, Paul maintained, despite any number of offered opportunities from eager beautiful women, he was faithful to Dot. Dot was his life. Without her and the kids he had nothing.

That I could believe. A school janitor has few things going for him. A wife, children, a home were the best he could hope for. Shit, if Dot cast him adrift, he'd drown.

With glasses empty, magnanimously I ordered another round, mentally calculating I'll be leaving a week's pay at Cavanaugh's.

Feeling it was also my turn to defend my wife Pam I mentioned my happy marriage to the best wife, a fantastic woman and mother.

Mendaciously, Tony brought out my tet a tete with Toni Brite over drinks and dinner. Weakly I mentioned her trying to be my literary agent as an excuse.

Receiving laughter and crude comments the excuse deserved, I backtracked mentioning she was fantastically hot as a more plausible excuse.

Agreeing, Paul told a disbelieving audience she wanted him to go to her place to discuss a book deal. Needless he amplified his fantasy, "And you know what was deal she really had in mind."

Starting to pass from good fellowship to ego enhancement, highball Tony said, "Yeah, she could sleep with a janitor like I'd screw that old Dina Saw broad."

To help in recovering our bon homie, Ray asked me if I knew how the imposter Hedja Hussan got to run the Memorial. "Shit, what kind of security is there when a wacko character can just go on stage, give orders and have everybody obey him."

Tony added, "He's like a politician."

From my self assumed pontificating position, I lectured the group, "Security depends on paper. The majority of people, your middle class, are basically honest in filling out paper forms and reciprocate with readily accepting the truth of paper they receive. If you have paper you have the world. Without it you're just a reader, accepter and believer. This Bernie Fuchs, aka Hedja Hussan, employed printed credentials. He made up on paper a bogus Federal Internal Security, with himself as his chief officer. With such bogus self generated paper with gold embossed seals accompanied by illegible signatures of nonexistent entities proclaiming his authority and with plastic encased IDs with his picture, can anyone doubt his authority. Who could not believe a store bought gold shield to buttress all his paper credentials. Who would dare question him. You doubt the certifications? He gives you the ID badges. If you continue your perverse doubts, the badge glistening gold with the letters FIS in black enamel quickly puts you right. Only cynical negative people would dare doubt him, as he had more paper than everyone else, more even than legitimate authorities. If you have a sufficient impressive barricade to proclaim yourself, no one will question your bonifides.

After he passed the initial casual screening, easily accomplished given his powerful paper position, he overcame successive barriers employing the knowledge prior scrutiny had validated his paper. Easily hurdling the successive security barriers he moved upward 'til standing among the highest, and from such a perch no one would dare venture to question him. All prior acceptors of his paper will die before admitting they were wrong and had been had, and therefore will defend him and his posturing against all doubters. Through their acceptance comes their belief and his paper becomes their paper. Belief in paper is the foundation of all Ponzi schemes including social Ponzis."

Putting down an empty glass Paul Palante said he didn't understand in tone and voice suggesting his perceptivity had decided I talked nonsense.

Irritated I gave an example. "If some person unknown to you presents a Ph.D. diploma from MIT as an accreditation of his acumen, buttress with reference letters from authorities, along with confederates or prior dupes swearing to the person and his papers' verisimilitude, you would accept it and by accepting it will readily accept all that may flow directly or indirectly from such acceptance."

Paul impolitely said I was long winded and boring.

Nervously noting the near empty glasses, Tony agreed with me saying the reverse is true. If you find out a guy's a phony, a bullshitter, you never believe anything he says.

Impishly I amended, "Except politicians. No one really believes them but they say such beautiful lies before dipping into your pocket for your money and vote, it would be nasty not to believe them."

With the sagacity confirmed by his ownership of several McDonald's, Ray felt the need to doubt my premise, in fact sneering at it, declaring it all absurd..

Hell, our group was leaking all our alcohol fueled comradeship. Defending I said, "Ray, if on filling out an application for a job in one of your restaurants, the applicant checks the box 'no' to having been convicted of a felony, checks 'yes' to high school diploma, checks 'no' to communicative disease, do you check, or do you accept him as his paper purports? After all, if you had a sexually transmitted disease, never saw the inside of the ninth grade, served time for theft, would you be honest? Would such an impulse to lie on paper be so foreign and sinful to a dishonest person? The application is useless as the dishonest will put down the same answers as an honest person."

Ray didn't back down but easily lied maintaining he checks up on all applications. He owed it to his patrons to insure reliable servers.

Obviously it would take a few more Martinis to drag Ray down to the level of honesty.

Tony, feeling he and I were now in a combative tournament, interjected his argument that my example was trivial. "No one checks minimal wage applications."

Damn him. Illogically agreeing with me he's using our agreement against me.

Defensively I said, "Tony, you maintain you're a licensed plumber with insurance. Are you?"

That got a rise out of him. "Certainly, I've got a State license and carry an insurance card."

"No doubt, but are they real? Or did you just print up facsimiles, and if anyone doubts your word use those pieces of paper to smother any doubt."

"Look, are you saying I'm a phony, not a licensed plumber?"

The guy was getting belligerent, so soothingly I suggested another round on me. Both Tony and Paul looked relieved as it was definitely one of their turns to buy.

My waving to the bartender caught other eyes. Just entering, Tom Applegate waved back and joined us in time to order a straight highball on me. Damn it, I'm going into next week's salary.

In the respite of giving bar orders, removing empty glasses, and impatiently waiting for refills, feeling I was generously buying out of turn, I felt justified in continuing my argument. "Hell, do you question a doctor's diploma, a lawyer's diploma, a politician's war record?"

Tom, recognizing he owed me a drink, mentioned a woman politician who went through life posing as a native American, getting all sorts of affirmative aid in her career, ending up as a US Senator. Of course she was all just a big bullshitter, but even when exposed, the people duped to excuse their being duped excuse the liar.

The arrival of the drinks put a period to that sad snippet of information.

The sober one of the group, Tom, was the first to pull his nose out of the alcohol to complain, "I'm through coaching kid's football." He said it as if we deeply cared and would be horrified. Believing in our caring and shock, rhetorically he asked, "Did you see the team on stage? They screwed up the simple run through the four hole, and then they all disappeared, leaving me looking like a fool."

Even though he was critical of our kids, we extended several sympatric 'too bad's which had him amplifying, "After that stupid Memorial service several parents complained of an absence of supervision. Hell, one parent threatened to sue me 'cause her son left the stage and was missing for over four hours."

Between our sipping, we gave him more 'that's not right' which encouraged him to continue venting his anger. His anger and disappointment moved from the team to a more personal level. "You know, my three children, Pierce, Myanmar and Matt aren't mine. All are stepchildren, Robin's by prior marriages. At least she said she was married, but now I doubt it." Raising his glass to the ceiling he offered the toast. "I thank my good fortune I never married Robin. She and her kids have no holds on me. I'm a free man."

Somehow his saying he was free made the rest of us envious.

"What are you planning to do?" Tony asked.

"Shit, leave the whore."

Ray repeated, "Whore?" As if it was a little too harsh.

"Yeah, I said whore, and that's what she is. When I got home after spending hours rounding up a team that enjoyed busting my ass playing hide and seek around the hall, more than playing football, she accuses me of seeing someone. Here I'm spending my afternoons and evenings looking for her little bastards, and instead of thanks I get lip, hard, mean lip. Shit, I don't have to take it from her."

Paul Palante argued over how Tom couldn't say for sure the children were illegitimate which incited Tom to continue ranting against Robin. "When I moved in with her she claimed she had married to an abuser, a manipulating sexual deviant from whom she eventually was able to escape. In love and with great sex I didn't question her, but in time began to see her true character, and questions started to come to mind. She couldn't provide marriage licenses nor divorce papers, so the three kids are bastards. Once I suspected her of lying I looked hard at the children. The girl Myanmar is Arab dark. The eldest boy is red headed and Mitt has a proboscis a monkey would be proud of. How could I have been so blind. Three bastards by three different men, and she's badgering me to marry her and adopt all her bastards. Guys, to be honest, in the beginning I was tempted, but some self preservational caution in the back of my mind made me procrastinate. Shit, I shudder at the mess I'd be in now if I did what I thought was the right thing to do. Can you imagine, having to support all of them. Hell, talk about slavery."

Taking a long swallow he announced, "Fellows, look for a new football coach next year. I'm bailing out of the whole father thing."

We sympathized as a group. We were turning into crying bitchy drunks.

Paul Palante was the first to leave, stating his wife Dot would be worried about him being with one of the nurses. Uncharitably I thought his exit was propelled by the possibility of his having to buy the next round. Like a nuclear chain reaction, once one of the group leaves the rest have an irresistible impulse to leave.

I was next, saying we had to get together again. Enthusiastic agreement brought forth alcoholic vows, same time next week. Everyone solemnly vowed to be there with all the sincerity of the unemployed on benefits swearing they're diligently looking for work, just can't find it.

CHAPTER 42

American Marriage

Being a city worker I still had an additional week off to recuperate from the Roach. Being a city worker, though being fit for work, paid not to work, I didn't work. Being a city worker I felt simultaneously lucky having an undeserved paid vacation and a little dirty knowing the money was undeserved.

My week was empty of pleasure, void of accomplishment, yet being a city worker, staying off the job, doing nothing except lose a little self respect. If a person loses a little too much self respect, hating himself he easily becomes a welfare bum.

Recovering from my night at Cavanaugh's with Brite and the table 12 guys, possessing a hangover of monumental proportions, head in a bucket experiencing dry heaves, swallowing at least six aspirins, the morning was spent in biblical misery. Where it all came from is a little vague. Remember ordering a drink or two after Brite, but then - oh, what the hell. I suffered a blackout. One moment I'm at Cavanaugh's talking to the guys, next waking up sick as a dog. I tried to pass off the blackout as some sort of oddity, not to be connected with my drinking.

The early afternoon came bringing some relief, sufficient relief to wander downstairs, gulp down orange juice and make some serious virtuous abstinence vows. Pam tried to nurse me, walking by me on cat's paws quietly asking about any needs I had however in general, kept out of sight. Of course I saw her disappointment in every gesture, shame in every whispered offer of help, and feeling her reproaches were justified made me angry at her. Yes, even as I growled at her ministrations I knew I was actually deep in self loathing. Where would we be without psychiatry.

The bell rang at the weakest link in the day's chain of pain where tired of the day, one eagerly waits for the night, Woody with Ronni in tow arrived. Damn him, like a jackal he smells weakness. Trying to keep him out, Pam being too polite to slam the door in his face allowed Woody to gain the foyer and with the wall breached he came loudly into the living room shouting he had great news, ostensibly great for me, but I knew Woody.

The sight of me in the lounger, pjs on, a waste bucket nearby, hanging on to life, he manufactured one of those sympathetic faces people give dying rich relatives while wondering when they can order the flight to Vegas.

Ronni was better at looking solicitous but kept her distance in case I up heaved. I suffered two, possibly three sentences from them explaining how bad I looked, how I shouldn't drink so much, ending with hints of AA intervention. They tossed AA between Pam and me for one of us to catch and run with implementing the idea. The suggestion, without comment was silently dropped into the waste basket. Woody, suggesting we had business to discuss Pam left to get some coffee. Only an innocent newlywed would believe she wasn't planning to listen.

Woody announced, "Look Mac, as I've been made Captain of the Anti Homophobic LGT Division I want you to join me and Lt. Ronni Deutsch as part of our team."

My 'no way' answer delivered with all the vim and vigor a dying man can manage passing easily by the two, exited the room without a whisper.

"Mac, before you answer, listen to Woody," was Ronni's advice.

"Yeah Mac, since we've come out of the closet things are opening up, even Lt. Ronni had come out as a lesbian."

"I'm thinking of putting in for a sex change operation with City money, along with a year's leave to recuperate," was Ronni's contribution.

Knowing Ronni had a pair of hard brass ones I greeted the need of surgery with, "How can they give you, er, man's equipment?"

Giving me a sly smile Ronni sent a little bit of knowledge my way, "There's a lot of City and Federal money available to help people who are sexually undecided and need counseling."

Ronni's comment explained it all: free money, free time, eat up 'til you burst.

"I get the picture," I said.

Woody distraught at being conversationally shunted aside said, "Ronni we all know where you're going with that." Then smirking he added, "And you know I'll support you in any decision you make.

"Now Mac, the reason I'm, er we're here is to enlist your help in the Gay Lesbian Transgender task force, the GLT Ronni and I created. It's going to operate outside all the other gay task forces and my approach will be eclectic in scope. I need an officer to back up Ronni and me in this important outreach program. Someone who will have our back when we are out of town. Like now I'm off to Key West to address the Anti Defamation Association for the LGT at their convention, then it's off to San Francisco to give the keynote address at the SFPD monthly meeting to discuss ways to rectify prejudices against gays in San Francisco police department."

Ronni said she was off to Tahiti to address the female inhabitants of the advantages of coming out. If they feel persecuted because of coming out they can seek asylum in America and after located in government housing they'll be instructed in such progressive ideas as negative income tax, food stamp credit cards, gay marriage, and free cell phones.

Woody added, "You know Mac, it's hard to convince primitive people that America's progressive caring is real and not some kind of con."

Sarcastically I told the two they certainly had a busy schedule but I couldn't see where I came in. Actually deep into my self loathing hangover state and with all my weaknesses, I still felt I possessed more pride than to join them.

Woody lamented, "Being out of the City so often, attending meetings, conventions, study groups and conferences on the multitude of problems gays face, I can't do the basic job of my Task Force; education children to create gay acceptance and gathering gay hating crime data."

Although Lieutenant to Woody's Captaincy, Ronni didn't feel inferior, rather believed she was superior, and she was. She jumped in with amplifications, "Mac, all you have to do is go to the City schools and at their assemblies, lecture the students not to bully gay students, and for gay students to come out of the closet and be proud of their gayness."

My disgusted look forced Ronni to add, "And Mac, in our absence you'll be in charge of hate crimes against gays."

"Yes," Woody added, "We're commissioned to investigate any crime against a gay person and determine if it's a hate crime. Nothing is more despicable than a hate crime, not even murder. You'll be working with Captain Moses' team fighting black hate crimes and with Captain Mohamed's task force investigating Muslim hate crimes. Of course, Major Jose Gonzalez's unit investigating hate crimes against Hispanics is a world unto itself."

Ronni added, "And all hate crimes against successful women. You'll be in charge of deciding if a crime is a sexist hate crime. If a person is robbed, you'll have to determine if he was gay, if he is, it's a hate crime and as such entered into the hate crime data base. If a person is run over, if gay, it's a hate crime. If a person is beaten up in a bar, if gay, a hate crime. Of course any gay murdered is automatically elevated to a hate crime. Murdering a person is terrible, but murdering a gay person is so much worse, being a hate crime. Thank goodness being classified as a hate crime doubles the punishment."

Woody said, "the same goes for hate crimes against blacks, Hispanics, Muslims, Chinese, Koreans, er - who did I leave out?"

"Women, abused, raped, forced into prostitution women," Ronni added.

"Anyway," Woody said, "There's a promotion for you. Who would have the balls to deny a gay guy fighting prejudice and hate a promotion and risk being labeled homophobic, lose his career.

"Oh, did I tell you, I'm getting married to Bubba Harrison, a Sgt at the City Commission for Diversity. He's as gay as I am. Hell, he's such a sex dog, he's known as the police department's Bill Clinton, but it's going to look great on our resumes and applications for promotion. He's already lined up some lucrative University speeches on the importance to the nation of legalizing gay marriage. Mac, ignorant people think walking on the moon is an indication of our greatness. Let me tell you history will record America's legalizing gay marriage as the capstone of our progressive greatness. What do you think of that?"

He expected a 'great' so I gave him a great with a smile, saying not great. Listening to Woody and Ronni was not helping my hangover. "Look Woody, I appreciate the offer. (I didn't.) and I wish you the best (I didn't) and I think you marrying Bubba is a great idea (I didn't) but what if you want to marry a woman?"

"Mac, that's the beauty of it all. Bubba and I are planning to get a divorce. We'll be the first gay couple getting a divorce. Two guys getting married is getting old hat, has no shock value any more. Being the first two guys to get a divorce, being so progressive will be a great publicity gimmick. By divorcing it will show we had a normal marriage."

Ronni said, "They can go on talk shows explaining how with similar careers they experienced difficulties having quality time together, they grew apart. *Oprah, Dr. Phil, the View* and all the other talk BS shows engaged in nonsensical girly talk will love to hear of the difficulties two married gay policemen encountered within their marriage. How their gay marriage was the cause of their receiving hate from the department, leading to difficulties in their relationship. Questions like, 'are you planning to marry another man? are you discouraged to your search to find happiness' in a gay hating world?"

Ronni concluded, "Mac, you know I may marry a woman. There's no downside. Commander Hillary who was sitting judgment on your trial has proposed and I'm thinking it over."

Woody cautioned Ronni, "I hope after your marriage to Commander Hillary you're not planning to co-opt Bubba and my divorcing."

Slyly Ronni denied any intention of divorce saying they plan to have children.

"Yeah, well Bubba and I thought about it, but it would complicate our divorce."

With all the gayness about I said, "Look, I'm happy to be out of the closet as long as Pam knows it's not true. In the immediate future I'll dive back into the closet and declare my normalcy."

"Normalcy," Woody shouted. "Shit to say heterosexual is normal is to infer homosexual is abnormal, even deviant. Mac, gay is the new black. As a gay, you tell a joke and everyone has to laugh. You drop a meatball in your lap, no one dare notice. Women are elated if you come on to them hoping they're so powerfully hot they can transform you and are dying to try, go down on your knees thanking heaven if you let them, and let them succeed. You enter a group and by your 'special' sexuality you become special. The one advantage blacks have is they don't have to show their 'special' color. I'm forced to get my gayness into the conversation without being too obvious. Let me tell you, it's a hard job to wedge it in." Wistfully Woody lamented to be black, gay and a woman is the royal road to success in achieving the American dream.

Pam came in with coffee and slices of coffee cake. With her presence talk became trivial except for Woody pressing me on how I was making out on solving the Roach Poison Case. Lying he said he and Ronni were making progress and if I had any information, no matter how minute, they'd appreciate hearing it.

Lying I said I had made no progress, but in my mind was a name.

Leaving, Woody reminded me how joining his and Ronni's GLT gay task force would be a great career move for me. Again I declined. As Woody left, Ronni delayed ostensibly having trouble with her coat to ask if I had any information about the poisoner I should call her or come over to her place to share ideas. She said this with Woody standing on the sidewalk, said it with her hand in mine, lightly squeezing with meaning, suggesting rewards, definitely not gay.

CHAPTER 43

Getting Brite

The disadvantages of piece work ... you have to work to get paid; the advantages of government employment ... such burdensome strictures are missing. Free, walking about under the city's overly large sick-leave umbrella, I still had a good week of time and energy to engage in various unproductive self destructive pursuits, one of which was the pursuit of Toni Brite.

Catching my interest with her agreeable, well developed body and sympathetic mind, I thought a symbiosis between us was established at Cavanaugh's. Additionally her hints of possessing Park Avenue wealth and Manhattan's sophistication was a bonus, although in my mind she was well below me in intelligence and the real knowledge only experience can impart. The Friday after our Cavanaugh connection, and being sufficiently recovered from my liquor indulgence, I put to use her business card to arrange for drinks at her place for that night. The goal was to bed Brite, an ego enhancing conquest and a libido exercise. My expectation was our loosening up with sharing drinks at her place accompanied by chit chat exchanges preparatory to her bedroom, a room feet away easily traversed and the awkwardness of moving there, quickly and easily overcome with walking hugs, kisses and whispered nonsense women find irresistible.

For some reason, all my mental expectations vaporized at her apartment's door when Brite, coat on, came rushing out before I could press the bell a second time. Passing me she explained she heard of a fabulous watering hole she was dying to visit.

I just had time to glance over her shoulder at her apartment's miniscule interior, an interior suggesting the couch was the bed. Forestalling my attempt to enter by slamming the door, she turned and in her wake informing me our reservations were for nine and we'd have to hurry.

Damn it, the bed suddenly moved miles away and she was taking me to 'her' place, 'her' venue. Was this the modern liberated 'take charge' woman: or just a woman trying to impress with her night life sophistication; or a woman hoping to present herself against an enhancing background; or was she distancing herself from her bedroom to play coy and innocent; or was she upping the price of entrance; or was it because her apartment, although at a prestigious address was embarrassingly small; or was our initial Cavanaugh's instilled sense of intimacy a delusion on my part? In any case I wasn't pleased she moved the goal post further away, necessitating additional time, energy, and most important money to get her to the bed post.

On the sidewalk my accusatory 'what reservations' elicited an accusation in return.

"You didn't say where you wanted to dine and in Manhattan on Friday night you absolutely must make reservations to insure having a table so I took the liberty. You don't mind."

Dinner reservations! I certainly did mind. My simple thoughts of strong booze, soft music, whispered words, silk sheets, smooth skin, quick exit was getting unexpectedly complicated. I was beginning to feel Brite was playing a board game and I was the token being moved from space to space.

She continued her assault. "Not knowing your favorite restaurant I took a chance and chose The Tides."

As a dollop of cuteness she added, "It could be 'our' restaurant."

Shit, I hadn't had my feet in her apartment, my ass on her couch, head on her pillow, and we already have 'our' restaurant chosen by her. What next ... our song, our joke, our favorite day of the week, when were we to have our favorite position.

Located In Soho, The Tide, with several empty forlorn tables outside surrounded and protected by a wrought iron fence attempted a faux pretentious Parisian sidewalk cafe. Inside, next to a podium, a tuxed maître d' stood guard over a large leather ledger. Running a Monte Blanc pen down the ledger's list he announced in tones similar to announcing one's entrance to heaven: the Brite party was there in the book and could enter, but not to eat. We were told we must wait at the bar and answer the buzzer to eat.

Sitting at the bar what could one do but order drinks. Obviously I had to pay in order to wait to eat. Brite had a Cosmopolitan costing a Cavanaugh's roast beef sandwich. My highball equaled a fifth of my house whiskey

Eyes bright, looking around she commented, "I don't see any famous people. I've heard Dustin Hoffman and Beyonce eat here often."

"Really!"

"Read it in The Times magazine section. Must be an off night for celebrities."

I didn't hide my sarcastic laugh, but Brite was too busy trying to uncover a name, no matter how obscure, to talk about tomorrow at work

Eyeing her Cosmopolitan level, fighting the urge to down mine and face another fifth in cost, the buzzer sounded, and like lap dogs we hopped off the stools and eagerly raced to the maitre, oh the hell, head waiter.

We serpentined our way past white linen draped tables inches apart to be delivered to a table feet from the kitchen. Obviously Brite didn't possess the weight she believed she had or hoped to have. Unlike Cavanaugh's basic red and white checkered cloth used to cover the table's scars, here gleaming linen provided a spotless white canvas for a series of numerous stem glasses of various volumes, and a gilt edge plate guarded by an imposing battalion of military aligned glistening silver. You had to wonder what could be the possible purpose of the multitude of silverware and glasses on display.

Sitting down Brite arranged us so I faced the kitchen and she could observe the crowd for a celebrity sighting. Waiting for our server I gloomily countered: the white starched linen adds twenty to the bill, each glass adds at least two bucks, the military parade of silver, a dollar a soldier, and the empty gilt plate added fifteen to the bill. From free drinks at her place on her couch leading to bed wrestling and quick goodbyes, I was seated here looking at a kitchen door realizing Brite thought herself very dear, possibly too dear for me, certainly overpriced. There is no more true measure of desire's strength than the effort and cost it commands to be possessed.

Our server Mosidek was stunned when we declined wine. To be correct, I quickly announced for Brite and myself we were wine abstainers, suspecting a glass of wine resting in her mind was moving down to her lips. With no wine, and my decline of imported spring water, our stemware instantly disappeared, except for one forlorn glass each.

Mosidek presented a large leather folder containing a two sheet menu without price (either The Tides were too proud or too ashamed) with all the panache of St. Peter asking who on the list would you chose to be worthy of saving. As I perused the difficult to read artistic script sprinkled with French adjectives, excited Brite announced a Mr. Woerle, a senior partner at MAD said we must simply order The Tide's filet mignon with The Tide's secret sauce. "Mr. Woerle guaranteed the meat, cuts as easily as the clouds, tastes simply heavenly. Mr. Woerle said The Tides' angus beef imported from Japan was never frozen, and fed only organic grains."

Casting an eye at the menu, found the meat surrounded by French words but again sans price. The lack of price added at least twenty, and each French word was provided at a dollar a syllable. Shit, where was this going! To the poor house where I was going and not to her house.

With the steak ordered, the silverware army was gathered up to guard other plates on other linen battlefields. In their place a large steak knife made its entrance. The size and heft suggested the flown in beef from Japan may not be as soft as the cloud, able to be cut with a fork.

Brite ordered a shrimp cocktail with the house's special sauce followed by a salad with house dressing. I passed on both ordering a double Canadian Club, straight up. My growing apprehension of the bill needed to be quieted with a double Club and going to the poor house I may as well go in comfort.

As she nibbled on three shrimp the size of frankfurters, Brite went on and on about the beef. I could only wonder where the hell were veggie women when you need them. If Brite thought all this dinner presentation BS would impress me, it didn't, being cognizant of who's paying for it. Unlike government welfare programs, the coming bill was neither hidden nor delayed but soon inextricably will be placed in my hand demanding payment in full. Feeling being used, feeling I was overpaying for the use of her room for a few hours, I felt I was being played for a sucker.

With Brite lamenting over our lack of wine, I felt it as a putdown suggesting cheapness. Apparently she never put a piece of beef in her mouth without gargling before and after with some vintage French red. Being a mile from her bedroom I was totally disinterested in catering to her BS movie and TV acquired pallet. Drinking my double I amused myself watching the coming in and going out of the kitchen door.

Dipping the frankfurter size shrimp into the house sauce Brite raved over her shrimp trio, gushed over the house salad dressing while I ordered a second double commenting The Tide thank heaven had an unseen strong steady pouring hand. Her enthusing over the shrimp and salad I thought was to make me feel either the cost was worth it (it wasn't) or feel good in giving her pleasure (I didn't) or making me feel bad at missing out on an epicurean experience previously enjoyed only in heaven. (Crap, it was only shrimp and lettuce.)

Brite's dinner conversation was spiced with 'awesome', 'fabulous', 'amazing', 'fantastic', 'marvelous' this or that object or person. Her eyes lit up when a piano player gave out with dinner music. I thought she'd have an orgasm. The only orgasm for me, now miles away and retreating with each awesome. My 'awesome' was the bill. I feared it will be heaven's sentence ordering me to hell for my sordid desires.

The meat, being so rare as to be considered precious possessing the size of a diamond, was set in a dollop of sauce. The two didn't have the weight or protein to smother Canadian's double buzz. Brite again tried for a cravat of wine grossing over angus being unaccompanied and wasn't it a shame.

I felt angus could make it down to the stomach without any help. The meat gone, the dishes running away, I saw Mosidek coming with some severe leather which I surmised was a disastrous dessert index.

Quickly I practiced a preemptive strike, announcing after all that food we must be too full for any more. Brite eyeing intently a hairy guy in torn jeans asking if that isn't Leonardo DiCaprio missed the import of my comment and distractedly agreed with me. To forestall Mosidek from presenting more leather I said we were full, couldn't eat any more, just coffee and the bill.

As a disappointed Brite was sipping a demitasse, I was licking the bottom of my third double.

Finally the day of reckoning. Mosidek came with a leather enfolded wallet, with all the sad restraint of one empathizing with your pain. Now knew the expression of a warden arriving to announce your stay isn't coming.

Sliding my credit card into the folder, I lacked the courage to see what The Tide brought in. In truth, doubting my ability to maintain savoir faire, I feared I would devolve into a weeping ghost condemned to the hell of bankruptcy. My 'give yourself twenty percent' Mosidek tossed to the floor saying the usual twenty percent gratuity at The Tide is automatically included. He held the leather packet under my nose for a poignant moment suggesting additive percents would not only be not amiss but was customary.

My getting up and asking, "Toni, are you ready to leave?" was needed to get the bill from under my nose.

Finally back at Brite's studio apartment, not really in the mood for libido action, (having to pay for it and pay large does not stimulate intimate desires,) but damn it, the cost stiffened my resolve to get what I paid for. Brite said I should help myself to a drink while she freshened up.

Finally, a free drink, which hopefully will dilute in some small measure the evening's overall cost and revive desire. After eyeing the convertible couch wondering how awkward it was to open, I turned on the TV for world news noise. Sipping, I watched TV's rendition of the exciting rescue of a dog stranded in a mud hole followed by being bathe in TV warm oil listening to the mother and child saying how happy they were that little Waffles was saved and how eternally grateful they were to the emergency squad. Viewing such TV news' exciting cliff hangers intros followed by cashmere endings, I had to make myself a new one, to the rim.

Dropping her soft smile at the uplifting dog story's ending, the mascara eye lashed newswoman, looking straight at the camera's eye with wide eyed horror reported on a devastating mud slide killing at many as ten thousand (more likely ten), destroying villages (maybe a couple of shacks) in the suburbs of Porto Novo (what's that?) and major city of Benin (where is that?.) Wherever it was, whatever it was, to give the viewer the intimacy of an eye witness on the ground right at the exciting happening of this devastating news, I had the pleasure of Miss Ubi Tubi. The color suggesting the what and the where were in Africa. Standing in front of a roiling muddy river she gushed tears over the devastation the muddy river was causing. Serendipitously an outhouse floated by allowing the camera in close up to follow its horrific passage.

In tremulous voice the studio newswoman asked if anything was being done to help Porto Novo's people in their catastrophic situation. Before answering this usual TV follow-up question to a horror story, Ubi had to bring in the proverbial crying children who were dying or about to die in the muddy river for your living room inspection and titillation. A black child, sitting in a mud puddle was rewarded with a close-up. Scared by the camera, the crying child was picked up by the mother who asked you, in your living room what she could do. (Not knowing what she could do, I was confused at her asking me a thousand miles away and marveled at her command of English.)

The newsreader in the studio knew what had to be done, that always had to be done. Assuring the mother and a concerned Ubi copious special meetings of the Western countries were convening in

Geneva to discuss how aid can be sent to Porto Novo to relieve the suffering of hundreds of thousands (maybe a hundred). In case Ubi felt meetings in Geneva were inadequate to meet the immediate dire situation, she was also assured at that very moment, in Brussels, the UN Relief Commission was meeting and help was on its way.

After telling a hopeful, though still concerned Ubi, for her to stay safe as if she was standing on the Titanic deck, the studio moved to a hot weather babe (are any TV babes not hot) who was now going to give today's weather in case you died in the morning and missed observing it. As I suspected she reaffirmed my observation, it was a damp nasty day in the forties.

A returning Toni disappointed me big time. She hadn't taken off anything nor slipped into something easily taken off. She partially assuaged my annoyance by making us drinks, mine the Club, hers wine. (Finally she had her wine.) On TV, the hot weather babe wearing her worried face mentioned it was the wettest November New York City has experienced in the past twenty four months. (Let's hear an amen for global warming and say a prayer for polar bears.) Despite this anxiety causing data I was sufficiently able to control myself and not go into a paroxysm of fear for the world's future.)

Going to turn off the TV so I could make profitable use of the buzz I was striving to keep alive all night, Toni stopped me halfway across the six feet separating couch and TV. She wanted to hear tomorrow's weather forecast. Hesitating, complaining being the item most germane to our life, the future weather forecast was always placed at the news' ass. (Ass, that was the Club talking.)

Seeing her take off her shoes and on the couch curl her feet under her ass I left the TV on and refreshed my drink. That was a mistake. The buzz was becoming the goal in itself and not the instrument to open the couch. Just one of a mistake filled evening. Still, at the time feeling my desire had been battered down by the evening's expense I felt the need to reinforce my spirit with additional spirits. Suddenly the TV screen became psychedelic with flashing lights announcing a news alert necessarily repeated, repeatedly flashed several times in case you blinked and missed the first alert. In an impassioned voice one expects to be employed if the market in dropping ten thousand points had Wall Street brokers opening windows announced the alert concerned pantries for the poor. Apparently they were depleted and in dire need of being refurbished lest people go hungry for Thanksgiving and Christmas. A grandmother type, in a red Santa apron, the type of granny you never had, and was probably hired from a talent agency, appeared in front of some empty shelves. Lamenting the empty food pantry she prophesied children will starve, kitchens feeding the homeless will have to close and the homeless (winos, druggies, and worthless bums) will be dropping dead of hunger. (Though they never do.)

It was here where the critical mistake was made! The Club buzz wouldn't let me keep my damn mouth shut. If I had to talk, given the current intimate situation I should have cried over the empty shelves, been aghast in horror of the immediate advent of starving people dying. Like a politician I should have voiced my love of the poor, my desire to feed the poor, and my outrage at people who are so heartless as to not feel the pain desperate single mothers and their starving children experience. Brite and I could then sitting together sharing noble impulses, elevating ourselves over the heartless, and sharing emotional concern we could share touches, lips touches, and discuss how to open the couch.

Unfortunately buzz was king and the ego crushed the libido. I had to say, "Shit, (another Canadian Club word.) it's Thanksgiving and Christmas time and like the annual appearance of phony snow and plastic pines, these phony charity stories annually blossom forth. I hate this blatant cynical manipulation of people into caring or giving a damn. Apparently people don't starve in the summer."

In disbelief, a startled Toni asked if I really believe no one was going hungry in America and didn't need help, especially at the holiday season. She was showing her Park Avenue sophistication with her unshakable belief that hundreds of thousands of people were moments away from dropping dead in the city gutters only a mile from her apartment. It was only her caring, her concern, her loose change that was the fragile shield in keeping needy people alive. Most of the year the starving stood in the dark waiting to be pulled into the light whenever sophisticated people feel the need to bring them forth especially in TV Sweeps Week..

As I suspected, Toni thought in clichés, those often said popular beliefs, and having bed aspirations I should shut my mouth, finish my drink, sit on the couch and get soft words working. Of course, with the buzz's strength I stayed standing, sipping and talking. "Toni, do you believe people are seasonal starvers, only getting hungry when in the fall they start to drop like leaves? Christmas stories of hunger are traditional, and like Dickens' *Christmas Carol* are an expected part of the season with as much substance. It's put on display to make you feel more human and to increase your enjoyment of the season. After all, what could increase your Thanksgiving appetite and dinner enjoyment without soup kitchen stories that eventually have a happy ending with some bum munching a drumstick."

Toni's feet came out from under her ass. "You can't really believe that here, in America, there is no real hunger. That's so unAmerican."

The feet coming out of her ass area said sex was in serious jeopardy. To salvage it I had to shut up. Of course I didn't. Damn the Canadian Club. "Toni, how could a country be starving when the first lady with wisdom above all women is worried about obesity being rampant among children especially poor children, poor black children. A country filled with TV ads touting weight reduction ploys, a country awash in food stamps talk seriously about starvation. No one is starving save anorexic girls."

Toni stiffened her back, sat straight on the couch, her warning shot across my bow was to give me an opportunity to abjure my statements by again asking, "Mac, you really can't believe people aren't going hungry in America, especially at Thanksgiving."

I didn't say apparently no one suffers at Labor Day barbecues, but it almost slipped out.

Her language: body, tone and words were flashing warning red sex lights and would you believe it, I accelerated. Damn the Club.

"It makes me laugh at all the fools who ring bells, cook and serve meals, collect and distribute free food, free turkeys with all the fixings (can't give a starving person just a turkey sandwich) to the unemployed bums. (I believe the Club actually made me say bums).Toni, if the starving poor are unemployed, virtuous innocent victims of a malicious fate, why aren't they ringing the bells, soliciting food, working the foot pantries, cooking and serving the Thanksgiving dinners? They don't cause they don't work. Only people who work, or have worked, work to feed those that don't work."

Finally, my ego clubbed my libido to dust.

In shock disbelief Toni said more to herself than to me, "You can't really, can't really believe what you're saying. No one can believe what you're saying. Everyone knows people are starving. You see it on TV every night, especially during the holidays."

Her shoes were on; all was lost. There was no chance in hell any abject denials by me would get those shoes back off her feet. Damn the torpedoes, full steam ahead. "If you read Dickens's Christmas Carol you'll see a much aligned scrooge. The quintessential capitalist diligently working at his business striving to build it up, saving and investing his profits. The liberal visiting ghost and the story's characters all revile him for not giving money to the poor, not raising wages. Not only giving money away but the ghost insists he lead a debauched life his nephew was leading, attending parties with the aim of pleasuring himself rather than work. If Scrooge followed such destructive advice he would end up joining his employees in the workhouse. You can only have poor if you have workers to support them. If the workers become poor all are poor, and by poverty's definition, none are poor. Universal poverty is the only way to cure poverty. It's Socialism's great solution."

Standing up, telling me I was being ridiculous, mentioning it was late, traveling the eight feet to the front door, Toni announced she had a busy day at work.

In attempting an enjoyable miniature Gotterdammerung I asked if she was going to ring bells next to a kettle outside of Macy's on Christmas Eve.

She answered by opening the door with all the drama of sending a fallen angel into eternal darkness. To make it clear, my punishment was total expulsion from enjoying her heavenly delights and she ordered me not to call her.

Any struggle between ego and libido, the ego must triumph.

CHAPTER 44

Getting to Cavanaugh's

After the fiasco at Brite's, it was strange I wasn't angry at her. Yes 'bitch' and 'whore' were among the frequent colorful descriptions connected to her name, but my real bitterness was directed at myself. Played for the fool; I played the fool. With aims shallow, foolish and worse, I allowed myself to be gamed by a fool. Bitterly feeling myself better than that, I resented allowing myself, no worse, was a willing partner to being made to jump from place to place only in the end failing to reach my meaningless goal. I was seduced into playing sex monopoly with loaded dice, she, counterfeit money, believing if I won I would have something real, a significant objective would have been achieved.

Hell, something was achieved; my self examination revealed all my poisonous fantasies, and if not curbed the extent to which they dragged me down. You don't have to be a tattooed drug addict running about the city gutters, begging other life losers for something to forget who you've become, not to realize their motivation is yours. Begging for Brite's tattooless ass, I was addicted to the country's prevailing drugs and sex. I had been reduced to running with fools, begging losers for a drug to forget my emptiness.

After spending most of the weekend in self flagellation, I decided to rid myself of meaningless goals corrosive to the self, and strive for that which the self with pride could applaud. One step on the road to recovery was to be attentive to Pam, a person woefully mistreated. She and I were linked, we had mutual obligations to answer, and I intended to be true to those obligations. She was true, rock fast, and I've been mistreating, disrespecting and unappreciative of her love.

Once I've solved the Roach Murder, if not to judicial convict, at least convict in my mind, I resolved to be more attentive to Pam.

Why should I bother solving the Roach Murder? Forget abstract justice which loses definitional precepts once it gets personal. Forget respect for the law which is interpreted, amended, cancelled with every contemporary change in fashion. Forget airy contradictory ethical theories which like veins of fool's gold elicit excitement 'til another vein is announced drawing away the first popularity. Forget all the popular easily digested moral platitudes advanced on TV and in print. It's in the particular individual where a sense of justice resides.

Within me, by my human nature, there exists a need to correct a perceived wrong; to leave it unaddressed is a serious blemish to my ego's sense of self. What is the foundation, the support of axiomatic theories of law, ethics and morality if not righting injustices done to you. If those theories can't or if in practice they leave your injustice unresolved, they become more than meaningless. They are chains keeping you from seeking your own redress needed to restore painful imbalances in your life.

To that end I did some research into the lives of the men at table 12, the modern way, browsing through Twitter, Google, Facebook and direct telephone calls. I wasn't interested in the victims per se, but how the wives and girlfriends viewed their relationships with the men.

I discovered Robin, Applegate's mistress, revealing on Facebook how she saved Applegate's life with her intuition springing from her feminine psyche. On the way to the banquet she begged Tom not to sit at table 12. According to her Facebook, she felt someone was going to meet a tragic fate. It was only through her pleading on the way to the banquet that Tom consented to move to the kid's table and out of danger. If this fantasy actually occurred, it cleared her of being a suspect. The only problem was Tom saying in our interview his decision was made at the banquet. This discrepancy had to be clarified. Their existed the marriage barrier for her to collect Tom's money. Not being married blocked Robin's legal access to a dead Applegate's estate. Anyway, through his almost wife I extended an invitation for Applegate to join me at Cavanaugh's Saturday night.

The Palantes had no interest in showing their lives to the world. Dorothy, a sensible mother needing no electronic fame to validate her life forced me to use the phone. Knowing janitor's hours, I easily reached Dorothy on the phone. After identifying myself as a police officer I asked if she was aware of her husband having a relationship with another woman. Damn it, she laughed, actually laughed at the suggestion before apologizing for her rudeness. After allowing her to decry any suggestion of Paul's extracurricular activities, I pressed her for reasons why she was so sure.

"Mr. Detective McCoppin, do you know his hours doing janitorial work?"

Confessing ignorance she told me, "Three in the afternoon to nine at night, cleaning an entire 900 student school. It's almost ten before he arrives home tired and hungry."

"The weekends, what about the weekends?"

"He stays home with me and our children."

"Every weekend?" I asked.

"Do you know how much a school janitor makes, how much he actually brings home?"

"No."

"Let me tell you, it's insufficient to allow Paul to go gallivanting about and getting into trouble. He gives me his salary and I know where each precious dollar goes."

Realizing from personal experience how costly pursuing sex fantasies can be, expensive both in time and dollars, I thanked her for her time, mentioning I was planning a meeting of table 12 fathers on Saturday night at Cavanaugh's.

"You needn't tell me, Paul will tell me and share what happened as soon as he comes home."

"The expense will be mine."

"Please, I can give Paul some money. I don't want him to be embarrassed."

Hanging up the phone I thought, shit, talk about a puppet master, talk about a woman's ideal husband. I wondered if she could entertain a revulsion towards such a pliant spouse. Damn it, I didn't like Palante, didn't respect him, thought him a clown, but you need hate to kill and a stay at home mother with three children couldn't afford to kill that bi-weekly janitorial check.

After talking to Dorothy I called the school district, found out employees had a ten thousand dollar insurance policy, no double indemnity. Dorothy and her three children couldn't last six months on that, and in talking to her she struck me as that rare mother of low income who despises welfare for what it was, charity paid by people forced to contribute.

Next up was Geroni, and Facebook was informative about Zoe Birnsten, Geroni's extracurricular girlfriend. Apparently the world at large was as excited as she to find out she met a simply wonderful man who has become a significant person in her life. According to her electronic public diary, Ralph was a wealthy neurosurgeon separated from his wife. He and Zoe were planning to sail around the world on his yacht as soon as the divorce became final. The date of the posting was the day before the poisoning. If true, with a new matrimonial fantasy hopefully soon to be unencumbered by a wife, she wouldn't be interested in seeking revenge against Geroni. Of course, days after the poisoning, she warned the female world at large on her Facebook page that Tony Geroni was married, wasn't an executive at Koehler plumbing, was a liar, a cheat, impotent, an abuser and a despicable abuser of women.

Ray Brothers, my main suspected targeted victim, indeed cashed in his million dollar policies, and from his insurance agent found out I was the fourth person to inquire about the status of his insurance. The day before the poisoning, a woman named Courtney, claiming to be Ray's wife, found out about the cancellation. She was quickly followed by Eleanor, Ray's wife, who was devastated to find out her husband, insurance wise, was uncovered. A third woman, Ray's daughter, called to check on what her mother told her, and was equally horrified to find out her dad was naked insurance wise. Since Ray now had no life insurance, the agent was hoping wives and daughters would spur Ray to reinstate his policies, so he was glad to share the information, emphasizing Ray's nudity was putting all in jeopardy. They must do the right thing towards achieving their peace of mind and get Ray to buy insurance.

With black Rufus being interviewed by MAD for his life story of his heroically enduring and surviving in racist America, I got Dagmar, his black pudding on the phone. Knowing her heart and mind, I identified myself as an officer of the minority police division. To sell it I gave out with black English, a lot of 'you know what I'm saying' and sliding over consonants and vowels that required effort, i.e., 'da' for the, 'ya' for you. I was able to overcame her suspicion of authority, but it took my suggestion that Rufus was being investigated for drug trafficking to gain her attention. She didn't wait for the punctuation before screaming racism, hate crime, and drugs never entered her home, and she'll sue.

Remembering her hospital conversation, I mentioned talking to Jimmy, and he was being very informative.

"Jimmy! Did you say Jimmy?" she fearfully shouted before ending with, "Who Jimmy? Don't know any Jimmy, and look,da drug business was only a few Acapulco gold ounces for medical purposes. Rufus has a bad back driving that cab all day and needs a joint once in a while."

"Are you saying he drives a cab while high on marijuana?"

"Shit, no. Don't know what you're talking about. Look, we're getting a lot of money so Rufus and I are getting married. We don't need to sell drugs, which we never did, and I may even decide to get off State assistance."

There was a pause. I didn't really have much to say. In fact, I really didn't know why I actually called her. She had nothing to gain with Rufus' death.

A little surprising she came out worrying, 'Do you think, now that we have some money, the state would be mean enough to expect us to pay back the little assistance Rufus and I received for the past twenty five years?"

"They could," I said, thought they should, knew they wouldn't, the State being preoccupied in getting my money to give it away .

Dagmar said, "I've got to talk to my lawyer O'Malley and straighten out any problems. It's not right for the government to rob people just because they have some money, just isn't right.

"Now look, got to hang up, da wedding arrangements and O'Malley - ya know he's negotiating a lot of money for the sale of da video of our marriage to *Entertainment Tonight,* and pictures of me in my bridal dress will be *on Bride Magazine's* cover, but only if they come up with at least a hundred grand." Before I could say goodbye she hung up.

My last call was to Scott's wife, Joy. After identifying myself as the officer in charge of investigating her husband's death she asked if I was with the FBI.

"No."

"CIA?"

"No."

"Federal Security Agency?"

'No."

"Special state investigators?"

"No."

"Justice Department lawyers?"

"No."

"Congressional Investigators?"

"No."

"FIS?"

"Never."

"Then who the hell are you, if not one of them?"

My, "City police" brought, "big deal. I've been interviewed by really important people and I'm not interested in talking to City cops."

Sensing the phone about to leave her ear I shouted, "I have information you and Zapp are lovers."

"What did you say?" she said as if she became momentarily deaf, the usual play for getting thinking time. "I don't understand you," she complained as if I spoke in a Mongolian dialect.

I repeated, "I have reliable information that you and Zapp are having an affair."

First she went to a woman's basic ego defense, "Him? Zapp? Do you really think I'd be interested in someone like him?" before going to her virtue, "Look officer, I'm not the type of woman to engage in sordid affairs." Finally she brought out her vows and love for Jim, "I never would be unfaithful to my husband - I loved him - he was my son's father and my entire life."

I persisted saying my source was reliable.

"I know your source and you can tell Murry Zapp I never was interested in him. You know recently he's been trying to establish a relationship with me, and poor Jim still above ground. Well I told him he was being very disrespectful to Jim's memory and I found his attention disgusting and inappropriate, and I'm planning to get a restraining order.

"Now Mr. City cop, I've got to attend a conference at MAD to arrange for poor Jim's burial ceremony so it will receive the tasteful publicity such a national event deserves, and then I've got to go to O'Malley's to negotiate my compensation for the TV video rights to the funeral, and the stipends for in-depth interviews on my son's and my pain, and how we're dealing with the loss of a father and husband, as well as - ."

My last thought about her was how lucky Jim was.

After investigating the suspected woman poisoners, I called all the men connecting with table 12's roach poisoning to meet me at Cavanaugh's. To provide sufficient enticement, I suggested a conference to investigate methods we could use to increase our compensation for our victimization.

Approaching each individual, I inferred it would be a meeting just between the two of us. All were receptive to various degrees, subject to various enticements. To most the mention of more money, free undeserved money, sufficed.

In addition for black Rufus, to overcome his suspecting I wanted to get in on all his black rewards, I had to hint Ebony was going to be there to do a cover story. (Yeah, he actually believed it, then again it could actually had been true.)

Ray Brothers, possessing money, needed to be enticed by suggesting a revelation of something outrageously perverse or criminal connected to his daughter Amber's black boyfriend Derek. And again it could be true.

Geroni the plumber was coming, expecting inside information on a city plumbing job. Being one of the many men giving up on going somewhere on his own legs, he was a believer in luck's lightening striking him: the lottery ticket, the dream of kicking a stone and finding oil, the unknown dead relative leaving wealth. Like many, he became glassy eyed over lottery winners' stories and bored by stories of the success men earned by hard work. In the past, men dreamed of making their millions. Now they dream of finding their millions. So my hint of millions to be made on inside information of a massive city plumbing project was all that was needed to entice the naive believer in stories of fortune's sudden appearance.

Paul Palante needed only to hear hints of mysterious women interested in meeting and talking to him, but only to tell them being married he was unavailable.

Pep Boy Zapp responded to my hints of hot new information about Jim Scott's widow, spiced with inside dope on Pep Boy's great plans for his future employment..

My suggestion that high school football teams were interested in him for coaching positions got Applegate to Cavanaugh's.

As additional enticement. I promised all of them the food and drinks would be on me. The poor are susceptible to the magnetic pull of free food and drinks, as are the rich to tax deductions..

Anyway it took lies to get them to fall in with my plans. Today with ghosts talking to you through a flat screen box, lies are acceptable. Untruths to the gullible get politicians elected, sell weight reduction pills and exercise gimmicks, and are the main staple of fan magazines.

Planning to spare no expense, reserving a large table in Cavanaugh's private room, I put in orders for roast beef and pulled pork sandwiches accompanied by pitchers of ice beer to be readied.. Seated at the head of the rectangular table so conversation would be channeled towards me, with drink in hand I waited for their individual arrival.

Ray Brothers was the first to arrive and as behooves men of wealth, demanded I immediately get to the point. What did I know about that nigger Derek; would it be sufficient to pry his daughter from her degrading infatuation. Suddenly with an eye of hope he asked if I could get dear Ali in jail for life. He groaned, "My Lord, she's out with him right now. Can you imagine what he's doing to her?"

I could, after all there was my Brite fantasy. He was so agitated it took me time to stop his walking about the table and get him seated and order a stiff drink.

I said, "I called this meeting to discuss who poisoned table 12."

"You've evidence it was Derek!" Ray gleefully shouted.

Thank goodness Geroni came in with Palante, both looking confused at being in the same place with each other. Eyeing Ray suspiciously, Geroni asked him about the plumbing job, what were the specifications, and why was big Mac involved in city plumbing.

A confused Palante looked about the room, most likely searching for love smitten women he would let down in a sensitive manner.

Each being disconcerted, it was easy to get them into chairs and drinks in their hands. Ray started to tell them that a nigger had poisoned them, when a nigger coming in, peering about the room asking where are the *Ebony* people, where are the black photographers, where are the black models, why are only whites here, are they trying to get in on his *Ebony's* cover? Moving from bewilderment to anger, he yelled, "No way in hell are you whites going to get in on my heart wrenching black story of how I'm a victim of racism."

Ray stared at Rufus wondering what was the connection with Derek. Geroni vowed he'd eat shit before posing for a black magazine.

Hearing black models, Palante hoped they would be TV and movie blacks, milk chocolate, a few shades from tanned white, straight nose, soft long hair, and he'd be glad to pose with them, free, and autograph the pictures. He was also concerned about this being a bathing suit shoot for *Ebony*. If it was to be a swim suit layout he'd have to go home and get trunks. All staring at him, Palante's bazaar comments brought everyone to silence

In the silence Zapp arrived asking me why were they all here, and would Joy be coming.

I said, "Zapp, this is stag. Now look, everyone take a chair, have a drink on me and let me explain."

In the confusion of ordering various drinks, on me, no surprise, doubles were very popular, Applegate came in. His eyes traveled from corner to corner of the room, most likely searching for high school athletic directors. He even check behind himself in case there were some about to surprise him. Quick off the mark, Applegate commented, "You guys aren't recruiting football coaches. You're the guys that tried to get me fired. Hey Mac, where are the recruiters?"

Fortuitously, the waiters came in with trays of roast beef and pulled pork sandwiches accompanied by pitchers of ice beer, which I previously ordered. They also took drink orders, when I said the 'Open Sesame' words of, "It's all on me." Telling Applegate to take a seat, I told the group I'll be explaining everything after we have a bit to eat. Loud sipping, noisy munching allowed only dilatory table talk.

A discussion on fantasy football teams was initiated by Applegate. Investigating the dangers minimum wages poised, was Ray's contribution. Palante was concerned over contemporary women's turpitude where a man isn't safe to walk the streets, Geroni waxed heavily over the dangers of poor plumbing and women who don't trust and check on their plumber's reputation. Most were preoccupied wiping barbecue and beef gray off lips between bites. After all was satiated and they were on their third round of drinks, doubles giving way to singles, I introduced the night's real topic, my attempt to reveal which wife, girlfriend, mistress or daughter tried to poison table 12.

CHAPTER 45

Resolutions - Sort Of

With plates and platters removed, with glasses nearly empty, with conversation heavily diluted with pauses and non responses, with eyes staring blankly about the room, I felt it was time to start the evening's real business.

Starting on a high note I begged everyone to drink up and reorder. Energized, all in good cheer, everyone obeyed. (No surprise there.) Filled glasses in place, fingers and lips cleaned, men's room visits accomplished, I introduced the night's actual agenda after tapping on a water glass. "Gentlemen, if I may have your attention." And I got it whether it was the tap on the glass or my being paymaster. "Our purpose," (the royal 'our'), "for getting together is to answer an important question, a question critical to each of us. Someone tried to poison one of us, and succeeded in killing poor Jim Scott. Even those absent from table 12, being expected to sit with us, could have been the actual target for the poisoner, and could have easily ended up in the emergency room getting pumped out from both ends as some of us did."

While Applegate, Zapp and Geroni gave knowing smiles at their good fortune, as if their luck was the result of personal intelligent divination, the rest looked at me in curious anticipation. There was no unsettled doubt or question, everyone accepted my initial premise.

People always feel comfortable and secure when presented with the obvious they expect, what conforms with previous experience. (No wonder political oration is boring and TV Shows sterile.)

Having their attention I continued with more of the obvious. "Let's face it guys, the poisoned salsa on our table wasn't put there by some terrorist, nor was it a random act of a deranged person."

Interrupting, Ray mentioned that the CIA felt strongly it was a terrorist attack.

Hearing Ray forced Geroni to jump in with how the FBI felt it was an insane act by a bipolar nut.

With these interruptions, Palante felt obliged to mention the 6:30 news reporting it was a Tea Party attack to disparage the Democratic party. In case anyone doubted, he nailed the factitious news by saying Diane Saw had a three minute news segment interviewing democrats who sagaciously explained how it could be true.

Damn it, you could say the world is round and some ass will contest the statement by referencing the equatorial bulge.

To keep us on target and not allow fools to talk just to talk, I lied. (Should have gone into advertisement.) "Being a lieutenant in the New York City Police Department, I'm the detective in charge of this poisoning case and I have, on the most reliable information, the fact that the terrorists, the deranged, the tea party are emphatically discounted."

Geroni wouldn't let it go asking if I was sure, mentioning on *The Letterman Show,* a psychic interviewed by Dave said definitely --

"Absolutely, my information is from impeccable sources."

When Ray again began putting out terrorism, I had to stand up, authoritatively stating my sources, and they were numerous, occupied the highest places in the investigation.

"Who are they?" Palante asked.

"Can't reveal their names, they're confidential, but you can believe they're absolutely reliable sources, and if I named them they would be instantly recognized by all." (Shit, I should be a reporter for *The Times*.)

With their fantastic ideas of the insane and terrorist silenced, I restated the obvious, "The killer wanted to kill one of us, and didn't care if we all died."

Feeling left out, to hear his voice, Applegate suggested we could all have been targeted by a gang of assassins, sort of like the Wilkes Booth gang conspiring to kill Lincoln and his cabinet.

Before I could politely handle Applegate, Ray said it was nonsense, Geroni said it was stupid, Palante asked who was the Booth character and was he poisoned.

They were moments away from leaving me and starting a liquor fueled meandering among themselves. I had to quickly reign them in with some intelligence, repeating, "It's obvious one individual was the target. Someone wanted one of us dead."

The idea of someone wanting to kill them struck each as an interesting anomaly with the probability of being true, equal to being struck by lightning. We acquire knowledge, either true or false, with repetition. (Political ads win elections.) I again reiterated, "Look, someone put sufficient roach poison on table 12 to poison each one of us, and it did kill poor Jim Scott. As a group we have nothing in common, so the target couldn't reasonably be seen as wanting to kill all of us."

In any meeting where discussing isn't explicitly prohibited, there has to be an Applegate to state a ridiculous counter argument. "Mac, we were all fathers of players on my football team. We certainly had that in common."

Zapp came in with tangential nonsense. "You were a lousy coach. Every one of us thought so. In fact, Jim had a petition to --"

Defensively Applegate loudly answered, "Are you saying I killed Scott because of some ridiculous petition?"

Zapp answered, "Well you didn't sit at table 12, and you were supposed to sit there."

Sighing I thought, *shit, you need a whip to keep these characters on point. Some educated people actually believe democratically run committees can really be productive.* "Look, to want to poison our group someone had to have a strong motive against us all, and there isn't anyone, so can we--"

Silent 'til now Rufus had to drag out and lay on the table his raison d'être. "Racism is a strong hatred. Some racist could hate how good my son played and trying to kill me, didn't mind if you white guys were collateral damage."

Geroni told him he was being stupid, to which Rufus called him an ignorant racist.

Ray told Rufus his idea was idiotic.

Rufus answered, threatening a black boycott of his restaurants.

I was pleasantly surprised when Paul Palante innocently interjected sex into the table's ramblings. "Hey guys, it could have been a woman who had the hots for one of us." (No question who was the one.) " After all, poison is a woman's weapon."

I almost ran over to give him a big wet kiss. "You're right Paul, one of us was the target and the poisoner was one of the women in our lives. If we value our lives, we have to find out which woman is guilty. After all, if Scott wasn't her target, she could try again."

Ray put forth Scott as the target. After all, he's the one dead and so we're all safe.

Suspecting a renewal of prior suspicions, Applegate defensively maintained his innocence, saying he recently had offers from high schools to coach football. His glancing behind at the door indicated he still harbored a forlorn hope.

Out of fatherly love, from hatred of miscegenation, Ray put forth Derek as a candidate. "My misguided daughter is dating a worthless nig -, er," a quick look at Rufus, "black, and I'm standing in the way of his cohabitating with my young daughter."

Feeling everyone having strong instinctive aversion to interracial dating, even Rufus mumbled about rich white bitches seducing strong black men sympathizing with Ray. Political correctness inculcated, everyone allowed Ray's daughter and black Derek to slide off the table with no one interested in picking up on them.

Before the couple disappeared, Palante hearing girls told anyone who is interested (no one was) he wasn't interested in black women, said it with all the profound sadness of one denying Harlem's female population the opportunity of his company to their everlasting despair.

This meeting was akin to racing the Iditarod in Alaska with a team of rabid dogs. I told them, "Look, let's stay focused. Sad to say it was one of our wives, girlfriends, or relatives who is the poisoner. To start, let's address Rufus' Dagmar."

"Hey, that's my slave name. I'm now Abdullah, and why are we starting with me and Dagmar? It's because of racism. You see it everywhere. Well let me tell you, Dagmar loves me and I love her."

"Yeah," Ray commented. "With all that love between you two why aren't you married?"

Enjoying adding to the chaos, Geroni had to answered with a rhetorical question, "Wouldn't all the free welfare disappear with the appearance of a marriage license?"

Standing up, an outraged Abdullah angrily defended, "Welfare! There's no welfare. It's temporary assistance for people in need."

Someone laughed.

Flaying his arms about Abdullah continued, "Besides we deserve every dollar we get, we've earned it."

Geroni angrily told him, "Rufus or Abdullah, or whatever, cut the shit, every damn dime you get comes out of my pocket and if it was up to me you wouldn't get a dime."

Banging the table, Abdullah yelled, "Now it's out in the open. You're all racists and want little black children to starve." His accusatory outburst didn't bring the expected frightened 'oh no, not me, I respect and love all blacks,' but did bring the waiter. Despite my attempts to wave him off he walked about taking orders, with doubles returning with a vengeance.

Abdullah's righteous anger didn't stop him from ordering a double shot of Jack Daniels. The table had achieved a consensus, all were thirsty. Even Palante left diet beer for a double, but only after checking with me, "It's still on you."

Everyone held their breath looking expectantly at me when I nodded, allowing all to breathe. Damn it, thinking of the bill, I briefly thought of climbing out the bathroom window. Reading my mind, mumbling bathroom needs, Zapp went out with the waiter and returned with a new double. He quickly downed it so when the reordered drinks arrived with his new double he wouldn't look like he had a drinking problem.

With ordering finished, a calmer Abdullah sat down to announce Dagmar and he were getting married and *Entertainment Tonight* was videoing the event for some big money. Then to share their bliss with the rest of the world it will go on sale for everyone to watch just like Hollywood weddings. Not only that, *Brides* Magazine was devoting an entire issue on Dagmar's bridal shower, her dress, and all that other shit along with a follow-up layout of their Jamaican honeymoon in a travel magazine.

Applegate voiced everyone's conclusion, "Crap man, you're making some serious money."

'Yeah man, this poisoning shit has been the greatest thing for me and Dagmar."

Paul Palante suggested the poisoner could be Dagmar in order to get all this money.

Before I could politely refute the idea, Geroni told him and the table that Paul was an idiot, as no one could predict all the money some people were getting.

Realizing anyone connected with Hollywood entertainment, such as agents, could have easily predicted the deluge of money I said, "I think it's safe to eliminate a money motive in Abdullah's situation. His death could not forseeably translate into money for Dagmar."

Still hoping for a black connection Ray doubted we could eliminate Dagmar.

Patiently I explained, "Look, with women it's all about money and marriage. The hope of getting the two, the fear of losing the two. In Abdullah's case, since they weren't married, there could be no inheritance money, and as for love, I maintained Dagmar would be angry to receive a marriage proposal due to the welfare money she'd lose being the single mother of many."

"It's assistance," corrected Abdullah, "and we're getting married."

I continued, "Dagmar had neither money nor a marriage motive to poison Abdullah."

"Amen to that," Abdullah answered, and everyone paused as the waiter arrived with the drinks.

As with all group meetings it was hard to move these asses from current hackneyed topics to consider something different, so it was no surprise to hear Palante ignoring a topic's death asking about Dagmar fearing losing Abdullah's love, tried to kill him.

Smiling broadly, showing a single tooth where at least eight should have been, with a wave of his hand Abdullah dismissed Paul's point, as we all quickly did. Thinking, if married, Dagmar may kill to get rid of Rufus but who would kill to get him.

Expressing his thanks for the table's exoneration Abdullah said, "Glad to see you racists failed to convict an innocent black mother."

Deep in all this black talk excited Ray to question whether Derek could have been the poisoner, mentioning Derek had both motive in the money he could expect to get out of Amber with her father dead, as well as the love of an innocent young girl.

Patiently I explained Derek wasn't at the banquet. Given his color, no way could he have blended in with all the white there.

Rufus explained, "Yes, that's right, the beloved Louis Farrakhan is right as he always is. It's an example of racism with us blacks always excluded and -"

Ray told Rufus to get over himself. It's not about him, no one gives a shit about him and his being black.

"Yeah, well tell me, I know on Martin Luther King's birthday, you didn't close your restaurants to show respect for one of the greatest black Americans?"

Using Zapp's going to the bathroom ploy, Geroni somehow got another double, probably ordered on the way in to the men's room and picked up on his way out. Stepping out of his social self to reveal the inner man, he angrily told Rufus, "Look, I don't give a shit for your Martin Luther King. He's one hell of an overrated bullshitter who did nothing to help me."

Rufus' hand shook as he cried out, "I can't believe I'm here with all these racists. What next, disrespect for Nelson Mandela, a saint who saved South Africa."

Palante, in honest confusion asked the table who's this Nelson guy, and if he's an American, what the hell was he doing in South Africa.

Rufus sputtered, "You ignorant bastard."

Getting into the spirit Applegate had to sarcastically add, "What next, a national Mandela holiday?"

"If you want my opinion people just don't give a damn about these hyped up characters, it's all media generated buzz," came from Ray.

A furious Rufus yelled, "Who the hell gives a shit for your white racist opinion?" and with back straight, indignant pride in every step taken to the door, he exited, but not before turning and giving us a parting finger saying something about Farrakhan's Muslims, hearing about Martin and Mandela's disrespect were going to be angry.

To his back Geroni yelled, "You notice, he's leaving after he's had his fill of food and booze, just like all freeloaders."

Thinking true, but given Geroni wasn't going to reach deep into his pocket any time soon I felt the comment was hypocritical. Turning my attention to Geroni I asked how Zoe, his mistress was doing.

"That bitch? She's history. Was a lousy lay, and such a phony trying to pass herself off as a cosmetology scientist when all she did all day was put face powder on old ugly broads aimlessly wandering about the mall looking for something that isn't there."

Ray, being also sufficiently lubricated to shed some of his social skin unkindly said, "She probably dumped you."

Before Ray's dart could be buried into Geroni's flesh, I interrupted saying Zoe's and Tony's breakup was after the poisoning. Believing in Tony's bullshit about his getting a divorce, she had no motive to poison him. In fact, if Babs, his wife was poisoned, we'd know who to suspect.

"Can you imagine, that bitch Zoe didn't trust me and checked with Kohler Plumbing headquarters about me"

Palante asked if Tony's wife was aware of his fooling around. She could be mad enough to kill him.

Emphatically Tony replied, "My Babs loves me," as if like the speed of light, her love for him was an uncontested constant.

Reasonably I dismissed Babs as a potential mass killer, repeating my thesis the murder was either love inspired or money inspired. "Tony, is there any possibility Babs has another man in her life?"

"Look, she understands me, loves me. Yeah, I fool around a little. Who doesn't? But she knows I love her and wouldn't divorce her."

With pride Palante had to tell us he never fooled around, though it wasn't for the lack of opportunity. Hope he liked hearing himself saying that to maintain his self delusion; the table was totally uninteresting and in complete disbelief.

Again I asked Tony if his wife Babs had any admirers.

"She's a slob, likes her wine, a year from forty and with a kid. There's no chance for her to attract anyone."

Ray said, "So you're her only future and you cheat on her. That's not right and it could be a motive for her."

Tony argued, "We've got a child. She hasn't any education or career. She's got nowhere to go. I'm a professional man. Where is she going to get another professional man."

I asked if there was any money in his death.

"Hey, I'm self employed and things are temporarily tight. Hell, times are tough. The plumbing business is hurting, and I don't want anyone disrespecting my wife. She's a great wife and mother."

Ray asked about insurance on his life.

"Shit, I'm barely making it, never mind paying insurance premiums. Look, I'm only a dollar a day and an ounce of self respect away from following that Rufus character and live on welfare."

I concluded, "So with no prospect of a new love, no insurance, no money. I can't see your Babs making any move to get rid of you. She's stuck in her situation and hanging on for dear life."

"Hell, screw you guys. I don't have to sit here (he was standing) and take this shit. My Babs is a hell of a great wife and she loves me and I love her and I'm going home to tell her that, and screw you all."

At the door, turning, he told us if anyone from the city planning board shows up, he's in the book. Leaving, I noticed, to show self respect, he angrily didn't toss any green on the table. When self respect costs money, self respect is always shallow.

Looking about noticing two had left, registering there remained besides himself Ray, Applegate, Zapp and myself, Palante felt the need to leave. "Look fellows. It's been a great night. Thanks Mac for the drinks and food but it's getting late and my wife Dorothy will be worried about me."

Getting up, draining his glass, he apologetically repeated he had to leave as if en mass we'd plan to physically force him to remain.

I asked, "Paul, do you think Dorothy would be interested in killing you?"

Pausing, thinking it over, he decided he liked the idea, "Well, she does have cause with all the chicks coming on to me. It's only natural to be jealous, but let me tell you, I've been true to her. She has no cause to be jealous, at least on my part." He stood there, looking at us, waiting for our response. Like one who swears he's seen aliens, there can't be a response only stares, hoping the person will suddenly shout 'fooled yah.'

Looking at a school janitor, I dismissed money as a possible motive and anyone so tolerant, no, so disinterested in her husband's flights of sexual fantasy, she couldn't generate the energy to kill. If anything, just walking away would be the more likely course Dorothy would employ. Still I couldn't see her leaving her children without a father because of her piqué at their father's foibles. As far as a lover, I thought she wasn't the type of woman to engage in such betrayal. If I was wrong about her personality, if she had betrayed Paul, she wouldn't keep it from Paul but would use it as a chastising whip in responding angrily to his flights of sexual fantasy, responding with something real to counter his delusions. However, if she did leave him it would be quiet, no drama, just a letting go. Of course Paul would be devastated without her and that may be a chief reason for her staying, sort of motherly pity.

With Paul standing, confused by our silence, I released him. "Look Paul, let's keep in touch and give my best to Dorothy."

He left in half steps unsure if he should leave. Was there something he should say or do, was it really alright for him to leave. I didn't think paying for his dinner and drinks ever entered his mind.

The exodus had begun. Applegate got up saying he had to attend to numerous coaching applications he received.

I asked him, "So you and Robin decided it would be best if you sat at the head table with your son on the way to the banquet."

"Huh? Yeah, well actually it was Robin's idea. Thought her son would like to sit next to me. Besides, left to their devices the team could get unruly. Remember the practice when they all went into the clubhouse bathroom and locking the door wouldn't come out. Spread toilet paper all over the room and everyone left it to me to clean it up."

Obviously there was no money, no grand passion here and with Robin not only knowing but suggesting he move from table 12, he wasn't the intended victim. Giving him permission to leave I told him, "Good luck on all your football applications and it made good sense for Robin to want you to sit with her son and the team. Hell, I'm surprised we were able to keep the mothers from sitting next to their sons."

At the door, as a farewell he said, "Well, er, tell Scott's widow I hold no grudge against Jim for his petition. You always have some parent upset over the coaching of their kid."

In the role of Joy's representative, Zapp told Tom Applegate that Joy wasn't mad at him..

After giving the room a quick searching look, probably still hoping for those elusive football scouts, he left.

Couldn't help reflecting sadly on the fact none so far had even offered to pay their share, at least contribute to the tip, or pay for his drinks. Yet given the cards I was dealt, could I have expected anything else.

Now a trinity, Zapp, Ray and myself, I turned to them saying, "One of you was the target."

Zapp argued he had no connection with table 12 and the women involved.

Ray asked more hopefully than realistically if I thought it could possibly have been Derek.

Answering Ray I said, "Forget Derek. It's your trio, Eleanor your wife, Amber your daughter, and Courtney your mistress."

"Not Derek?"

"No, he wasn't there, and your money wouldn't go to Amber but to Eleanor. Now, as to Courtney, she found out before the banquet you cancelled your insurance so she didn't have the money motive, and keeping you interested in her was the only way she could keep her mall fashion store. Her main interest was to keep you happy, get you divorced and exchange vows with her. Even though she was at the banquet, we can eliminate her."

"Anyway, I'm through with her," was Ray's comment. She doesn't know it but I met DesIree, a really fantastic looking woman who really loves me, unlike Courtney, whose only interest is in my money." He paused and reflected on what he just said. "Still, DesIree knows I've got three McDonald's franchises and I know women are interested in money." He announced the last as if revealing to Zapp and me a deep hidden truth. Ruefully he concluded,." Sometimes I think paying for prostitutes would be cheaper and more honest, so even though she was at -"

Zapp interrupted suggesting, "There's your wife Eleanor. Still married to her she'd get all your money."

I added, "Also Ray, though separated, you haven't started divorce proceedings which suggests indecision on your part. How far have you gotten? Seen a lawyer yet?"

Standing, preparatory to leaving, he told me they hadn't reached the lawyer stage, were just at the 'we need time apart to find ourselves' stage. With regret he confessed to moving out of his home and renting a house with Courtney. There had been no talk of divorce. Although it was after the fact knowing Courtney's personality, he now regretted leaving Eleanor. Maybe Amber wouldn't be involved with that black loser if he had stayed with Eleanor. Teen agers need a father. Up to puberty children need a mother's love. After that what's needed is a father's strength and discipline.

Zapp concurred, maintaining single mothers are losers, trying to act like they're heroic winners.

I summed up Ray's personal revelations, "As far as Eleanor is concerned, you're going through a faze, a sort of fever which will hopefully pass."

"You know, this DesIree is just like Courtney. The hell with them. Yeah, and you know, I'm going to Eleanor tonight and beg her forgiveness. Shit, I've been led by my crotch, not by my mind. I lost all sense of balance. My daughter needs my guidance, my son needs my love, my business needs my attention. Shit, what's more important to a man then his business and family.

"Mac, I know I've had one drink too many, but sometimes you need that one too many to see what's real and now I see clearly. Just want to say thanks for this get together. It really helped clarify things for me."

Hell, he's drunk, drunk on my dime, and though too proud to ask, I had the hope he'd volunteer to split the night's cost. Unfortunately so immersed in good intentions, the renewal of his life and in his fervor of confessional cleansing, he's going to stiff me. Couldn't ask him to pay something, yet knowing he'd gladly pony up, my silence was costing me dearly.

He left, a new man, a resolute new man going out to do what's right. He left me with the bill, and eyeing Zapp, my Pep Boy tire changer, knew I had no hope of help.

Being the last left, possibly the thought of having to pay something or at least offering to pay propelled Zapp to mumble something about having a busy day tomorrow, as if without his professional attention the wheels of industry would fall off.

Shit, and again shit, I had no intention of releasing him, knowing how he imbibed on my tab each time he went to the bathroom for another drink to be quickly swallowed before returning, and he snuck out several times. Currently he was more than double the legal limit, probably three times, yet I still ordered another round. Tire changers at Pep Boys don't readily refuse a free drink so he stayed put.

With a fresh drink keeping him, Zapp waited on me. I gave him nothing, forcing him to start. "Er, Mac, great party, you, er-"

He had trouble saying 'you paid for' and to force him to continue gave him silence.

"Well look, I really got to go, so -"

"So," I told him, "we both know Joy is the poisoner."

"Hey Mac, where are you getting that? Joy loved Jim and wouldn't-"

Hoping the booze was my strong ally I told him, with all the emphasis and sincerity politicians generate promising you something that will cost nothing, "There's no doubt Joy killed her husband. We can see all the other women didn't have the motive or personality to kill. Joy does."

Zapp walked a step or two away from me, asking for some proof,

I told him, "First, after all is said and done, who was actually killed?"

"Er, Jim, my best friend."

"Zapp, cut the bullshit. It was obvious from my first interview, you two were having an affair. You were screwing your best friend's wife."

Liquor came to my aid. After a brief expected outrage over how anyone would think he'd do such a thing, the booze spoke. and he ended with, "And what if we did sleep together. What about it?"

Before he could take back the admission I pressed, "Look, man to man, I know she came on to you. You're not the type of guy to come on to a friend's wife. She had to make the first move."

"Damn right. Said Jim abused her, raped her, beat her with his fists."

I gave out a loud, "Really!" Only a tire changer watching too much TV could believe Joy's bullshit and I didn't work at Pep Boys.

"Yeah, he hit her where bruises wouldn't show."

My liquor consumption let slip a sarcastic, "So you never saw a bruise."

Being deep in justification of betraying a friend, he took me literally "Yeah, Joy was too embarrassed to show all the welts."

"And you didn't have it out with Jim about his abuse 'cause Joy begged you not to make an issue of her being abused."

"You got it. She said if I mentioned it to Jim or to anyone, Jim would just beat her more."

"And when you suggested she leave him she said what?"

"Too afraid. She was sure he'd track her down and kill her."

"Ah yes, the word kill and the idea of murder suddenly was in bed between you."

"Huh, yeah, well it all seemed reasonable. She had no other options but to get rid of Jim permanently. And after all, there were the children to consider. She told me he abused them."

"Sexually, of course, in additional to physically and mentally," I said.

"Yeah, believed it at the time but now I don't know. You know she tossed a lot of bullshit at me."

"Yeah, I believe putting your nose in it she rubbed it all around the BS. I suppose after she was free of Jim, you two would get married and live happily ever after."

A disappointed Zapp revealed, "She said we'd have to wait a decent time, she's big on social proprieties."

"Especially if Jim was murdered."

"Yeah, there was that."

"And there was Jim's Pep Boy's life insurance, double indemnity in case of accidental death."

Eagerly Zapp informed me Joy had an additional insurance policy which would pay off the mortgage in case of Jim's death.

I asked if he would have moved into Jim's home.

"Hell no. What do you think I am. I couldn't move into Jim's home, sleep in his bed. Never. Joy was planning to sell the house and buy a new one in Florida, one with a pool, tile floors, stainless steel kitchen appliances, walk in closet, and -"

"A dream house for the two of you."

"And of course, Jim's kids ... and there are Pep Boy's stores throughout the country. I could transfer down there and not lose seniority."

Deciding it was time to move the conversation up a notch I asked, "So Zapp, did you poison the salsa?"

Wrapped up in giving excuses and causes for the love affair, he had lost track of their effects. Shocked tinged with fear he shouted, "No never. I'm not the type of guy who'd kill his best friend."

I knew if he had murdered Jim, he never would have admitted his affair with Joy. In fact, if the future fantasy life he had in his mind was still viable, he'd never loosen up. He was deep into pressing a vat of sour grapes. It was just necessary to press him, push down on the Joy button to have him continue blathering like a teenage girl over an false girlfriend.

I pressed down, "If it wasn't you, it must be Joy. She killed Jim. We know it's true, and she'll be arrested within the month. We're waiting 'til after the holidays for public relations reasons. The question is, how much liability exposure you had."

Booze, guilt, inherent cowardness joined me in wringing him like a wet paper napkin, reducing him to a scared fearful informer mumbling how great a guy Jim was, how he loved him like a brother, despite abusing his wife.

It was time to shred that paper shield he was hiding behind by mentioning Joy referred to her husband as a 'should' man, a man who did what he 'should' do, what was expected of him, and today such men are killed. How could she describe him in such a way and maintain he abused her.

"Look Mac, if Joy had such a guy, a guy who did all the right things, why in hell would she kill him."

He was still in his defensive mode, so I tried a new approach. "Tell me, who do thieves hang around with?"

"Er, other thieves."

"Who are the best friends of bums, drunks, and druggies?"

"I guess other drunks."

"Who are liberals friendly with but other liberals. If you wish to know how your child is doing academically, check the grades of his closest friends."

A confused Zapp asked, "What's your point?"

"Jim, at least in Joy's eyes, was a good man, or as she put it, a 'should' man and she couldn't hide her dislike even loathing him because he was a moral man. By hating his morality she convicted herself of her own immorality. The person an atheist can't stand is the person of faith. The degenerate person hates the good and seeks out more congenial companions."

Offering as a counter proof, Zapp said he was her friend.

Thinking case proven I gave him, "There's always the exception."

We took time out to sip and think. Suddenly Zapp came out with, "I had nothing to do with poisoning Jim."

I reached the area where finesse had to be employed. "Look Zapp, if you had nothing to do with the poisoning, it's time to distance yourself from Joy. She's going down for murder. You don't want to be the one holding her hand all the way down."

"Certainly not. Let me be honest with you. (Zapp, have you been dishonest 'til now? Okay let's proceed with some booze generated honesty). It's true we were intimate and I'll confess I'm not proud of myself with sleeping with her. But I really believed Jim was abusing her and she really needed someone to care for her."

I gave a, "Yeah," to his mushy TV crap to keep the flow going.

Zapp continued, "You're right. It was all so much blow. Now I realize she's a liar. (As if screwing with Zapp behind Jim's back wasn't a clue to her dishonesty.) She's changed since Jim's death. With all the attention, with all the money she's going to get, with all the contracts worth millions she's signing to tell about her happy past with Jim, her despairing present without Jim, her hope for future happiness, you know, MAD and O'Malley are talking millions and she's changed.

"And you wouldn't believe the donations she's getting from the suckers."

From what I've recently seen I could honestly tell him I believe the money was flowing.

"Anyway, with all that money coming in, she's gotten cold towards me."

Sarcastically I said, "No!" Damn the booze. Still, thanks to the booze he couldn't recognize nor interpret the getting of the finger, unless it was stuck up his nose, so I still had him talking friend to friend.

"It's true. Won't return my calls, answer my texts, respond to my emails. In fact she's threatening to get a restraining order against me if I try to get in touch with her. Can you imagine money changing someone so much."

"No!" he again missed my sarcasm.

"Yeah, she's turned into one mean bitch."

"That suddenly!" sarcasm again missed.

Wistfully he related how great a life he and she could have had with all the money. If she wanted him to quit Pep Boys he would, and they could enjoy life living together in Florida.

I had to observe, "If you two married, there could be a good chance you'd end up, ass up in the pool with a lily sticking up out of your crack."

"I still can't believe Joy really went through murdering Jim."

"Look at it soberly," whoa, Freudian slip, "She had you as a future replacement for Jim. She had insurance making Jim a hell of a lot more dead than alive."

"Still, I don't–"

"She disliked Jim so much she had affairs"

"Affairs, plural?"

"Did you think you were so special? Anyway, here's the clincher, at the hospital she said she didn't know about Jim's acute ulcer, and yet you knew. She had to know. It's not something you keep silent about, like herpes. It's a prestigious ailment wealthy men get for eating too much rich food. Knowing Jim's vulnerability she had to know roach poison would shoot through his ulcer as if on a freeway. That lie is her main mistake which will eventually convict her. Now (here I lie) I have several people saying you put the salsa out on the table, and remember your reason for not sitting at table 12, that crap about being Jim's superior in tire changing for Pep Boys, won't stand up to a jury. Zapp, look at it. You're having an affair with the wife, motive, people see you with the salsa in your hands and you know about Jim's ulcer vulnerability, and didn't sit at table 12 but inexplicably moved to another table."

"Look, I didn't do anything."

He was about to do anything I wanted. "If Joy says you talked of killing Jim, if Joy says you confessed to her how you murdered Jim out of passion for her, well, you can see how vulnerable you are."

"Shit Mac, you've got to believe me. (I really didn't.) Yeah, I was the one who put the salsa out on table 12 but on my mother's life I didn't know it contained poison. Joy gave it to me telling me to put it on table 12 and warned me not to sit there. No way did I know what she was doing."

"If she denies giving you the salsa what have you got to refute her?"

Frantically Zapp asked, "Let me think," then as an indication of his desperation asking for another round, he offered to pay.

Knowing his 'buy' was figurative, I went out to the bar and got our drinks, mostly to give him time to bury Joy.

With drinks in hand, Zapp proceeded to dig Joy's grave. "Okay, here is how it went down. Joy bought the poison at Home Depot and

I'm sure they have her on camera and the stupid broad paid by credit card, so there's a record. In addition, for days preceding the banquet, she kept talking about killing Jim, how sweet our lives would be when he is dead. Mac, I thought she was just talking, sort of pillow talk."

He stopped to consider whether he was still griping Joy's hand or not on her way down. Needing a goose I told him it wasn't enough.

He frantically kept digging the grave. "I could swear she talked about how with Jim's ulcer, the doctored salsa would be dangerous for him."

I gave him another goose, "And-"

"She said if the salsa had even a little poison it would kill Jim."

"And-"

"Look, if I get immunity I could swear she said she poison him. In giving me the bowl of salsa she told me it would be Jim's last meal. What do you think about immunity?"

"Why not. Look, I'll arrange for you to give a formal statement to an officer in charge of granting immunities. If this officer gives you immunity you can never be charged."

I left Zapp telling my back he had nothing to hide. Joy will regret dissing him and looked forward to telling the truth. (Like people actually do.)

CHAPTER 46

Down One, Up One

Next day I woke depressed, so depressed it took the combination of: sheer willpower, Pam's exultations, a phone call from Ronni Deutsch, a visit from Woody, and most effective, a call from nature to get my covers tossed and roll me out of bed, and the 'me' who came out of bed was neither energetic nor pleasant.

After answering nature's pressing call I yelled down to Pam to tell Ronni I'd call her back. Midpoint between bed and bath Woody intersected me, and yes, he was in my bedroom trying to act solicitous while simultaneously showing insulting disrespect and superiority: disrespect by being in my bedroom uninvited, dressing his gross inopportune with the flimsy excuse good friends of long standing need not stand on ceremony: superiority in one being impeccably dressed exuding good cheer to one unshaven standing in wrinkled pjs just minutes after answering nature's call, and possessing a stomach complaining with sour notes and emitting ominously unpleasant embarrassing noises.

Woody ignored my 'I've got to dress,' observing, "Mac, you don't look good," as if I had no idea my outside 'me' didn't have a suspicion of my inside's terrible condition.

Knowing Woody's ego, I continued getting dressed, for if I returned to bed he'd still stay and talk because he was here to get something, and any of Woody's needs, no matter how trivial, take precedence over anything else.

Returning to the bathroom to dress, I also took the opportunity to respond to a sudden unexpected second call from nature. Dam it, nature getting too familiar was refusing to keep a proper distance.

Dressed, emerging from the bathroom, I did feel better; better, not good, certainly not great. Let's say my mood, starting in the third basement at nature's first call, was now standing in the lobby staring at stairs, praying for an elevator.

Joining Woody and Pam in the kitchen for coffee I briefly thought of the efficaciousness of a bracer in the coffee, sort of the tail of last night's dog who bit me, but with my stomach telling my mind it was an insane idea and out of anger threatening to react by tossing everything, it was coffee, black. Drinking it I glared at Woody happily munching a prune danish. With each bite I winced, with each wince his prune enjoyment doubled. Doubled, shit, last night's doubles bill came close to reaching four digits. The thought of money spent reinforced my sour mood and digestion, in tandem driving me to hell.

Wiping clean lips of prunes' ghost, Woody left the danish to explain why he was here in my life. "Mac, the reason I'm - Pam, this is one hell of a prune danish. Did you make it?"

With a blush admitting she did, fulsome praise emitted from Woody, praise frequently uttered to her, almost as frequent as his suggestions I should have one.

In any group of three, either one lectures the two or the two conversing together exclude the third, who must play the role of an observer. I interrupted Pam and Woody's prune talk, "Look Woody, why the hell are you here?"

Since he had reasons for being here, I knew if I retreated to any room, even to the bathroom, he'd follow me. Closed door wouldn't serve to bar him. He had his needs and mine were inconsequential.

"Yeah, well Mac, just wanted to see how you and your wonderful wife are doing."

"Fine, is that all?" I answered knowing it wasn't even close to being all.

"I feel we're still a team despite Ronni being temporarily assigned to work under me in your place."

Unable to decide if he was implying I was now working under him, I said nothing. Anything said would delay his leaving.

"Mac, I'd like to exchange information with you on this Roach Case, (anyone talking exchange is planning to go deep into your pocket), and I feel it only right to keep you abreast of the department's progress."

"Which is what Woody?"

"I feel we need to talk," (anyone needing to talk has something they definitely want to say to you).

Too tired to respond, too depressed to be annoyed, saying nothing forced Woody to continue, "Well Mac, you know of our negative progress, the progress of elimination. Well the department has been making fantastic negative progress, progress I really can't reveal in specifics but trust me, it's been tremendous."

Negative progress - it's like the exercise you decide not to do, money you decide not to save, work you decide not to do.

I answered Woody's revelation, "Don't mind not knowing what's definitely been excluding," I spitefully said with double negatives abounding.

"Glad you understand. Some people hate to be out of the loop. Now if you have any ideas about the case I'll be glad to listen to them."

Shit, the guy's here begging for my ideas and he's close to getting me to beg him to let me help him. The guy's good, should be running for public office. Sipping my second cup of coffee where hopefully unnoticed, slipping a little of the dog's tail to give the coffee some bite, I remained silent. Silence is a conversational strength when the other conversant wants something from you, a mighty weapon, a nothing that's something.

Forced to continue, Woody expounded on negativity. "The multi agency task force for the time being has eliminated the possibility of a terrorist being responsible for the poisoning."

Woody was a common type of self assured idiot; less assured idiots listening to him would swear he's brilliant. Anyone possessing minimal intelligence would know he's selling BS, and my urge to yell bullshit was irresistible. "Woody, that's all bullshit."

With my disbelief filtered through his firm belief of being always right I ipso facto became an unsound mind and was certainly pitifully dense. Employing the TV's talking head's ploy of twisting your denial of their propositions against you by reversing your denial into a positive position, such as denying long term unemployment benefits benefit people, is tossed back at you as you're not wishing to help the desperate poor who lost their jobs."

In this case Woody argued, "Well numerous agencies, independently are still pursuing the terrorist angle, and many in the media feel there definitely may be a racist component. Remember, one of those poisoned was an African American."

I firmly stated all agencies are wrong. It wasn't a deranged mad man and certainly wasn't a racist attack on the Rufus character.

"Mac, can you really believe a person capable of trying to poison numerous men is fully rational, and in trying to kill a black man is not racist."

Refusing to argue with a fool whose mind, train-like travels on rails laid down by other fools I waited for him to continue.

"Mac, here's an idea that's getting some serious traction with important political commentators, pundits and social analysts. What're your thoughts about the Tea Party? You know, fanatical far righters."

What absurdity, Here supposedly an educated man, well dressed, articulate possessing some influence, blabbering nonsense as if when opened to examination it would reveal hidden kernels of sense. Not by the consideration of facts nor by logical analysis of facts, today's truth is found by the weight of media's time spent expounding nonsense, by heavy self bestowed reputations uttering the nonsense and always with sly deceptive use of semantics to hide their stupidity when revealed.

Enough. I couldn't talk to the man. We occupy not just different worlds, we live in opposite universes.

Having Joy as the murderess and Zapp her disgruntled former lover ready to give her up, I decided not to give Woody the treasure I unearthed. Would he appreciate it, only 'til he put his coat on. Would he share credit with me, only 'til he stepped out the front door. Gratitude from a recipient to a giver is measured by the few quick passing moments on the way to hate. Remembrances of past beneficences resurfaces only when the next dire need arises. If nine cured lepers didn't give thanks, can you expect anything more.

Leaving the Tea Party he coaxed me again to share any insights I had gleamed, stressing we were a team.

I was in limbo as to what to do with my discovered treasure: Zapp wanting to spill his guts in revenge for being dissed by Joy. To whomever I revealed my discovery, I realized I would soon be a forgotten man. Possessing no copyrights I would eventually become an invisible footnote to the case's solution as higher ups possessing visible voices could easily claim my discovery. After all, was it Balboa or some unknown sailor who first saw the Pacific.

Standing up Woody asking if I was sure I had no ideas about the Roach Case no matter how insignificant, showed the poverty of his mind. Continually pressing me, becoming more demanding, less the petitioner, he suspected my protestations of poverty were false out of my jealousy of him. I was refusing to assist him, to give him what he wanted, what he deserved. Still if someone says they're stone broke you have to either leave it like that or by pressing with continued demands, infer they're lying and are very nasty.

Woody left empty, but left behind false smiles, false friendship wrapped in happy words. Between the smiles, friendship and happy words he again inserted a request that if any ideas came my way I must share them with him. As he closed the door I sadly reflected on how sterile minds unencumbered by ideas not universally shared and approved, remained barricaded against reality.

Unable to rouse myself I sat for a good fifteen minutes staring at the closed front door. In those melancholic fifteen minutes contemplating my life I felt aimless lassitude. Damn it, it all seems so useless. Nutrition goes in, shit come out, and all for what purpose. Fully aware of the symbolism an unbidden picture of a caged running hamster came to mind from some unconscious cavern. Tried to toss the hamster back to where he came from, but once in awareness it was impossible to will that rodent back into the darkness. The hamster drove me to the kitchen and to Pam, even tried a quick bite of prune danish, but my stomach was far too alert and it quickly shouted 'stop' with impolite noises. The stomach's noise being sufficiently loud kept Pam from suggesting a brunch of eggs and bacon. Sitting down with a new cup of coffee, still black, with a little tail added, Pam asked what was troubling me, as if it was on a monitor ready to be printed out for us to read and analyzed.

Since I didn't have a culprit to point to or perhaps too many to single out one, I shrugged her off with "nothing's bothering me." which convinced neither of us. Either my heart wasn't in my denial or the hamster desired Pam to continue pressing me, to open the cage 'cause I wanted to open up to her.

She continued, "Mac, ever since the poisoning you haven't been the same."

While repeating, "Pam, nothing's bothering me," I added as a half hearted excuse, "maybe it's the after effects of the poisoning, but I'm all right."

Shit, feeling I dipped a toe into something illogical, still I did believe the poisoning had nothing to do with my malaise, at least I didn't think so but I'd be the last to know.

With half a cup drunk, with clownishness attempts at casualness I walked to the living room for more of the tail as if the goal of my steps was a mystery to Pam and the hamster. The tail began to stir some energetic optimism in me. People talking about alcohol being a depressant never enjoyed a pick-me-up, never experienced one too many. Throwing a lot of mental dead weight overboard it allows the ship to ride high on the waves.

With me back, sitting down at the kitchen table Pam almost succeeded in hiding her unsaid opprobrium. Feeling such condemnation was both undeserved and deserved I challenged her, "If you have something to say, say it."

Now, possessing a couple of tails, I was armed for argumentation.

She said, "We should get away for a while."

Like to think I'm quick witted, mentally agile, but her observation had me and my tails totally confused. Expecting an attack on the tails I asked what she meant, as if she was speaking in tongues.

"You've got a lot of sick leave left. We could go away someplace nice for a week to rest and recuperate."

One tail wanted to pounce on recuperate, to argue what the hell was she implying, rehab! Was she saying, in drinking too much I've got a problem. The second tail got all excited by the idea to go away, to get away from the here and now, leaving today's me to rediscover a younger rejuvenated me. The later tail wagged the harder. "Pam, it's a great idea." Then like Woody I took the suggestion as mine asking Pam, well actually out loud asking myself where we should go. Pam quietly suggested Disney World in Florida. I repeated, "Disney Land!. Mickey will love it. We'll go to Disney World." Both tails were now excitedly wagging over the prospect. Pam enthusiastically fell in with my idea, or was she leading me on by saying, "The Disney people combine a resort stay with a cruise to the Bahamas. We could spend a week at Disney and cruise on the Disney ship for five days."

Cruise ship! Twelve days! Mentally I came up short trying to get my mind around the two. Could we afford it especially after the Tides and Cavanaugh's fiasco. Could I get away for twelve days. Pam wanting both justified them as something I needed for health reasons, and I deserved and earned from years of work. With Mickey growing up it may be the last time to generate memories of our family having fun together.

Getting up I went to the living room and came back with a cup carrying the tail along with the dog who I scolded with a dollop of hot coffee. Not only was the dog energizing me but the hound was an optimistic devil. I told Pam, "Damn it, let's do it."

With the ease of a car salesman Pam slipped brochures, cost approximations and time lines next to my cup of dog's breath. Shit, where did all this come from. I was being manipulated and I had to go along as it was a great idea. I needed a break, needed to get my head straight, needed to put a choke collar on the dog who was pulling me all over places leading to nowhere. Besides being manipulated is not controlling; I had the husband prerogative of delivering the final yes or no in my family and the dog backed me up on that. After giving Pam my presidential affirmative vote to her plans, reservations appeared from between the glossy brochure pages. Did she know me that well or was she gambling, risking the month's rent on the turn of a card. Couldn't say but we spent an excited hour making and renovating plans and dreams.

CHAPTER 47

Turn Out The Lights

I suspect Pam and I could have spent happy hours creating twelve days of fun extrapolating from a single brochure's pictures day long trips to happiness, and from a single descriptive paragraph a book length narrative of beautiful dreams, if the phone didn't ring. At that moment, energizing my coffee with a little tail in the living room, I took the call and was quickly brought from Florida's warm sunshine to a cold wet New York November. It was Ronni Deutsch employing a health giver's voice supposedly calling to see how I was doing. Telling her I was feeling great, the caregiver now became an intimate friend, a best friend you always think you have 'til tested, then becomes a disappointment.

Relieved to hear I was doing great she confided in a little girl's voice her distress over my well being costing her nights of sleep, but thank goodness her rest was now assured. Her concern over my family's wellbeing affected her appetite to the extent of not being able to eat a single morsel, but now hearing Pam, my son, and I were doing fine she could risk a dinner.

Speaking of dinner, an unexpected idea struck her from out of the blue, a fabulous idea: how about she and I have dinner together to discuss the case. She had some real important information she shouldn't share, but with our friendship she'd take the risk. It may risk her job but she felt I must hear it.

After her sleeplessness and starvation came her gifts, Illicit gifts for me alone. Shit, standing, phone to ear, listening to her, I thought 'desperate.' Laying it on too thick she was going over the top, touching the clouds, and had as much substance. "Yeah Ronni, maybe some time we'll get together, but not right now,"

"What about tonight? I have some fantastic new information about the poisoner."

"Tonight! Look Ronni, I'm not interested in catching the poisoner. I know all I want to know."

"You do? You have some knowledge!"

Hell, she almost had an orgasm at my hint of possessing a possible solution. To splash cold water on her heated breath and dinner out invites I told her. "Look Ronni, I'm busy. I don't wish to discuss it."

A big cat smelling a prey's scent, she continued to press, "Mac, look, you know you could trust me (a politicians trust before an election). Can you give me even a hint as to how you're thinking?"

"Not over the phone."

"Right, right, we have to get together. I've got a lot to share with you. Together, working as a team we could solve this case."

I had no intention of sharing Joy with Ronni. If you're going to play me for a fool, at least I expect some subtlety. "Look Ronni, like I told Woody, I'm not interested in the roach poisoning solution."

"Woody! He's been there?"

"This morning."

"You told him nothing."

"Nothing."

"Sure?"

"Yes."

A pause on her side of the ether as she digested Woody's visit; on my part I paused to devise a polite way to hang up.

"Mac, you're being uninterested in the solution of the roach murder means you have some very definite ideas," she said.

"Look Ronni, Pam's got lunch waiting. I've got to go."

"Mac, don't hang up. Look, we have to have dinner together. I'm really feeling alone. I really need to see you."

Her needs were sent to me as a lover needing the presence of her desired one.

Feeling it would be uncharitable to slam the door in the face of her urgent need, I told her I'd love to see her, but it was impossible.

"Mac, I really think we make a great team."

As police or love team was a toss-up, but she had silk sheets in her voice. Love those sheets.

She continued to press, "How about eight tonight. I'll expect you at eight and we'll have a nice friendly dinner."

'Friendly' was heavily bathe with promise. Having just recovered from the Brite fiasco, I gently washed the friendly silk sheets from my mind as being more air than mattress.

After telling Ronni dinner was definitely not going to happen, she let several seconds of blow time between us before she came back with drinks.

"We could go out for quick drinks."

She was very near offering to pay and I expect she would have, if she didn't feel I was the type of man to be insulted at the offer, and despite all my Brite experiences was still that type of man. Brite had illuminated the dangers of these types of teases: pleadings, perfume, promises, all emptiness costing an arm and a leg.

"Sorry Ronni, I really can't get out of the house." Sounding like I was hen pecked by Pam I amended, "Got a lot to do around here."

"Mac, I really really need to see you. (double reallys!) Certainly you could stop by my apartment for a quick drink. I make an absolutely great Manhattan."

Her apartment, Manhattans, double reallys, all combined to promise something very real. I hedged like a reluctant girl needing to be dragged and coaxed to the bedroom. "I don't know if I can spare the time."

"A half hour, we'll have a few drinks, hors d'oeurves, talk about the case and share information."

My 'really Ronni, I don't have the time' was said not as a door slamming but one now ajar. I held out for a few more 'reallys' expressing desperation in her pleas 'til I was sure of her. I relented with the appropriate hesitation of a virgin visiting a roué.

It was just five when I rang her bell with carnal anticipation. My anticipation was tempered by my Brite's experience, but still with the smell of her desperation emitting from all her 'really's' I felt confident.

In a red cocktail dress, low cut on top, skirt cut high, her dress was like a band of fancy red wrapping around her middle leaving top and bottom free to breathe and to be seen. Barely made the middle of the living room before I was handed one of her 'fabulous' Manhattans floating two cherries. The drink wasn't particularly 'fabulous' but it had the strength of two.

On the couch, she on one end, I the other, neutral cushion between us, she constantly leaned over giving me lascivious eye treats. She spent one half of our Manhattans dissing Woody, who was indicted as being selfish, egotistical, definitely not a team player.

Unable to argue over her take on Woody's character, my agreeing with her allowed her to lean over and pat my hand.

For the life of me I couldn't understand how those ripe melons kept from falling out.

With Woody disposed of as a mean bastard, and moving the conversation to her loneliness, she moved to the middle cushion. Apparently people thought, being a successful, attractive career woman she lived a happy life, but her career wasn't fulfilling; as a woman she needed companionship in her life.

Couldn't possibly say what kept me from jumping up, picking her up and take her in my arms, offering her needed friendship and companionship on the way to the bedroom door. Most probably I was hindered by the drink in my hand, and by the time I finished it and was able to get both hands into play, she was handing me another drink, stronger than the first. Was she trying to get me drunk to have her way with me? If so, it was needless, a waste of liquor. Another leaning over would easily do the trick.

After handing me my drink Ronni returned to the middle cushion, fretting over how strong she made the drinks, confessing she was feeling light headed.

I suspected after our copulation she'd regain her virginity, swearing the booze made her do it, doesn't remember the 'it,' but 'it' was wonderful with me.

She may be light at the waist, light in weight, but was heavy on top and definitely was never light in the head.

Tossing my hand across the couch's back with studied casualness, I attempted to initiate the usual subtle encircling movement but to no avail.

She stood up saying she forgot to put out the hors d'oeuvres and returned with a bowl of potato chips.

Like a red sky at sunset I saw rough water ahead. Her counter movement was definitely not a positive feminine ploy of enticement but a negative statement hard to ignore. My mood was easily mirrored by my frown, and leaning back on the couch brought her back to the couch. After placing the damn chips on the coffee table she sat at the end of the couch leaning over to get a chip.

Damn it, those melons had to be glued to her half bra. How can so much showing still keep the nipples hidden.

With knowledge recently gained from Brite, suspicious, I tested the waters suggesting she show me around the apartment. Since the apartment was eight hundred square feet, the only room left to see was her bedroom. Once in I expected to exit after an hour, well with a Manhattan, definitely a half hour.

She said, "Oh, my bedroom is such a mess. I'd be ashamed for you to see it."

The only disorder I noticed so far was the staleness of the chips. What I heard her saying was 'no action for you.' Still, with strong drink in hand, my ass in the hands of a soft pliable cushion, and her constantly doing deep waist bends to secure the smallest potato chips, I decided to give her some more time. Possibly she expected more finesse for forms sake, certainly not to overcome timidity. We were definitely playing a game, and with my goal obvious, only her goal was still to be revealed. Optimistically the goal was me, with my charming personality, intelligence, looks, and masculine magnetism hopefully I expected she'll validate my opinion in bed.

Her first move was the right move, saying how she admired me and my work. I returned the compliment saying I admired her. My leaving out what suggested it could be her body or her mind. Still, with my eyes going up and down each time she bent for a chip, I suspected she easily read what I admired. After all why were we here if not to copulate. She knew it and I knew it. What was left was the necessity to wrap up and hide the sex for as long as possible. Watching her wrap the sex in chiffon and keep the deed hidden doing potato chip calisthenics, I had to grab some stale chips.

Apologizing for not having any dip, she proceeded to do a graceful dip. Damn it what the hell is keeping them from dropping out, nipple and all.

"Mac, please drink up. I take pride in my Manhattans. Don't you like them? Do you like the cherries in your drink?"

With my stomach empty as a progressive's mind, I felt the first two drinks, and feeling good, definitely frisky, sufficiently frisky to investigate those gravity defying melons, should have said no to another Manhattan, but the first two said they needed a backup, a third leg, as it was, to stand level. I'm sure there was Vermouth in my third visit to Manhattan, but the Vermouth could have moved to Brooklyn.

I told Ronni this is my last, feeling more could lessen my performance. Obviously she was getting me drunk but shouldn't it be the reverse? Hats off to the liberated woman; more man than woman.

Leaning back on the couch's arm she pushed the goodies skyward. I was still able to enjoy the view without appearing lascivious. Shit, we're both sitting on the couch admiring her body and its careful teasing display.

After a few moments of letting me fawn and leer over her physical attractiveness, she made her first critical move in our game, "Woody was here yesterday."

"For what purpose?" I quickly asked fearing it was my purpose and worried he got a tour of the apartment.

Correctly reading my hurried question she moved quickly to counter my concerns. "Poor Woody, desperate to solve the Roach case, he tried to get me to help him.."

"And did you?" I asked knowing she only serves the libido, arousing and relieving it.

"Mac, you're the only one I'd share ideas with about the case. I just sent poor Woody on his way. Don't you feel he's so ineffectual?"

"We may think that, but more important, he doesn't and never will. Like rich political do gooders, after picking your pockets, when eventually proven wrong are able to twist and turn 'til it's proven they were right in being wrong. After all, the hard part isn't saying it was wrong, the hard part is saying I'm responsible for what went wrong Being in the public eye is defacto proof of never being in the wrong. If they did admit fallibility like an irritating speck would be quickly removed from the public eye. We like to believe in their infallibility ."

Taking a sip of her drink Ronni agreed, "Hey, if you admit you're wrong who the hell would listen to you?"

With her taking a chip I followed her chip's journey from bowl to lips and wondering how her glistening red lipstick didn't mar her teeth. She had bright red lips making her mouth a bull's eye. In case I missed the bull's eye, she glided her tongue over her lips to taste any salt deposit.

"Mac, I'm going to tell you something in confidence. Can I trust you?"

"Certainly," I answered. What the hell did she expect me to say; 'no, don't trust me, I'm a world class gossip?'

Next she asked if I'd respect her; after all she promised not to say anything.

"Absolutely," what did she expect before the bedroom, 'no, not respecting you I'll think you're a cheap lay.'

"It's just that I have a great opinion of your knowledge and experience." She baptized her opinion with a bend and an arm touch. Straightening up she took a sip as if to gain courage to continue. I was sort of expecting the follow up word 'love' peeking out of the next undergrowth of words, but was confused whether I or she should drop it. Continuing her whispering she confided, "Between us, I've heard the CIA has definitely ruled out terrorists as being responsible for the poisoning.,"

Confused as to where love and the bed had disappeared I confided that I had it on the most reliable sources it wasn't the act of a deranged person. Somehow sharing Woody's nonsense made me feel foolish.

"Really!" she said. "That's very interesting," in a tone saying very uninteresting. Bending she took a wafer size chip, bit casually licked her lips as if we both didn't know I was watching.

Starting to lean towards her, preparatory to going physical, she picked up the chip bowl, and placing it between us urged me to take some. We were close enough I could reach out and grab her, but decided tossing the chips and bowl across the room would destroy the intimate ambiance. Such nonsense works in girly shows but somehow not here, not now, not with her.

Letting her lean back to the couch's arm I said, "Still waiting to see your apartment. I'm sure it's not so disarranged." I said it with as much innocence of purpose as I could summon.

She answered by noting with feigned horror my glass was at low tide, too shallow to float my forlorn Manhattan cherry. The cherry may have been in my glass, certainly not in the room.

Demanding I must have another I was proud of myself in refusing. Inexplicably either she didn't hear me or didn't believe the seriousness of my denial and what could I do but accept a new proffered drink placed under my nose and over my crotch. The Vermouth now was visiting Long Island.

"Mac, I've got so much respect for you, for your intelligence, and I'll confess I've never met a man of your abilities."

Swallowing my need to modestly deny what was a replication of my own opinion, I took a deep stroll down Manhattan. Not only was she hot but very perceptive.

Ronni continued, "Tell me how your investigation is proceeding. Hear you've been interviewing all the principals involved in table 12."

I swallowed any need to reply with another taste of Manhattan, taste buds fruitlessly searching for the missing Vermouth.

Her choice of topic sobered me up, an ice cold psychic bath. It wasn't my personality, my looks, conversation, intelligence, character, or sexual magnetism, it wasn't me she wanted. She wanted my buried treasure. My pride was grievously punctured. Did she think a half view of her boobs, a few drinks and stale chips can easily flip me open like a soda can?

Normally I'd like to have walked out saying to myself 'screw her'.

Normally I might have tried with promises to get into her bed, then afterwards in revenge walk out saying to her and myself, 'screw you.'

Normally I might play at fly fishing, casting my treasure bait to watch her jump for my fly, then keep it zippered up walk out saying to myself 'screw her.'

Sensing my tensing up, my contemplating getting up, she again bent over but now it only annoyed me. I threatened to leave, mentioning pressing business. Suddenly her melons lost all their appeal and became powerless lumps of fat. Power, like flowing electricity was switched from her to me. With easy divorce and feminist free love, women become desperate, it's a man's buyers market and so it became on that couch.

Wrinkling her face powder, pursing her red lacquered lips with concern one would employ inquiring if they were entering heaven, she asked if she did anything to trouble me. She hinted at a quid pro quo arrangement, I give up my treasure and she'd let me handle her well squeezed melons.

I suspected if I gave in first she'd suddenly develop virginal innocence and welch on her part. employ that insincere time honored excuse 'certainly you didn't think I'd do that, I'm not that type of woman you dirty bastard, Now get out.'

Knowing this I continued fly casting, mentioning my suspicion she only invited me to find out what I learned.

She jumped at the bait with a loud denial.

Casting out my fly again I told her I really respected her but she was disrespecting me.

Again she jumped out of the water or rather it was out of the couch crying out a 'no.'

I was enjoying myself. She deserved to be punished. Obviously she had no idea who she was dealing with. I cast a colored fly into her rippling waters, "Don't want to boast (believe it and you're innocent of human nature) but I've been successful in identifying the poisoner."

Shit, at that fly my hottie fish literally flopped down to my feet literally asking who did I think was the murderer and how sure was I.

Taking her supplicating hands in mine I looked down at her glistening anticipating eyes and played with the hooked fish. "Listen to this Ronni, not only do I know the murderer but I've got someone who will testify against the murderer."

"Really, really, you really, really have evidence?"

Her pathetic 'reallys' were like little guppies sucking for air.

"I just don't know how to make the arrest, what with all the competing agencies. You could easily get stumped to death walking among these excited elephants."

"But Mac, if we both make the arrest we could stand up to them."

With the water now so roiling I cast my line asking if I could see the rest of her apartment.

Leaning back on her knees, perky melons wrapped tight outlining the nipples, she asked if I really wanted to see her small apartment.

A little negativity, a show and tell. I tell first, then she shows, maybe. It was all so sordid, cold, a business exchange like any street prostitution. I wanted her body, she my mind. There were no real people involved.

It was all so soulless and inhuman. I had to fight to free my legs from her grasp in order to stand. She almost tackled me as I moved from the couch. "Look Ronni, it's getting late. I'm making plans to go on vacation."

Getting to her feet, blocking the door, she now was eager to show me the apartment. Normally I'd walk into her bedroom grinning but it wouldn't be me in her bed, it would be my treasure. Normally I'd like to believe I'd just walk out with dignity, advertising my victory over her seductions.. She was so pathetic, so needy, so willing to sell herself cheaply. It all became so beneath me. Anyone possessing what I had could be me in her bed. I had to rise above these circumstances and on a whim, a grand gesture to stand above her, Woody and them all, I blurted out, "Look Ronni, Joy is the poisoner."

"Joy!" she repeated. "Joy. Do you really think it's Joy? Jim Scott's wife?"

I patiently explained, "Who died? Joy's husband who had a perforated ulcer guaranteeing he'd die from the poison and remember, she denied knowing about her husband's ulcer. An extremely incriminating lie."

"That's true ... she did lie about that," then as if a revelation from Olympus came upon her she repeated, "and it was her husband who died."

I continued, teacher to pupil, "She had life insurance, double indemnity on Jim's life, along with house mortgage insurance."

Ronni agreed, "Yes," adding, "we found out about everyone's insurance background. You know Mac, you have a lot of insurance."

I took that last item as a little girlish nastiness. I continued, "Joy has a lover."

"No - really - who?" Ronni asked.

Strange, the women who sleep around the most are often the most shocked at the revelation others are doing the same. Apparently the knowledge of other's conduct cheapens theirs, tarnishes their love, their free spirit, their hot desirability.

"Joy's boyfriend is Zapp."

"The Pep Boy!. The tire changer?" Ronni said in disbelief. "He just puts tires on cars."

Obviously Ronni participated in the ethos it's not the frequency of sex that's unsavory, it's giving yourself to bums that's degrading. Sex with a millionaire is to be published. Sex with nonentities is to be hidden, sex with a famous actor, singer, athlete no matter how fleeting the duration becomes a lifelong fulfillment all must know about.

"Ronni, Joy has broken up with Zapp. Thanks to Jim's death she has become rich, in the money, and decided Zapp is not worthy of her."

"Are you sure of this love affair between Zapp and Joy? I find it hard to picture them together. (what she meant was picturing them naked in bed together)."

I explained, "Zapp is pissed off with the treatment Joy is giving him since she's gotten rich on the publicity of Jim's death, and he's willing to turn state's witness, if he gets immunity. All you need to do is get the government to give him a free pass and he'll kill Joy for you."

"How much evidence does he have?"

"He'll give the place where the poison was purchased, with Joy on the film buying it. He'll say Joy gave him the salsa to put on table 12, warning him not to sit there."

"So he was helping her."

"Well Ronni, the way he tells it he had no idea, no suspicion, not the faintest whisper of Joy's intentions, and hasn't come forward sooner because he's afraid Joy will kill him."

In joy she grabbed me around the neck and tried to go mouth to mouth. If my mouth was open, my teeth would have received a vigorous tongue cleaning. I pushed her away. Once it was obvious as to her purpose in inviting me, and in her eagerness now to make payment, I felt asexual, above all this sordid mess. Screw her, screw it all. With her hanging around my neck, with my hand on the front doorknob, I told her she could make the arrest. I'm going to Disney Land.

"I'll give you credit. Mac, I promise I'll give you full credit," she vowed as I opened the door. Stepping out into the hallway I told her I was sure she would. The door closed and I went home to plan for Disney Land.

CHAPTER 48

Cold Shower

Can't say what was the cause of the malaise which crept into my spirit unbidden, unnoticed, inexplicable after my first enthusiastic reaction to our initial vacation plans. Peering into my mind's various rooms I searched for reasons to make my mood more reasonable. Could it be the failures in my sexual adventures with Brite and Ronni? Would like to pin the reason on those two tails, but the mind's hotelier would have none of those tales. Instead it pointed to another suite where joy should reside but didn't, namely solving the Roach murder to my satisfaction.

Failing to fill me with anything near ego satisfaction, my being the cause of bringing a murderer to just retribution brought only a 'so what' shrug. Nor could my parting grand gesture in giving Joy to Ronni give me any joy, denying my creative intellectual product was more a self flagellation gesture, tossing loose change to an undeserving hungry needy Ronni. Neither was there any pleasure in her willingness to lay down for me, nor could I find moral satisfaction in denying myself the pleasures of her body. Such pleasures were alloyed with her desperation, by her shopworn goods currently discounted, and in future years will be displayed at flea markets. Feeling all this I walked away from her to escape her, rather than playing at being the noble moral man my hotelier and I like to think we were.

Thank goodness for Pam's enthusiasm and energy in getting us to Disney Land for I was just another suitcase she had to pack and carry with her. Somehow the fog of depression lifted in the matter of one day after our arrival. When feeling good do we ever examine the why, go into the minutiae of the causes, or is it sufficient just to say 'I feel great' and the matter is fully explained. When in low spirits, like basset hounds, we eagerly search outside ourselves for a scent, a clue as to the cause of our woe.

In any case the trip was a brisk cold shower for my psyche. In the land of fantasy, of carefree pleasures, guilt free leisure, seeing Pam and Mickey's joy were my joy. Love is measured by the depth of your pleasure in giving pleasure to others; true enmity's depth is plumbed by the envy you feel at another's pleasure.

Anyway, we returned as a united family, a family tied by threads of numerous memories of shared pleasures, memories more permanent than any photo. Instead of looking beyond myself to find myself I rediscovered myself in my wife and son and such trivial insights bitch slapped my awareness and renewed me. What is there if not you and your blood, only strangers who hold no love for you. Reality is a circle containing you and your beloved. Outside its circumference is nothing, which if mistakenly you think it's something will eventually break the circle leaving you alone and in misery.

We were back after two weeks, in debt and unlike the Tide, not suffering from buyer's remorse. Tired yet energized, happy memories at the just past vacation, smiling at a hopeful future, having two more days of sick leave I decided to rest and amuse myself by catching up on the Roach Case.

In my lounger I read in sequence, as one would read a mystery, two weeks of delivered newspapers. Bemused I felt an alien reading about the trifling quibbles of an inferior race. It was a race mesmerized by print and electronic nonsense: enjoying feeling scared from scary stories, feeling good with feel good stories, feeling amazed at bizarre or fictional feats of unknown persons, feeling anxious or relieved at star gazer's prognosticating stories of the future, feeling shocked at stories about human depravity, feeling exciting about today's stories that will be gone tomorrow, feeling intimate with stories of the doings of stars circling above your world as if they and their stories were real or important. The hoopla of all these stories revealed nothing, as if it was something.

In the first chapter of the Roach Mystery, the media, as well as the political (is there any real difference) were thrown into confusion at Ronni's arrest of Joy Scott for her husband's murder. Without flourishes, the straight story of the arrest was presented on the first day; void of hyperbole, shorn of adjectives and adverbs, lacking commentary, the poor reader was left without a clue as to how to react, what to think.

One could sense editorial and media pundits asking each other where are the hidden terrorists we've been writing about; TV producers in e-mail huddles querying each other, where is the hook to catch the public, how can our afternoon TV blatherers be deprived of manifestations of racist hate, where is the exciting horror of terrorists, where is the narrative of an upcoming apocalypse nailing the listeners with pseudo anxiety to flood our ratings, where indeed is the raw meat in the simple narrative of wife poisoning husband. There is no joy in such a simplistic tale; this cannot be all.

Fortunately, by the second day the media was able to inform confused you, they and you were horrified at the case of poisons' availability. Papers aimed at the more educated reader expressed deep horror over the ease of availability of rat and roach poisons, bleach and anti-freeze liquids, insect repellents, poison mole pellets, all accessible to children without a prescription. To prove the point, to hammer down the truth, statistics were given of hundreds of children dying after digesting readily available poisons. Hard hitting, take no prisoners investigative reporters posing as underage high school students were able to easily buy several bottles of bleach which if ingested could cause serious health problems. On TV, the hosts of ubiquitous women talk shows spent days interviewing parents of children killed by ingesting poison. A nineteen year old identified as an adolescent child blinded after getting drunk on after shave lotion was bounced from one day time talk show to another, from one network to the next, generating tears, tears in abundance, real and manufactured, poured over numerous plush studio couches.

The analysis of Joy poisoning her husband had to wait 'til the third day. By the third day the cause was revealed by the insightful media to be the evil profit driven ruthless chemical corporations with all the unanimity of global warming theorists. From pompous pundits, to late night laugh track driven comics, to blubbering sob sisters, in fact to all who talk at you, it became an uncontestable fact, profit driven corporate heads motivated by lucrative stock options were responsible for Jim's death.

By the fourth day a plethora of congressional hearings were announced as well as three Presidential blue panels were being appointed to investigate the rampant availability of deadly poisons. The democratic politicians were the first to propose legislation to protect the health of the children. Concomitant was their outrage to discover the republicans were in the pocket of child killing corporations and they should publicly apologize to all the dead poisoned children and their parents.

It took almost a week for those who tell you how to think, how all must think about Joy. The cause for the delay was the difficulty arising from Joy's sex. NOW feminists and numerous dike organizations wanted to shout 'right on girl', 'stick it to the man.' If men could murder women, in equality, women should be able to murder men. They wanted a strong woman standing up for herself. Joy should be butch.

Unfortunately a divergent cultural current demanding villains, victims and heroes needed to label the dramatis personae of the day's play and Joy was anointed as victim and heroine, Jim the villain. White men de facto are the oppressors, all the rest are their victims. With such axiomatic article of faith, Joy became a weak wife, too good, too caring, too loving, who out of her goodness allowed her husband to belittle her, manipulate her, verbally abuse her, physically beat her, rape her. Why, he was frightened and envious of her accomplishments. The dichotomy of feminist 'I am woman hear me roar' just watch me fight the Taliban hand to hand in the trenches, and the 'good woman done wrong by her man' was quickly resolved on the seventh day. Joy was beaten and abused by Jim 'til the strong feminist spirit within all women's breasts ignited by daytime TV talk shows shouted 'no more abuse' and she had to kill Jim. Obviously if Joy is victim and heroine, Jim was cast in the role of villain. Poor dead Jim, the husband Joy dismissively described as a 'should man', a man who did what a man should do, had his character tossed into the darkness where all vile creatures crawl about doing wild things.

In America, (color her pink) Joy was made a victim, a helpless victim, a courageous victim, a sympathetic victim, a motherly victim, an angelic victim as well as a manufactured heroine. As a backdrop for such virtue minds had to find a villain. The murdered husband automatically a wife beater being inconveniently dead was deemed an inadequate villain. This brought to the fore Zapp.

It didn't take Woody, diversity lover, hater of haters and all similar people of judgment in the media to realize there was no joy in Joy without a live villain and quickly turned to her fellow conspirator, Zapp. Here Woody as head of the GLT anti discrimination, anti hate task force was first to lead poor bewildered Zapp on a prep walk, a six block walk crossing several streets from the police car to the jail's front door, each foot of the sidewalk populated by TV cameras and perky TV girls telling you what you were seeing in case you were blind, the arrest of the mass murderer Zapp. Of course 'alleged' was the seasoning liberally sprinkled over the commentary.

Stripped of the ubiquitous coat over the head, Zapp walked bare headed, guilt spoken in every furtive twist of his head, in his downward gaze, in his stooped shoulders. Alleged indeed. they may say alleged but need recliners put such a legal nicety to Zapp. Woody quickly hid him in a basement storeroom as numerous high officials and politicians fruitlessly searched the police headquarters' interrogation rooms for the prize. In the cellar's depth a perspiring Woody couldn't get Zapp to confess, to change his story of being an innocent ignorant pawn in Joy's diabolical murder game the Jezebel played. Of course with Woody trying to reason with Zapp to get him to approach some honesty was bound to fail. All he got was appeals for lawyers to which Woody couldn't hear. Woody reasoned, how could Zapp reasonably expect intelligent people on the jury to believe his lover, after giving him a bowl of salsa, warned him not to sit at table 12, and he wasn't suspicious.

"Where is Mac? Mac told me I'd be given immunity if I talked,"

Zapp cried, alternating between asking for a lawyer and vowing on his mother's life he was as innocent as when he came out of her womb, more innocent as he was born illegitimate.

Ronni, breaking off from the frantic herd tearing police headquarters apart searching for Zapp, possessing a mind as torturous as Woody's, found Woody's locked basement storage room. After putting ear to the door, banging loudly, she announced it was Ronni, and she knew Zapp was in there. With threats of bringing the herd thundering down on him, a defeated Woody let Ronni in.

First thing Zapp said to her was his desperate need for a lawyer, stating the law said he need not speak without a lawyer holding his hand whispering to his ear, 'say absolutely nothing.' Ronni proving as deaf as Woody to his pleas decided to crack this nut with talk of castration, reminding Zapp in prison lurked hulks thirsting for his soft white ass, how in almost killing children he may be handled with care by courts, prison murderers know what to do with child murderers; they don't live long.

Zapp screamed my name, "Mac, where is Mac? I'll only talk to Mac. He understands me, he'll get me a lawyer to protect me."

The poor simpleton might as well be orating before a deaf assembly, as to penetrate the two conveniently insensible interrogators. Woody pushing aside Ronni and her gelding approach dropping reason, picking up bribery hoped to buy Zapp's vote. "Look Zapp, confess and I promise you'll spend maybe a year at a prison farm riding around on horses and growing alfalfa. If you don't tell all this very moment you'll spend the rest of your life in Attica. This is your last chance, your only chance to get this fantastic deal (Woody has the ability to sell used cars). In response, all Zapp would say was my name as if lost in a religious trans was praying for my miraculous appearance.

Ronni hipped Woody aside and laid out the case against Zapp. He was a dirty bastard for sleeping with his best friends wife. What kind of creep would do that to a friend.

"She slept with me. Joy made the first move," a plaintiff Zapp countered.

"How despicable," Ronni said. "blaming your depravity on a woman, a woman who was vulnerable, who was hurting, whose husband abused her, and you, a slimy viper slithered your way into her bed."

Woody, picking up on Ronni's narrative continued, "Poor Joy, having the misfortune in marrying an abusive manipulating husband, in her dire desperation finds herself enmeshed with a murderous villain. A man who when faced with the guilt of his crime cowardly tries to blame an innocent woman, a woman who innocently out of love and her needs makes bad choices in men."

"She bought the roach poison, bought it at Home Depot," Zapp argued. "then got the salsa at a neighborhood deli. She never told me what was in the salsa, just asked me to put it on table 12 and if I wanted to see another day and sleep another night with her I mustn't sit at table 12."

Woody expressed his incredulity at the picture of an absolute innocent Zapp carrying salsa to table 12.

Bending into Zapp's face, Ronni simply told him he was a bull shitter, he stole the roach poison out of Joy's kitchen and poisoned her husband so he could have his lascivious way with her.

Leaning back away from her Zapp cried out, "Mac, Mac, I need you, a lawyer, I need a lawyer, I have a right to get a free lawyer."

Banging the table Woody shouted Zapp was the most despicable of men, killing his best friend in order to sleep with the widow.

A shaken Zapp cried, "Look, I'm a Pep Boy's man. We don't do things like that, and where is Mac? When will I see my lawyer?"

Suddenly a thunderous crash at the door silenced the trio. Heard with loud shouts from outside, "We know Zapp is in there. Let us at him. You can't keep us out. We're the Sensitivity and Diversity Department, and if refused entry well have you up on charges of being insensitive and adverse to diversity. Let us in under the pain of being labeled."

"Shit," yelled Ronni. "It's the SAD Gestapo."

"What will we do?" screamed Woody.

Since Woody was facing Zapp, Zapp answered. "Crap, let them in. It must be Mac and my lawyer."

As the door vibrated with hard fists raining against it, as screams and curses passed effortlessly through wood, Ronni and Woody stared speechlessly at each other as Zapp, getting up opened the door to let in the SAD committee of three. Quickly tossing Ronni and Woody out, the three surrounded Zapp, a poor deer in the headlights. What happened after Woody and Ronni left the basement storage room is open to conjecture but within three hours Zapp made a full confession, swearing it was freely given, didn't know who Mac was, and he eschewed his right to a lawyer. You may look at Zapp, a Pep Boy using the word eschewed and wonder, but in wondering you run the risk of being called a cynic.

Poor Zapp, wrong sex, wrong pigment. Needless to say I never saw the poor bastard, and never wanted to see his sorry ass. As for the media buzz, all the promised excitement was vaporized by Zapp's average appearance, his unglamorous Pep Boy job, his mundane sordid motives, particularly when all attempts to make Joy either a femme fatale or a Mary Poplins, failed to elevate a thirtyish housewife to talk show quality.

Zapp got life with parole; Joy, being the real victim, forget dead Jim her husband, was given a stiff ten year probation from attending midget football games and absolutely forbidden to buy, make, serve, or eat salsa during her ten year probation.

Many people hearing Joy's sentence were shocked at the severity, thinking the penalty grossly unfair. Though confessing to roach seasoning the salsa but only under the hypnotic Svengali control of the Pep Boy tire changer most women talk heads, with crossed legs sitting on studio couches thought the ten years too harsh. They seriously told each other and you if Joy lived for five years, free from poisoning salsa was more than sufficient. After all, with Jim dead having no husband Joy wouldn't be a threat to poisoning another man. All agreed Joy and her son needed extensive psychiatric counseling. I heard the caring professional who previously diagnosed Pam and Mickey as being in desperate need of extensive treatment was seen visiting Joy individually and in groups on numerous occasions while making the tour of TV talk shows.

My tenure as Lieutenant in the Hate Crime Division was mutually terminated. In informing me of my return to my previous lower rank Woody confessed after fighting hard for me to keep my lieutenancy he was eventually defeated by immoveable unknown personages too high, too strong, too powerful, for him to thwart. Besides, he confessed his opinion I wasn't fully committed in fostering diversity and it was best I go back to my old rank and job. I was better at serving the public in catching ordinary criminals. Agreeing with being uninterested in fighting hate, I also announced rediscovering my heterosexual self made my unqualified.

Woody regretfully confessed, as a Captain in the GLT division he couldn't come out as normal man, and poor Ronni, as Lieutenant in the Lesbian Squad had to be very secretive in her dating.

Knowing Woody, understanding Ronni, I was sure they were having furtive illicit sex with each other.

With no media interest, with no monies present, the Roach Case disappeared, pushed aside with video of a forest fire destroying a thousand acres and killing a hundred in Togo Land. Especially heart wrenching were pictures of a little girl crying over her charred Raggedy Ann doll. Shit, what an age in which a man is condemned to live, work, and dream. At least I discovered my family and my life revolves around them and catching the occasional criminal.

THE END